from Pasta to Pigfoot

D0270211

First published in this edition in Great Britain 2015 by
Jacaranda Books Art Music Ltd
5 Achilles Road
West Hampstead
London NW6 1DZ
www.jacarandabooksartmusic.co.uk

A CIP catalogue record for this book is available from
the British Library

ISBN: 987 1 90976 220 6
eISBN 978 1 90976 221 3

Typeset by Head & Heart Publishing Services
www.headandheartpublishingservices.com

Printed and bound in Great Britain
by CPI Group (UK) Ltd, Croydon, CR0 4YY

From Pasta
to Pigfoot

Frances Mensah Williams

JACARANDA

Daddy, this one's for you.

Part One

PASTA

*When two cultures collide is the only time
when true suffering exists*

Hermann Hesse

1

Cultural Collisions

'*For Christ's sake, Faye*! Give it a rest, will you? How many times are you going to play that bloody record?'

Six feet and a half-inch of highly irritated black man stood in the doorway of his sister's bedroom, rubbing his receding hairline and taking in the mess in the room.

Faye reluctantly turned down the volume, nearly knocking her iPod off the dock on her crowded dressing table in the process, and glared back at her irate brother.

'It's not a "bloody record"', she retorted crossly. '*Natural Mystic* is a classic, I'll have you know! You should listen to it instead of yelling at me.'

She turned back to her bed and resumed her task of sifting frantically through the pile of clothes strewn across the rumpled duvet. 'Michael says it resonates with the essence of the Rastafari message,' she added.

'Well, all it's doing is resonating against the essence of my hangover. Look, I don't care how much of a genius you think Bob Marley is – just keep it down, okay?'

William sighed and shook his head as he watched his

sister trying to smooth the creases out of a black cardigan covered with bits of white fluff. 'Why can't you hang your clothes on hangers like the rest of civilisation? And please don't tell me you're wearing that top out?'

Faye struggled into the offending piece of clothing without comment, buttoned it quickly and brushed at the front with impatient hands.

'William, I don't have time for a lecture,' she said firmly. 'I'm meeting Michael in Brixton in thirty minutes and I haven't even done my face yet.'

'Well, it looks like you're going to be late – as usual.' William sighed, but this time with a smile. 'Faye, you really *are* the limit.'

He watched in amusement as his younger sister tried frantically to brush some life back into her hair, all the while muttering curses against the South London hairdresser Michael had recommended. Unfortunately, *Sharice of Streatham* had managed to turn her usually silky straightened hair into a mass of tight curls.

'I look like I stuck my finger into an electrical socket,' she said, gazing into the mirror in despair.

The mournful mocha-coloured face looking back at her was strikingly like William's, although its oval shape softened the chiselled profile that worked to such devastating effect on her brother. Her high cheekbones and almond-shaped eyes, with their long sweeping lashes, looked almost Asian, and rather at odds with her full African mouth.

'I wouldn't worry about it,' William said dryly, glancing down at Faye's long limbs and high round bottom emphasised by her tight black jeans. 'I don't think Michael's going to be looking at your hair much anyway.' He laughed and ducked as Faye threw her hairbrush in his direction. With her lean build and slightly awkward walk, his sister's legs looked like those of a young colt learning to take its first steps. Facing the full-length mirror, she turned sideways and sighed as her silhouette came into view.

'Michael says my bum is the only part of me with ethnic integrity,' she said musingly. William looked blank.

'You know, a real African bottom,' she explained.

William snorted contemptuously. 'Michael is, as usual, completely full of it! The guy went to an English public school, for crying out loud. What does he know about ethnic anything? And how on earth you have the time to listen to the pseudo-intellectual garbage he's always spouting is beyond me!'

Faye picked up her hairbrush from the carpet and prudently changed the subject before her brother could launch full steam into yet another of his periodic rants against her boyfriend.

'Never mind my backside. How come you have a hangover at 8 o'clock in the *evening*?' she asked curiously.

Her brother gave a soft groan and pushed the clothes on Faye's unmade bed aside before throwing himself across it. Although he was only three years older than Faye, William was usually so confident and self-assured that people assumed that he was much older. It was not like her usually super self-controlled brother to be the victim of anything, Faye thought, much less a hangover.

William yawned widely and rubbed his head again. 'I know, mad isn't it? You know Lucinda and I went to a legal

3

seminar this afternoon? You're usually lucky to get a glass of cheap plonk afterwards but these guys really pushed the boat out. Nice canapés and waiters walking round with trays of champagne. One of them must have seriously fancied Lucinda because he just kept hanging around. In the end, we had to empty his tray to get rid of him.'

'Well, I can't say I'm surprised,' Faye replied absently, back to brushing furiously at the tight curls on her head. Lucinda was William's girlfriend and was also a lawyer. She was also stunning, with model looks that led her opponents in court to frequently underestimate her ruthlessness in defending her clients, an advantage she exploited shamelessly. When they were out together, the contrast between William's dark good looks and Lucinda's blonde beauty never failed to turn heads.

Giving up on Sharice's handiwork with a sigh of exasperation, Faye grabbed a hair band and pulled her hair back into a short ponytail. Grimacing at the thought of the lecture Michael was going to give her when she finally made it to Brixton, she grabbed her faded leather jacket and the pink satin bag she had discovered at the local craft market and headed for the door.

'Will, I've got to run! Make sure you shut that door behind you; I could do without a lecture from Dad on the state of my room,' she babbled breathlessly. 'Don't forget – when he gets back, tell him I've gone out and that I won't be back too late, okay? *Don't forget*, Will – you know what he can be like.'

Ignoring the pained expression on his face as he stood up and tripped over another pile of her clothes, she ran down the stairs and out of the door, sliding quickly into her car and starting the engine. Though the windscreen was misty and she could barely see the road in front of her, she was too worried about being late to wait for the heater to do its work. With a frustrated glance at her watch, she frantically wiped an old tissue that had been shoved into the glove compartment across the foggy screen and was rewarded with streaks of damp tissue fluff across the stubbornly opaque glass. Sighing impatiently, she turned the heater up full blast and crossed her fingers before pulling out into the road.

Driving through the dark streets of Hampstead, she sang loudly along with Coldplay as they belted out 'Paradise' through the one speaker in her car that still worked. *I wonder what message this song resonates with*, she thought flippantly, making a mental note to hide the CD, and its obvious lack of ethnic integrity, from Michael before she got to Brixton. One rant was more than enough for one evening, she decided, and listening to Coldplay was more than likely to send Michael over the edge. She pushed the engine of her little Fiesta as hard as she could, and sent up a silent prayer of thanks for the unusually light traffic on a Saturday night. Keeping a nervous eye on her rear-view mirror for any flashing lights as she dashed through Swiss Cottage and headed down through St John's Wood, she sped up and slowed down expertly, grateful for her familiarity with the road and the speed cameras on her route.

She heaved a sigh of relief at the surprisingly light traffic in central London and sped around the tangle of streets through Victoria, screeching up to the traffic lights at Vauxhall Bridge in fifth gear. Taking her chances, she dashed through the amber light and onto the bridge, for once managing to stay in the right lane for Brixton.

It was quarter to nine by the time Faye pulled up in front of the tube station where Michael had instructed her to pick him up. She pulled in to the side of the road and switched on her hazard lights, ignoring the irritated toots of the cars now forced to drive around her. Concentrating on removing the offending Coldplay CD, she jumped when Michael rapped impatiently on the window of the passenger seat, gesturing vigorously for her to unlock the door.

'Oh, sorry Michael, I didn't see you!' she said, rolling down the window on his side before releasing the lock. She watched him slide his solid legs into the suddenly small space of her car, smiling brightly at him as she furtively pulled the sleeve of her sweater over her watch. It didn't work.

'Faye, you're late again. I've been waiting for ages, girl!' Michael sucked his teeth in annoyance before reluctantly leaning across to give her a brief kiss on the cheek. Sitting back, he rubbed his cold hands together, then pulled down the sun visor to check his neatly corn-rowed hair in the mirror before turning his attention back to her.

'I'm really sorry,' she said hastily, trying to placate him before he could get started. 'Honestly, you wouldn't believe the traffic on the roads – and literally *all* the lights were against me.' She avoided his disbelieving eyes by leaning out of her window and making a show of checking for oncoming traffic before pulling back out into the busy road.

'Which way should I go?' she added quickly, hoping to stem yet another lecture on her punctuality, or rather the lack of it.

Michael didn't answer immediately. Gripping onto his seatbelt as Faye narrowly avoided a collision with a transit van that had appeared as if from nowhere just as she'd pulled out into the road, he had to take a couple of deep breaths before he could speak.

'Just keep going straight – there's a left turn coming up soon. Yes, that's it! Turn in here and take the second road on the right.'

Faye followed his directions and eventually turned into a narrow street of terraced houses. None of the homes seemed to have curtains or, if they did, the occupants didn't seem to feel the need to draw them. In the darkness, the lights shining through the windows seemed to glower at her like the eyes of a pack of unfriendly dogs. At Michael's instruction, she pulled into a parking space halfway down the street and switched off the car engine. The faint strains of reggae filtered into the now silent car and she reached behind to grab her bag from the back seat. She glanced across at Michael who was once again staring into the mirror, frowning in concentration as he tilted his head from side to side.

Nothing changes, she thought, mentally shaking her head as she watched him give his hair a final pat. In the first flush of their relationship, Faye had found Michael's near obsession with his appearance sweet. But after almost two years together, dealing with his vanity was less about endearing than enduring.

Swallowing an irritated sigh, she quickly reminded herself how lucky she was to have a boyfriend and how, in spite of his sometimes annoying qualities, Michael was still around. Life 'BM' (before Michael), as she labelled it, had been a series of mostly one-off dates, followed by insincere promises of 'I'll call you' or vague excuses about hectic work schedules. Living in an area like Hampstead didn't offer many dating options other than the privately educated posh boys who occasionally asked her out, often seeing a date with her as being as close as they were going to get to being considered a rebel. After a few dates, and with their foray into the exotic satisfied, they were usually ready to return to the familiar comforts of the Chloes, Pippas and Amandas they had grown up with. Far too unsure of herself to try online dating, and fed up with the well-meaning attempts of her friends to fix her up with the same kind of men that they had all grown up with, Faye had watched from the sidelines while her old school friends settled down and moved in with their partners, one or two of them already starting families. Just as she had given up hope of ever having a decent relationship with any man, let alone one of African ancestry, she had met Michael at William's public school reunion dinner; the last place she would have expected to find Mr Right. Lucinda had been down with flu, and to keep William quiet, as well as break the monotony of yet another evening watching EastEnders with Lottie their housekeeper, Faye had agreed to go with her brother.

When they arrived – late, thanks to the two hours Faye had spent getting ready – dinner was about to be served and they were quickly ushered towards the dining tables. The large banqueting hall where the dinner was being held was dark and cavernous, with faded portraits of Lansdowne School's celebrated alumni decorating the walls. Over two hundred Old Lansdonians, along with an assortment of wives and girlfriends, had been crammed onto narrow tables. Following William to their table, Faye slipped into the remaining empty seat. She found herself sandwiched between a wolfish-looking dark-haired man who looked as if he'd already made inroads into more than one bottle that night, and Michael, who was one of the few black faces she had spotted as she walked across the room. Seemingly oblivious to the din of loud aristocratic accents filling the air, Michael sat silently, his smoky brown eyes thoughtfully observing his former classmates. Under his well-cut black suit, Faye could see a waistcoat made from a brilliantly blue *kente* fabric, while his glossy natural hair was twisted into short locks, framing a square jaw.

Immediately drawn to his brooding good looks, Faye mumbled a greeting and tried not to stare. But, as if Faye's shy but obvious interest had animated him, Michael more than made up for his earlier silence by talking endlessly throughout the meal. Faye had pushed the dry roast chicken and watery vegetables around her plate in silence and let Michael dominate the conversation, most of which centred on his devastation at being dumped by his girlfriend after almost two years together.

Ignoring William's exasperated eye-rolling from across the table, Faye had picked her way through the increasingly inedible four course dinner, listening sympathetically to

Michael's unstoppable analysis of his failed relationship. Forced to remove the hand of the man seated on her left from her bare thigh every few minutes, she edged ever closer to Michael, hoping her chair wouldn't tip her over into his lap. After the waiters had cleared away the remains of the tasteless meal and the attempted speeches had been sabotaged by drunken heckling, Michael led Faye away from their table and pinned her against the wall at the far end of the room. Taking her through every painful aspect of his recent break-up, he continued to bare his soul, ignoring his former school mates bouncing around raucously on the dance floor.

As the night wore on, the combination of the loud music and even louder party animals made any kind of conversation impossible. Fed up with being jostled by drunken dancers, Michael dragged an unresisting Faye out of the hall to sit on a low stone wall in front of the building.

Out in the cool night air, Faye listened intently as Michael described how he had abandoned his original plans to become a doctor after he had grown close to a group of Caribbean artists shortly after graduating, and had become aware of his cultural shortcomings.

'My parents were a bit upset when I told them I'd changed my mind about medical school,' he said, dismissing his family's fury at the school fees wasted on his education with a philosophical shrug of his broad shoulders. 'But the truth is that I was just living a cultural lie – do you know what I mean? Honestly, living with those guys who were so *real* and so *connected* really showed me how out of tune I was with my culture and my spiritual roots. They taught me about black music, literature, art – all the stuff I'd never learnt growing up. I mean, look at the people I went to school with,' he nodded with derision in the direction of the hall. 'Anyway, I didn't want to be a doctor. I decided I wanted to do something that would keep me close to my ethnic consciousness.'

Faye had never met anyone like Michael. Black consciousness was not a big topic of discussion in Hampstead, and she listened, mesmerised, as he spoke. 'So I took a course in African-Caribbean Discourse and Communications and then applied to one of the local papers for a job,' he explained. 'It was just a trainee position to start with, of course. Most of the time, I was sent out to report on events like the meetings between the police and the local Afro-Caribbean community leaders, which really taught me a lot about what was going on with our people. But after a while I wanted to do more creative reporting – especially when I really got into the cultural stuff. Anyway, I got lucky after a couple of years and got an offer from *The Black Herald* – where I'm working now – to do their arts and culture reviews. I've also got my own column and I blog on a number of black consciousness sites,' he added, trying to sound modest.

Faye was oblivious to the cool October night air blowing up the very short dress she had worn that night as she sat listening to Michael. The combination of the two large glasses of red wine she had absently downed during the long meal, and the hypnotic effect of his penetrating dark eyes, made her uncharacteristically bold. Almost as if it were someone else speaking, she heard herself offering to cook him a meal the following weekend.

'Hey, that would be great!' he said enthusiastically. After a short pause, he eyed Faye thoughtfully and added, 'Would you mind very much coming over and cooking at my flat? It's just to save me having to get across town when I'm still feeling, well... emotionally down, you know?'

She didn't, but Michael, assuming her silence to mean that she had agreed, then changed the subject back to his theme for the evening. Shaking his head slowly, his voice dropped and a pained expression crossed his face. 'I still can't believe it. After all I did for that woman, how could she just walk away like that...?'

Faye listened without interruption until William came looking for her, dragging her off before she could say more than a hasty goodbye to Michael and punch his number into her mobile.

All that week at work, she had buzzed with excitement at the thought of an evening alone with Michael and on Saturday afternoon she spent an hour in the supermarket, happily blowing her budget for the week on food. Laden with two carrier bags, she had driven down to Michael's flat in Streatham ready to cook away any memories of his old flame.

As a self-confessed addict, as far as Faye was concerned, pasta was the obvious answer to any situation. Celebrating good news always called for a generous plate of fun, shoestring-like stringozzi, while a big bowl of steaming linguine with clams was guaranteed to ward off any looming depression over credit card bills. A hard, unsatisfying day at the office was best forgotten with a bowl of soup packed with cavatappi, her favourite corkscrew-shaped macaroni,

12

while, as far as she was concerned, the antidote to any form of heartache was always to be found in the soothing curls of garlic-infused tagliatelle.

Taking no notice of Michael's worried expression when she looked blank at his request for saltfish and ackee, she banged around his tiny kitchen preparing her speciality dish of tagliatelle with prawns in a creamy tomato sauce. Lost in her Jamie Oliver fantasies, she cleaned the prawns and chopped liberal quantities of garlic and fresh parsley for the sauce. While the pasta cooked, she drizzled a liberal glug of garlic and olive oil dressing over a huge green salad and warmed up a mound of garlic bread in the oven. Dessert was a creamy tiramisu. After they had eaten Faye stacked the dishes into the dishwasher while Michael carefully packed away the leftover food, revealing what looked like a hundred plastic takeaway containers in his cupboard. She made two cups of coffee with the freshly ground, ruinously expensive Brazilian beans that had been her final extravagance, taking the drinks through into his small living room, where they sat while he played track after track from what appeared to be a huge collection of reggae, blues and jazz CDs.

It was an hour before her reward came – in the form of an invitation to an exhibition of watercolour landscapes by a newly discovered Jamaican artist that Michael was reviewing for his paper the following week.

'You'll like his stuff,' he said. 'And it will give you a chance to see some of the work that's coming out of the Caribbean these days.'

Faye was so excited at the thought of another date that

she barely noticed the less than romantic perfunctory peck on the cheek as he said goodbye at his front door when she finally, reluctantly, got up to leave.

After the art exhibition, more dates followed, although it didn't take Faye too long to realise that they invariably centred on events that Michael had been sent to cover by his paper.

But if she occasionally wished that they could go to the cinema, without Michael tapping review notes onto his iPad for his column while the other couples around them held hands, or – just once – go to a concert that Michael *hadn't* been given free tickets to, she would remind herself of the boring loneliness of her boyfriend-less days. Truly terrified at the idea of being alone and once again standing on the sidelines while romance passed her by, Faye choked back any protests and dutifully attended exhibitions, concerts and films by mainstream and obscure Caribbean and African artists, while Michael took it upon himself to fill what he called her 'huge cultural gaps'. And if Michael didn't exactly overwhelm her with passion or, if she was honest, any real affection, she mentally shrugged it off. After all, she would tell herself as she firmly silenced the doubts that occasionally pushed through, a good relationship was much more about mental compatibility than what he described as 'all that fake, Eurocentric, lovey-dovey stuff'.

Tonight's date was different, however. Instead of another work-related event, this was the first time Michael had invited her to meet his friends. Despite looking forward to this evening all week, she was now feeling the heavy weight of his expectations on her slim shoulders. Now, almost shivering with nerves despite the warm interior of the car, she cleared her throat and tried to sound calm and confident. This was not the time to provoke another lecture from him about the lack of self-confidence that had probably been engendered by her separation from the proud peoples of Africa.

'Michael, just remind me again. Whose house are we going to?'

'Faye, I've told you three times already – you really should pay more attention.' He tutted impatiently and flipped the sun visor back into place before reaching for the door handle. 'Luther and Philomena.' He said their names slowly and clearly as if dealing with a demanding toddler.

'Wait!' She seized his arm and fought back the rising feeling of panic. 'Okay, tell me again how you know them? *Please*, Michael. I don't want to look like a complete idiot when we get inside!'

He heaved a loud sigh of exaggerated patience but turned to face her fully for the first time since getting into the car.

'Okay, so you know I lived with a group of artists for a while after I decided to leave uni, right? Well, Luther was one of them. When we shared a house, he was going out with Philomena. They stayed on here and got married after the rest of us moved out.'

He stopped speaking and peered at her through the near darkness.

'Faye, what's that white stuff on your sweater?' His voice rose in annoyance as he brushed his hand over the

15

front of her black top. 'You need to make a bit more effort with your appearance, you know,' he said, now clearly irritated.

Brushing an imaginary speck of dust off his own immaculate chocolate-brown suede jacket, he ran a gentle hand over his neatly coiffed hair before glancing over at her.

'So, can we go now?' he said. 'It's getting cold in here and we're late.' Without waiting for a response, he pulled his arm away and opened the car door, sliding his legs out of the small space.

Faye took a deep breath and climbed out of the safety of her beloved car. She locked it quickly and ran after her boyfriend as he strode ahead towards one of the shadowed front doors, then stood awkwardly behind him as he rang the doorbell.

When the front door opened, her first impression was of a large dark silhouette in the doorway with its head nodding in time to the thumping rhythms of what was now very loud reggae.

'Mi-chael!' the silhouette screeched, its voice rising in joyful volume with each long drawn syllable. 'Luther! Come quick now, it's Michael and his lady friend!'

Faye watched in astonishment as the normally reticent Michael threw his head back and laughed happily; a deep belly laugh almost as loud as the music. Throwing his arms around the silhouette, he rocked them both from side to side with a loud 'whoo-oop' that made Faye jump nervously.

'Philo, girl, long time!' he exclaimed when he finally released the woman. He dragged her inside into a narrow hallway and turned back to Faye who was still standing on the doorstep, smiling politely and waiting to be asked in. He beckoned to her impatiently and she stepped into the house, immediately overcome by the overwhelming combination of noise, heat and light.

The next moment she found herself wrapped in a warm embrace and, once released, was looking into the face of one of the darkest women she had ever seen.

'Welcome to our home, Faye!' she said. 'I'm Philomena. We have been simply *dying* to meet you, girl!' Her voice was rich with a strong Caribbean accent that sounded almost musical as she spoke.

Philomena's skin shone black with an almost blue sheen, into which her jet-black hair, which had been cut into a short, curly style, seemed to blend with no obvious hairline. Her warm dark eyes twinkled as though she had just heard a great joke and her head continued to rise and fall in time with the music that now sounded louder than ever. She was a little taller than Faye and considerably wider, and the embroidered red caftan she was wearing was loosely cut to drape around her generous curves.

She turned her head slightly and without any warning screeched again impatiently, her sculpted dark lips barely moving. 'Luther!'

Faye blinked as a short man suddenly appeared in the doorway of the front room. He rushed towards Michael and the two men hugged each other hard. In almost ridiculous contrast to his ebony coloured wife, Luther was so pale he could have been mistaken for a white man. His fair hair hung in long dreadlocks over a short-sleeved African print shirt that reached below his knees, while a pair of torn jeans and scuffed trainers completed his outfit.

He pushed Michael aside gently and turned to Faye.

'Well, now', he said, looking her over appraisingly. 'So this is the lady that's been keeping you away for so long, Michael.' He spoke very slowly and deliberately and, like his wife, his accent was strong. 'Welcome, Sister Faye – you see I remember her name, my brother.'

He winked at Michael with a broad smile before turning back to her. 'It's nice to meet you at last.' He took her hand in both of his and pumped it up and down vigorously.

Turning back to Michael, Luther hugged him again and pushed him into the front room while Philomena followed close behind him, clasping Faye's hand tightly in hers.

Stepping into the large front room Faye was instantly transported a thousand miles away from the dark September evening in South London to a magical, exotic place. Looking around, there were no sofas, armchairs or, in fact, any formal furniture to be seen. Instead, piles of brightly coloured soft cushions were scattered around covering almost the entire surface of bleached hardwood floor. In blazing colours of scarlet, gold and green, the cushions were covered with small squares of brightly coloured fabric and *kente* cloth. There were no curtains covering the slightly open bay windows; instead, gold and cream striped blinds hung suspended from the ceiling, reaching down to cover the top half of the glass. It was like walking into an Aladdin's cave of jewels and light. The pulsing beat of the incredibly loud reggae music coming from the strategically positioned speakers and the intense heat of the room added to the exotic atmosphere.

Utterly entranced, Faye gazed around in amazement

before turning to Philomena. 'What a fabulous room!' she exclaimed. Her nervousness was forgotten for a moment as her eyes, wide with incredulity, took in the fantastic decor.

Philomena's twinkling eyes creased at the corners as she beamed at Faye's enthusiasm. 'Thank you, girl! We like it like this, you know? It helps us feel like we are back home.'

Not quite sure where that was, Faye lapsed into silence. Folding her long legs together, she sat down on an emerald-coloured cushion, silently hoping that it wouldn't clash with her handbag.

Gesturing impatiently at Luther to turn the volume down, Philomena turned her attention to Michael.

'Michael, since you told us you were coming over tonight, I called Wesley and Jiggy and they both say that they'll pass by – it's been quite a while since you all were together. Also, I thought it would be nice for Faye to meet them at last,' she added, smiling warmly at her. 'So now, what y'all want to drink?' she asked.

Without appearing to need an answer to her question, she immediately walked out of the room, her wide curves swaying rhythmically under their vibrant covering.

The sudden piercing ring of the doorbell, loud enough to be heard over the music, had Michael leaping to his feet from the cushion he had been sprawled across. He waved Luther down as his host made a half-hearted attempt to get to his feet.

'I'll get the door, man. I can't wait to see those guys!' His handsome face was split wide by a broad grin as he loped out of the room.

Alone with Luther, Faye searched for something to say.

Typical, she thought ruefully. *The first time Michael introduces me to someone he's not being paid to meet, I go dumb.*

She stared back at the pale Jamaican who, judging from his calm expression, seemed under no pressure to make conversation. Instead, he continued steadily examining her features as though he needed to remember every detail to paint some future portrait.

Above the noise of the throbbing music reverberating around the room, she could hear the sound of loud voices in the corridor. She cleared her throat nervously but still Luther said nothing. He seemed content to nod his head in time to the reverberating bass notes of the wailing melody, his long locks swaying gently, and to let his eyes wander over her face and the length of her legs, now crossed defensively in front of her.

To her intense relief, Michael burst back into the room, an even wider grin across his face.

'Man!' he exclaimed happily, 'it's just like the old days!'

He was followed by two men who were also laughing as they walked into what Faye had now privately christened the rainbow room. The shorter man was wearing a short-sleeved African-style blue and white striped cotton smock over a black wool crew neck sweater with frayed cuffs. His dreadlocks were short and framed his dark chocolate-coloured face like a halo.

The other man was white. Not a pale African, but white. Caucasian. European. White. Tall with curly fair hair that thinned at his temples, he had pale blue eyes that gave nothing away. He nodded briefly at Faye before turning back to Michael who was asking him a question.

The shorter man slapped Luther on the back, giving him a brief hug, before turning his attention to Faye. His eyes were a surprisingly light brown and contrasted strikingly against his dark skin. Like Luther, he took his time to look her up and down before speaking.

'So, Michael', he said finally. 'I take it that this is *the* lady?'

Michael broke off his conversation with the taller man and glanced over at Faye, who was still sitting cross-legged on the cushion.

'Yes,' he said. Barely suppressing his impatience at having to interrupt his conversation, he quickly went through the formalities. 'Faye, this is Jiggy. And he', he added, gesturing towards the man in front of him, 'is Wesley. Jiggy is an artist from Trinidad. Wesley comes from Grenada – he's a sculptor and also a very talented musician.'

Faye smiled awkwardly at the two men, trying not to feel intimidated by their credentials. She murmured what was meant to be 'pleased to meet you' but, having sat without speaking for so long, the words came out sounding more like those of a frog suffering from chronic laryngitis. As she racked her brains – unsuccessfully – to find something charming, or at least witty, to say, Michael turned the music up. At the same time Philomena came back into the room carrying a tray on which she had balanced two tall dark bottles and several glasses in colours as vivid as her cushions.

'Okay,' she announced loudly, her lilting voice somehow penetrating through the din. 'Drinks are here, people!'

Clearing a pile of magazines from a low table, she deposited the tray on its surface and stood up straight, her hands planted on her generous hips.

'Faye, what are you drinking, girl? The men can help themselves.' She twinkled conspiratorially at her and gestured towards the tray. 'We've got some mighty good rum here, straight from home.'

Faye smiled back at her hesitantly, shifting uncomfortably on the cushion, which was now proving to be lumpier than she had first realised.

'I'd like a rum and coke then, please', she said politely, just as Michael stopped the music.

As though the move had been choreographed, the heads of the four men in the room swivelled in her direction. Jiggy was the first to speak, his strongly accented voice breaking into the sudden silence.

'Huh! What's that, Faye? You want to mix our sacred nectar with a Coca-Cola drink?' He looked incredulous and his short dreadlocks bounced in outrage as he turned towards Michael. 'Michael, what have you been teaching her all this time?' Although he tried to keep his tone light, it didn't take a genius to pick up the disapproval now flowing from him.

'I'm not a very big drinker', Faye said defensively and threw a look of appeal at Michael, silently begging for support. Swiftly distancing himself from her cultural anarchy, he just shrugged and glared at her as though she were a tiresome child he had been forced to look after.

'Go on, Faye, just try it and see. This is real Jamaican rum, you know, not that rubbish you get in Hampstead pubs,' he snapped.

Quailing in the face of this unexpected cultural

onslaught, Faye found herself nodding meekly.

'Fine. Philomena, I'll just have the rum please,' she said. Taking a generously filled florescent-pink glass from her hostess, she touched the dark liquid inside to her lips and smiled brightly at the row of faces still staring at her, forcing herself not to grimace at the taste of the strong liquor. Thankfully, Wesley put on another CD and the men turned their attention back to the tray, filling their own glasses with generous measures of rum. Left to her own devices, Faye sipped the fiery drink slowly, letting her eyes wander over the stunning décor. The end of the next track was followed by silence as Luther ejected the disc and rummaged through a huge stack to find its case.

Once again, it was Jiggy who broke the silence.

'So, Faye, where you come from, then?' he asked, thawing slightly as he saw her take another sip of her drink.

With her mind still on the clever contrast of colour combinations used for the floor cushions, Faye replied distractedly. 'North London'.

The choreographed head spinning routine went through a second rendition.

This time, however, it was Michael who led the charge. 'Faye, *nobody* of your colour comes from North London! I thought you'd learned by now not to buy into that ethnic re-colonialism crap.' Not bothering to disguise his irritation, he turned his back and sucked his teeth loudly while he flipped through the stack of CDs, his body language screaming rejection at her.

Oh God, Faye thought wretchedly, *I'm embarrassing him in front of his friends. I cannot believe this is happening!*

From the questioning look on his face, she realised that Jiggy was still waiting for an answer to his question and she replied quietly.

'Well, my family is from Ghana.'

The music had started playing again, almost drowning out her soft voice.

'What's that you say – Guyana?' Jiggy asked, cocking his head towards her as though it would improve his hearing. Tutting at Wesley who had been responsible for turning the music up this time, he marched over to the stereo and turned the volume down to its lowest level since she had arrived, before turning back to her expectantly.

'No, Ghana,' she repeated, adding quickly, 'You know – in West Africa?'

She took another sip of the heavy rum and felt the liquid burn its way down her constricted throat. It had been several hours since she had eaten and she was beginning to feel distinctly light-headed from the homeland nectar.

Philomena had flopped down onto a cushion next to Faye and was comfortably settled into its generous depths. The outline of her caftan blended into the fabric, giving her a slightly disembodied appearance. She was slowly sipping her rum and gave a start of recognition as Faye spoke. Her midnight blue features were sharply defined against the scarlet background of her cushion as she turned towards her husband.

'Luther!' she exclaimed.

'What?' He looked up from the CD that he had been studying.

'You remember that woman Tony used to live with?'

Philomena asked excitedly, her broad forehead creasing into rippling dark furrows as she frowned in an effort to remember. 'What's her name, now – was it Abena? Wasn't she from Ghana too?'

Shaking her head impatiently at Luther's blank expression, she turned back to Faye.

'You know Abena, Faye? She lives in Tulse Hill.'

'No, I'm afraid I don't,' Faye said, looking apologetic. Anxious now to restore her rapidly depleting stock of cultural credibility, she quickly added, 'Actually, Abena is the name given in Ghana to a girl born on a Tuesday.'

Looking up from the colourful Burning Spear album he had been examining, Wesley spoke for the first time, his pale blue eyes staring at her dispassionately.

'Is that so? That's interesting. It's Faye, is that right?' He paused for a moment, continuing after she nodded in confirmation. 'What about yourself – you were born on which day?'

To Faye's surprise his accent was, if possible, even more pronounced than Jiggy's. She collected her thoughts as best as she could through the rum-induced fog that was fast enveloping her.

'Thursday. My 'home' name is Akua. It's spelt A-k-u-a but you pronounce it like "a queer".' She started giggling as the powerful rum hit her. She didn't notice Michael's frown as she took another sip of the rum and carried on, now determined to reclaim her cultural credentials.

'There are names for boys too. Like Kofi Annan? You know, he used to be the Secretary-General of the United Nations. Well, he's from Ghana and Kofi is the name for a boy born on a Friday.'

Everyone in the room had now stopped to listen to her. The only sound to be heard in the room was the wail of Maxi Priest begging someone to 'Make My Day'.

'Well, fancy that now,' Philomena said, clearly impressed with her guest's knowledge of her cultural heritage. Heaving herself off her cushion with surprising agility, she swayed over to drinks tray and, without stopping to ask, generously topped up Faye's pink glass, now almost empty.

'Go on, Faye, share some more of your culture with us,' she said as she settled herself back into the immense scarlet cushion. 'If I come across Abena, I'll be able to tell her I know something about her homeland,' she added, chuckling comfortably.

Faye shifted her almost numb, but at least ethnically correct, backside against the cushion that was now a far cry from its initial apparent softness. She still held the floor and as even Michael was now looking at her with newly appreciative eyes, she hardly needed Philomena's encouragement to keep on going. She took another sip of the rum, her voice getting louder as her confidence grew.

'There are also special names given to children, depending on the order they were born in. For instance, if you are an Ashanti, the third boy in a row in your family is quite likely to be named Mensah. In our family, my dad's younger brother is called Mensah Bonsu because he was born after my father who was the second son.'

Luther nodded. His eyes were bright with interest as he listened to the impromptu lecture. 'It sounds like you know quite a bit about your culture,' he said soberly, respect clearly visible in his pale eyes.

Wesley's intent stare wasn't quite so friendly, although his tone was neutral. 'So what kind of music are you into, Faye?'

She stared back, her thoughts immediately flying to the Coldplay CD hidden away in her glove compartment. She glanced at Michael and bit her lip at the look of naked pleading on his face.

'I'm pretty open – I like a lot of different kinds,' she said casually. 'Michael introduced me to Bob Marley's music – actually I was playing one of his albums earlier this evening.'

Her boyfriend visibly relaxed and carried on chatting to Luther. But it was soon apparent that Wesley hadn't finished with his line of questioning.

'So what kind of music is popular in Ghana, then?' His eyes stabbed at her, belying the casual tone of his voice.

Faye gulped at her rum in an effort to buy time and was saved by Philomena marching back into the room clutching two large bowls of snacks.

'Sorry, people, I didn't get time to cook today – my women's group meeting went on longer than usual. Faye,' she turned to her guest with a smile. 'I've got some plantain chips here for you.'

Faye took the bowl on offer and crammed a couple of the chips into her mouth. She savoured the sweet crispiness of the snack and ate a few more in quick succession, hoping to soak up the powerful rum. *Too little, too late*, she thought, as the room swayed gently before her eyes in a kaleidoscope of colour.

Desperate to fend off Wesley's questioning, she turned

to Philomena. 'These chips are really tasty – where did you buy them?'

'All the shops around here sell them.' Philomena sounded puzzled by the question, but her smile was friendly as she settled back into her cushion. 'You don't have them where you live?'

Faye shrugged, not about to admit that plantain chips were not the usual snack of choice in Hampstead shops or that, thanks to Lottie, she rarely did the grocery shopping.

Wesley leaned back in his cushion. His eyes almost matched the light sea-blue tones of the fabric, and his voice sounded lazy and relaxed.

'So, you and Michael...'

'Ye-es?'

'You've been seeing each other long?'

'Almost two years,' Faye said slowly. She took another sip of her rum, wondering what was coming next.

'So, then, is it serious?' His tone hadn't changed and he sounded like someone discussing the weather and not delving into personal territory with a virtual stranger.

Philomena chuckled and waved a lazy hand in Faye's direction. 'Girl, just ignore him! You don't have to be telling any of us your business.'

Wesley shrugged and grinned, although the humour stopped short of reaching his eyes. 'Hey, just curious, you know.'

Without warning, he switched topics. 'I hear there are good things happening in Africa these days – how's Ghana's economy doing?

What the hell is this? Who Wants to Be a Millionaire

28

time? Faye gritted her teeth, wishing she could phone a friend or, preferably, a hit man who could remove this intensely annoying man.

She tried to shrug off the numbing effects of the rum and opened her mouth to speak. Her tongue suddenly felt heavy and wayward, as if it had a mind of its own and was ready to do its own thing. She focused hard on her words and forced them out carefully. 'Well, from what my dad says, the economy is going through some challenges at the moment. But the country has a lot of natural resources, so things should pick up over time.'

Michael and Luther had also been listening and to her relief, Luther smiled and nodded. Michael, on the other hand, was eyeing the half-empty glass in her hand with alarm.

But Wesley wasn't finished. 'Do you get to go back home often?'

Stopped in her tracks, she stared back at him and groaned in silent agony.

Okay, Faye, you big mouth, kiss goodbye to all the brownie points you just scored!

As her now captive audience was still waiting for her response, she tried one or two sentences out in her head before answering. Then she took a deep breath.

'Well', she started, sounded awkward, and stopped. She squirmed uncomfortably on her cushion. Taking a swift gulp from her glass, she tried again, trying hard not to sound apologetic.

'Well, my father, my brother and I came to live in England when I was five after my mother died. My father travels a lot for his work and, well, we've never really had the chance to go back since...'

Her voice trailed off as she took in the expression of barely disguised scorn on Wesley's face. Desperate to avoid his eyes, she took another sip of her drink and stared fixedly down into her glass.

The taste of the rum was now beginning to make her feel very sick. It was patently clear to everyone that Faye's moment in the spotlight was over and Jiggy and Michael quickly turned back to the music selection spread out in front of them. Before long they were in the middle of a loud and obviously familiar row over the lyrics of the Steel Pulse track that was now playing. Wesley, on the other hand, continued to stare at Faye while she studiously gazed into her glass and wished herself a thousand miles away from her present situation.

'You know,' he said thoughtfully, as though in answer to a question she had asked him. 'One thing you must understand is that it's crucial for us black people to know our motherland. Back in the colonial days, all the white people went out chasing after other people's lands. They bought our brothers in Africa – but, you know something?'

Faye didn't and, at this point, the throbbing in her head induced by the drink was leaving her with very little desire to find out. Her bottom was now almost completely numb and, although desperate for the toilet, she had to fight her increasing need to ask Philomena for directions to the bathroom, miserably aware that she might not be able to stand up.

Wesley's brooding blue eyes were still fixed on her.

Completely oblivious to her dilemma, he continued his lecture.

'Even when they set up their colonies, the white people I mean, they always remembered where they came from. They never said "We are Indians" or "We are Africans". Oh, no!'

His voice was getting progressively louder as he spoke, either not noticing or not caring about Faye's growing discomfort and her surreptitious attempts to pinch some feeling back into her now nerveless backside. With scarcely a pause for breath, Wesley continued his lecture on the history of the slave trade and the dispersion of the 'proud black peoples of Africa' around the world. While the others carried on with their conversation, Philomena listened enraptured to her friend's rich, lilting and – to Faye – almost incomprehensible accent, her head rising and falling in time with the music. While Wesley's voice went on relentlessly, Faye was feeling dizzier by the minute.

Struggling to concentrate through the hazy alcoholic stupor that was threatening to engulf her, she realised that Wesley had finished with history and was now talking about the present day mental colonisation of black people by whites. The insinuation was crystal clear as he stared fixedly at her, his face flushed with passion.

'So, today, if we black people don't know our homelands, we have allowed ourselves to become cultural slaves.' The accusation in his voice was unmistakable. His reproachful expression suddenly reminded Faye of the look on her physics teacher's face on the day she had unwittingly set off a minor explosion in the school lab.

'It is our responsibility to stay close to home as much as possible. That's the only way we can keep our souls connected to our roots. You don't do that, then you're just a slave to the white man!' Wesley ended suddenly and loudly, the unexpected volume of his voice instantly recapturing her flagging attention.

She later decided that it was the shock of the loud voice as well as the patronising tone that did it. As it was, the combination of the rum and, in Faye's opinion at least, the undeserved glare of accusation levelled at her from Wesley's piercing blue eyes wreaked devastating results. Crushed by the weight of her defensiveness at this unwarranted attack, her usual tact and diplomacy vanished. Once again the music conspired against her and there was absolute silence as, in complete exasperation and bewilderment, she blurted out indignantly.

'But you're white yourself, how can you say that!'

Philomena's broad smile vanished. Luther, who was about to start playing a new CD, froze. Jiggy and Michael's conversation stopped abruptly, Michael staring at her in mortified disbelief while Jiggy slowly shook his head from side to side. Only Wesley looked unperturbed.

Now feeling very sick, Faye looked blindly at the blurred faces staring at her and tried to stand up before she passed out. The others seemed frozen and, as no one came to her assistance, she gritted her teeth and willed her bottom to cooperate, finally managing to struggle to her feet unaided. She did not remain standing long.

After taking a couple of steps, the last thing she heard

before her legs gave way and she collapsed gracelessly into an amethyst yellow cushion was Wesley's strong lilt proclaiming disdainfully,

'Girl, let me tell you something: black is not a colour; it's a state of mind!'

2

Cultural Dilemmas

'Wake up, child!' The loud voice reverberated through Faye's head without mercy. The dark room suddenly flooded with light as the heavy raw silk curtains were pulled back.

Faye groaned and tried to raise her head. But her head might as well have been made of iron and the pillow a magnet because after a couple of feeble attempts, she gave up and sank back under the duvet.

'What on earth were you up to last night, young lady?' Lottie said in the rich Scottish accent that sounded as though she had left Glasgow for London the previous week, instead of more than twenty years earlier.

Faye's only response was a weak groan. Unmoved, Lottie pulled the heavy duvet back a few inches and tried not to laugh as Faye clawed frantically at the covers, trying to crawl back into her warm cocoon.

She took one look at Faye cowering miserably under the duvet and she shook her head without sympathy.

'Look at the state of you,' she said sternly. 'Come on, up

with you – you'll feel better after a nice shower!'

Finally realising that Lottie had no intention of leaving until she had been obeyed, Faye crawled out of the comfort of her bed and staggered into the adjoining bathroom. Her head was throbbing and her hand shook as she brushed her teeth before returning to her room where Lottie was bent over picking up the clothes strewn across the floor.

'Oh God', she wailed, sitting on the corner of her bed. 'I'm dying!'

Dressed in one of William's old T-shirts that barely reached her knees and with her hair sticking out in all directions, she looked like a long-legged street urchin. Lottie's expression remained unmoved and Faye knew better than to argue, even if she had had the strength to try.

Tall and angular, with greying brown hair cut into a severe bob, Lottie had been part of the Bonsu family since Faye was six years old.

Born Charlotte Cameron, Lottie was the fourth of seven children and had grown up in a small and very crowded terraced house in Glasgow. Unlike her brothers and sisters, who had left school at the first opportunity, Charlotte, who dreamed of becoming a teacher, had stayed on, eventually winning a scholarship to study at the leading teacher training college in the city. While her mother openly grumbled about where all this education would lead, Charlotte's success was warmly welcomed by her proudly working class father who basked in the heightened status his daughter's achievement brought him. Barely literate himself and having left school at fourteen, Jim Cameron was from a long line of dock workers, as were most of his friends. When she finally qualified, 'our Charlotte, the teacher' gave him something to boast about to anyone at his local pub who would listen. Excited at the whole new world now open to her, and having read about the shortage of good teachers in the English capital, Charlotte decided to move south to London where she soon found a teaching job. However, after three years of fruitlessly trying to force English and history down the bored and uncooperative throats of the inmates of an East London comprehensive school, Charlotte came to the sad conclusion that teaching was not after all the vocation for her and gave in her notice. Her father did not hide his disappointment when she decided instead to train as a nurse and managed to secure a trainee position at a teaching hospital in Tooting.

'What do you want to be doing changing bedpans and catching diseases from all those poofs and bloody foreigners?' Jim had grumbled, finally starting to wonder if his wife didn't have a point about too much education.

Charlotte was halfway through her final year at St Luke's when she met and fell in love with Olu, a handsome Nigerian doctor who had joined the hospital on a six-month contract. Soon the romance was public knowledge and when Olu proposed four months to the day after their first date, the other student nurses in her hostel clubbed together to throw a party for them.

Olu insisted that they had to visit Lagos for Charlotte to meet his parents and to see his country before they got married.

'You will love Nigeria, Charlotte,' he would say constantly, his dark brown eyes gazing deep into hers.

'And my family will love you very much.'

Deliriously happy, Charlotte swallowed her apprehension about Jim's likely reaction and finally found the courage to tell her father her good news.

'You want to *marry an African*? Are you off your head, girl?' he had asked in incredulous disbelief, too shocked to tell anyone except his wife.

'She should have stuck with working in the local factory like her sisters, Jim. I told you so!' was the furious response he got from her. Even though she had finally been proved right, her mother was too upset to tell any of Charlotte's sisters. After all, there was no sense in putting any ideas in *their* heads either.

Charlotte, however, was determined not to let anything destroy her happiness. Ignoring her father's pleas to come to her senses and see things from his point of view, she refused to feel any guilt for what he now saw as his complete lack of credibility down the pub if any of this ever came out. She was even more determined to put aside Jim's pleas because, as she made the travel arrangements for their trip to Nigeria, she hid a secret but very strong feeling that she was pregnant.

The afternoon before they were due to leave for the airport, Olu failed to show up for his final shift. No one at the hospital had any idea where he was and after yet another phone call from the hospital administrator, Charlotte was starting to panic when he rang the bell at the flat in the hostel that she still shared with two other student nurses. Her initial relief on seeing he was safe faded quickly as she took in his haggard appearance, rumpled clothes and a strong smell of stale beer, so completely at odds with his usual impeccable appearance. Filled with dread, as he pushed past her and made for her room, she remained standing.

Olu, who clearly couldn't, sat down heavily on the small bed, waiting until she finally walked into the room. Keeping his red-rimmed eyes fixed to a spot on the floor between his feet, he remained silent while she stared at him, too afraid to even ask what was wrong.

'Charlotte, please forgive me,' he said eventually. His voice was muffled and his speech slightly slurred but the shame in his voice was unmistakable.

'We cannot go to Nigeria,' he said slowly. 'I already have a wife, Charlotte. She lives with my parents in Lagos.'

Charlotte looked down at him, numb with shock and unable to say a word. After a brief glance up at her, he lowered his head again and continued haltingly.

'You know, I have wanted to tell you so many times and, God forgive me, I couldn't do so. But you must believe me... I had planned to leave her and to marry you – I swear to you!' His voice became more animated as he went on. 'I phoned my parents today to tell them about you but they told me that my wife is pregnant with our first child. Apparently, she's been waiting for my return to surprise me with the news. Charlotte, my beloved, please try to understand...'

His voice tailed off into silence at the icy contempt blazing at him from her eyes. She stared stonily down at the hunched figure sitting on the bed as though he were a complete stranger and, without uttering a word, walked out of the room.

When Olu eventually left the house, Charlotte took refuge in her bed and stayed there, unable to speak to anyone. Refusing to see Olu, or answer his frantic phone calls, or even talk to her anxious friends, she lay staring silently at the ceiling, only getting out of bed to use the bathroom or to go to the kitchen to make yet another cup of peppermint tea to relieve the nausea that constantly threatened to overwhelm her. This continued for several days until one of her flatmates, coming home from her shift, found her lying in a heap on the kitchen floor and frantically called an ambulance. By the time they reached St Luke's, it was too late to save her baby. Following an overheard phone call with his wife, who was anxious to find out why his return had been delayed, Olu's guilty secret was soon public knowledge. Unable to stand the undisguised contempt of the hospital staff, he abruptly terminated his contract and returned home to his unsuspecting wife.

Confessing to her flatmates that she felt alone and couldn't bear to go home to face the inevitable "I told you so's" from her parents, Charlotte decided to escape the hospital and its memories of Olu. She scoured the newspapers and the cards on the windows of the local newsagents, desperate to find a job that would give her the chance for a new start, until finally she spotted a small advertisement in the daily paper for a housekeeper. The job involved looking after a widower who had recently come to England with his two young children and, intrigued by the sound of the vacancy, she phoned the recruitment agency.

At her interview, Dr Bonsu, who was already impressed

by Charlotte's obvious intelligence and nursing background, was won over when he saw Faye's reaction to the tall young woman with sad eyes. His daughter had suffered the double trauma of losing her mother and changing countries, and was still extremely wary and shy around people. For Charlotte, the tiny five-year-old with huge eyes and stubby plaits covered in multicoloured ribbons could have been an older version of the baby she had pictured in her mind so often during her short-lived pregnancy. To her father's astonishment, and as though somehow sensing their mutual need for comfort, Faye had immediately taken to the angular dark-haired woman with shiny brown eyes, and spontaneously reached up to hug her.

Dr Bonsu explained to Lottie that, as an international medical consultant in a very specialised field, his job required him to travel constantly.

'When my children and I first arrived here,' he explained, 'we were accompanied by my cousin who was supposed to live with us and look after the children. Unfortunately, Sophia missed her friends and the active social life she had enjoyed in Ghana too much.'

Sophia, the doctor admitted, had complained incessantly about the cold weather – it was mid-July – and had eventually packed her bags and taken the next flight back home.

Shortly after her interview, Charlotte was offered the job and moved immediately into the large house in Hampstead with the Bonsu family, where she was soon known simply as Lottie. Although she never mentioned his name, Charlotte's experience with Olu had left her extremely bitter and cynical about the intentions of every member of the male sex. Making it clear to anyone who approached her that she had absolutely no time for men in her life, she instead concentrated her efforts on making sure that her adopted family was well cared for.

Now, shaking her head as she took in Faye's misery, Lottie dumped the clothes she had retrieved from the floor into a nearby chair and turned back to face her.

'I don't know *what* is going on in this house. How do both you and William end up with hangovers this morning when neither one of you hardly ever drinks?' she asked in exasperation. Although her tone was stern, her soft brown eyes showed her concern.

'Michael was here about an hour ago to return your car, by the way,' she added. 'Your father answered the door before I could get to it. You, needless to say, were out for the count!' She removed the car keys from the pocket of her well-worn brown skirt and dropped them on the pine dressing table with a loud clatter.

'Don't, Lottie!' Faye clasped her head between her hands, cringing as the noise sent vibrations reverberating through her head. When the noise in her head had died down slightly, she peeked up through her fingers at the older woman.

'Did Michael say anything about last night?'

Lottie sniffed. As far as she was concerned Michael was a complete waste of her breath.

'He made some comment about you overdoing it with rum,' she said abruptly. 'I expect *he* was responsible for letting you drink, although you should have known better since you were driving, Faye!'

This time Lottie couldn't hide her anger. Ten years earlier, her sister had been hit by a car while on her way back from work. The driver, a young salesman on his way home after a long session at the pub, had escaped with a fine while Moira had been sentenced to life in a wheelchair. Lottie's views on people who drank when driving were, if possible, even more venomous than her views on men.

Faye's lips trembled perilously; Lottie was hardly ever angry with her. After the trials of the previous night and in her present weakened state, she felt completely unable to cope with any more guilt.

'I'm sorry,' she pleaded miserably. 'Please don't be angry with me, Lottie.' The drummers that had taken up residence in her head were almost forgotten in the face of Lottie's rare display of anger.

The housekeeper's face softened. 'Okay, Faye, but you know how I feel about alcohol when it comes to driving.'

She sat down on the bed and eyed the younger girl curiously. 'So what *did* happen? Were you not meeting some friends of Michael's last night?'

Faye nodded and immediately regretted it as a wave of nausea washed over her. 'He took me round to some friends that he used to live with. It was fine until I screwed it all up.'

'How do you mean?'

'They seemed like nice people – well, except for one of them who was really winding me up,' Faye sighed. 'I don't know, Lottie, I felt a bit out of my depth, to be honest. They were all really intellectual and do a hundred different things and are really into black culture and music and stuff. And I suppose me knocking back neat rum on an empty stomach didn't help.'

Lottie raised an eyebrow in disbelief. 'Rum! Seriously, Faye, what were you thinking? Why on earth didn't you just ask for some wine if you wanted a drink?'

Faye shrugged. 'You should have seen their faces when I asked for Coke to go with it – Michael looked like he was going to have a heart attack!'

She groaned again as she remembered Michael's exasperated glare and the concerned look on Philomena's face as he had bundled her into the car to drive her home. 'Oh no, Michael…! He's going to be furious with me. I really thought we were moving on to the next level – he's never taken me out to see his friends before. I can't believe I've messed it up!'

Lottie repressed a shudder at the idea of what the next level with Michael might involve. 'Well, it sounds like he could have been a bit more supportive – and you could certainly have been a bit more assertive. I know you wanted to make a good impression on them, but you don't have to force yourself to drink strong liquor to be accepted, Faye.'

Before Faye could answer, there was an abrupt knock at the door. Lottie took one look at the alarmed expression on Faye's face and walked swiftly over to the door, opening it slightly and blocking the entrance with her tall narrow frame.

'Oh, Doctor, it's you!' she said smoothly, stepping outside the room and closing the door gently behind her. For several minutes all Faye could hear was the murmur of

43

voices in the corridor and when Lottie came back into the room, her face was grim.

'Well, you've got some explaining to do to your father as well, young Faye. He's waiting for you downstairs. Well, I had better get on – I've got plenty to do. We'll talk properly later, okay?' With that, she hastily left the room.

It took a few minutes of waiting for the room to steady itself before Faye managed to heave herself off her bed and stagger to the bathroom. After a long, almost boiling hot shower she dressed slowly in a pair of skinny jeans and a plain black sweatshirt that she had rescued from the local charity shop.

She stared miserably at her reflection in the mirror, dreading the inevitable lecture coming up from her father. *Thank God it's Sunday today – there's no way I could have faced a day at Fiske, Fiske & Partners*, she thought. She sighed as she headed slowly out of her room.

Eating breakfast together on Sunday was one of her father's commandments and as the drumming in her head had now subsided to a leaden pain behind her eyes, she reluctantly started downstairs, walking into the large airy dining room where her father had long finished his breakfast. Hearing her enter the room, he put down the news supplement he had been reading and frowned at her through thick tortoiseshell glasses.

'Morning, Dad,' Faye mumbled, taking her place at the polished dining table and wincing as bright shafts of morning sun shone through the French windows almost directly into her eyes. She shifted her chair slightly before cautiously pouring herself a cup of black coffee, clutching the pot tightly to prevent her shaky hands from trembling.

'Good morning' was the short response from her father, who had removed his glasses and was rubbing the bridge of his broad nose while watching her steadily.

At five feet nine inches, although not a tall man, Kwame Bonsu radiated an air of authority. Widely acknowledged as one of the leaders in his field of medical research, he had graduated at the top of his class at university in his native Ghana before winning a full scholarship to Harvard Medical School, where he specialised in paediatrics. Credited with groundbreaking research into childhood diseases, he was a sought-after expert who spent a good part of his time travelling around the world lecturing and publishing his ongoing research. Her father's high profile role had earned him the title of 'the Nelson Mandela of medicine' from his daughter. Despite her good-natured teasing, Faye was fiercely proud of her father and his achievements – although, she had to admit, she was totally disgusted at the unfairness of William being the one to inherit their father's impressive mind.

Inevitably, the doctor's frequent travelling meant that Lottie had often been left to be both mother and father to his children. It was at times such as this morning that he felt particularly guilty about the effect these absences might have had. Although he had little to worry about with William, who was an ambitious and extremely disciplined man, Dr Bonsu had become increasingly worried about what he saw as Faye's lack of drive or direction. Convinced that she was capable of doing more with her life, and frustrated that she didn't seem to realise it, he had tried several times to pin her down to at least identifying a career she would enjoy. Each attempt was no more successful than the last, he thought, casting his mind back to their last conversation on the subject.

'Faye, you shouldn't be discouraged – there are plenty of careers you can make a go of,' he had said kindly. 'You're not unintelligent. You're just… a little less academically motivated than William, that's all.'

'Is that a diplomatic way of explaining away why I couldn't get any further than A levels and a computing course?' she had quipped, giggling at his earnest expression. 'Dad, let's face it, William is the brains in this family, not me.' She had quickly changed the subject, reading out a joke her friend had texted her, which soon had him roaring with laughter.

This morning, however, as he took in her wan appearance, he was in no mood for jokes. Replacing his glasses, he looked directly into her eyes.

'Are you not feeling well?' He stared pointedly at her trembling hand as she raised the coffee cup to her lips.

Faye, only too aware of her father's feelings about alcohol abuse, cast around furiously for something to say. She was saved by William's entrance. Happily oblivious to the tension in the air, he greeted both of them cheerily and sat down across the table from Faye.

'What's wrong with *you*? You look awful!' he peered closely at her while taking a bite of his father's leftover toast.

'Thanks.' Faye muttered, trying without success to kick his ankle under the dining table. The physical effort immediately set off the throbbing in her head again and she glared angrily at him.

Dr Bonsu took his glasses off again and turned to his son.

'I was just asking her the same question. And, since you are also here, William,' he added mildly, 'perhaps you can both explain to me why we have missed breakfast *and* church today.'

As a devout Catholic, Dr Bonsu was uncompromising about church attendance. Although both his children were fully grown adults, he still expected them to attend mass with him every Sunday morning whenever he was home, whatever their own views on the subject. Dr Bonsu was a firm believer in the Ghanaian tradition whereby children respected and obeyed their parents' wishes so long as they remained under their roof. This morning when neither William nor Faye had shown up ready for their usual nine o'clock mass, he had been alarmed and then irritated – a feeling that was not helped by the unexpected and unwanted arrival of Michael with Faye's car keys in hand.

William swallowed the rest of the toast and looked affectionately at his father.

'Sorry, Dad. I was feeling pretty tired last night and overslept,' he said smoothly. 'We'll go to the six o'clock mass this evening. That is', he added, grinning at his chastened sister, '*if* she's able to walk.'

'Very funny, William!' Scowling furiously at her brother, Faye quietly apologised in turn. Her father was a great believer in discipline and was constantly complaining about what he saw as the total disrespect shown by British children towards their parents. '*I* will never tolerate such displays of unacceptable European liberalism,' he was quick to remind them if he thought he saw any symptoms of this particular disease.

Now, he simply nodded slowly and gave a gentle sigh.

'It's times like this when I sorely regret taking on the kind of profession that has made me travel so much,' he said soberly. 'I sincerely hope that this is not the start of the slippery road to...'

Moral decadence, Faye finished off silently in her head having heard the same sentence more times than she could remember. She studiously avoided William's eyes, only too aware that he was probably silently mouthing the words as her father spoke. This was not exactly the best time to burst out laughing.

With a final sorrowful shake of his head, the doctor rose from the breakfast table and very firmly plucked his magazine from his son's grip. After reminding them about their promise to attend evening mass, he excused himself and shut himself off in his study to finish reading his papers in peace.

Once the door had closed behind him, Faye aimed again and this time made contact with her brother's shin.

'Ouch! Bloody hell, Faye. That hurt!' Glaring at his unrepentant sister, William rubbed his leg hard.

'Serves you right for landing me in it.' She poured another cup of coffee and was glad to see that her hand had stopped shaking, at least for now. Notoriously unable to hold her drink, Faye usually stuck to wine when she went out and hardly ever touched spirits, making the impact of the powerful dark Jamaican rum from the previous evening particularly devastating.

'Hey, I didn't say anything he couldn't figure out for himself,' William muttered defensively. 'He *is* a doctor, you know, and I'm sure he's seen more than his fair share of alcoholically challenged people over the years.'

Rising quickly to avoid another attack on his shins, he grabbed an apple from the fruit bowl on the dining table and, keeping well out of reach, grinned at her cheerfully, his good humour restored.

'So, little sister, what did you and your cultural guru get up to last night?'

Her face dropped as she remembered the hideous turn the evening had taken.

'I don't think Michael will ever speak to me again! I got more than a bit drunk and ended up collapsing at his friend's house – and I think I was a bit rude to one of them,' she sighed deeply. Frowning slightly, she went on. 'I don't remember too much after that except being practically carried out. Michael just dumped me at home and drove off – in *my* car!' she added indignantly.

William chewed thoughtfully on his apple. 'That doesn't sound like you – being rude to your beloved's friends, I mean.'

Ignoring the implication that being drunk, however, *did* sound like her, Faye shrugged. 'Oh, it was just this one guy there who really got on my nerves. He basically accused me of being a slave to the colonialist mentality and cut off from my cultural roots. I know Michael can be a bit much sometimes, but you should have heard this one going on. You know, the usual "you don't know where you come from" rubbish.'

'Well, sounds like he had it coming then,' was the swift response. Gesturing with his half-eaten apple, William added with a grin, 'You know, this is what comes of hanging around with Michael Duncan. That man's got enough chips on his shoulder to feed an entire army. Ever since he got into this whole "I'm black and I'm proud" thing, he's become even more of a prat than he was when we were in school.'

Deciding this was not the moment to tell William that her boyfriend considered *him* to be culturally extinct, Faye bit her lip and drank her coffee without comment.

She put the empty cup down and stared thoughtfully across at him. In his fitted jeans and with his lean muscular torso covered with a grey polo shirt, William looked fit and, as usual, extremely self-confident.

'Will, don't you ever think that maybe we don't have enough of a connection to Ghana? I mean, you even have a white girlfriend. Don't you *ever* worry about people thinking that you've sold out culturally?'

William gave a snort of pure contempt. He wolfed down the rest of the apple, grabbed his plate and stood up. 'Faye, the moment you start worrying about what other people think, you really will be lost!'

He headed for the door, almost bumping into Lottie who was coming in. Turning back to his sister, he added more gently, 'Look, just be yourself. You know where you come from, so what do you care if someone else has a problem? I'm going over to Lucinda's now but I'll be back by six, in time for mass. If you don't want another lecture from Dad, *don't* be late!'

Winking cheekily at Lottie, he strode out of the room,

leaving her staring after him in bewilderment.

'Now, what was *that* all about?' She asked, completely perplexed. She turned back to Faye who had moved over to the French windows and was looking thoughtfully out into the garden. The apple trees that yielded so much fruit during the summer now looked barren. A few pale rays of sunlight had managed to struggle through the clouds and succeeded in casting a gentle glow over the impeccable green lawn. Although it was a chilly September morning, the picture through the glass doors was altogether one of warmth and serenity.

'Faye?' Lottie's voice was sharp with concern as she watched her staring forlornly out of the window.

Faye turned back to her with a wan smile. 'It's okay, Lottie. I'm fine, really.'

Lottie poured herself a cup of coffee from the pot on the dining table and grimaced as she tasted the now lukewarm drink.

'Ugh! I don't know why I torture myself trying to drink this stuff – I hate coffee!' she said in disgust. 'Now listen, my lass, I know you about as well as I know myself and I know when something's not right.' She sat down and gestured to the chair next to her. 'I've got a few minutes to spare and you look like you have plenty on your mind.'

Faye sighed and, after a moment's hesitation, took the chair on offer. 'I was just thinking about last night and having to deal with Michael. His friends really matter to him – what if I've pushed him too far?'

Lottie's nostrils flared with outrage. 'Are you saying *you* don't matter to him? Because if he doesn't think you're more important than his friends, why on earth are you wasting your time with him?'

'I'm not saying I don't matter. It's just... oh, I don't know!' Anxiety and frustration mingled as she struggled to voice her feelings. Her head ached and she forced herself to calm her rising panic. 'Lottie, I don't want to lose him. I know you hate him but he can be really sweet when he wants to be, and I don't see anyone else chasing after me, do you?'

'Maybe if you spent less time worrying about that man and more time with some of your other friends, that would change,' Lottie muttered under her breath. She took in Faye's miserable expression and her voice softened. 'You've had your ups and downs with Michael before, but I've never seen you this upset. There's something else, isn't there?'

Faye hesitated for a moment, almost afraid to give voice to her own suspicions. 'Yes, there is. I *am* worried about Michael; this isn't another silly argument, he's finally let me meet his friends and I know he's going to be furious at me for getting drunk and showing him up. But I can't shake off the feeling that something else was going on last night. One of his friends really seemed to have it in for me from the start. We were talking about culture and I started explaining about Ghana – I'm not sure what happened, but it all seemed to go downhill from there.'

'What were you saying about Ghana?' Lottie leaned forward with interest.

'I was trying to show them that I knew something about *my* culture which, as it turned out, wasn't the smartest idea. Because then they all piled in and started asking me questions that I couldn't answer. And this one guy, Wesley, for some reason was practically interrogating me the whole evening. Then, as if I didn't already feel like a prize idiot, he starts having a go at me and basically accusing me of being clueless about black culture. The funny thing was, he's white and *he* had the nerve to start lecturing me about not keeping in touch with my black identity!' As she thought back to Wesley's condescending remarks, she felt her temper starting to rise.

'Well, maybe he's right,' Lottie said mildly.

'What do you mean, maybe he's right? Lottie!' Faye stared at her in disbelief, completely outraged by this unexpected betrayal.

Unperturbed, Lottie took another sip of her coffee and grimaced again before putting the cup down firmly and pushing it away.

'Calm down, Faye', she said evenly. 'Look, what I mean is that maybe he has a point. You *have* lived in England almost all your life. You know more about English history than African, you barely speak any of your Ghanaian language and you've not been in Ghana since you were a wee lass. *Not* that I agree with him being rude, I can assure you – although, what else can you expect from a man, for pity's sake! – but from his point of view, you probably are cut off from your African identity.'

Faye leaned back in the chair and closed her eyes, casting her mind back to what she recalled of her country of birth. Although the details of life in Ghana were now mostly a distant blur with occasional windows of clarity, her memories remained rich in texture: the noise of raised voices speaking in different languages, the pungent smells of spicy food, the intense heat of the afternoon sun, the dust so thick that it would swirl around and coat every surface, exhilarating music throbbing with rhythm, and colours made even more vivid by the blazing sun were all the things that came to mind whenever she tried to remember her time in Ghana. If she pushed it – which she rarely did – she could remember laughing with her brother as they played outside in the sun and even feel again the warmth of their mother's soft embrace. When she forced herself to do so, she could still remember how her mother had seemed to just disappear and how she had cried for days after overhearing her father's older brother saying, 'Poor, poor Annie! Dying so young and leaving those children alone.'

She could also remember the early days after their arrival in England and how she and William had clung together, seeing each other as allies in a world that had suddenly changed into a literally cold and very alien place, at least until Lottie had come into their lives.

Faye remembered how Lottie had forced them to go for picnics on Hampstead Heath and encouraged them to run and play and shout again as they used to back in Ghana. She smiled, remembering how Lottie had dragged home a young Kenyan nanny she had met in the park and begged her to show her how to braid Faye's unruly curls properly. It was also Lottie who had comforted her when she sobbed because the white girls at her exclusive Hampstead primary school wouldn't play with her and called her dark skin 'dirty'.

While William had commanded respect at his private school, at first with his fists and later with his outstanding brainpower, Faye, with far fewer academic talents, had just desperately wanted to be accepted. When she moved on to secondary school, it was to yet another institution for the elite of Hampstead. Despite Lottie's pleas to let Faye go to a more culturally mixed school, Dr Bonsu had refused to listen.

'I'm sorry, Lottie,' he'd said firmly. 'But I cannot sacrifice a good education for my daughter on the grounds of what, quite frankly, I consider to be quite spurious ethnic considerations.'

At her new school, Faye was one of only a handful of black pupils in her year. Wanting to fit in with everyone around them, the dark-skinned girls had not formed a group. Instead, they had sought out friends among the white students and were soon accepted by the others girls as being 'just like us'.

It was at school that Faye had met her best friend, Caroline Duffy, a cheery redhead whose Irish father, a working class builder, had made a fortune during the property boom. Brendan Duffy was determined that his children would have the best of everything life and his wealth could offer and, although he was initially taken aback by his daughter's choice of best friend, he and his wife had quickly grown fond of Faye, who over the years spent almost as much time in Caroline's house as in her own.

It was when she was fifteen that Faye first began to realise that her assimilation had, in some ways, been a little too successful. It was a rainy Saturday afternoon and she and Caroline were listening to music in her friend's huge bedroom. Mrs Duffy's sister, Eileen, who had been visiting from Australia where she'd emigrated with her husband, had walked into the room as Faye was teaching Caroline a new dance move that she had picked up from a music video.

Watching the leggy teenager move gracefully around the room, Auntie Eileen remarked admiringly, 'My word, Faye, you dance well. Mind you, they do say you people all have marvellous rhythm!'

Faye came to an abrupt stop, embarrassed by the woman's careless remark. Even more confusing, however, was Caroline's response. 'Which people?' she asked her aunt curiously. 'What, you mean the girls from my school?'

Later that evening, after telling Lottie about the incident, Faye had struggled to explain her feelings.

'*I* know I'm black, Lottie,' she said. 'But, it's like Caroline and the other girls see me as white because we've all been friends for so long. You know, it's like it's a compliment that they don't see me as any different from them, but why can't they just like me *and* see me as black?'

It was a question that neither Lottie nor anyone else had ever been able to answer for her over the years.

Now, at almost twenty-six, despite having found herself a black boyfriend, she stood accused of being racially rootless and, to add insult to injury, she thought indignantly, by a man even paler than Caroline.

'And where was Michael in all this? Didn't he stand up for you?' Lottie's expression showed that she already knew the answer.

Faye sighed. 'You must be kidding. He just kept rolling his eyes and glaring at me like *I* was the problem.'

'So, if he won't stand up for you, Faye, when are you going to stand up for yourself?' Although her tone was mild, her flushed face showed that Lottie was trying hard to keep her emotions in check.

Faye looked at her curiously. 'What do you mean?'

Lottie sighed. 'Faye, you are twenty-five and sometimes you act like you are still a teenager. You let Michael get away with murder and I don't know when you are going to realise that you don't have to put up with him. I know you've had a sheltered life—' She raised her hand to stop Faye's protest. 'No, hear me out. You weren't brought up on the streets of Glasgow like I was – you've gone from a private school in Hampstead to working in the same quiet little company for years. You've had your father, William and me looking out for you and coming to your rescue all your life. Look, I understand better than anyone that you've not had to deal with the real world in many respects, but Faye, it's time for you to grow up!'

Faye's eyes reflected her shock and hurt at Lottie's words. 'But it's not *my* fault that I don't have a clue about their culture,' she burst out. 'You should have heard him, Lottie! "It is our responsibility to stay close to home – you don' do that, you jus' a slave to the white man!"' She tried – and failed – to mimic the strong lilt of Wesley's accent.

She sucked her teeth in complete exasperation with a loud and authentically ethnic 'tchhh', and stood up, smoothing back her hair.

'Anyway, I still think he was rude,' she said huffily. 'I

mean, what the hell am I supposed to do, for goodness sake. Just get up and go to Ghana?'

Once again, Lottie's reply was unexpected.

'Well, why not?'

3

Working Cultures

Faye stared moodily out of her office window at the grey October weather. It had been raining for three days in a row and, with no word from Michael since Saturday evening, she was getting steadily more depressed. She had tried his mobile a hundred times and was ready to scream if she heard his voicemail message again.

Knowing Michael's talent for sulking, she was convinced that he was deliberately refusing to take her calls, making her even more frantic in her attempts to get through to him. Surreptitiously checking to see if her boss, the junior Mr Fiske, was anywhere around, she pressed the redial button on her office phone. Once again, after the sixth ring, it went to his voicemail. Deciding against leaving yet another message, she hung up the phone and turned back with a sigh to the legal agreement she was supposed to have prepared for her boss's meeting that morning.

Resisting the impulse to check Facebook, both to relieve her boredom and to see if she could find any clues about what Michael was up to, she forced herself to continue with her work. She had just finished the last page and saved the document when her mobile buzzed. Praying it was Michael she grabbed the phone, fighting back her intense disappointment when Caroline's name flashed up.

'Faye?'

Swallowing hard, Faye forced herself to try and sound normal. 'Hi, Caroline. How are you?'

Her best friend knew her too well to be taken in by the perky sales tone.

'Well, I'm fine, but you certainly don't sound it,' she replied bluntly. 'Have you still not heard from him?'

Faye gave up any pretence at indifference and dropping the cheery tone, she let her voice sink in misery.

'No. I've tried his phone a million times and he's not answering. I know he can be a bit sulky, but it's been four days now!' She tapped moodily on her keyboard and resisted the urge to bite her nails, a childhood habit she had broken until she met Michael.

Caroline, whose opinion of Faye's boyfriend was far closer to Lottie's point of view than to Faye's, swallowed her misgivings and concentrated on trying to soothe her distraught friend.

'Don't worry, he'll call soon,' she said gently. 'He's probably just trying to make you feel really bad before he decides to forgive you.'

She changed the subject quickly before Faye could make any further comment. 'Anyway, the reason I called is that Dermot's band is playing again tonight at that Irish pub in Kilburn and Marcus and I have promised to go and watch them. Why don't you come with us and forget about

Michael for a few hours?'

Despite her misery, Faye couldn't help but smile. Caroline's nineteen-year-old brother had a huge crush on Faye and could always be counted on to boost her spirits when she felt low. Sabotaging his father's dream for him to go to university and become a lawyer, Dermot had instead formed a rock band with three Irish boys he had met in a pub after leaving his expensive public school the year before. To his father's disbelief and intense annoyance, the group – Guns in Clover – had found almost instant success on the small club circuit and were being snapped up to play by club owners around the country. Although his mop of mad, curly red hair made Dermot look more like a comedian than a musician, his cheeky smile and undeniable talent made him an irresistible front man. The band's fan base was growing daily and Dermot was proving particularly popular with the young girls that queued up for hours to get into their gigs.

Faye sighed with regret. 'No, Caro, much as I love Dermot, I don't think I would be very good company at the moment. Besides, I'm sure Marcus wouldn't mind an evening out alone with you for a change,' she giggled. 'Actually, just getting you out of the house at all will be excitement enough! You two are such a boring couple and you've only been living together for a year.'

'That's not true!' Caroline said indignantly. 'We go out loads of times.'

Faye was silent for a few moments waiting for her friend's honesty to get the better of her. Caroline was legendary for her total dedication to the cause of lounging.

She loathed any kind of physical exertion with a passion and had even been known to pretend not to hear the fire alarm at her office because she couldn't bear the thought of climbing down four flights of stairs. She loved watching television as much as she hated physical effort and was guaranteed to be found on the sofa, TV remote in hand, within minutes of getting home from work.

'Okay,' she admitted reluctantly. 'So I can be just a *teeny* bit addicted to watching telly.'

Faye snorted with laughter. 'A *teeny* bit?' Speaking with a fake whine in her voice, she went on. '"I'm sooo sorry, Faye, Corrie's on tonight and I'm already recording two other TV shows, so can we go to that exclusive concert that you've only got once-in-a-lifetime tickets for another day…?"'

'Okay, okay, point taken,' Caroline laughed. 'Mind you, now that Marcus and I are together, we don't need to go out looking any more. So why bother?' She sighed blissfully, her voice dripping with smugness.

Faye rolled her eyes but had to admit that Caroline had a point. Marcus O'Neill was a successful stockbroker who met all of Caroline's father's marital aspirations for his daughter. Marcus was both Irish and very wealthy, having co-founded a successful hedge fund in his early thirties and Mr Duffy had fallen in love with him at first sight. Fortunately, Caroline had also followed suit and, after two years of dating, she had moved into his spacious bachelor pad, having first insisted that he order a bouncy new sofa and the full Sky TV package.

Dr Bonsu, who was fond of Caroline, had shaken his head in sorrow when Faye had excitedly broken the news to him. Like many Africans of his generation, the thought of his daughter living with a man without the benefit of marriage went against both his Catholic upbringing and the norms of his society. Although William and Lucinda had been seeing each other for over three years, William continued to live at home, although only in deference to his father's wishes. Any suggestion of moving out to live with Lucinda inevitably led to the 'road to moral decadence' speech from the doctor. As far as their unrelenting father was concerned, both Faye and William would live with their future partners only after marriage.

Just then Faye spotted her boss approaching her desk with more speed than his heavy frame usually allowed.

'Caro, I've got to go!' she whispered urgently. 'I'll call you later!' Sliding her phone under the papers on her desk, she smiled guiltily up at her boss.

'I'll just print the agreement out now and bring it through to you, Mr Fiske,' she said brightly, trying to sound efficient.

Peering at her anxiously through his round rimless glasses, her boss made no move to return to his office and continued to hover at her desk. The meeting with his client was scheduled to start in ten minutes and the signing of this agreement was the main reason for the appointment. Faye glanced across at him and felt a pang of guilt as she saw him look at his watch yet again. There was now very little time for him to read through the final document and his agitation was increasing visibly.

Referred to among the staff simply as Junior, the younger Mr Fiske was an extremely large man and prone to anxiety attacks whenever he felt under the slightest pressure. Faye had worked for him for five years as, despite her heavy hints to HR about the possibility of working for a more dynamic boss, he was actually the only partner at Fiske, Fiske & Partners who was prepared to put up with her constant daydreaming and 'creative' typing skills. Junior, despite the occasional panic attacks brought on by her lack of concentration, was fond of Faye, and found her extremely soothing and comforting to be around, as well as always ready to listen to the detailed descriptions of his numerous health problems. Although the senior Mr Fiske, the son of the firm's original founder, had technically retired almost five years earlier, he had prudently retained his hold on the company. His only son was, therefore, still only one of the several '& Partners' on the company's letterhead – a key reason for the firm's continued success.

Just as the last page of the agreement curled out of the printer, Faye's office phone rang. Snatching the receiver, she muttered impatiently, 'Faye Bonsu speaking.'

'Faye, it's me, Michael.' His voice was cool and he sounded less than friendly.

Pushing the sheaf of papers impatiently into Mr Fiske's outstretched hand, Faye turned her back on him and hissed into the receiver.

'Michael! I've been trying to get you for days. Why haven't you called? I've left loads of messages on your phone!'

There was a brief pause before he spoke.

'I've been up in Manchester covering an arts festival,' was his frosty response. 'Besides, I needed some time to think some things through. Your behaviour on Saturday was appalling.' His self-righteous tone wiped away any lingering guilt about her part in the Brixton fiasco and she felt her blood starting to boil again.

Struck by the difference in his accent now that Wesley and Jiggy weren't around, Faye listened without interruption, chewing on her nails and trying to hold her temper in check.

'You've been on at me for ages about wanting to know my friends,' he said, his voice thick with reproach. 'And when I take you to meet some of the most intelligent, *conscious* black people – that frankly it wouldn't hurt you to spend more time with – what do you do?'

Not pausing for an answer, he carried on while she listened mutinously until a soft cough from Junior sounded behind her. She turned back to her long-suffering boss who was now pointing frantically at several errors on the agreement that he had marked with a red pen. Faye seized the pages and nodded at him with vigour.

'Michael, hold on just a minute.' Cutting into her boyfriend's interminable tirade, she tucked the handset under her chin and looked up at her boss whose forehead was now covered with a light film of moisture as he glanced anxiously and repeatedly at his watch.

'I'll just make the corrections and bring this right into you, Mr Fiske,' she said, in what she hoped was a soothing tone.

'Please do so, Faye,' he said heavily, the light film turning into distinct drops of moisture as he spoke. 'I'm sure Mr Carmichael will be here for the appointment momentarily.'

Wiping his wide forehead with a large white handkerchief, Junior lumbered back towards his office.

Her eyes on his retreating figure, Faye spoke back into the phone. 'Michael, I've got to finish a document for my boss. Can I call you back in five minutes?'

His voice was glacial. 'Well, I'm very sorry to interrupt your busy schedule.'

Faye sighed loudly, scrolling up and down the document on her screen as she searched for the pages where she needed to make the changes. Finally sensing her growing impatience, his tone now sounded slightly more conciliatory.

'Anyway, I was calling to see if you wanted to come with me on Friday. I'm reviewing a new Caribbean restaurant for the paper and I've asked Luther and the other guys along. I know they'll love the food and...' he paused and added, 'I think it will give you a good opportunity to apologise.'

The sight of Junior's client, Mr Carmichael, stepping out of the lift and heading towards her desk cut off Faye's instinctive response to that suggestion. Opting for the path of least resistance, she quickly agreed to Michael's invitation before slamming down the phone and hastily printing out the corrected document.

Later that afternoon, she slipped into the small staff room, replaying the phone conversation over and over in her mind as she made herself a strong cup of coffee. While she felt less than happy at the thought of another close encounter of the Wesley kind, it was a relief that Michael had finally called and that they were back on speaking terms. Maybe it was time to be gracious and try again with Wesley, if only to keep the peace with her disgruntled boyfriend.

Clutching her mug, she looked around the poky room, optimistically described as the 'Staff Sitting Room' by the Partners, and wondered for the umpteenth time what she was doing in this place. Unlike William, who had always known that he wanted to be a lawyer, Faye had left school with absolutely no idea of where her future career lay. Trying to please her father, she had looked up multiple possible training courses to take at college and ended up even more confused than before she had started.

Finally deciding that even she could handle office work, she had signed up at a local college and to her own surprise, and the secret astonishment of her father, actually completed the one year IT and secretarial course. The real challenge came after she had registered with a few agencies hoping to find an entry level job. Some of the other girls on her course, well connected to the right social networks, quickly found themselves jobs in advertising, media and PR firms, with the others almost effortlessly finding PA roles at investment banks in the City. Faye's job applications, on the other hand, seemed to come to more dead ends than she could have believed possible. Despite the fact that he lacked the type of contacts she needed for an admin job, Faye's father was totally against nepotism of any kind and resolutely refused to get involved in her job search. Trying desperately not to care about the number of jobs that she had been 'perfect' for during telephone conversations but which were subsequently 'not really very suitable' once the recruitment consultant had actually laid eyes on her, Faye had nevertheless persevered.

She still winced whenever she thought about her first

real interview. The job was for a PA in a fast-growing advertising agency and she had stayed up half the night researching the latest issues in the industry and Googling information about the founders of the agency, absolutely determined to impress the recruiters and show that she was up to date with the sector.

But from the minute she entered the luxurious reception area of YMBJ Ads in Chelsea, Faye had felt distinctly uncomfortable. Dressed in smartly tailored navy trousers and a cream top, teamed with the striking navy and gold Hermès scarf her father had given her the previous Christmas, she knew she looked fine but she still felt out of place. Her uneasiness increased tenfold when the elegant blonde sitting behind the reception desk smiled frigidly at her and gestured back towards the lift from which she had just emerged.

'The interviews for the facilities department are being held on the ground floor,' she said. 'You'll need to take the lift back down, I'm afraid.'

Resisting the urge to box the woman's pearl studded ears, Faye had politely but firmly insisted that she was there to interview for the PA vacancy for the Creative Director, standing her ground until the disbelieving receptionist finally phoned through to the Human Resources department. One look at the HR Officer conducting the interviews, a glossy blonde called Petra who spoke with an accent that could have cut a two-inch pane of glass, told Faye that this was not going to end well. Petra seemed slightly taken aback at the sight of the young impeccably dressed black woman waiting for her, but smiled brightly and gestured for Faye to follow her into her office.

When they were both seated, she continued smiling vaguely in Faye's direction as she offered her coffee, looking slightly relieved when Faye shook her head. Continuing to avoid direct eye contact, Petra rattled through a series of questions, barely waiting for the answer to one question before firing the next one.

After ten minutes, Petra sighed, leant forward and shook her head, her smooth blonde bob bouncing gently in sympathy. Gesturing helplessly with long pale fingers tipped with nails elegantly coated in rose pink varnish, her voice took on an earnest and almost conspiratorial tone.

'Look, the thing is that Conrad – that's our Creative Director – is *absolutely* insistent that he needs someone with at least two years' experience doing this kind of thing. I'm *positive* I told the agency about that. So, Fern, I'm so sorry but you're not really—'

'Very suitable,' Faye interrupted her grimly. Fighting back tears, she held her head high and scrambled to her feet, leaving the office without another word. Reluctant to wait out on the street for William, who had offered to meet her and take her out for a celebratory drink, she was forced to sit in the reception area, where she tried to ignore the smug 'I-told-you-so' expression on the receptionist's face. She sat bolt upright in a very stylish and equally uncomfortable armchair and buried her face in one of the glossy magazines featuring horses, dogs and very large country homes that were scattered carelessly on the glass-topped centre table.

When her brother strode into the reception area twenty

minutes later, she had her revenge. The receptionist, taking in at a glance the tall athletic man with the handsome chocolate features and strong muscles clothed in a beautifully cut dark suit, immediately sat up straighter to emphasise her cleavage and patted her already perfect hair. Smiling invitingly at William, she was just about to ask how she could help him when Faye jumped to her feet and walked quickly towards him.

'Darling!' The word came out in a seductive husky voice totally unlike the normal tone she adopted with her brother. Before the startled William could say a word, she had flung her arms around his neck and whispered urgently in his ear. 'Bitch alert!'

Instantly picking up on his sister's signal, William turned to the receptionist, whose smile had now frozen comically on her heavily made-up face.

'Looks like I've found the one I was looking for,' he said, grinning engagingly at the now sulky blonde, before turning back to Faye. 'All set, angel? Are you ready to leave?'

Tossing her head, Faye slipped her hand inside his arm and said loudly in the most affected accent she could manage, 'More than ready, darling. I've had quite enough of this place – it's really *not* very suitable!'

Although the sight of the receptionist's livid face as she stalked out of the office kept Faye laughing long enough to avoid the threat of tears, she had been terrified of any further rejection. To avoid any more traumatising interviews, she signed up with a temp agency and was sent to Fiske, Fiske & Partners to cover for a PA who was away on maternity leave. After six months, when Karen returned to work, Faye was offered the chance to work with Junior to cover for his secretary, who had left the previous week to travel round the world – or at least as far around it as she could get from her boss. At the end of her two-week holiday, she sent an unapologetic email to say that she would not be coming back, and Faye had needed little persuasion to stay on permanently.

Junior was a dedicated hypochondriac and, once he discovered that Faye's father was a doctor, hardly a week went by without a plea from him for her father's advice about whichever symptom was plaguing him at that particular point in time. Having only accepted the job to prove to her father that she could actually stick at something, Faye had little choice but to put up with him. To her surprise, as time went on, she found herself growing fond of the bumbling solicitor who, despite his quirks, was happy to let her do pretty much as she liked. His father's quiet pleas to the other partners meant that Junior was rarely overburdened with any serious legal work and, consequently, apart from the very occasional moment of stress like this morning, both Faye and her boss usually led a quiet life during office hours.

Now, looking around the so-called sitting room, she felt the familiar feelings of frustration welling up and wondered yet again how she had allowed herself to become so stuck.

Her dead-end job was probably about the only subject that William and Michael agreed on – although, typically, for different reasons. William was appalled that Faye could spend so much time in such a staid, old-fashioned and unchallenging job while Michael was equally appalled that Faye was supporting 'a bourgeois legal system that works to oppress the people of colour'.

Waving aside Faye's protests that Fiske, Fiske & Partners were involved in conveyancing and property law and not in civil rights litigation, Michael had cornered poor Junior during the Christmas staff party and lectured him sternly for allowing Faye 'to collaborate with the system'. While Faye had squirmed in embarrassment, Junior, who had been too busy collaborating with the sherry to understand a word the excitable young man was saying, had smiled politely at him while his eyes roamed around in search of a waiter. After patting Michael on the shoulder several times and muttering, 'Yes, yes, indeed, my good fellow!' he had finally given up all pretence of listening and headed straight for the bar with as much speed as his heavy form allowed.

Forcing her mind back to the present with another deep sigh, Faye finished her coffee and rinsed out the blue "It's better in the Bahamas" mug that Michael had given her for their first Christmas together. As she turned to leave the room, the door opened and a small middle-aged lady entered. The only other "person of colour", as Faye laughingly described her, at the firm, Miss Mildred T. Campbell had worked at Fiske, Fiske & Partners for almost twenty years. Until his retirement, she had been the senior Mr Fiske's private secretary and, although she now worked for one of the other Partners, she still carried herself with the same majesty she had acquired in her former role.

Such was the awe she inspired among the staff that she was only ever referred to as "Miss Campbell" and it had been nearly three months before Faye had discovered that her first name was Mildred.

'Oh, Faye, there you are!' Miss Campbell exclaimed. 'Junior Mr Fiske is looking for you.'

Guiltily aware that her fifteen-minute tea break had stretched to nearer thirty, Faye moved quickly towards the door but was soon stopped by Miss Campbell's genteel voice.

'Actually, he asked me to let you know that he was on his way out to see a client and should be back in an hour or two.' Miss Campbell walked towards the coffee machine. Aware of the younger girl now hovering awkwardly in the doorway, she added cheerfully.

'Since your boss won't be back for some time, dear, why don't you keep me company while I have my coffee.'

Faye perched on the edge of the faded chintz sofa that took up one side of the room and watched Miss Campbell's precise movements as she made herself a cup of extremely sweet coffee and selected several biscuits from the biscuit tin in the cupboard.

Barely five feet tall with dark skin whose smoothness was only now beginning to show signs of the encroaching years, Miss Campbell reminded Faye of a neat little mouse. Her clothes were all of the same style – a simple A-line wool skirt reaching just below the knee, a pale blouse that tied at the neck in a loose bow and a soft cardigan that matched the colour of the skirt. In the summer the wool skirt was exchanged for one in brushed cotton, while the cashmere cardigan was replaced by lacy cotton.

Settling herself on the sofa beside Faye, Miss Campbell placed her coffee and the saucer of biscuits carefully on the glass coffee table and turned to Faye.

'So, how have you been, my dear?' She peered at Faye through the small gold-rimmed bifocals she always wore. Miss Campbell's voice still held more than a trace of her native Jamaican accent, although the years spent working with upper middle class English lawyers had added a clipped precision to her words.

Despite the age gap, a warm friendship had developed between the two women since Faye had come to work at Fiske, Fiske & Partners. Miss Campbell tended to keep to herself and had precious little time for the other secretaries in the company.

'No sense of decorum, my dear,' she would say to Faye, tutting in distaste. 'Most especially the younger ladies – just look at those short skirts and showy necklines. As my mother used to say, "A woman who shows her geography tells her history!"'

Rarely exchanging more than a nod with the younger admin staff, Miss Campbell had been nevertheless charmed by the tall, slightly gawky Faye with her compulsive good manners and ready smile. Having worked for his father for many years, Miss Campbell knew only too well the poor opinion the older Mr Fiske had of his son. But she had always had a soft spot for the clumsy younger lawyer whom she had known since his school days. Seeing how kindly Faye handled him had brought her up in Miss Campbell's estimation.

Faye watched the older lady cautiously sip her sweet coffee.

'I'm very well, thank you, Miss Campbell,' she said, suppressing a smile at the look of sheer bliss on the older woman's face as she took a sip of the syrupy warm drink. 'Are you having a busy day?' she added politely.

'Oh not too bad, you know. These days the work is nowhere near as busy as it was in Senior Mr Fiske's day. And what about you? Although I probably don't need to ask if you're busy,' she chuckled. 'How are things with that young man of yours?' she added with a conspiratorial smile, taking a delicate bite of her biscuit.

Miss Campbell had also met Michael at the staff party and while, in her private opinion, she'd thought him to be an ill-mannered and extremely self-centred man, she had treated him with the same formal courtesy she extended to everyone.

'He's fine, thanks.' Faye answered automatically. Glancing across at the placid figure seated next to her, she asked impulsively, 'What made you decide to come to England, Miss Campbell?'

Startled by the suddenness of the question, Miss Campbell choked slightly on the coffee she had been swallowing. Turning to look at Faye, she asked curiously, 'Why on earth would you be interested in the details of my unexciting life?' The gentle smile robbed the words of any sting.

'It's just that I had a cultural clash, for want of a better word, with a friend of Michael's at the weekend and now I can't stop thinking about what he said to me,' she admitted with a sigh.

She narrated the events of the previous weekend to Miss Campbell, who listened intently and without interruption. By the time Faye had ground to a halt, the older lady had finished her last biscuit and was sipping the dregs of her coffee.

'So he said you were culturally disconnected,' Miss Campbell summarised in her slightly clipped tones. 'But, even if you choose to believe him, what does that have to do with my coming to this country?'

'Well, I suppose I'm just curious about why you chose to leave Jamaica,' Faye said. 'I came to England because my father brought me here as a child. But you once mentioned that you were a grown woman when you emigrated from your country.'

The older woman nodded slowly and settled back as best as she could on the overstuffed sofa. 'You're quite right, Faye,' she said with a small smile. 'I was a grown woman when I came here. So you want to know why I left?'

She paused thoughtfully and her eyes were unfocused as her gaze wandered over the slightly tatty striped paper covering the walls of the small room. In a low voice and with her Jamaican accent suddenly more marked, she continued.

'Well, I was born and raised in Kingston, as I may have told you. My family had a very successful small business in town – they printed stationery and business cards and sold all kinds of office equipment. My mother would work out front in the shop while my father spent most of his time in the printing shed at the back. Now, Mummy was a woman who just loved people and loved to trade gossip.

She must have known half the town. From the salesmen who came to have cards made up with big titles to impress their clients, to the buyers for the big companies who came to order their office stationery. They always knew that at our shop they could get good prices as well as a fresh cup of coffee and some juicy tidbit of gossip!

'My sister Millicent – we are twins, you know – and I would help Mummy out in the shop whenever we were on holiday from school. And when we finished school, we both came to work full time at the business. We got used to seeing many of the successful people in town and, it's fair to say, we also knew more than our fair share about the goings-on in Kingston society!'

She laughed and patted Faye's knee gently.

'Now, you see Faye, my sister and I took after my father in looks. Daddy was probably one of the shortest men around and as dark as toasted molasses. He had fallen in love with Mummy right from when they were in school and he pursued her like crazy until she just gave up and said yes. It took everyone by surprise, because Mummy is from a light-skinned family and nobody had expected her to end up with this short, dark man.

'Anyway, they were married before her family had time to finish telling her all the reasons why she was making a big mistake. Daddy's business grew quickly and Mummy was soon able to boast to her sisters that at least *she* had a man who earned enough money to buy them their own house right in the centre of town!

'Anyway, to answer your question, I never thought I would leave Jamaica. I loved my home and my sister was my best friend. I wouldn't have imagined living anywhere without her close by. But then, you see, things changed after I met Harry Coleville-Smith.

Miss Campbell's voice tailed off and, shaking her head slightly, she carried on.

'The Coleville-Smiths were a very rich family, Faye, and very well known in Kingston. Mr Coleville-Smith – Harry's father – was the son of a half-Jamaican, half-Irish woman and an Englishman who had been sent out to the island by his father (if you believe the town gossips, he was an aristocrat of some kind) after running up a pile of gambling debts. Anyway, the man must have mended his ways when he got to Jamaica because by the time Millicent and I were teenagers, the Coleville-Smith family owned a large sugar processing factory on the island and Coleville's, one of the most popular department stores in town. Harry's mother came from Bermuda and she and Harry's father were both very light-skinned people. Harry's mother managed the department store and because they bought their office supplies from us, she would occasionally come to the shop herself to place an order.

'Harry was the youngest of their three children and most definitely the apple of his mother's eye. It was easy to see why. I tell you, Faye, he was so handsome he could stop traffic! His complexion was like a girl's – all soft and creamy. He had lovely wavy light-brown curls with little gold streaks everywhere and looked just like an angel. Sadly, though, he had the most terrible stammer I'd ever heard and it took him the longest time to say the most simple sentence! His family tried everything to help him get rid of it but nothing worked. Once in a while his mother would send him over to our shop with an order and, if Millicent or I happened to be working, we would fight like cats to be the one to serve him!

'Anyway, one day I was in the shop alone when Harry came in. Millicent was down with a bad cold and Mummy had refused to let her leave the house in case she passed it on to a customer. Harry was in no rush to leave – in any case, with that stammer, it usually took him quite a while to place his orders – and we chattered together for ages. Before he left, he asked me out to a dance that weekend. I said yes, of course! I was so excited and I couldn't wait to tell Millicent. That Saturday night I wore my best dress and even though Millicent almost died of envy, I went to the dance on his arm. Oh boy, we had a marvellous time...

'Thinking about it now, Faye, we must have looked quite a funny pair. There he was, so tall and fair-skinned, and then me, so small and dark. But we had fun together, you know. After that first dance, he asked me out again and again. He felt so comfortable with me that he would hardly stammer at all when we were alone together.

'In those days, my dear, when you went out with a man on a regular basis, it was expected that you were heading for marriage. Even though Millicent and Mummy had warned me that the Coleville-Smiths were out of our league, I knew how Harry felt about me and I refused to listen. Harry and I talked about a life together and how happy we would be.'

Miss Campbell paused again and Faye leaned forward eagerly, totally absorbed in the story.

'Well, things came to a head one afternoon. Clarence, the clerk from Coleville's, came to our shop to collect the stationery supplies they had ordered earlier. I had been helping Daddy in the back and was coming into the front of the shop when I heard Clarence saying Harry's name. Clarence was so busy sharing his gossip that he didn't hear me come through the door. I went back quietly behind the door when I heard Harry's name mentioned and was horrified to hear him tell my mother that Mrs Coleville-Smith had secretly arranged for Harry to go and stay with her family in Bermuda, to work in her brother's business. Clarence – Lord! I can just see him now with his big eyes rolling and his round head weaving while he drank his coffee – then told my mother how he had overheard Mrs Coleville-Smith on the telephone to her brother planning how to get her son away from "the social climbing dark-skinned mouse Harry has taken up with" and that "if she thinks she has hooked my boy, she had better think again!"

'After that, Faye, everything happened so quickly, I couldn't believe it. Before I could blink, Harry was in Bermuda and I was on my own, with everyone staring at me wherever I went. Oh, child, I didn't mind the gossips too much, but I *did* miss my Harry!

'Mummy was furious. She soon got fed up with everyone gossiping about us for a change and decided that I should come to England to stay with her younger sister who was studying in London. To be honest, Faye, I didn't care *where* I went. Nothing about Kingston made any sense any more and I was happy to come over here. So I stayed with Auntie Angela and went to secretarial school.

Mr Fiske hired me shortly after I got my qualifications and I have been here ever since.'

Miss Campbell stopped speaking and there was silence for several minutes. Visibly shaking herself back into the present, she smiled at Faye.

'You see, my dear, even an old lady like me was once in love. Just like you are with your Michael!'

Faye had been listening in fascination to the older woman's story and trying to reconcile the prim little mouse before her with the image of a passionate young Jamaican girl pining for her lover. Now, as she stared into Miss Campbell's twinkling eyes, she wondered wryly, and not for the first time, if what she felt for Michael could really be described as love.

Miss Campbell looked at her watch and tutted as she realised the time. Rising nimbly to her feet, she brushed the biscuit crumbs from her coffee-coloured cashmere cardigan, pushed her glasses back onto her nose and quickly rinsed out her coffee cup.

Having said a gentle goodbye to Faye, she was just about to leave the room when the younger girl asked suddenly.

'Miss Campbell, since I've been so nosy already, can I ask you one last thing?'

'What is that, my dear?' Miss Campbell asked indulgently.

'What does the T. in your name stand for? I've always wondered,' Faye said curiously.

Miss Campbell's eyes twinkled as she turned the handle of the door.

'After what I've told you today, Faye, I would have thought you could guess.' With a final wave to a mystified Faye, Miss Campbell said as she left the room, 'Actually, I was named after my mother's family, Faye. The T. stands for Truelove.'

4

Pigfoot or Pasta?

Travelling on the London Underground during the evening rush hour is, at best, a test of human endurance. On a Friday evening, however, Faye thought moodily, the rush hour made the most hideous picture of hell seem pretty acceptable.

It had been one of those rare days when Faye and her boss had genuinely been under pressure. With two of the other partners away, Junior had been called upon to handle far more than his usual negligible workload and, as a result, Faye had been swamped with documents to produce, check and update.

When she had finally managed to escape her exhausted boss, the hands on the large clock in the reception area showed it was past six o'clock. Oblivious to the cold, she'd raced along the dark cobbled streets to the tube station, feeling the sweat prickling her skin under her wool coat. Once again, Michael had arranged to meet her at the tube station in Brixton and she had less than two hours to get home and prepare for the evening.

To her annoyance the Edgware bound tube she wanted was sliding away from the platform just as she galloped down the stairs at Tottenham Court Road station.

'Crap!' Panting hard from the unaccustomed exercise, she watched in frustration as the train moved off, the red lights at the back disappearing into the dark tunnel. A quick glance at the platform indicator showed that the next train was due in twelve minutes.

Pacing up and down the platform, Faye mentally ran through her wardrobe and tried to remember where she had last seen her favourite black jeans.

Five minutes later, in true London Underground fashion, the platform indicator still showed a twelve-minute wait for her train. Glaring at a cheerful busker in a woolly hat who seemed determined to serenade her, she elbowed her way through the fast-thickening crowd to stand further down the platform.

Despite the twelve minutes still showing on the indicator, a sudden rush of air accompanied by a distant rumbling signalled the arrival of another train. Faye stood as close as she dared to the edge of the platform, determined to get onto the train even if she had to push someone under it first. With a loud rumble, the train rolled into the station and she positioned herself directly in front of the double doors, bracing herself for the rush of the descending crowd.

'Stand clear of the doors, please. Stand clear of the doors!'

The mass of people crushed inside looked in dire need

of oxygen as the train ground to a screeching halt. As soon as the doors swept open, the cooped up occupants spilled out, gulping in the semi-fresh air. Faye stood firm against the mass of passengers streaming out from the congested train and those pushing her from the rear. Then, seizing her moment and ignoring the outraged cries of the tube prisoners still waiting for release, she nipped smartly through a small gap in the human traffic and into the overheated carriage. She spotted a row of recently vacated seats and sat down on the one nearest the door.

The tube moved slowly between stations, disgorging bodies and replacing them immediately. Faye's frustration increased by the minute and turned to fury as people getting on and off the train trampled on her ruinously expensive Russell & Bromley leather boots, still an outstanding item on her credit card bill. Finally, the train pulled into Hampstead station, releasing her from the stuffy carriage.

Relieved to see the lift to street level was working, she resisted the temptation to give the doors a helpful push as they slowly slid open.

Almost dropping her keys in her haste to open her front door, she dashed in and cannoned straight into a tall blonde figure standing in the hallway.

'Oof! Sorry, Lucinda... Hi.' The apology-cum-greeting was delivered between gasps as Faye attempted to struggle out of her coat and kick her boots off at the same time.

'Hi to you too,' was the amused response. 'No, wait, don't tell me – you're supposed to be somewhere in ten seconds from now and you're late. Am I right?'

Lucinda Bennett and Faye had been good friends for years despite the differences in their personalities. Where Faye often lacked confidence, Lucinda was never at a loss for words and had yet to meet anyone who intimidated her. Unlike Faye who usually hung back, Lucinda was a firm believer in going after what you wanted, as long as no one got too hurt in the process. Having first spotted William when he had reluctantly showed up at a dinner party at a mutual friend's house to give Faye a lift home, she had made an instant beeline for him. William, who had never had any trouble dealing with unwanted female attention, had been reduced to adoring putty in her elegant hands before he knew what had hit him. Unlike William's previous girlfriends who were usually intimidated by his father, Lucinda had given Dr Bonsu's outstretched hand a miss when she was introduced to him, and instead hugged him like a long lost friend. Her genuine enthusiasm about everything combined with her stunning good looks made it difficult for anyone to dislike her, including Lottie, who had never believed that any girl was good enough for William.

'And they say blondes are dumb,' Faye grinned in reply to the question as she headed towards the stairs. 'Actually, I'm meeting Michael in Brixton in about—' she glanced at her watch and squealed in horror, taking the steps two at a time.

'I was just leaving – do you want a lift anywhere?' Lucinda called after Faye's disappearing back. Hearing a muffled scream from upstairs that she took to mean yes, she went back into the kitchen where Lottie was putting the finishing touches to the chicken pie she was making for dinner. Carefully placing the brimming pie dish into the oven, Lottie looked across at Lucinda.

'I take it that was Faye?' she said, jerking her head in the direction of the dull thuds coming from above the kitchen. 'Late again, I suppose?'

Lucinda's smile was answer enough.

'Well, I know Faye won't be in for dinner tonight,' she said. 'What are you and William up to?'

'We're going to try out a new wine bar that's just opened up in town,' Lucinda said. 'I'll wait and give Faye a lift before I head home. William's working late and says he'll pick me up when he's done.'

A few minutes and several loud thumps later, Faye crashed through the kitchen door, still fastening the buttons on her black jeans, their tight cut and her spiky boots making her long legs appear endless. Ignoring Lottie's pursed lips as she took in the low cut strappy black top visible under her leather jacket, Faye was almost wringing her hands in desperation.

'Lucinda, let's go! *Now* or Michael will go ballistic!' Her agonised plea was wasted on Lottie who simply sniffed scornfully.

'Faye, when will you stop letting that boy bully you? You've only just now got in, for goodness' sake! At least sit down and have a cup of tea or something before you rush out.'

Lucinda grinned at the distaste in Lottie's voice when she referred to Michael. The older woman had never quite recovered from the lecture he had once given her when he warned her that 'reverse colonialism through domestic service to the formerly colonised peoples of Africa' could never atone for the centuries of slavery and oppression that had been practised by her people. Although at the time she had pointed out that the only oppression she had ever seen in Glasgow had come from rival football fans against the rest of the community on Saturday nights, her already poor opinion of Michael had sunk to an all-time low.

Taking pity on Faye who was now literally hopping from foot to foot in agitation, Lucinda slid off the kitchen stool and snatched up her car keys and coat in one fluid graceful movement.

'Okay, let's go! Lottie, I'll come over at the weekend. I want to know all about that couple that's just moved into number 28. I've seen them a couple of times now and, quite honestly, the man looks pretty dodgy to me.'

Blowing Lottie a quick kiss, Faye followed close on Lucinda's heels as they hurried out of the house. She slid into the padded leather passenger seat of her friend's sleek silver Mazda convertible, which, rather like its owner, was gleaming and immaculately maintained. Faye looked around the pristine interior and sighed enviously. Her own Fiesta, littered with Mars bar wrappers and old issues of *The Black Herald* that she had never quite got round to reading, made her car look like a seedy bed and breakfast compared to this luxury five star hotel.

As they drove off, Faye checked her watch again, now completely despairing of being on time. It was nearly seven-thirty and the Friday night traffic into town was moving at a slow crawl. It was clearly time for a change of plan.

'Luce, just drop me off at Euston, if that's okay? I'll get the tube down to Brixton. With all this traffic, the Underground is bound to be faster.'

Lucinda nodded. Barely pausing to indicate, she turned left into the road leading to Euston station, cutting confidently across the choked lanes of traffic with supreme disregard for the irate drivers forced to give way. She weaved expertly through the cars slowly inching their way along the Euston Road until they reached the entrance to the underground.

'You are a *star*! Thanks a million – I'll see you later.' Faye gave her friend a hurried kiss goodbye and slid out of the car.

For the second time in less than an hour she was back underground. The platform indicator showed the next Brixton-bound train was due in four minutes. Yet less than a minute later, clearly having reservations about its original information, the indicator now showed that the train was due in six minutes.

Faye turned around to find herself surrounded by a small group of women dressed in flowing skirts with shawls tied around the shoulders. Two of them were carrying babies tightly swaddled in coloured shawls. One of the women leaned forward to try to pin a purple posy wrapped in tin foil onto the lapel of Faye's coat while another held her baby up to her. With a smile that revealed several missing teeth, she held out a rather grubby hand, palm upwards.

Trying really hard not to grimace at the unmistakable smell of a baby in urgent need of a nappy change, Faye turned her head away from the smelly infant and scrabbled in her coat pocket for change. Clutching gratefully at the fluff-covered coins dropped into her palm, the woman gave another flash of her discoloured smile and hugged her protesting baby to her chest.

The sound of the approaching train gave Faye the opportunity to slip away, and she moved quickly down the platform as it thundered into the station. This time the train moved quickly and smoothly between stations, arriving at Brixton without incident.

Well, twenty minutes isn't *that* bad, Faye muttered under her breath as she tried to check her make-up in the smudged mirror of her compact while walking up the moving escalator. *Of course, Michael could just buy a car and save me from this endless rushing around all the time*, she thought moodily. *It's not like he can't afford it.*

Although Michael constantly scorned the need for a car, blaming car owners for every possible environmental problem, he never had any complaints about her driving them everywhere or even using her car himself when it suited him, Faye thought irritably. Look at Lucinda – the lucky cow just sat at home and waited for William to pick her up whenever they went out.

'Here, Faye! Over here!'

She turned to see Michael waving vigorously at her. He was wearing a long black leather coat over fashionably baggy jeans and a black woolly cap covered his hair. Her resentment was quickly forgotten as the familiar warm rush of pleasure at seeing him swept over her.

She sighed as she looked into his brown eyes, fringed

with the thick long lashes that always reminded her of a cuddly puppy. *I know he can be difficult*, she thought, *but he is* so *gorgeous.*

Resisting the urge to hurl herself on him, she hugged him tightly and pressed her warm eager lips against his cold mouth. Only briefly returning the pressure, Michael patted her awkwardly on the shoulder before quickly disengaging himself and rubbing his hands together against the night chill.

'Hey, what's up?' he said casually. 'Well, for once you're not *that* late,' he added with a smile. 'Come on, let's go.'

Propelling her out of the crowded station and up the stairs, he draped an arm around her shoulders as they set off down the street at a brisk pace.

'So, like I said on the phone, I have to do a write-up for the paper on this new restaurant that opened up last week. The owner is Jamaican and from what he told me when I spoke to him, his vision is to offer really authentic home food. If we like the food tonight, I'll set up an interview for him with a couple of food writers I know – I'm sure he'll appreciate the publicity.'

As they walked, he moved his arm away and hugged himself against the cold. Wanting to stay close to him, she tried to slip her hand inside the crook of his arm but his hands remained resolutely clamped against his forearms. Sighing, she gave up and pushed her hands into the pockets of her jacket, forcing herself to concentrate on what he was saying. Struck by his unusual cheeriness – Michael usually needed a lot of jollying to emerge from a sulk as prolonged as his recent effort – Faye looked up at him with narrowed eyes.

'You're very chirpy tonight,' she remarked. It was also out of character for the Michael she knew not to have made any further reference to the previous weekend.

He gave a careless shrug and carried on without comment.

'So who's coming this evening?' she said a few minutes later, interrupting his flow again.

He put his arm around her to steer her away from a tramp staggering towards them, clutching a can of lager. When they were safely past, he released her and continued at a brisk pace, his hands buried deep inside his coat pockets.

'Well, Philomena can't make it,' he said. 'She's got a poetry evening with the Brixton Caribbean Women's Circle. She's the main organiser, so she couldn't get away.'

'So it's just Luther, Wesley and Jiggy then?' Faye asked slowly, looking forward to the evening less and less by the minute. Michael didn't answer immediately and she looked across at him curiously.

'Well, Wesley's sister, Jasmine, will probably come with them,' he said casually. 'I invited her as well.'

'*Who?*' Faye stopped walking and stared at him.

Reluctantly forced to stop, he sighed with exaggerated patience. 'Jasmine. She's Wesley's younger sister,' he repeated. 'She's a part-time lecturer at a college in Balham. She's nice – you'll like her.'

He slipped his arm through hers and pulled her along with him as they walked around a corner and into a small side road, past dark vacant lots and shabby-looking terraced houses with huge satellite dishes fixed to the roofs.

Her LK Bennett boots had been designed to be easy

on the eye, not the feet, and she was now beginning to feel their pinch. To her relief, the restaurant was only a few minutes away and they were soon in front of a building with a large sign bearing the words *Pigfoot Etcetera* in pink letters above the image of a large platter of pink pigfoot nestling on a bed of dark green spinach leaves.

Walking into the restaurant, Faye was immediately hit by the smell of fresh paint combined with the musky scent of lighted candles and the unmistakable odour of paraffin. Inside the poorly lit room, about fifteen wooden tables had been laid and in the centre of each one was a small bouquet of blue silk flowers and matching pink salt and pepper mills. Paraffin lamps set on metal stands were dotted around the room, adding to the odd and old-fashioned décor.

At the far end of the restaurant, she could see a narrow bar topped with an array of glasses and manned by a slim black man wearing a white shirt under a black and white waistcoat with a matching bow tie. As she and Michael moved into the restaurant, the bartender pushed a CD into a player behind the bar and reggae music softly filled the room.

Faye turned her attention back to Michael who was exchanging loud greetings with a tall dark man in his early thirties striding towards them.

'Faye, this is Trevor Royal,' Michael said, grinning at the other man. 'He's the owner of the restaurant.'

Trevor smiled broadly at Faye, the gold tooth at the front of his mouth glinting in the muted lighting of the room. Faye shook his outstretched hand and, conscious of his expectant gaze, she cast her eyes around the restaurant trying desperately to find something positive to say.

'I've never seen anything like this place before,' she said truthfully.

Trevor's smile was now even wider and he stroked the small gold hoop earring in his left earlobe thoughtfully.

'Yeah, we wanted something a bit different, you get me?' he said, gesturing broadly around the room. His voice was deep and his accent pure South London. He pointed to one of the paraffin lamps.

'See those lamps there, yeah? That was my girlfriend Angie's idea – she's the chef. When they was growing up in Jamaica, that's what they used to keep in the house for when the power went off.' He burst into a huge roar of laughter, slapping Michael on the back until he joined in while Faye watched them both in bemusement. After a moment, Trevor abruptly stopped laughing. Placing a heavy hand on Michael's shoulder, he led them to a large table in the middle of the room.

'All right then, Mr Reporter,' he said loudly. 'Here's your table for tonight. Best one in the house – know what I mean?' He winked at Michael knowingly and burst into loud laughter again.

Trevor threw his arm around Faye's shoulders and shouted towards the bar.

''Ere, Phil, come and find out what Mr Reporter and his woman want to drink!'

Wincing at the sudden volume so close to her ear, Faye slid out from under Trevor's arm and pulled out a chair, having learned long ago that there was no point waiting for Michael to do any such thing. According to him, pulling out chairs and holding doors open for women was an insult to their equal status with men.

Trevor walked over to the bar to prod Phil into action and Michael took a seat across the table from Faye. Frowning slightly, she looked across at him and whispered.

'Should you have told him that you're a journalist?' She ignored the darkening expression on his face. 'I mean, aren't you supposed to be undercover to see what their food and the service is *really* like?'

Whatever response he was going to make was cut off by Phil's arrival at their table. Waving a languid hand in the air and with a stubby pencil and small notebook at the ready, he smiled politely at them. Up close, he was even thinner than he had appeared half-hidden behind the bar counter and Faye stared enviously at the tiny span of his waist. His voice, when he spoke, was soft and strongly accented and with a pronounced lisp.

'Welcome to Pigfoot Etcetera and a good evening to you. I'll be back to take your food order but what are you all drinking now?' He nodded in the direction of the bar. 'We've got some *divine* rum from the islands.'

Frowning at Faye's involuntary shudder at the word rum, he tossed his head and added somewhat petulantly, 'Or maybe I can fix you a nice fruit cocktail? I can recommend the Tropical Island Sunset. It's fresh pineapple juice with a touch of cherryade and just a hint of crushed mint?'

Anxious not to offend further, she nodded in agreement and absently fingered the waxy vinyl table-cloth while Michael ordered a glass of Jamaican rum that Phil assured him was 'full-bodied, rich and honeyed on the nose'. Although it was now well after eight o'clock, with the exception of the owner and bartender, she and Michael were still the only two people in the restaurant. Suppressing a sigh, she followed Michael's cue and picked up her menu, a small, laminated card stuck in a wooden stand next to the improbably blue flowers. The short list of dishes was almost without exception centred on the main ingredient of pigfoot.

'Pigfoot Royal, Island-Style Pigfoot, Spicy Rice with Pigfoot, Pigfoot Supreme...' Faye read out the list with dismay. Towards the bottom of the card, in smaller print, was a short selection of non-pigfoot dishes and two types of dessert.

I suppose I should be grateful they don't have Pigfoot ice cream, she thought morosely. She leaned across the table, keeping her voice low.

'Michael, this place isn't exactly heaving with people. Don't you think it's a bit risky setting up a restaurant for only one type of food?'

He looked up from his menu. 'Maybe you don't eat this kind of food in your cosy Hampstead world,' he said, his words laced with sarcasm, 'but down here this is part of the culture.' He looked at his watch. 'Anyway, it's still early; it probably gets busier later on.'

Chastened by his dismissive response, she subsided into her chair and went back to scrutinising the menu. She looked up as a cold shock of air wafted across the overheated room and cut straight through her flimsy blouse. Wesley stood in the doorway of the restaurant and was holding the front door wide to let Jiggy, Luther and a

96

petite girl with a mass of red gold curls through.

Jasmine, I presume, Faye thought curiously. The girl slipped her coat off as soon as she walked in, revealing a short red skirt and a close-fitting white top.

'Hey, guys! Over here!' Michael's voice sounded overly loud in the empty restaurant. Without waiting for them to reach the table, he rushed over to greet them, hugging the girl and kissing her warmly on the cheek before shaking hands with the men. As she watched the small group heading in her direction, Faye's stomach muscles tightened involuntarily in alarm.

Clearly relieved to see any paying customers, Trevor Royal also rushed over to greet the new arrivals and stopped them to shake hands before they could reach their table. His loud booming laugh reverberated around the room as he rubbed his hands together joyfully.

'Welcome to our little piece of home, my brothers and my sister, right here in London town!'

Faye watched in disbelief as Michael moved swiftly to their table to pull out the chair next to his and help Jasmine into the seat. What the hell had happened to the "insulting the emancipated female" line, she thought furiously, glaring at her boyfriend who studiously refused to make eye contact with her.

Aware that the other new arrivals were eyeing her somewhat warily, Faye forced a smile and rose to her feet. She shook hands quickly with the three men, mumbling what she hoped sounded like a polite greeting.

'I hope you're feeling better today, Faye?' Wesley said pointedly, his pale blue eyes fixed on her face. She resisted the sudden urge to punch him and contented herself with a polite smile and nod before taking her seat again.

Michael cleared his throat as though he had an important announcement to make. 'Faye, let me introduce you to Jasmine Baptiste, Wesley's sister,' he said with a broad smile. 'Jasmine, this is Faye Bonsu, a very good friend of mine.'

A very good friend? Faye arched an eyebrow questioningly at her partner, who smiled innocently back at her.

She gave a weary sigh; it was clearly going to be a very long evening. Forcing a smile at the girl sitting in front of her, Faye leaned across the expanse of white vinyl and shook hands. Jasmine's hand was as small and dainty as the rest of her, making Faye feel like a clumsy giant in comparison. The candlelight picked up the burnished gold highlights in the girl's hair, giving the impression of a speckled halo around her head.

She clearly doesn't go to Sharice of flipping Streatham, Faye thought sourly, fighting back the temptation to smooth down her own hair, which was only just starting to recover from Sharice's very expensive and very damaging hot steam treatment and curl.

The men sat down and Faye found herself sandwiched between Luther and Jiggy, while Wesley settled himself between Luther and Michael. Luther gave a friendly nod and asked how she was, his eyes showing none of the hostility she always sensed from Wesley.

Jiggy, whom Faye had secretly dubbed the silent one since he rarely had anything to say to her, smiled politely and asked if they had been waiting long. His short dreadlocks glistened in the lamplight and once again he was wearing an African-style smock, this one in a striped black and white fabric.

Jasmine snuggled up next to Michael, pushing him playfully with her elbow and giggling with excitement. He didn't seem to mind and her soft curls grazed his cheek as he bent his head closer to hers, laughing as she made a comment clearly meant for his ears alone.

Faye frowned, bewildered by Michael's behaviour and feeling more than a little hurt by the obvious attention he was paying to Jasmine. She responded absently to a question from Jiggy about the menu and watched with growing anger as her boyfriend casually smoothed back an errant curl that had fallen over Jasmine's eyes.

The waiter wandered back and dumped Michael's rum on the table. Rather more carefully and with a dramatic flourish, he placed a tall glass of a dark yellow liquid with a sprig of mint floating on top in front of Faye. Taking out his notebook and pencil, Phil asked the new arrivals for their drink orders and, without missing a beat, the three men ordered the Jamaican rum.

Phil looked pointedly at Michael who was laughing at something Jasmine had just whispered to him.

'Would your lady also like the rum, sir?'

Faye choked on the sip of Tropical Island Sunset she had just taken and glared furiously at Michael, waiting for him to correct the waiter. Michael kept his head down and, unable to make eye contact with him, Faye looked round to see Wesley looking at her, a half-smile playing across his lips.

Jasmine made no effort to correct Phil either and

instead turned towards Michael and lightly caressed his bare forearm, her glossy lips curved into a little pout.

'Oh, I don't know! I can never make up my mind what I want to drink,' she purred. 'Michael, what do you recommend – you're the expert at eating out.'

Faye watched in fascination as Michael's chest literally swelled before her eyes. *If I had asked him that, he would have told me to stop being pathetic*, she thought, as he paused to give Jasmine's question a few moments of serious thought. His suggestion of a rum cocktail, which Phil huffily explained was called the Island Rum Delight, was met with an ecstatic response.

'That sounds wonderful!' Jasmine smiled sweetly at Michael and her eyes shone with appreciation.

Oh puh-lease! Get over yourself, woman, it's only a drink! For a moment, Faye thought she had spoken the words out loud. In the few minutes since she had met her, she was already irritated at the other girl's wide-eyed innocent act and proprietary attitude towards Michael, and even more annoyed at her boyfriend who seemed to not just welcome, but actively encourage her attentions.

Faye took another sip of her tepid drink, trying not to grimace at the taste of the sickly sweet liquid. Well aware that she had already embarrassed herself enough in front of them, she decided not to risk making a fuss by asking for ice and instead watched as the group of old friends around the table chatted easily amongst themselves. She felt uncomfortably like an outsider crashing a private party; a sensation that Michael's behaviour was making even more intense.

After the waiter had deposited everyone's drinks, the men sat back, drinking their rum and laughing at each other's stories. After a quick visit to their table to check on his customers, Trevor left them to their own devices, retreating with a farewell laugh to a small room behind the bar. Phil hovered in the background for several minutes but when it became clear that they were in no hurry to order, he shrugged and returned to his post behind the bar, apparently quite content to polish the same glasses over and over again.

Faye glanced surreptitiously at her watch and wished she were anywhere but in her current location. Luther, although friendly enough, was caught up in a lively debate with Wesley about Jamaican politics. After their initial exchanges, Jiggy had lapsed into his customary silence, and Michael was barely acknowledging her existence, let alone behaving like an attentive partner. For the first time since meeting him, she found herself wondering whether having a boyfriend was really worth going through this agony. Is sitting at home watching EastEnders really worse than this? *What the hell am I doing here?*

'So, Faye, what do you do?' Jasmine's silky voice roused Faye from her brooding. Even in the dim light of the restaurant, Faye could see she had eyes almost identical in colour to her brother's and with the same slightly hypnotic quality.

'I work for a firm of solicitors,' she replied coolly.

'Oh, really,' Jasmine cooed. 'That sounds interesting. Are you a lawyer, then?'

Michael laughed. 'No, Faye's a secretary, Jas. Not quite

101

as demanding, is it?' He grinned at Faye and she glared back at him, outraged at the blatant put-down. She gritted her teeth and bit back the angry response on her lips, fearful of causing another scene. Conscious of the other girl's scrutiny, she forced herself to smile.

'What do *you* do, Jasmine?' she asked politely. Before Jasmine could answer, Michael jumped in again.

'She's a lecturer in Caribbean History and Culture.' He looked down at the golden halo of curls brushing against his shoulder and said proudly, 'There's not much Jasmine here doesn't know about the islands. She's even writing a book on the history of slavery in Grenada, aren't you?'

Perfect, Faye thought sourly, *a cultural genius to boot*. And how did Michael know so much about her, anyway? She took another sip of her Tropical Island Sunset, immediately regretting the decision, and returned to her study of the pig-themed menu. Despite having read it so many times that she could have recited the names of the dishes without looking if anyone had asked her, Faye still couldn't pick a single one that appealed to her. While she loved many Caribbean dishes and since meeting Michael could now cook an acceptable jerk chicken with rice and peas, she simply couldn't stand pigfoot. The texture of the bony pink meat didn't appeal to her in the slightest and actually left her feeling slightly nauseous. Knowing what Michael's reaction would be if she dared to voice this, she looked longingly at the other options on the menu before returning with a sigh to the restaurant's signature dishes.

Taking advantage of a lull in the conversation between him and Wesley, Faye turned to Luther and asked after

Philomena. His smile was warm and when he spoke, he sounded quite affable. 'Oh, she's doing fine. She has her women's group meeting tonight so she couldn't come along.'

'Philo is *so* committed to bringing Caribbean women like us together. You should join, Faye; we have some really interesting talks and lectures with artists and writers from back home,' Jasmine's smooth voice interjected. Then she gasped dramatically before the other girl could speak.

'Oh, silly me!' she said, her tone sweetly apologetic. 'Sorry, Faye, I forgot you're not from the Caribbean. Michael said you are from Africa, is that not so?' A careless toss of her mane set the golden highlights dancing in the candlelight.

'Yes,' Faye replied, her voice curt. 'My family comes from Ghana.' She turned to Luther again. 'Do say hello to Philomena for me. I really enjoyed meeting her and seeing your lovely house.'

Luther nodded politely and returned to his conversation with Wesley.

'Yes, they do have a beautiful home, don't they?' Jasmine spoke out again, her tone casual. 'I always love spending time there, don't I Michael?'

He gave her a brief smile and glanced at Faye almost nervously before hastily directing a question to Jiggy.

Jasmine's eyes were fixed thoughtfully on Faye. Almost colourless in the dim light, they reflected the flames from the scattered lamps and candles in the restaurant. She slowly reached into her handbag and daintily extracted a pack of cigarettes. Faye stiffened and waited for the inevitable explosion from Michael, who hated smokers with a passion.

It was clearly to be a night of surprises. As Jasmine stood up, obviously intending to step outside to smoke, Michael's hand closed over hers. He broke off from his conversation and clasped the small hand gently while shaking his head in mock sorrow.

'Don't tell me you still haven't given up smoking, Jas!' He gently plucked the packet of cigarettes from her fingers and tossed it back into her handbag in one deft movement.

Jasmine sat down again and pouted prettily as he ruffled her curls in mock apology. 'There are *lots* of things I haven't given up on, Michael,' she said, a cryptic smile replacing the pout.

She turned to Faye who had been watching them silently. 'Do you have any vices, Faye?' she asked slyly, her eyes glinting maliciously as she took in the set expression on the other girl's face.

Faye shrugged, determined not to rise to the bait.

'Who hasn't?' she said coolly. *Although* mine *don't include behaving like a man-stealing bitch*, she thought furiously. Fed up of Jasmine's needling, Faye decided it was her turn to smile sweetly at Michael and she turned towards him, raising her voice to get his attention.

'Although, speaking of vices, I'm surprised Michael is being so tolerant about you smoking. What is it you always say, *darling*?' Ignoring his warning frown, she continued, her voice deepening in imitation of his masculine tones. '"People who smoke are disgusting, selfish polluters of the universe who should all be made to live together on a desert island!"'

Jasmine's eyes darkened in anger and she stared back

at Faye, for once apparently lost for words. Wesley's voice suddenly broke into the tense silence. His pale eyes were fixed on Faye as he spoke.

'I don't think there's too much he don't know about Jasmine and her vices,' he said coolly. 'After living with her for over a year, he should be used to her smoking, you know?'

Faye didn't know and, for one stunned moment, she couldn't breathe. The background music that had been playing softly suddenly sounded much louder as the pieces of the puzzle started to fall together. Michael's sudden animation and change of behaviour, Wesley's hostility and even Jasmine's proprietary behaviour now all made sense. Feeling like a fool, she stared blankly at Michael and tried to swallow the huge lump that had suddenly appeared in her throat. She shrank back into her seat and pinched her thigh hard to stop the threatening tears.

I will not *cry in front of this woman*, she thought grimly, only too aware of Jasmine smiling smugly as she scanned the menu she was holding.

Michael glared angrily at Wesley before ducking his head in an effort to avoid Faye's gaze and pretended to scrutinise his menu. The other men quickly did the same, clearly relieved that a scene appeared to have been averted.

There was quiet while everyone read through their menu until Michael broke the silence.

'Are we all ready to order?' he said, looking round the table, his eyes not quite meeting Faye's. 'Don't forget I have to write about this place so let's all order different dishes so I can get a good idea of what the food is like.'

He gestured to Phil who glided over immediately with his spiral notebook poised for action. Lisping through the specials, he waited expectantly. Michael was the first to speak, choosing the Pigfoot Royal.

'The house speciality – an excellent choice, sir.' Phil nodded in approval.

Wesley finally decided on the Chilli and Ginger Pigfoot, while Jiggy chose the Pigfoot Island Style. Luther and Jasmine spent several minutes arguing over who should order the Pigfoot Paradiso – Jasmine won – and with a good-natured laugh, Luther settled for the spicy pigfoot served with a medley of vegetables.

The waiter tapped his pencil impatiently on his note-book as Faye wildly scanned the list again. Nothing looked in the least bit appealing and all eyes were on her now.

Oh great, she thought, trying to focus on the words printed on the card in front of her; no pressure then. A quick glance around the table didn't help.

Jasmine's expression could only be described as scornful as she took in Faye's rising confusion. Michael's face had the familiar look of impatience that Faye sadly realised he only ever seemed to reserve for her. The others, now silent, waited impassively.

Phil cleared his throat and shifted his feet restlessly.

'Perhaps madam would also want the Pigfoot Royal?' His tone was condescending as he looked down his shiny nose at her.

Faye looked round helplessly and with increasing desperation, her stomach now twisted into knots. Wesley's eyes met hers and he stared at her, making no effort to disguise his dislike, while his sister smiled openly at Faye's obvious discomfort.

Phil cleared his throat again.

Sitting up straight for the first time that evening, Faye raised her chin defiantly and said coolly to the waiter, 'I'll have the Pasta Carbonara.'

5

Roots Culture

'It almost choked me, but I ate every last strand of that bloody spaghetti!' Faye gazed moodily into her empty coffee cup as she finished recounting her ordeal to a riveted Caroline.

Pushing aside the rubber gloves she had been wearing while she cleaned her kitchen, Caroline asked impatiently. 'So what happened? What did Michael say?'

Faye shrugged. 'Nothing – he just looked daggers at me. Jasmine gave that silly gasp of hers and said "Oh!" Honestly, you'd think I'd murdered someone the way they all stared at me! As soon as I finished eating, I just threw some money onto the table, smiled sweetly at everyone and left, saying that I had an early start in the morning. Michael didn't move – not even to see me to the door!'

Her rising indignation subsided as her despair at the turn of events threatened to overwhelm her again.

Caroline gave her friend a quick squeeze of sympathy and refilled the coffee pot, giving Faye a chance to pull herself together. She poured some of the fresh brew into Faye's cup and perched on the stool next to her.

'So what are you going to do now?' she asked gently. She hated to see Faye so upset and although, as far as she was concerned Faye would be well rid of Michael, seeing her best friend look so miserable, she resolved to hold her tongue for now.

Faye's eyes were red and puffy and it was clear that her tears were still close to the surface. 'I don't know,' she wailed, rubbing her swollen eyes with the back of her hand. 'I just can't believe that Michael could do that to me!' Sniffing, she took a gulp of the coffee and shook her head.

'I mean, Caro, when was he going to tell me that she was his ex?' Faye's voice started to rise again as she relived the humiliation of the previous night. 'If you knew how many *hours* I spent listening to him rant and rave about what an ungrateful bitch his ex-girlfriend was when we first started going out. I didn't even know her name because the only thing he ever called her was "that ungrateful bitch..."' Her voice tailed off as she shook her head once more in disbelief.

Caroline was sipping her coffee thoughtfully. 'Well, after all his lectures on cultural purity, it's quite funny that his old girlfriend's as white as me,' she observed. 'Funny how he didn't mention *that* either!'

Faye giggled, her misery temporarily forgotten. 'I can't wait to see William's face when I tell him – after all Michael's snide comments about Lucinda!'

Caroline gave a snort of laughter and, swallowing the rest of her coffee, retrieved her rubber gloves and continued with her cleaning, swinging her arms widely. Faye ducked hastily before Caroline swept her off her stool and moved over to sit in the old rocking chair that took up a full corner of the small modern kitchen. Despite the fact that it was completely at odds with the sparkling chrome and white kitchen fitted with every possible labour and space saving device, the chair was always the most popular item in the room. The reason lay partly in its history as the original rocking chair that Marcus's nanny had sat in to rock him when he was a baby. When he left home, Marcus had carried it off to university and then to the house he had shared with two former university friends before moving into the apartment. But the main reason for the usual mad scramble everyone made to sit in it was that after a hard day's work, its rocking movement never failed to soothe the spirit.

Faye propelled herself back and forth with her long legs and soon felt the comfort of the rocking slowly start to ease the raw pain in her chest. She looked on in fascination as Caroline whipped a mop out from a tall cupboard and mercilessly swiped at any germs that had dared to visit her kitchen floor.

'What's with you and all this cleaning?' she asked, puzzled. 'Can whoever's taken my friend away, please bring her back!'

She grinned at the determined expression on her friend's face as she pushed the mop over the spotless tiles. 'Besides, didn't Mrs Vance come and clean only two days ago?'

Caroline was so relieved to see Faye smiling that she

stopped, tossed the mop back into the cupboard, and sat down again.

'Well, I read this article online that said housework is really good exercise,' she said ruefully, pinching the generous fold above her waistline. 'I've put on loads of weight lately and you know how much I hate the gym – all those skinny girls in cropped tops standing around posing and making you feel like an elephant!'

Caroline's battle with her weight had been her biggest preoccupation since their teenage years. At five feet two, she had an abundance of dark red-gold hair and generous curves that unfortunately promised to follow in the mould of her plump mother.

'Well, you may hate exercising,' Faye said with all the smugness of someone who had never had a weight problem, 'but all the experts agree that if you want to lose weight, you've got to exercise.'

'I *do* exercise!' protested Caroline.

'I don't think getting dolled up in designer lycra and watching an exercise DVD with a glass of wine in one hand and a cigarette in the other is quite what they had in mind,' Faye retorted dryly.

'Well, they were *really* expensive leggings,' Caroline muttered defensively. 'I didn't want to get them all sweaty.'

She looked with envy at her friend's lean frame. 'You're so lucky, Faye. If I had legs like yours I'd wear mini skirts and shorts every day – even in the middle of winter!'

Faye laughed aloud, her battered self-confidence perking up slightly.

'Thanks, babe, but even if you had my legs, you'd still

need to wear high heels to kiss Marcus. Talking of Marcus, where is he this morning? I've been so busy crying into my coffee, I forgot all about him.'

Caroline had washed out her coffee mug and was now looking around for her next target. Faye instinctively tightened her hold on her own cup before it found its way into her hands.

'He's gone off to play golf again,' she replied absently. After scanning the spotless kitchen fruitlessly, she shrugged and settled herself down on a bar stool, smoothing down the baggy denim dungarees she always wore on her 'fat days'.

'I told you he'd started playing golf with that client he could never get to show up at his office for meetings, didn't I?' Faye nodded and she continued. 'Yes, well now *he's* hooked on the game and it looks as if I'm going to turn into a golf widow before I'm even married!'

Barely pausing for breath, Caroline changed the subject. 'Never mind Marcus,' she said impatiently. 'What are you going to do about Michael?' Having tried to appear neutral so far, she could hear disapproval creeping into her voice. 'I know you probably don't want to hear this, but I really think you've got to make a decision about this relationship before he hurts you even more.'

Steeling herself against the bleak expression on her friend's face, Caroline forced herself to keep going. Having started, there was now no point in keeping the rest back.

'You know I wouldn't hurt you for the world, Faye, but it's time you woke up and saw what Michael is really like. You've been seeing him for what, nearly two years? And how much real time do you actually spend together

– unless, of course, he's got freebie tickets to some event or other!'

Faye remained silent, her head hanging down despondently. Caroline continued more gently.

'Look, Faye, I've tried to keep my mouth shut because whoever you want to see is your own business and as long as Michael made you even halfway happy, I promised myself I'd stay out of it. And sometimes you are so damned stubborn, no one can tell you anything! But, you're not happy and it's not just about last night. Don't forget, I've known you for years. You are a loving, caring, funny person who is fantastic to be around. You've got your own style – a bit weird, mind you, but it's all your own. Michael's not a bad guy, I suppose, but you just let him walk all over you! Somehow he manages to turn you into an insecure bunch of nerves and makes you feel inadequate all the time. Don't try and tell me that's love.' Caroline paused for a moment before deciding to go for broke.

'And tell me *what* kind of boyfriend would rather watch some arty film than have wild sex. And if all that's not enough, he has the cheek to cuddle up to his obnoxious ex-girlfriend right under your nose *and* think that he can get away with it! Now what kind of relationship is that to hang on to – do you really love him *that* much?' She glared at Faye indignantly, her face flushed with anger.

Faye sighed and pulled herself up from the rocking chair. Taking her mug over to the pristine sink, she washed it slowly and placed it in the drainer before speaking.

'Look, I know you don't like Michael very much,' she said. She shook her head as her friend started to speak.

'No, it's okay,' she interrupted with a small smile. 'I can't honestly say I blame you – let's face it, he's not the easiest person to get on with.'

She leaned back against the sink, studying the sparkling white floor tiles abstractedly. 'The thing is, I really thought I meant more to him than just some black Eliza Doolittle that needed a cultural makeover, or a rebound girlfriend when the girl he really wanted dumped him. In some ways, I do love him – or at least some things about him. But maybe I put up with him because if I don't have Michael, there might never be anyone else out there for me. I mean, just look at all the idiots I went out with before him!'

She went on quickly as Caroline opened her mouth to protest. 'Yeah, I know – you think Michael's just as big a twat as Rupert and Boris and all the rest. And maybe I *have* been kidding myself about him – although, no matter what, after two years together, you'd think he would at least have the decency not to parade his ex-live-in lover in front of me! Anyway, I was up most of last night thinking and a couple of things have become really clear to me. One is that Michael doesn't love me and never did. The other is that *I'm* not happy and it's not just because of my crappy job that's going nowhere and my equally crappy boyfriend – also obviously going nowhere, after last night.'

Caroline pulled a strand of her red-gold hair from the untidy topknot on her head and curled it round her finger, her expression curious.

'Why? What else is wrong?'

Faye shook her head slowly as she considered her words.

114

'Well, even though I know Michael's behaviour is really hypocritical, I can't help feeling that he has a point about me being culturally, well...' She hesitated. 'You know... being in a sort of cultural limbo.'

Caroline groaned loudly and threw her hands in the air in exasperation.

'What on *earth* is this whole fixation you've suddenly developed about your roots, Faye!' Jumping off the stool, she strode over to the fridge and took out a bottle of mineral water. Her face was pink with indignation as she poured herself a glass and sat down again.

'Look, so you have a couple of lousy nights out with a bunch of judgmental people who don't know the first thing about you telling you all sorts of rubbish and you actually *believe* them?'

'Well, there must be something to what they said or I wouldn't be letting it bother me so much,' Faye protested. 'Come on, Caro, you know as well as I do that I haven't been back to Ghana since I was a little girl. That surely can't be right.'

Well, I haven't been back to Ireland since we buried Granny O'Rourke when I was twelve,' Caroline retorted heatedly. 'So what does that prove?'

Faye's response was cut short as a lanky figure with bright red hair strode into the kitchen.

Caroline clutched at her chest. 'I know you have a spare key, Dermot, but would it *kill* you to ring the doorbell or something when you come here? You scared the living daylights out of me!'

Grinning unrepentantly and with a triumphant whoop,

Dermot raced to the empty rocking chair and ignoring Faye's yelp of protest, threw himself into the old chair, clutching the arms dramatically and winking at his sister.

'So, what's all this about Granny O'Rourke? Don't tell me she *did* leave us some money after all?' he said, looking hopeful.

Caroline's indignation at his unceremonious entry dissolved into laughter as she watched her brother resist Faye's outraged attempts to drag him out of the rocking chair. After a brief tussle, Dermot pulled her onto his lap, his thin pale arms surprisingly strong.

'Okay, okay!' He gasped with laughter. 'Stop wriggling and we can share.'

When Faye finally gave up the fight and was sitting still, he asked again. 'What about Granny O'Rourke?'

Ignoring Faye's warning look, Caroline impatiently related the last part of their conversation to her brother who listened without interruption, rocking the chair back and forth with one arm loosely draped around Faye.

When Caroline finished speaking, Dermot nodded gravely and gave Faye a gentle squeeze.

'Well, Caro, I know what she means. It's easy for us to forget that Faye isn't totally British because we've known her for so long, but that doesn't mean she feels the same,' he said. Being serious was not something she was used to from Dermot and Caroline gaped at him.

Recovering quickly, she shot back, 'But she barely remembers Ghana – she's grown up here! Isn't that what's important?' she asked.

Dermot gently pushed Faye off his lap and stood up,

relinquishing the rocking chair. Opening one of the cupboards, he took out a mug and poured himself the rest of the coffee in the pot, all the while still arguing with his sister.

'Caro, that's just the point! She's grown up here but she doesn't come from here, and now she clearly feels that something's missing. Look,' he added impatiently, 'if you were adopted, wouldn't you want to know who your real parents were?'

As his sister looked baffled, he went on. 'As far as Faye's concerned, she's been adopted by Britain and now she's curious about where she really comes from. It's only natural, if you ask me!'

'Well, I'm sorry I did!' Caroline pouted.

Faye had been listening to their argument in fascination, her head swivelling from one to the other like a riveted tennis fan during a Wimbledon final.

'Hello, you two!' She interrupted at this point, stamping her foot. 'Can I remind you that I'm actually here?'

She turned to Dermot, who was drinking his coffee, his face now nearly as pink as his sister's.

'How come you understand so well and Caro doesn't?' She looked at him in wonderment. She had always seen Dermot as her friend's cheeky younger brother and it was proving a bit of a revelation to find out that he had turned into such a sensitive young man.

He shrugged, suddenly embarrassed at the intensity with which both women were looking at him.

'Let's just say I'm a musician and, as an artist, I'm more in tune with people's emotions than Ms TV producer here!' Ducking a pretend blow from his sister, he smiled winningly at Faye and reverted to the Dermot she was used to.

'Of course, you could always solve your problems by marrying me – the band's doing really well at the moment and I might actually be able to afford you. That is,' he added, 'if you've finally dumped that Michael character.'

Faye's face clouded over at the mention of Michael and Caroline kicked Dermot in exasperation. Ignoring his howl of pain, she marched over to the rocking chair and hauled Faye out.

'Come on,' she said with determination. 'It's time to blow the cobwebs away. We're going shopping!'

It was almost four hours later when an exhausted Faye finally returned home, her arms aching from the heavy carrier bags that were the usual result of a shopping expedition with Caroline. Laying her new clothes out on her bed, she realised ruefully that her salary for the month had been totally blown.

So much for trying to clear the credit card bill this month, she thought, running her fingers over a black silk dress that had cost her almost two weeks' salary. Piling on even more debt is all I need now and it's not as if I even have anywhere to wear this.

Her eyes filled with tears as the memory of Michael's face just before she had stalked out of the pigfoot restaurant the night before brought a fresh wave of pain. When she had stood up to leave, his jovial expression had swiftly changed to one of anger, but as she had stared down into his eyes, silently challenging him to make her stay, she had also seen an unmistakable hint of relief.

Her tears fell unchecked as she relived the humiliation of Jasmine placing a restraining hand on Michael's arm as he made a move to stand up, and the triumphant smirk that she made no effort to hide when he complied with her silent command.

A sharp knock on her bedroom door jolted her from her thoughts. Starting guiltily, she wiped her eyes and called out 'Come in' while hastily gathering together the leather skirt and cropped denim jacket she had been about to try on.

Her father walked in, shaking his head at the chaotic state of her room.

'Faye, how can you live like this?' He looked around the room in irritation. Without waiting for an answer, he went on. 'Have you seen Lottie?'

Faye shook her head. 'No, Dad. She's probably gone into town. She said something yesterday about doing her Christmas shopping early. I can call her mobile if you like?'

She bent down, as much to pick up some of the offending garments as to avoid his gaze. Her father could always tell when she had been crying and she was in no mood to discuss her cultural dilemma again today.

Her ploy failed when, instead of leaving, her father instead walked slowly over to her. Waiting for her to straighten up, he gently raised her head with his hand and scrutinised her face. 'You've been crying,' he observed.

She sighed. 'I'm okay, Dad. I'm just feeling a bit low, that's all.'

He looked at the clothes she was holding in her arms, the price tags still visible.

'It looks like your bank balance is probably feeling the same,' he said with a smile. Hugging her gently, he drew her over to the bed and sat down beside her.

'I've been so busy these last few weeks that you and I have not been able to chat properly for a while. Why don't we make up for lost time now?' he said.

His dark eyes were filled with concern and as Faye looked into them, she promptly burst into tears again. Clutching the lapel of his jacket, she sobbed until her head ached. Eventually, she calmed down and took the clean handkerchief he held out for her and wiped her eyes fiercely.

'Sorry, Dad, I didn't mean to fall apart like that.' She looked at the crumpled hanky she had been about to hand to him.

'I don't suppose you want this back, do you?' she asked with a weak grin.

Her father smiled and gently shook his head. 'You can keep it.' He leant back slightly to take a better look at her. 'I suppose it's that young man Michael that has upset you so much?'

Like most of the people in Faye's life who had come into contact with Michael, Dr Bonsu had received his share of lectures from the young journalist. Knowing that voicing his real opinions about Michael to Faye could be counterproductive, he had wisely held back and just prayed for the day when she would eventually see what everyone else had no trouble observing. But keeping his peace while Faye seemed reasonably happy was one thing; to stand by and see her so upset was quite another. Although by his upbringing he was not a demonstrative man, Dr Bonsu loved his children fiercely and was ready to deal with anyone who threatened their happiness.

Instinctively trying to protect Michael from her father's wrath, Faye shook her head hastily. 'No – well, yes, but it's not really all about Michael.'

Her father frowned in bewilderment. He wished for the umpteenth time that his beloved Annie were still alive to deal with these complex matters. While he could have written a book about the long-term effects of measles on a child's physiological development, he was completely at sea when it came to matters of the heart. He had only ever loved one woman and, luckily, she had felt the same about him. Since her death, he had experienced no more than a fleeting attraction for anyone else and he was totally baffled by the complex nature of romantic relationships in the West.

Hesitantly, Faye recounted the events of the last two weeks to her father. As she reached the point where Jasmine's status was revealed, her father clenched his fists, anger clearly visible on his face.

'Faye, please tell me you don't plan to see this man again, because I can assure you that he is not welcome in this house!'

She shrugged helplessly. 'I know, Dad. I'm furious at him myself but honestly, it's not just about what happened last night.'

'What do you mean?' Her father was baffled. From what he'd heard, Michael's behaviour was more than enough to justify Faye's tears.

'What really hurt was feeling like such an outsider,' she said. 'It was like they were all in this world where they *understood* each other. Even his ex that he's supposed to hate so much was part of the inner circle because she understands the culture. I just felt like I didn't belong – like I'm this disconnected, posh Hampstead girl who doesn't know anything about her culture and they're all really *conscious* and in touch with their roots and...'

Her voice ground to a halt and for several moments, her father didn't say a word. When he finally spoke, he simply said, 'Faye, I am so sorry.'

Taken aback by the depth of sorrow in his voice, Faye was quick to reassure him. 'No, Dad, it's not your fault. I'm just being a bit pathetic, that's all.'

Dr Bonsu shook his head and took his daughter's hands between his own.

'No, my dear, it is indeed my fault. I have been so busy taking care of other people, I stopped taking care of my own children.' He hushed her as she tried to interrupt him. 'No, Faye, it's true. I may have given you and William all the material things you need, but I have clearly neglected your cultural needs. I should have done more to keep you both connected to Ghana over the years. I just assumed that you had no problem coping with being both Ghanaian and British and didn't feel any conflict about doing so, but I see now that I was wrong.' He restrained himself from adding that it was even more soul destroying that it had taken Michael, of all people, to make him see this.

Faye sighed, now feeling guilty for upsetting her father. 'Dad, please don't blame yourself. Honestly, it's not an issue for me most of the time – I'm just feeling a bit raw after last night.'

When he still didn't look convinced, she dug deep and dredged up what she hoped was a smile of reassurance. 'I just need to be a bit more like William and stop worrying about things I can't change.'

With a deep sigh, he stood up and gave her a gentle pat on the shoulder. He shook his head once more at the clothes decorating the carpet, and left the room. Taking the hint, Faye tossed the piles of clothing onto her bed and started the monumental task of tidying her room. She had almost finished when her brother and Lucinda barged in.

'I see the practice of knocking on doors has gone out of fashion again,' she said sarcastically as the two of them hurled themselves on her bed. Oblivious to her tone, William grabbed a magazine that had been hiding under the crumpled bedclothes while Lucinda started trying on a denim jacket.

Faye's exasperation vanished as she recognised the magazine she had given up for lost.

'Oh is that where it was! William, don't take it away with you – I haven't finished reading it yet and you know what you're like!'

Cramming a handful of hangers draped with clothes into her packed wardrobe, Faye turned to admire Lucinda who was preening in front of the full-length mirror.

'That really suits you, Luce,' she said appreciatively. 'No, that doesn't mean that you can wear it before I do. I just paid a fortune for that.'

Lucinda pouted and reluctantly took off the jacket. Sitting on the edge of the bed, she crossed her shapely legs and tossed back her blonde mane.

'So, how did it go last night, then?' she asked. 'And how's the delightful Michael?' she added with a teasing smile.

'I think the delightful Michael is now my delightful ex-Michael,' Faye said with a grimace.

'*What!*' William dropped the magazine on the bed and punched his fist in the air with a triumphant 'Yes!' Seeing the hurt expression on his sister's face, Lucinda punched his arm and hissed at him to shut up.

'What's happened, Faye?' she asked in concern.

Faye ran her fingers through her dishevelled locks and groaned inwardly at the thought of going through the whole story again. But knowing William and Lucinda as she did, she knew that there was no way she was going to get away with anything less than a step by step account of the evening. She sat cross-legged on the carpet by her bed, took a deep breath and dutifully went through the saga of Pigfoot Etcetera for the third time that day.

As they listened, William's grin faded and, in an almost exact replay of his father's reaction, a look of intense fury crossed his face when Faye repeated Wesley's scornful remark about Jasmine. Although he looked ready to explode, he didn't interrupt, and listened until she finished speaking, his expression grim.

Lucinda was the first to speak. 'Well, if I were you, Faye, I'd have thumped him before I left the restaurant. What a *complete* pig!' she exclaimed indignantly.

'I know,' said Faye. 'Come to think of it,' she added whimsically, 'I should have asked for Pigfoot Michael when that waiter came round.'

William did not join in the girls' laughter. Slamming his

fist on the bed, he stood up and walked over to the bedroom window, intense anger clearly evident in his taut features. Lucinda and Faye exchanged glances as they recognised the prelude to a display of William's infamous temper.

'Just as well Michael's nowhere near here right now,' Lucinda whispered to Faye, glancing with apprehension at the silent figure at the window. She knew that despite all the teasing he inflicted on her, William was extremely protective of his younger sister. Added to that was his guilt at having been the one who had, albeit unwittingly, brought Michael into Faye's life.

In an effort to defuse the situation, Lucinda moved to William's side and hugged him gently. 'Calm down, darling,' she said softly.

William turned back and walked over to sit down on the carpet next to his anxious sister. He gave her an affectionate squeeze. 'Sorry, sis. You must be feeling bloody awful.'

Her eyes moistened again at William's concern and she leant against him gratefully for a moment. Then pushing him away lightly, she jumped to her feet and cleared her throat.

'Well, I'll survive, folks,' she said shakily, 'but thanks for caring. And listen, Will,' she added hastily, 'if Michael shows up here, I'm not in, okay? I really don't feel up to talking to him right now.'

William's response was swift. 'If he dares to show his face here, it will be the last thing he does for a long time!'

Lucinda intervened quickly before he started to work himself up again. Seizing his hand, she dragged him up from the floor. 'Come on, big guy. I think Faye probably needs some time to herself. Besides,' she looked thoughtful as her eyes strayed to the discarded jacket, 'I've just seen the loveliest denim jacket, so let's go shopping!' Blowing Faye a kiss, she walked out of the room, dragging her protesting fiancé behind her.

Grateful for the peace, Faye finished tidying up and looked around the room with satisfaction. The expanse of thick white carpet, now clear of clothes, brought an air of serenity to the large room. The white wooden wardrobes, crammed with enough clothes to stock a small boutique, took up the entire length of one wall while a large oil painting her father had brought her from Ghana several years ago took up most of the wall space above her bed. Faye sat on her newly made bed and looked up at the painting, examining it in painstaking detail for the first time in years.

Gazing wistfully at the market scene depicted by the artist, she marvelled at the graceful figures of the market women walking along, their bodies swaying in synchronised rhythm, babies tied onto their backs with colourful cloths and large baskets balanced on their heads. The colours of the fruits and vegetables piled high in the woven cane hampers were so vivid that she could almost taste the sweetness of the mangoes and feel the fiery tang of the puffy red and green chilli peppers. The whole scene was bathed in the golden light of a scorching sun set in a cloudless blue sky.

Faye closed her eyes and felt herself transported into the picture; she felt the sultry heat on her skin, smelt the pungent aroma of spices, heard the squeals of little children as they scampered between stalls chasing after errant chickens and the loud cries of the stall keepers sheltering from the sun under broad-brimmed straw hats.

Her reverie was broken by a knock at her door. She shook herself back to the present.

'Come in!' she called, her eyes back on the painting. The sound of her father chuckling made her turn around sharply.

Dr Bonsu was smiling broadly and rubbing his hands together in glee, looking just like William after he had won a tough court case.

'What have you been up to, Dad?' She grinned in amusement at the jubilation on her father's face. 'You look like you've just won the lottery.'

'Better than that, my dear', her father said with satisfaction. Chuckling again at the look of bewilderment on his daughter's face, he went on.

'I've just finished a phone call to my very good friend, Fred Asante – I'm sure I have mentioned him to you before. Well, he lives in Ghana, as you know, and he assures me that he and his family would be delighted to have you as his guest as soon as you are ready.'

Faye looked even more baffled and her father added triumphantly, 'My dearest Faye, it's all sorted. You're going to Ghana!'

Part Two

PIGFOOT

It is the highest of earthly honors to be descended from the great and the good.

Ben Jonson

6

Cultural Landings

The chaos at the airport was unlike anything she had seen before. Faye had travelled several times: holidays in France and Spain with Caroline and a trip to New York with William after he passed his bar exams. But standing in the check-in line for the flight to Ghana, she couldn't believe that this was same Heathrow Airport she had used in the past. The line of passengers waiting to check in was far longer than she had ever seen and harassed-looking officials moved anxiously around the check-in counters, dodging increasingly irritated passengers with barely concealed impatience.

Shuffling forward in the interminable line, Faye was overwhelmed as much by the intense activity in the airport terminal as by the pace of events since her father's announcement ten days earlier. She could still hardly believe that she was finally off to visit the country of her birth, a place that only three weeks before she had regarded more as a distant dream than a living reality.

After her father's bombshell, Faye had spent the rest of the weekend in a daze. William, who was still racked with guilt at having been the catalyst that brought her and Michael together, had urged her to take advantage of the opportunity on offer.

'You've hardly taken any time off this year, so why not spend a couple of weeks in the sun at Dad's expense *and* get your cultural identity sorted out while you're at it,' had been his pragmatic contribution.

She hadn't taken her holidays, Faye realised with a pang, in the vain hope that Michael would suggest that they go somewhere together. With the exception of a long weekend spent with Faye at a music festival in Cornwall at Easter, Caroline's holidays were now invariably spent with Marcus. Lucinda and William usually took short breaks once or twice a year and a longer holiday in the summer. But despite Faye's heavy hints, Michael had continually dodged the topic of a romantic getaway, insisting he was far too busy to take the time.

William's enthusiasm and Lottie's excitement about Mr Asante's invitation to Ghana notwithstanding, Faye had still felt inexplicably reluctant to go. Even Caroline's envious 'You lucky thing – I'd love a free holiday in the sun!' hadn't swayed her. In the end, it was a conversation with Miss Mildred Truelove Campbell that made up her mind.

Since her revelations about her life in Jamaica, the two women had grown closer. Their tea breaks were often spent together in the shabby staff sitting room with Miss Campbell reminiscing about her youth and Faye listening transfixed to her stories of growing up on the far away island.

It was during one of those breaks early in the week that Faye had hesitantly told the older woman about her father's offer to pay for her to visit Ghana. Instead of the instant excitement that the news had produced in the others, Miss Campbell had sat deep in thought for several moments before speaking. 'How do you feel about going? I must confess that if I were you, I'd probably be terrified!'

Faye gazed at her, stunned for a moment into silence. 'How on earth did you know?' she asked finally, amazed at her perspicacity.

The older woman's smile was gentle. 'Well, it's not too hard to imagine. You've been putting yourself under a great deal of pressure about your imagined alienation from your homeland, Faye.' The lilt in her accent seemed more pronounced to Faye these days. 'Now you have the chance to go over and meet your people,' she added musingly, 'you might well be worried about whether you will fit in and be accepted by them. Of course, it's also natural to worry about whether they might consider you to be a stranger and reject you – which would leave you feeling like neither fish nor fowl, so to speak.'

She paused and a look of sadness crossed her face. 'I wonder sometimes whether I would still fit in if I were to go back to Jamaica. Although we speak to each other regularly, our lives have been so different since I left that even my beloved Millicent might now consider me a stranger, you know.'

It was the first time that Faye had acknowledged the real reason for her reluctance to snatch up the chance to go home. She was brooding over Miss Campbell's words when the older woman gently patted her cheek.

'But, you know, my dear,' she said with a teasing smile. 'If you don't face your fear and take this chance, you will always wonder what you would have found. You're not an old lady like me, Faye. Go on, visit your country and find out where you come from so that no one can ever make you doubt who you are again.'

It was after that discussion that Faye found herself asking Junior for three weeks off. Riddled with anxiety at the thought of his working life without Faye, her boss reluctantly agreed, finally persuaded by Miss Campbell's offer to supervise a temp to cover for her.

Taking advantage of her newly discovered courage, she had also finally phoned Michael. She had ignored his calls since the night at the restaurant and dreaded the thought of speaking to him. Just as she thought the call was going to his voicemail, he answered, his voice icy as he said 'Hello'.

'Michael – we need to talk,' she said bluntly, avoiding the usual niceties.

Taken aback by her directness, Michael didn't answer straight away. After a long pause, he spoke, his voice sounding cautious. 'Talk about what?'

Faye sighed in irritation and resisted the urge to cut off the call. 'Michael, you can't possibly believe that things are okay between us – not after what happened last Friday?'

The exasperation in her voice quickly drew a response.

'Well,' he replied coolly, a note of annoyance now creeping into his tone. 'If I remember right, you didn't behave yourself too well when I took you out. You really shamed me in front of my friends with the way you behaved.'

Her outrage at this statement literally took her breath away and for a moment she couldn't speak.

'*You* were shamed...!' she finally squeaked in indignation. 'How the hell do you take me out to dinner, bring along your ex-girlfriend – *who* I might add, you've slagged off all the time I've known you – and then spend all evening flirting with the... the... silly cow right under my nose!'

'Jasmine is *not* a silly cow, don't be so stupid!' Michael's voice was cold.

'No, you're right, she's not a silly cow,' Faye shot back, stung at being called stupid. 'She's – what was it you always called her when I first met you? – "an ungrateful bitch!"'

The silence on the line told her she had hit home and when he spoke, he used a more conciliatory tone. 'Look, Faye, I can't deny that she and I have had our issues in the past, but she's a very intelligent woman and if you were to take the time to get to know her, she could teach you a lot about Afro-Caribbean culture.'

'Well, I could teach her a lot about manners!' Faye countered, a surge of pure rage rushing through her as Michael continued to defend Jasmine. 'And that includes not draping yourself all over your ex-boyfriend when *his* girlfriend is around.'

She paused as a new thought suddenly struck her. 'That is, of course, assuming she *knew* I was your girlfriend? You didn't tell her, did you? Why, Michael – were you hoping to get back with her again?'

Her suspicion was confirmed by the long pause at his end. The sheer audacity of his behaviour had her literally hopping with rage with her phone clenched tightly in her palm. Then suddenly, in an instant, her anger evaporated. In its place, she felt nothing except, strangely, an overwhelming sense of relief.

Her voice was calm and slow. 'Michael, we are *so* finished.'

For the first time in the conversation, she detected a note of alarm in his voice.

'Faye, don't you think you are overreacting?'

This time she was the one who remained silent. Clearing his throat, he continued, now openly pleading. 'Okay, fine, maybe I should have mentioned who Jasmine was – and, you're right, I should have told her I was with you. The truth is I saw her a couple of weeks ago for the first time since we broke up and, well… I didn't get a chance to mention it to you. Look, there's nothing going on between me and her. So maybe I wanted her to see what she was missing by letting me go, and maybe I got a bit carried away – but it's nothing to get upset about. You know how special you are to me! The important thing here is that I really think she could be helpful in introducing you to more of our culture. I mean, seriously Faye,' he went on unguardedly, 'look at how you went ordering pasta – in a Jamaican restaurant, for God's sake! What on earth do you think they thought of you?'

As she listened to him dismissing her feelings, Faye could just picture him standing there with his impeccable cornrows, soulful eyes and fashionable clothes. Beneath all his cultural double-talk, what she now saw was complete heartlessness. A line from a poem she had learned in school floated into her mind. *A brain of feathers and a heart of lead. Yes*, she thought, *that was certainly Michael.*

The pause lengthened and she realised that he was still waiting for her answer.

'What do *I* think they thought of me? Frankly, Michael, I don't give a crap about what they – or you – think about me any more. You're right, I am stupid, or at least I was. Stupid enough to think that you were worth hanging onto when all you've ever done is talk down to me and treat me like some kind of pet project. Seriously, Michael, you should *hear* yourself! Who the hell goes out with someone so they can *educate* them?'

She cut him off as he started to speak. 'Michael, you know what? I don't want to hear anything you've got to say. You and Jasmine are welcome to each other because if anyone hasn't learned their lesson, it's you. So good luck when the ungrateful bitch dumps you again!'

It was after that call that she had finally asked her father to accept Mr Asante's invitation. During her lunch break she had booked her flights and at home that evening, had rummaged through her wardrobe in a frantic search for clothes suitable for the tropics.

Now, as she slowly inched forward in the never-ending queue to check in her large suitcase, she started once again to feel the pangs of apprehension she had suppressed since her conversation with Miss Campbell. She looked around for her father, who had offered to drive her to the airport and then promptly disappeared once she had taken her place in the queue. Just then, his well-groomed salt-and-peppered head came into view.

'Dad, have you seen the amount of luggage some people are taking?' Faye whispered incredulously. Directly in front of them, a young couple had two trolleys, each laden with a wobbling tower of suitcases, canvas tote bags and cardboard boxes firmly secured with masking tape. The woman was carrying a handbag on top of an even larger shoulder bag, while trying to push a smaller wheeled suitcase that was clearly intended to be her hand luggage. Her partner held a large red and white striped bag that was so heavy that rather than carry it, he simply pushed it forward with his feet.

Dr Bonsu chuckled as he nudged Faye's trolley forward.

'It never changes. When Ghanaians are returning home, they always take huge amounts of luggage. It's almost a ritual for people to try and get away with more than their baggage entitlement.'

Looking at his watch and at the queue of people in front of them, the doctor sighed and shook his head in apology. 'Faye, my dear, I'm afraid I will have to leave now – I have a conference call scheduled for this afternoon that I have to get back for.'

Faye shrugged, trying to hide her sudden panic at being left alone. Forcing a smile, she hugged her father tightly and kissed his cheek.

'It's okay, Dad,' she said lightly. 'I'll manage. I'm a grown woman, don't forget.' She nodded towards the queue with a wry grin. 'And, judging by the speed this queue is moving, I'm going to be a lot older before I leave London.'

He kissed her warmly on both cheeks and, after checking once again that she had Mr Asante's phone number in case of any problems, he set off back to the car park.

As she continued her slow shuffle forward, Faye looked with interest at her fellow travellers and slowly felt her panic receding. She realised with wonder that it was the first time in years that she had been surrounded by so many people of her own skin colour. By the time she reached the check-in counter and dropped her suitcase on the conveyor belt, a glow of excitement had begun to burn in the pit of her stomach.

Once she had checked in her suitcase, Faye wandered into the newsagents for some magazines and mints before striding through to the departure lounge. She had worn her favourite black trousers for the flight with a white cotton vest and a lightweight linen jacket. Her black leather duffle bag was slung over one shoulder while her hair, now free from the attentions of *Sharice of Streatham*, had reverted to its usual straightened bob and was held back from her smooth high cheekbones by a pair of smoky sunglasses perched on her head.

Her flight was displayed on the departure screen as ready to board and she followed the signs to the departure gate, her sense of adventure growing with every step. At the gate, she showed her passport and boarding pass again to the flight staff and edged her way around toddlers, pushchairs and large sharp-edged boxes masquerading as hand luggage, until she found a seat in an empty corner of the rapidly filling lounge.

It was not quiet for long. The sharp nudge of an elbow in her side jolted her out of her reverie.

'Oh! I'm so sorry, my sister!' The young man who had

slipped into the hard bucket seat next to hers exclaimed apologetically as he slid a large tote bag securely between his legs.

'That's okay,' Faye muttered automatically, rubbing gently on the injured spot. She picked up one of her magazines and flipped to an article on how to check if your partner was still in love with you.

I should have read this article weeks ago, she thought as she mentally ticked off each of the warning signs that spelled disaster and found that she had answered yes to eight out of ten of them.

'So where do you stay in Ghana?' The man next to her was now settled comfortably in his chair and he smiled at her, a look of open curiosity on his face.

She hesitated and then smiled back. 'I'll be staying with friends in Accra.'

Her neighbour nodded vigorously as if she had answered a very complicated question. 'That is good. And, if I may ask, where do you come from in Ghana? Are you a Fanti?'

Faye shook her head. 'No, I'm an Ashanti.'

Although she had lived outside Ghana for most of her life, she was well aware of the different ethnic groups in the country. She knew from her father that the Ashantis, a proud tribe with a long and distinguished lineage, were the largest of the Akan-speaking people of West Africa. With the end of colonialism, the vast majority of Ashantis now lived in Ghana, which had once been a British colony known as the Gold Coast.

'But that is wonderful – so am I!' With a happy cry, her neighbour stretched out his right hand to shake hers, pumping it hard, and then released her fingers with a gentle click of his thumb and middle finger.

'My name is Kwabena Nti,' he said. After she had introduced herself, he asked curiously. 'Where is your home town?'

Again, Faye heaved an internal sigh of relief for her father's lectures on the subject. She knew that by asking her this question, Kwabena was asking where her mother came from, as the Ashantis trace their lineage through the female line.

'Ntriso,' she replied firmly. 'It's about a hundred and fifty kilometres from Kumasi.' Her reference to the capital of the Ashanti region appeared to have firmly established her ethnic credentials as Kwabena sat back in his chair, apparently satisfied with what he'd heard.

She checked her watch and realised that the flight should already have taken off, but remembering her father's warning that flights to Ghana often left later than scheduled, she went back to reading her magazine. The other passengers continued to flood into the lounge, many of them now leaning against the walls or sitting on their bulky hand luggage. Some of the younger children, restless at the delay and clearly excited at the prospect of getting on a plane, were running around the crowded area, ignoring the hissed instructions from their frustrated mothers to sit down.

Twenty minutes later, a flight official announced in a relieved voice that it was time to board and the suddenly energised passengers quickly gathered up their belongings. Faye watched with amazement as the crowd held back while mothers with young children and the elderly and infirm made their way forward first. Kwabena Nti rose from his seat and, hoisting his heavy tote bag over his back, politely offered to help her with her things.

'Oh no, it's okay,' Faye stammered in surprise. 'I only have my handbag and the magazines, but thank you.' He flashed a last smile at her and headed hastily towards the exit, his boarding pass in hand.

As she walked into the aeroplane, Faye once again felt a sense of suppressed excitement creeping over her. Although she knew she was in for a long flight, she could hardly wait to feel the soil of her home country under her feet.

Maybe Wesley wasn't so wrong after all, she mused, I should have made this trip ages ago. Her seat was by the window and as the other passengers made their way to theirs, she gazed through the small round window at the activity taking place on the tarmac below. A middle-aged woman paused in the aisle and, after checking her boarding pass, sat down wearily next to Faye. She was wearing the traditional Ghanaian dress of a long skirt in printed cotton with a fitted top, known as a *kaba*. As a concession to the English winter, she wore a warm heavy cardigan over the low cut top. A piece of fabric had been twisted around her head with a stylish knot holding it firmly in place.

After fastening her seat belt, the woman turned to Faye with a smile.

'Good afternoon. It looks like we will be at least an hour late getting to Accra,' she sighed.

Faye smiled and nodded. 'I was warned not to expect to arrive on time.'

They both laughed and the older lady held out her hand in greeting.

'I'm Mrs Patience Allotey,' she said. Her grip was firm as Faye shook her outstretched hand. She introduced herself and they both fell silent as the Captain's voice came over the speakers announcing the preparations for take off.

After the safety instructions had been demonstrated and the crew had taken their seats, the engines screamed in anticipation as the heavy jet taxied off the runway before hurtling up into the air to be buried in endless cushions of clouds.

Faye gave a sigh of relief and settled back into her seat, flicking through the in-flight magazine. She had never been particularly fond of flying and could never fully relax until the plane was safely up in the skies.

Mrs Allotey removed her bulky cardigan and also sighed aloud. She wiped her thin metal-rimmed glasses and put them firmly back on her broad nose.

'So, my dear, are you returning home or going on holiday?' she asked curiously. Faye watched as the woman opened a voluminous handbag, took out a clean cotton handkerchief and carefully wiped her face.

'Just a visit,' Faye replied. 'I haven't been back since I was a child, so this is a very special trip for me,' she added impulsively as another dart of excitement shot through her.

The older woman clucked enthusiastically.

'My goodness – is that so? Well, I hope you have a wonderful time,' she said, peering at Faye through her glasses. 'How long will you be staying?'

She sounded so warm and interested that Faye found

it impossible to take offence at the barrage of questions.

'About three weeks,' she replied, smiling in amusement as the woman practically squirmed with joy on her behalf. Deciding that she could also be nosy, Faye unfastened her seat belt and turned to face her neighbour.

'What about you, Mrs Allotey? Are you going on holiday too?'

The older woman shook her head vigorously, almost dislodging her colourful headgear.

'Oh no, Faye, I'm returning home,' she said with relief. 'I came to England to be with my daughter for a few months since she's just had her first child. But she is now back on her feet and able to cope, so I'm going back to Accra. My poor husband has been waiting for me far too long.'

'Oh, how lovely!' Faye exclaimed. 'What did your daughter have – a boy or a girl?'

Mrs Allotey was instantly the proud grandmother as she opened her handbag again and pulled out her phone. Going through what seemed like hundreds of photos, she gave a detailed explanation about the people in each picture and where each one had been taken. Faye cooed in delight at the pictures of the new grandchild – an extremely plump brown baby with masses of curly black hair and a wide toothless smile.

'You must feel really sad about having to leave them all behind,' Faye looked at her with sympathy.

Mrs Allotey sighed in agreement and switched off her phone, replacing it carefully back in her handbag. She pushed the bag under her seat and settled back once again.

'Yes, I shall miss them all very much,' she admitted,

her previously happy smile fading slightly. 'But, you see, Ghana is my home and I never like to leave it for too long.'

She grinned again as she went on. 'You know, I studied in England for a number of years – I'm a registered midwife, you see. Maybe for you young people who have grown up in England, it's different. But as for me, when I lived here I was never very happy.' She shook her head to emphasise her point.

The drinks trolley came round and Mrs Allotey asked for orange juice while Faye opted for a glass of wine. As they nibbled on the crunchy peanuts and sipped their drinks, Mrs Allotey regaled Faye with stories of her time in England. She had a sharp sense of humour and Faye was soon giggling uncontrollably.

'So you can imagine, Faye,' she said, finishing up a hilarious account of how she had survived her nursing course in Birmingham, 'my decision to return home was never in doubt. But even aside from my Abraham who was waiting impatiently for my return so that we could finally marry, there was also another reason.' She paused for a moment, deep in thought, and the smile left her face.

'In England, I always felt like a foreigner. My shifts were always longer than the English nurses' and when it came to ward duties, I always seemed to end up with the worst jobs.'

She made the comment without bitterness, a note of quiet acceptance in her voice. 'But in Ghana, it's completely different. Where I felt I had to beg for acceptance in England, in my own country total strangers address me with respect as "Madam".'

Leaning forward, she patted Faye's hand warmly. 'Don't mind me, though,' she added with a rueful smile, her warm brown eyes twinkling through her glasses. 'My daughter is always telling me that things are not like that for her in England and *she* can't understand how I put up with the inconveniences of life at home – the last time she and her husband came to Ghana, we had power cuts most of the time they were there!'

The conversation came to a temporary halt as lunch was served. Faye was ravenous and munched her way through a foil-covered dish of steak and potatoes followed by strawberry mousse and cheese and crackers. After the meal, the older lady removed her glasses and was soon fast asleep. Too excited for a nap, Faye put on her headphones and tuned into her iPod. She gazed out of the tiny window at the clouds, thinking wistfully of her family and friends now thousands of miles away, and smiled to herself as she remembered the raucous farewell dinner at Caroline and Marcus's flat the night before.

Between them, William, Lucinda, Caroline and Marcus had teased Faye mercilessly about her upcoming holiday. Dermot, who arrived halfway through dinner, had been in even higher spirits than normal.

'Don't go asking for pasta everywhere you go either, for God's sake,' he mumbled, cramming the creamy courgette and bacon stringozzi Faye had made earlier that evening into his mouth.

'Very funny,' Faye said dryly, dumping the basket of garlic bread by his plate. 'I'm glad you're all so amused by the idea of me culturally messing up all over the place.

We'll see who gets the last laugh when I come back and show you all up!'

There had been one solemn moment when William had risen to his feet and called out over the din for attention.

'Okay, now quiet everyone – I've got something to say,' he said peremptorily, suddenly every inch the barrister. Holding his full wine glass high, he cleared his throat and looked across at his sister who looked back at him, her expression wary.

'Faye sweetheart, on behalf of all of us here, I just want to say this.' He cleared his throat again. 'We all hope you have a wonderful holiday and that you find whatever it is that you're looking for when you get to Ghana. We'll miss you – and your ethnic backside,' he interjected with a cheeky grin, 'but we know you're going to have the adventure of your life. Here's to you!'

The unexpected toast almost reduced Faye to tears. Luckily, Dermot's attempts to eat Marcus's dessert while he was raising his glass broke the tension, and it was well past midnight when the party finally broke up.

Lost in thought, Faye felt it was only minutes later that the Captain's voice announced that they would be landing shortly. There was a last minute flurry of activity as landing cards were handed round and harassed mothers shepherded their tired children to and from the toilets.

Mrs Allotey sat up to re-tie her headgear and clicked open her powder compact to lightly dust her shiny nose. 'Well, I certainly won't need this for a while,' she said with relief as she folded her heavy cardigan into her handbag.

Faye, who had hastily run a comb through her hair and

repaired her smudged make-up, was trying to answer the questions on the immigration landing card.

'"Your Address"... I only have a post office box address for the Asante family,' she said aloud.

'Don't worry about that, dear,' Mrs Allotey advised. 'We hardly ever use street addresses in Ghana. Just write down the box number.'

Faye shrugged and did as she was told. She quickly filled in the rest of the form and tucked it into her passport.

The excitement in the air was now almost palpable and the plane started to circle in descent. Darkness had fallen and through her window she could see the twinkling of lights on the ground far below. The engines sounded louder than ever and the sudden noise of the wheels being released jolted her upright. The flight crew took their seats and the whine of the engines grew louder still as the plane made its way down to the runway. The huge jet landed on the tarmac with the lightness of a butterfly landing on a flower petal and the passengers broke into a spontaneous round of applause.

Mrs Allotey joined in the clapping, and then crossed herself quickly before reaching under her seat for her handbag. Overriding the commands coming through the speakers for passengers to remain seated until the plane had come to a complete halt, the impatient travellers were up on their feet, rushing to pull out their oversized cabin luggage long before the plane doors had been opened.

Faye quickly gathered her magazines together and rolled them into a thick wad. Pushing her passport into her leather duffle bag, she unclipped her seat belt and waited, almost trembling with excitement. Immediately the aeroplane doors opened, the crowd surged forward, their loud excited cries filling the air.

'Goodbye, Faye. I hope you have a wonderful holiday!' With a quick wave, Mrs Allotey was on her feet and, with a speed belying her advanced years, pushed herself forward through the queue of passengers and was out of the plane almost before Faye could respond.

Following more slowly, Faye was one of the last to reach the doors of the aircraft where the humidity of the tropical night hit her like a slap across her face. She walked carefully down the metal steps and joined the other passengers in the bus waiting on the tarmac.

The bus driver, after checking that the last passenger had boarded, sped off with a screech of his tyres towards the airport terminal where the weary travellers alighted to walk into the airport. Clutching her duffle bag and wiping her face, which was already moist from the humidity, Faye followed the crowd into the air-conditioned arrivals area and stood in the queue waiting to go through Immigration.

When it was her turn, she stepped forward and nervously handed her red British passport to the tired-looking officer. Despite the glass screen, Faye could see his large stomach poking gently through the gap between the buttons of his short-sleeved white cotton shirt. He stared at her for a long moment and then turned back to the pages of her passport.

'Miss Bonsu?' he asked ponderously, his bald head hardly moving as he flicked through the pages.

'Yes...?' Faye replied nervously.

'Your name is Bonsu, but you are British,' he said. His voice held no particular inflexion and Faye tried to work out whether it was a statement or if he was asking a question. She decided to keep it simple.

'Yes.'

The officer stared across at her for another few seconds and then stamped her passport. Suddenly his tired face lightened as he broke into a broad smile. Handing back her passport, he said gently, 'Welcome home.'

7

Cultural Homecoming

In comparison with Heathrow Airport's general air of calm, Kotoka International Airport was a frantic hub of activity. Faye stuck close to the other passengers heading towards the baggage collection area as busy officials rushed up and down barking instructions into mobile phones and uniformed security guards pushed through the throng of arriving travellers with barely concealed impatience, shouting across to each other in a combination of English mixed with other languages. Some, more obviously privileged, passengers were met by officious looking personnel and whisked off to a side room identified by a discreet sign as the VIP lounge.

Faye followed some of the people she recognised from her flight through to the large reclaim area. She walked past trolleys stacked against a wall and headed towards the baggage carousel.

'My sister, I hope you had a pleasant flight.' The voice came from behind her and, turning round, she almost bumped into Kwabena Nti with his ever-present smile.

'It was fine, thank you,' she replied. 'Have you got many cases to collect?' The carousel was still in motion although, as yet, there was nothing to be seen and she kept one eye on the moving belt as she spoke.

Kwabena shrugged amiably and said with a wry smile, 'Well, I have five sisters and they each gave me a long list of things to bring them. I can only hope that the goods have all arrived safely!'

Just then the first suitcase appeared on the carousel and the crowd surged forward, their trolleys banging against the metal sides as everyone struggled to identify their own. Kwabena manoeuvred his so that it was next to Faye and wriggled his wiry frame in front of it, ready to seize any of his belongings as soon as they appeared. Faye watched in amazement as he deftly collected a total of seven suitcases and three large boxes, one of them clearly marked with a picture of a microwave.

After a few more minutes, Faye spied her case and reached out towards it, but Kwabena got there first and heaved it off the carousel, placing it with great care in front of her.

'Here you are, my sister,' he said, wiping off the dust on his hands down the sides of his jeans. 'I am pleased that you have not lost your belongings.'

With a smile of thanks, Faye followed him as he navigated his overcrowded trolley through the crowd and walked confidently into the customs area. Just before they reached the exit, a portly shiny-faced official demanded to see their tickets and passports. Using a tired stub of chalk, the official scribbled an illegible mark on Faye's case with a flourish and gestured for her to carry on through the exit. As she moved off, Kwabena waved a cheerful goodbye and returned to his task of arguing with another official who seemed determined to go through each item on his trolley in painstaking detail before granting the white chalk seal of approval.

Faye tossed her duffle bag over her shoulder and wheeled her case out into the hot and humid night air, stopping for a moment to slip off her jacket and drape it over her arm. Before she had taken more than a few steps outside the building, she was mobbed by a pack of young men shouting 'trolley, trolley, madam!' and 'taxi, madam!' A few exhausted security guards tried to disperse the over-helpful porters but with little effect, as several others rushed forward to take the place of those who were pushed out of her way.

Just as Faye was wondering what to do next, she heard a deep voice shouting, 'Faye, Faye Bonsu... over here!'

Heaving a sigh of relief, she turned to see a middle-aged man moving rapidly towards her, followed by an attractive young woman. When the man reached her, he threw his arms out wide and gathered her into a warm embrace without saying a word. Releasing her, he prised her suitcase from her grip and propelled her away from the disappointed porters.

'Faye, I'm Fred Asante – your Uncle Fred,' he said, his voice loud over the cacophony. Gesturing at the young woman behind him who was smiling at her excitedly, he went on. 'This is my daughter Amma. Let's get you away from this commotion – the car is over here.'

The three of them walked down a flight of steps towards the car park and Uncle Fred briskly led the way to the car. Waving away some of the more optimistic porters who were still in hot pursuit, he opened the boot of the shiny 4x4 and manoeuvred her heavy suitcase inside with a short grunt before locking the boot carefully and coming round to open the car doors.

'In you get, ladies,' he said, opening the front door for Faye, who slid in gratefully, relieved to escape from the enthusiastic pack of porters still hanging around the car. Amma clambered into the back as her father settled himself into the driving seat before driving off slowly, carefully avoiding both the pedestrians and the porters milling around the newly arrived passengers.

Amma leaned forward from her seat in the back and rested her arm on the back of Faye's seat, almost bouncing with excitement. 'Did you have a good flight? We phoned from home to check if you would be on time but they told us that the plane had been delayed.'

Faye turned slightly to get a better view of the other girl. Amma looked remarkably like her father, with round brown eyes and soft full cheeks. She was wearing a long loose-fitting cotton shift dress with thin straps that accentuated a full bosom. Her sparkling white teeth glittered in the semi-darkness as she chattered on non-stop.

'Oh Amma!' her father protested after she had rattled through about ten questions without pausing long enough for Faye to answer. 'Give the poor girl a chance to get a word in.' He took his eyes off the road and glanced quickly in Faye's direction. 'Forgive her,' he said apologetically, 'she's a terrible chatterbox.'

Ignoring his daughter's indignant cry of protest, he gave Faye another quick glance.

'My goodness, Faye,' he said, a note of emotion creeping into his voice. 'I haven't seen you since you were a small child. We are so happy to have you here with us – the rest of the family are waiting anxiously to meet you.'

The warmth of the welcome she had received eased the anxiety that had begun to creep up on her as she left the airport terminal, and she settled comfortably into her seat, looking around her with interest.

With the windows rolled up and the powerful air conditioning blasting through the car, it was easy to forget the humidity outside. As they drove, mini buses crammed with people going home from work drove past them at full speed. The noise of car horns filled the night air as yellow and white taxis weaved in and out of their lanes, intent on picking up and depositing passengers and arrogantly dismissive of any other vehicles.

'Oh my God... Uncle Fred!' Faye exclaimed, wincing as she watched a taxi narrowly avoid a collision with a small van. 'How on earth do you manage to drive here and stay in one piece?'

Uncle Fred nodded. His expression was grim and he didn't take his eyes off the road for a second. 'These roads can be a death trap if you're not careful, Faye. I wouldn't suggest that you try and drive while you are here – between Amma, Rocky and I, you'll have plenty of people to take you around.'

At Faye's enquiring look, Amma jumped in. 'Rocky's my older brother,' she explained. 'Actually his name is Richard but his friends started calling him Rocky years ago because he was really into boxing at one time. Even though he gave it up a long time ago, the nickname stuck and it's what everyone calls him.'

Faye smiled at Amma's detailed explanation and said firmly. 'I've got no intention of driving while I'm in Ghana, Uncle Fred. Apart from the fact that I'm not used to driving on the right hand side of the road, I don't think I would last three minutes against these taxi drivers!'

As they drew up to a particularly busy roundabout, Amma pointed in the direction of one of the exits, where cars could be seen slowing inching along, bumper to bumper.

'That area over there is called Osu,' she said. 'We live in the centre of Accra and there are loads of pubs and nightclubs nearby. I'll make sure we go out a lot while you're here, Faye.' Her father rolled his eyes and Amma ruffled his hair affectionately as he shook his head in resignation.

'Actually, that particular road is known as Oxford Street, just like the one in London,' he said. 'And I can tell you that it's probably just as busy!'

They drove on through busy intersections and speeding traffic until finally they emerged into a quieter, more residential part of the city. The roads were darker and Faye could see the silhouettes of large houses behind high walls and securely locked gates, some of which carried signs with drawings of ferocious-looking dogs ready to tear any intruder into shreds.

'What's this part of Accra called?' Faye asked curiously.

Uncle Fred answered before Amma could speak. 'It's called Labone. In fact, we're almost home.'

Just as he finished speaking, he turned sharply into a short driveway and stopped the car in front of a pair of black iron gates. He gave a short blast of the car horn and seconds later the gates opened a little way and a dark head emerged and stared at the car.

'Togo, open the gate!' Uncle Fred shouted through his window. As Togo continued to examine the car without making any attempt to move, the older man pressed on his horn again, glaring at Togo with growing impatience.

Slowly Togo retreated and moments later threw back the gates, peering openly into the car at Faye as they drove inside. Uncle Fred parked under a corrugated steel canopy at the side of the house and came round to Faye's side to help her down. Amma slid out of the back and called Togo over to help with the suitcase.

Shuffling forward slowly, he made his way towards them. Staring at Faye, he raised his hand to his head in a brief salute and bared his teeth in a wide grin.

'*Akwaaba*, madam,' he said. 'You are welcome.'

Faye watched with amusement as he hoisted her suitcase up on top his head and shuffled off in well-worn rubber sandals towards the back of the house, his skinny legs protruding from wide shorts.

Amma followed her gaze, smiling with amusement as they watched him amble away. 'Togo's our gardeners-lash-security-guard-slash-general-handyman. He's been with us for years and knows just about everything that goes on in Labone. One or two of our neighbours have been burgled in the past, but it's never happened to us. Someone told my mother that it's because even the thieves in the area have heard about him and are too frightened to risk it.'

'It sounds to me as though you've got a perfect one man neighbourhood watch scheme going on here,' Faye giggled and they walked together towards the house.

They were still laughing when suddenly the front door was thrown wide open and a squealing figure came hurtling out, rooting them to the spot. As it reached where they stood, Faye had a momentary impression of a tall woman with high jutting cheekbones before she was crushed in a suffocating embrace. Focusing hard on trying to breathe, it was a few moments before she realised that the woman was weeping and laughing at the same time.

Just as suddenly, she was thrust back and found herself looking up into the woman's face. Faye gazed fixedly at the woman and felt the brief flicker of a long buried memory. The caramel-coloured eyes and slightly copper-coloured skin of the older woman brought with them a sense of *déjà vu* and for a minute no one spoke.

Then, wiping the tears away from her cheeks with an impatient hand, the woman spoke, her voice soft.

'My lord, I never thought I would see this day!' She stroked Faye's cheek gently and suddenly smiled. Despite the evening shadow, it was as though the sun had burst through the clouds.

'Faye, my dearest child, I'm so happy to see you at last! Your mother and I were like sisters.' Then suddenly her tone changed as she slapped at her forearm. 'Come on, girls – let's go in before the mosquitoes get us!'

Amma went ahead and her mother wrapped an arm around Faye and walked her quickly into the house.

'Welcome to our home,' she said as they entered a large hallway with high ceilings and a cool terrazzo floor. Moving ahead, she opened a side door and ushered Faye into what was clearly the living room.

The high walls of the room were painted white and decorated with large vibrant watercolours that reminded Faye of the painting in her bedroom. A long brown leather couch took up almost the length of one wall while a number of armchairs of soft matching leather were turned towards a large plasma TV. A profusion of brightly coloured flowers had been beautifully arranged in patterned ceramic vases all around the room, giving off a sweet fragrance. Two large fans suspended from the ceiling spun round quietly, creating an atmosphere of coolness and serenity.

Faye sat down in one of the armchairs, curling her legs into the soft leather, and sighed with pleasure.

'What a beautiful room, Mrs Asante,' she said, looking around the room with unconcealed admiration.

'Call me Auntie Amelia, my dear,' was the instant reply. Amma's mother slipped off her embroidered sandals and settled herself in the chair next to Faye, barely taking her eyes off her.

Amma remained standing. 'Faye, what would you like to drink?' she asked in her distinctive breathless voice. Without waiting for an answer, she rattled on. 'Martha's in the kitchen – I'll ask her to bring some drinks in so you can choose what you like.'

With that she left the room, almost bumping into her

father who was just walking through the door. Within what seemed like a few seconds, Amma was back, sounding even more breathless than before.

'Martha's on her way,' she announced, and crossed the room to sit next to her father on the long leather sofa. 'By the way, Mama, Martha said that Rocky just phoned to say that he'd left the office and should be home soon.'

Her mother shook her head in resignation. 'Why am I not surprised that he was at the office? Never mind the fact that today is Saturday.'

Amma grinned. 'You know he would work eight days a week, if it was possible.'

From where she sat, and despite their age and gender difference, the resemblance between Amma and her father was striking. Although her colouring was exactly like her mother's, she had clearly inherited Uncle Fred's shorter and more rounded frame.

'Fred!' Auntie Amelia exclaimed, her eyes back on Faye. 'Can you believe how much she looks like Annie?'

Faye shifted uncomfortably under the open scrutiny. Her own memories of her mother had largely faded over time. When she was much younger, she had spent hours poring over the few photographs she had of her, but had never seen any particular resemblance between her own childish features and her mother's graceful adult beauty. It had been years since she had looked at the old photographs but now, hearing Auntie Amelia's words, she felt a renewed curiosity about the woman who had given her life.

Before she could ask any questions, the door opened and a middle-aged woman entered carrying a tray laid out with several bottles. The drinks had clearly been well chilled and tiny droplets of water ran down the sides of the thick glass. The woman was plump and her pale blue polyester dress strained gently against her generous curves as she bent and placed the drinks on the glass-topped centre table.

'Faye, this is Martha,' Auntie Amelia said, standing up and walking over to the table. 'Martha is our housekeeper and has been a member of our family for many years.'

Martha smiled warmly at Faye, her smooth round cheeks impervious to any wrinkles. Her voice was pleasant and she spoke in strongly accented English. 'Welcome home. I hope you will enjoy being with us.'

She left the room and returned with a tray of glasses, briskly opened the bottles and served the drinks. After setting the bottles and glasses carefully on the smaller side tables, she picked up the empty trays and left the room.

Uncle Fred raised his glass and waited for his wife and daughter to follow suit.

'Here's to you, Faye, and to a wonderful visit back home.' His voice was solemn, but his twinkling eyes belied the serious tone.

Everyone dutifully took a sip of their drinks. Faye took a long gulp of the chilled Coke in her glass and then almost spluttered as the living room door opened again and one of the most handsome men she had ever seen walked in.

She stared wordlessly as the tall, muscular man greeted Uncle Fred and kissed Auntie Amelia on both cheeks before turning to her. Coughing to clear her suddenly constricted throat, she looked up into a pair of caramel-coloured eyes that were identical to Auntie Amelia's. But, although he had the same high cheekbones and dark-copper colouring of his beautiful mother, Rocky Asante's muscular frame and closely-cropped hair removed any trace of femininity from his appearance. He was dressed in a dark suit with a silk tie of a swirling pale gold design on a black background. His white shirt, unfastened at the neck, still looked crisp and pristine, giving no hint of the heat and humidity outside.

Staring blankly at the hand he had extended towards her, she dimly realised that she was being introduced and forced herself to concentrate on what Auntie Amelia was saying. She stuck a hesitant hand out to shake his, the unexpected strength of his grip once again throwing her mind off track.

'I'm Rocky,' he said coolly and with a brief smile. 'It's a pleasure to meet you at last – my parents have been so excited since they heard you were coming,' he added.

Not as excited as I am now... Swallowing hard, Faye stared up into his eyes, struggling for something to say and unaware that her hand still remained in his. Oblivious to the suddenly knowing glance exchanged between the two elder Asantes, neither Rocky nor Faye moved for several moments. Then, releasing her hand abruptly, Rocky turned to his sister, who had been watching them with great interest.

'Hi,' he said in greeting, gently swatting the top of her head. 'What's up?'

Without waiting for an answer, he picked up Amma's glass and took a quick sip of her drink before she could protest. He slipped off his jacket and sat next to her on the couch, one long leg casually crossed over the other knee, exposing dark socks and highly polished black shoes. Faye tried desperately not to stare but, despite her best intentions, her eyes kept straying back in his direction. Without the jacket, the breadth of his shoulders could be clearly seen and, as he further loosened his tie, the strong muscles in his upper arms pressed gently against the crisp cotton shirtsleeves.

Amma glared at her brother and picked up her drink hastily before he made any further inroads into it.

'By the way, Clarissa's called me about ten times today,' she said with a wicked smile, ignoring his sudden frown. 'She said she couldn't get through to your phone and to remind you that that her new commercial is going to be on TV tomorrow night, so don't miss it.'

Auntie Amelia leaned forward, her eyes widening with interest. 'Oh really, how exciting! Rocky, what will she be advertising?'

Rocky shrugged and ran his hand over his head. With a look of complete innocence that almost had Faye melting into the floor, he smiled at his mother disarmingly.

'Ma, you've got me there.' He shrugged helplessly. 'It's probably some hair product or cosmetic or something – I honestly can't remember.'

His mother snorted, disgusted by his obvious lack of interest in the subject. Turning to Faye, who had been listening intently to the exchange, she quickly explained.

'Clarissa is Rocky's girlfriend. She's a beautiful girl – she won the Miss Ghana beauty competition a few years ago. She's quite well known and is now an actress. She does quite a bit of modelling too, doesn't she, Rocky?'

Amma butted in before he could speak. 'I think you're a little behind the times there, Mama. She and Rocky broke up almost a month ago.'

'Really?' Auntie Amelia stared at her son in surprise. 'But Rocky, why...?'

Uncle Fred cleared his throat loudly, taking pity on his son, who was glaring angrily at his unrepentant sister, and suggested that Faye might want to freshen up before dinner.

Auntie Amelia rose gracefully to her feet and took Faye's hand. 'Come, my dear, I'll show you to your room.' Turning to her daughter, she went on. 'Amma, let Martha know we'll be ready for dinner in fifteen minutes.'

She led Faye out of the living room and up a broad flight of terrazzo stone steps. As she climbed the stairs, Faye admired the ebony-framed family photos hanging on the cream-coloured wall, most of which featured the Asante children. She smiled at one particular picture that showed a young Rocky leaning against a tree with Amma pulling on his arm. A huge portrait of a smiling chubby-faced Amma, aged around five, held pride of place at the top of the staircase.

When they reached the landing, Auntie Amelia gestured to her right. 'Our room is over there; if you need anything during the night, just come and look for me.'

They turned left and walked past three doors. Explaining that they led to Amma and Rocky's rooms and their shared bathroom, Auntie Amelia led Faye to the end of the passageway and opened another door.

'This is our guest room,' she said as Faye followed her into a large room with a huge bed in the centre covered by a thin white mosquito net draped over tall wooden posts at each corner of the bed. A cotton bedspread in a colourful tie-dye fabric and matching long curtains threw a cheerful glow against the white walls. The large windows, covered with mosquito netting, were fitted with slanted louvre panes, which had been left open wide enough to let through a cool breeze. There was an air conditioning unit in the far wall away from the bed, and two large built-in wardrobes and a matching dressing table and chair took up the right side of the room.

Auntie Amelia opened a door to the left of the bed and switched on the light. 'This is your private bathroom.' Pushing back a translucent white shower curtain, she quickly demonstrated how the shower unit worked and led the way back into the main room where Faye's suitcase had been deposited near the bed, along with her jacket and handbag. Suddenly desperate for a long cool shower, Faye closed the door behind her departing hostess and stripped off her clothes.

Fifteen minutes later, freshly showered and dressed in a sleeveless white linen shift dress, Faye went back down, sneaking a quick look at the family photographs as she came down the stairs. She walked quickly into the living room and collided with Rocky who had clearly been on his way out.

'Oh, sorry!' she exclaimed, stepping back in confusion. Instinctively, he reached out and held her arm to prevent her from falling. As he continued to hold on to her, she looked up at him, suddenly aware of his height. At five feet and seven inches, she was fairly tall and yet she barely reached his shoulder. He gently released her arm and inclined his head slightly in apology.

'I'm sorry, Faye,' he said, his tone formal. 'It's my fault – I wasn't looking where I was going.'

Forcing herself to tear her eyes away from his perfect features, Faye moved towards the sofa and sat down, conscious of his gaze following her. He had turned back into the room and watched her as she settled herself into the cushions.

'I was just on my way to get a cold drink from the kitchen,' he said. 'Can I get you one while you're waiting? I'm sure my parents will be down soon, although I can bet you Amma will be late.' He grinned as he said it and, once again, his smile threw her into a state of confusion.

'No, thank you,' she stammered shyly. Frustrated at feeling so tongue-tied, she frantically cast around for something to say. The silence lengthened as Rocky abandoned his mission and sat in the armchair across from her. He had changed out of his suit into a sports shirt and a pair of cotton trousers and he sat back looking relaxed.

I don't know what Clarissa looks like, Faye thought as her eyes strayed in his direction once again, *but with that face and body,* he *should be a model*. A picture of him posing shirtless suddenly flashed through her mind.

Rocky looked up suddenly and their eyes locked. For a moment no one spoke.

'So what do you do for a living?' Faye blurted out, flustered by the quizzical expression in his eyes.

'I work for an investment bank here in Accra. It's actually the Ghanaian branch of a British bank,' Rocky replied easily. 'I've been with them for a few years now.'

She nodded, trying – and failing – to look impressed. He laughed, clearly not offended. 'Yes, I know. Banking is not exactly the sexiest job in the world, is it? Aren't we all supposed to be heartless, money-sucking leeches?'

She tried to pretend the thought hadn't crossed her mind and smiled at him instead.

'Well, yes, if you were to believe all the horror stories about what banks have been up to. But I suppose it isn't fair to tar everyone with the same brush.'

He stretched his long legs out in front of him and looked curiously at her, causing her heart to flip over again. *Get a grip, Faye!*

'My father says you haven't been back to Ghana since you were five.' It was less a question than a statement and Faye nodded, feeling faint stirrings of anxiety at her cultural credentials being called into question again.

His full sculpted lips curved into a quizzical smile and she reluctantly forced her eyes away and tried to concentrate on his words. 'It must feel very strange to be back here; I'm sure you can't remember very much about the country.'

'To be honest, I never really thought very much about Ghana – I suppose because both my father and my brother are in England, there was never that urgency to find out more about the country.' She hesitated and then added quietly. 'I think losing my mother was so hard for my father that he found it too painful to come back home that often. Also, his parents died when he was young and without any grandparents demanding to see us, there was really no real pressure on him to keep bringing us home.'

Rocky nodded, his expression indicating that he understood. He was about to speak when his parents entered the room.

'Oh good, you're both ready for dinner,' Auntie Amelia said briskly as she bustled forward towards Faye. She had changed into a long mustard coloured caftan with gold embroidery around the curved neckline. She took Faye's hand and helped her up. 'Dinner's ready so let's go in and get started. Amma will just have to join us when she finally comes down.'

Uncle Fred and Rocky followed as Auntie Amelia led Faye across the hallway and into a dining room with high ceilings, dominated by a huge mirror with an ornate gold frame hanging on the far wall. A polished teak dining table had been set with white cotton place mats and gleaming white crockery and Faye was ushered to the chair next to Uncle Fred, who sat down at the head of the table.

Looking up, she found herself staring straight at Rocky who had taken his place directly opposite her. *Oh great*, she groaned inwardly. *How am I supposed to eat with him sitting right in front of me!*

Amma's sudden arrival gave Faye a moment to compose herself and by the time the younger girl had slipped into the chair next to her, Faye was able to smile and compliment her on the brightly coloured traditional Ghanaian dress she was wearing.

'Thanks,' Amma replied, and her voice sounded even

more breathless than usual after her rushed entry. 'My friend Baaba made it – she's a fantastic designer.'

Lifting the heavy cut-glass water pitcher from the centre of the table, she filled Faye's glass with ice-cold water before filling her own and passing the jug to her mother.

'Actually she sells a whole range of her clothes in Mama's shop – my mother has a boutique in town,' she rattled on, barely pausing for breath. 'If you really like this dress, we could go over to the shop on Monday and you can get one for yourself.'

Martha entered the room carrying a tray laden with steaming serving dishes piled high with food. She set them down carefully on woven cane place mats in the centre of the table and went back to the kitchen. Returning with more dishes, she arranged the serving spoons next to them and smiling sweetly at Faye, wished them all a good meal before leaving the room, this time closing the door behind her.

Faye looked at the mouth-watering spread in front of her. Not having eaten since the meal on the plane, she eyed the deliciously herbed tender chicken pieces, the steaming white rice, the bowl of rich red spiced tomato gravy and piping hot vegetables laid out on the table with appreciation.

Auntie Amelia passed the dishes round and the clinking of cutlery and the whirring of the ceiling fan were the only noises to be heard in the room until Amma finally leaned back with a sigh.

'That was delicious! I can't believe I ate so much; I'm supposed to be on a diet,' she groaned and looked at Faye enviously. 'Faye, you're so lucky that you're tall and slim – do you exercise a lot?'

Faye snorted with laughter, nibbling at the remains of a piece of chicken she had picked up from her plate. '*Me! Exercise*? Okay, to be fair, I did try going to the gym with my best friend Caroline for a while. But it was all too much effort for me and I was really glad when she got fed up and stopped after three weeks.'

Uncle Fred finished the generous portion of food his wife had heaped on his plate and wiped his mouth with a white linen table napkin. 'I don't think you need to worry about your weight, Faye. You have a lovely figure.'

He turned to Rocky who was briskly forking the last of his rice into his mouth, and added mischievously, 'Doesn't she, son?'

Rocky almost choked on his last mouthful. His mother hid a smile behind her hand while Amma giggled openly. Faye looked across at him, a challenging expression in her eyes, and he wiped his mouth slowly and stared straight back at her.

'Yes, Dad,' he said softly. 'She's got a great figure.'

Faye's eyes dropped in confusion and she felt a powerful surge of heat rise up into her face and all the way to her hairline, causing her scalp to prickle. Concentrating fiercely on slowly removing the last succulent piece of chicken from the bone, she only dared to look up again when Martha came back into the dining room to clear the table.

Amma rose and helped to stack the used dishes. Waving away Faye's offer to help, she carried the plates to the kitchen while Martha collected the empty serving dishes before following her out of the room. Amma returned after a couple of minutes and took her seat at the dining table.

'You look tired, Faye.' She peered at their guest with concern. 'I don't suppose you feel like going out anywhere this evening?'

Her mother gave a tut of annoyance and shot an impatient glare at her daughter. 'Amma, of course she doesn't feel like going out! She must be exhausted after the long flight.'

She turned to look at Faye, her voice reassuring. 'Martha is bringing some dessert in shortly and then you should get some rest. When we've finished dinner, you can call your father to let him know you've arrived safely?'

Faye nodded in agreement. Now that she had eaten, she was beginning to feel the effects of the day's events. She perked up slightly as Martha come back in, this time carrying a long platter, which she laid on the table with a flourish. Slices of golden yellow pineapple had been carefully arranged on the white platter and garnished with tiny sprigs of mint.

Faye gasped with delight as she tasted a piece of the juicy fruit. 'Mmm...! Auntie Amelia, this pineapple is fabulous – I've never tasted anything so sweet!' Her expression was one of pure rapture as she leaned back with her eyes almost closed, savouring the delicious fruit.

Rocky smiled at her uninhibited enthusiasm. Swiftly disposing of two slices of pineapple, he wiped his mouth on his napkin and leant back in his chair.

'You probably won't remember eating these when you

were a child but our pineapples are among the best in the world,' he said. 'This particular variety is particularly sweet and comes from Cape Coast – that's further west along the coast from Accra.'

He went on, his tone casual. 'If you have some free time while you're here, I can take you to see Cape Coast – they have some beautiful beaches there.'

Faye nodded dumbly, her appetite suddenly vanishing as butterflies took flight in her stomach at the thought of going out anywhere with him. She forced herself to eat her last piece of pineapple, now barely tasting its tangy sweetness.

The dessert was quickly consumed and when everyone had finished eating, Auntie Amelia ushered Faye into the study, another large room off the hallway and left her alone to phone her family. After a few minutes of conversation with her father and William, she exchanged a few words with Lottie and went back into the living room to find the older couple and Amma watching a film on TV.

'Rocky sends his apologies, but he had to leave,' Auntie Amelia said, patting the seat beside her in invitation. Faye sat down next to the older woman and burrowed into the soft leather of the couch. 'He has an appointment this evening with some business clients who are leaving Ghana tomorrow.'

Faye suppressed an unexpected pang of disappointment and watched the TV with the family for a few minutes, fascinated by the local drama involving a young village girl promised to the gods for a crime committed by her ancestors. But, despite herself, she soon found her eyelids drooping.

Uncle Fred nudged Auntie Amelia, who had been watching the film with barely concealed irritation at the storyline. His wife took one look at her tired guest and gathered her up from the couch.

'Look at me getting caught up in this foolish film when you are so exhausted!' she tutted in apology. After wishing Uncle Fred and Amma a good night, Faye followed as Auntie Amelia led the way to her room.

After her hostess had turned on the air conditioning unit and checked that fresh towels had been placed in the bathroom, she kissed Faye goodnight and hugged her. Once again her eyes moistened as she looked intently at the younger woman, and she shook her head from side to side as if she still could not believe what she was seeing. 'My dear, I am so happy to have you here with us at last.' Her voice softened. 'In a way, it's also like having Annie back again.'

Giving Faye a final hug, she released her and walked towards to the door. She turned back and added, 'If I know your father, I'm sure you are a regular church-goer?'

At Faye's rueful nod, she smiled. 'Uncle Fred and I go to the eight-thirty Mass and you're more than welcome to join us. But, if you're feeling tired tomorrow morning, just stay in bed – you can always go another time.'

With a final 'goodnight', she left the room and Faye quickly brushed her teeth and changed into a cotton T-shirt. Shivering slightly at the cool air blasting from the air conditioner, she quickly climbed under the mosquito net into the large welcoming bed. Her last conscious thought as she snuggled under the covers was of a pair of caramel-coloured eyes looking into hers – and they didn't belong to Auntie Amelia.

8

Social Culture

The incongruous sound of a cock crowing roused Faye from a deep sleep. She lay quietly for a few moments, wondering if she had dreamt it. The cock crowed again, its plaintive cry wafting in through the windows. The room was still in semi-darkness as Faye peered at the luminous dial of her wristwatch. Realising with horror that it was only five-thirty, she pulled the covers up under her chin and forced herself to go back to sleep.

When she opened her eyes again, the room was flooded with sunlight straining through the thin cotton drapes. Blinking at the incredible brightness of the morning sun, Faye sat up and stretched slowly and luxuriously. She slumped back against the pillows and surveyed her bedroom through the mosquito netting.

I'm really here!' she thought, squirming in excitement as the realisation of where she was finally hit her. Despite the gentle hum of the air conditioner, she could hear the strident toots of car horns, loud clucks from what sounded like an entire brood of chickens, and piercingly loud voices in a language she didn't understand wafting in from outside her window.

'I'm definitely not in Hampstead now,' she said aloud and plumped up her pillows before lying back against them. She thought back dreamily over the events of the previous evening and Rocky's face immediately came to mind.

She shook her head impatiently as if to dislodge the image, and wriggled out from under the mosquito net to walk over to the window. Pulling the metal tab, she peered through the louvre blades protected by the fine mosquito netting covering the window frames. Her room overlooked a large garden to the back of the house. At the far side of the garden, she could see part of a washing line with securely pegged clothes flapping lightly in the morning breeze. Directly behind the house, a green, neatly manicured lawn stretched back, surrounded by beds of brightly coloured flowering shrubs. To one side of the grass, a small open-sided structure with a thatched roof covered some tables and chairs. Alongside it was a large brick barbeque with a stand for a spit.

A knock at the door interrupted her survey of her temporary home.

'Come in!' she called, turning round to see who it was. The door opened slowly and Amma's head came into view.

'Good morning, Faye,' she said brightly. 'I'm glad you're awake – I didn't want to disturb you.'

Faye gestured to her to enter and she bounded happily into the room. Dressed in well-worn denims and a long white cotton shirt, she perched on the edge of the bed and looked at her guest critically.

'You look well rested this morning', she pronounced. 'I must say you were looking pretty tired last night. Which, I suppose is not surprising after flying all the way from London. I remember when we went to Canada a few years ago how tiring it was just sitting on the plane and doing nothing for hours!'

Amma's hair had been styled into a profusion of tiny braids that fell below her shoulders. She had twisted a bright red scarf into a hair band to keep the braids off her face and her soft round cheeks dimpled sweetly as she chattered non-stop.

'Rocky didn't get back home until midnight, you know,' she carried on, barely pausing for breath. 'Clarissa phoned me again after you went to bed and I could tell she didn't believe me when I said he'd gone out.'

'How long had they been going out before they broke up?' Faye asked, trying to sound casual. She lifted away the corner of the mosquito net to make space on her bed and sat down facing Amma.

'About a year or so,' Amma shrugged. She lowered her voice conspiratorially. 'She's still crazy about Rocky and is absolutely desperate to marry him. The trouble is Clarissa just doesn't know when to stop – she was always dropping hints and going on and on about marriage, which is about the worst thing to do with my brother. If you know Rocky at all, you know you can't make him do *anything* he's not ready to do.'

Faye held her breath as Amma paused briefly to clear her throat before continuing.

'Anyway, the whole bust-up happened because Clarissa decided that if she could get Rocky jealous, he'd go ahead and propose to her rather than lose her. So, what does she do? She starts flirting with Rocky's boss, Stuart. He's British – and a complete womaniser,' she whispered the last as an aside before continuing.

'Well, unfortunately for Clarissa, she got completely the opposite reaction. Rocky was furious when she started flirting with Stuart right in front of him *and* some other friends they were out with. When he took her home, he told her that he couldn't trust her any more and ended things there and then!'

Amma paused dramatically and Faye leant forward, completely forgetting to look uninterested.

'So what happened? How did she take it?' she asked impatiently.

Amma rolled her eyes in exasperation. 'Not very well at all, to put it mildly. She still thinks Rocky didn't mean what he said. Again, if you know my brother, you know he's as stubborn as a mule and *never* goes back on something he's said.'

Flicking back an errant braid, she went back to her story. 'So now she just keeps calling me or phoning the house line because he never picks up when she calls his mobile, and acting as if nothing's changed. I've told her to leave him alone for a while, but *she* thinks I don't really like her and that I'm trying to fix him up with my best friend Baaba, who's always had a huge crush on him.'

Confused at the sudden twist in the plot, Faye crossed her legs and shook her head in bewilderment.

'Okay,' she said slowly, trying to keep up. 'So, then how does Rocky feel about Baaba – I mean, is he interested in *her*?' She wondered why she was suddenly so interested in how Rocky felt about anything.

Amma gave a loud snort, slapping a hand against her plump thigh as she burst into hoots of laughter.

'There are not many things my brother's scared of – but Baaba is definitely one of them! He runs a mile whenever she's around. He calls her a man-eater, which isn't very nice. But it doesn't help that the first time he met her, she was on the phone and all Rocky heard was her telling the guy at the other end, "No finance, no romance!"'

Unconsciously releasing a slow breath of relief, Faye ran a hand through her dishevelled hair and looked down at her crumpled shirt.

'Well, it's getting late. I'd better have a shower and get dressed,' she said, getting up from the bed. 'Have your parents gone to church?'

Amma stood up reluctantly and moved towards the door. 'Yes – they'll probably get back about twelve,' she said. 'They usually visit one or two of their friends after church before they come back home for lunch.'

She opened the door and turned back to Faye, who was rummaging through her suitcase for some clothes. 'I'll be in the living room when you've finished getting ready. We can have breakfast together,' she said, before leaving the room.

Faye brushed her teeth, showered quickly and slipped into a pair of narrow cropped linen trousers she had bought in the summer sales. She teamed them with a white silk top that barely grazed the waistband of the trousers and brushed her hair vigorously, relieved to see that, despite the humidity, it still fell into place.

Sliding her feet into her canvas wedges, she grabbed a cotton handkerchief from the economy pack of ten Lottie had insisted on buying for her, and switched off the air conditioner before leaving the room.

Amma was stretched out on the couch engrossed in a glossy magazine when Faye walked into the living room. Without getting up, she lowered the magazine to look at Faye and shook her head enviously.

'I wish I had your figure,' she sighed. 'My thighs are much too fat to wear trousers like those. Let's go and get some breakfast.' With that she stood up, dropped the publication on the centre table and led the way into the kitchen.

Like the other rooms Faye had seen so far, the kitchen was large and sunny and with an array of shining modern labour-saving devices that reminded her of Caroline's kitchen. There was a large bleached-wood table in the middle of the room with several chairs pushed neatly under it. Pulling out a chair, Amma gestured to Faye to take a seat while she got to work. Explaining that Sunday was Martha's day off, Amma busied herself opening the fridge and cupboards, chattering relentlessly as she prepared breakfast.

'If it's okay with you, we can go to the beach after lunch.' She continued without waiting for a response. 'It's only a short drive away and it's a popular place on Sundays. You'll be able to meet my boyfriend Edwin and a few of our friends—'

'Some of whom you should avoid like the plague!'

Both girls jumped as Rocky's voice broke into Amma's rambling narration. He strode into the kitchen and pulled out another chair. Spinning it round, he straddled the chair, and rested his arms on the back, ignoring the look of irritation his sister directed at him. Instead, he smiled at Faye, his eyes taking in her long legs and the silk cropped top.

'Good morning,' he said finally. 'I hope you slept well.' He was wearing a loose pale blue cotton shirt with jeans and looked cheerful and relaxed.

Amma deposited a pot of coffee, slices of toast and a tray containing sugar, milk, cheese and an assortment of jams and marmalades on the table. Placing plates in front of Faye and Rocky, she gestured airily at the food.

'Go ahead, help yourselves.' She poured herself a cup of coffee, then sat down and sipped the black liquid slowly.

Rocky offered the plate of toast to Faye first and then liberally spread two slices with butter before pouring coffee for Faye and then for himself. He glanced at Amma as he bit into his toast and almost choked at the expression of longing on her face.

'What's wrong with you?' he demanded, when he could speak.

Amma shook her head and took another doleful sip of her coffee. Putting her cup down, she rested her elbows on the table and leant forward.

'Edwin says I'm getting fat. So I'm dieting until he stops teasing me, or,' she grinned at Faye, 'until I'm as slim as you.'

Rocky polished off a second slice of toast then shook

his head in exasperation.

'If he doesn't like you the way you are, just get rid of him,' he said bluntly. He added two teaspoons of sugar to his coffee and sipped the drink with satisfaction. Looking up, he caught Faye's eye; she was grinning and he smiled back.

'What's funny?' he enquired. His pale brown eyes watched her finish the last bit of toast.

'You two remind me so much of my brother, William, and me,' she laughed. 'He's always so critical of my boyfriend.'

The smile slowly faded from Rocky's lips and he continued drinking his coffee without comment. Amma's face, on the other hand, lit up with interest and she leant towards Faye excitedly.

'What's your boyfriend like, Faye? Is he English?' she asked.

'Well, I suppose I should say ex-boyfriend, really,' Faye admitted, aware that for the first time she didn't feel anything when she thought about Michael. She tested the feeling again, like a tongue probing against a once sore tooth. Again, she felt nothing.

Suddenly conscious of the two of them staring at her, she laughed again, a heady feeling of sheer joy sweeping through her.

Amma brushed the short explanation aside and repeated her questions impatiently. Still laughing, Faye raised her hand in surrender. 'Okay, okay!' She went on more soberly. 'Michael's British and his family is originally from Jamaica. We went out together for about two years. He was at school with my brother – which is how we met – although, to be honest, William never had much time for him.'

Swallowing the rest of her coffee, Faye thought back over the period she and Michael had been together. With hindsight, she realised how much their relationship had fallen into the pattern of Michael leading while she followed. At his own instigation, Michael had taken on the role of her culture guru while she had been content to shelter in the attention that it brought her even when that attention, as she now recognised, had been mostly negative and critical.

'Is the relationship really over?' Surprisingly, this time the question came from Rocky, his eyes hooded as he studied his own empty coffee cup intently. She paused before answering and he looked straight up at her, his eyes probing hers. She flushed at the unexpected intensity of the look but this time she didn't drop her gaze and stared back steadily at him.

'Yes,' she answered simply and smiled as he nodded his head in satisfaction.

Amma had observed the curious interchange with wide eyes and she rose from the table and collected the empty plates, for once lost for words. Faye forced her gaze away from Rocky and stood up to help clear the table and put the rest of the food back into the large refrigerator.

'Rocky, do you want to come to the beach with us this afternoon?' Amma had found her voice again and a new mission was taking seed in her fertile brain.

Faye concentrated on wiping the dishes the younger girl was washing and tried not to look interested in Rocky's reply. Having done what he considered his share of the clearing – carrying two plates to the sink – he had perched on the edge of the table, from where he watched them finish the washing up.

'I'm not sure,' he replied, his face expressionless. 'I have to go to the office for a couple of hours.'

'On a Sunday?' Faye looked at him in surprise.

'I have to write a report on the meeting we had with our clients last night. Unfortunately it needs to get to our London office tomorrow morning so I have to get it done today,' he explained.

Amma scrubbed hard at a coffee stain on the cup she was washing. 'We're used to it, Faye. Rocky often goes to the office at weekends – Mama says he works too hard and that he's far too ambitious.' She smiled mischievously at her brother. 'Anyway,' she added, 'if everything goes well, he's likely to get a major promotion at work soon.'

Glancing at his watch, Rocky stood up abruptly, interrupting his sister's seemingly endless flow of chatter.

'I have to go now, so I'll see you girls later. Amma, thanks for breakfast – and, if you've got any sense, you'll eat something yourself before you pass out.' He grinned at her, his expression teasing. 'Knowing you, I don't think you can survive until lunchtime on a cup of black coffee!'

As her brother strolled out of the kitchen, Amma glanced furtively at the look on Faye's face as she watched him leave and, apparently satisfied with what she saw there, smiled cheerfully.

With the clearing up finished, the two of them went back to the living room and spent the rest of the morning playing some of Amma's extensive music collection.

'Who's this by?' Faye asked curiously as Amma put on

a song that sounded like a mix of pop and reggae with a heavy horn section.

'He's called Daddy Lumba,' Amma answered, dancing in time to the music. 'He's been around for a long time, but I love his music – although the lyrics are a bit rude.'

'Dad used to play highlife music when we were kids,' Faye said, jumping up to dance as the beat of the music became impossible to listen to sitting down. 'He says that's the music he grew up with in Ghana. I like this much better – I must buy some CDs before I go.'

They danced around the living room, collapsing into giggles as Amma tried to teach Faye some of the popular dance steps. When Uncle Fred and Auntie Amelia returned home from church, they went to the kitchen to help make lunch – a simple meal of freshly grilled fish, rice and a rich vegetable salad, which Amma, all thoughts of her diet clearly forgotten, ate with gusto.

The sun was at its height and Uncle Fred and Auntie Amelia soon retired to their room to rest. Mindful of the heat outside, Amma and Faye stayed in the cool living room where they read magazines and newspapers for another hour before going up to get ready for the beach.

Faye changed into a navy blue and white polka dot bikini and slipped a pair of brief cotton shorts and a white short-sleeved shirt over her swimwear. As she came down the stairs, she glanced at Rocky's picture and shivered slightly, remembering the look in his eyes at breakfast that morning.

Oh Faye, stop it! She berated herself impatiently. *You're here on holiday – not to get involved with anyone.*

For once Amma was ready first and Faye found her waiting in the hall. Her long braids were tied back and she had changed into a white cotton dress. She was carrying a plastic mat folded into a neat square, and a large bag.

'I won't be swimming but I've brought a couple of towels and some body lotion in case you want to go into the water. I've packed some bottled water as well.'

She pointed to a wide-brimmed straw hat on the hall table. 'You'd better take that, Faye. You really don't want to get sunstroke on your first day here – it's very hot outside.'

Faye seized the hat gratefully and followed Amma outside to where her car was parked. The humidity was striking after the coolness of the house and even the short walk to the car caused beads of moisture to form on her forehead and upper lip. She slid into the front passenger seat of Amma's small car and heaved a sigh of relief when the air conditioner started to hum.

'It is seriously hot!' She sat back in her seat, letting the blasts of air from the vents cool her heated skin.

Amma drove skilfully, weaving her way in and out of the traffic and cleverly dodging the careless taxi drivers who stopped without warning to drop off and pick up passengers. Faye scrutinised the passing landscape with interest, amazed at the contrast between the smooth modern dual carriageway and the wide-open gutters alongside. At one point, Amma was forced to slow to a halt to allow some errant goats that had escaped their shepherd to cross the highway.

Imagine a bunch of goats crossing the North Circular Road as you're driving through Finchley, Faye thought in amusement, turning round to watch a young boy racing after the animals in his charge.

They turned onto another dual carriageway and sped down, past rickety shop fronts and kiosks, most of which were closed. Faye gasped with delight as the sparkling blue of the sea came into view. She could see the white foam at the edge of the waves curling into the sand, while further out to sea a couple of small boats bobbed lazily on the water.

Amma slowed the car down and turned off the main highway onto a narrow roughly pebbled road. They bumped along slowly until they reached a clearing where a number of other cars were parked.

'Oh good, Edwin's here – look, that's his car.' Amma parked alongside the sleek dark blue car she had pointed out and turned off the engine.

'Nice car,' Faye remarked with admiration, 'What does Edwin do?'

'Well, nothing at the moment,' was Amma's candid response. 'We've both just finished our National Service.'

At Faye's enquiring look, she went on. 'It's a year of community service that every graduate has to do. Edwin was away teaching maths at a primary school in the north of the country for most of the past year.' She turned off the engine and added with a wry grin. 'The car belongs to his mother – she usually lets him use it at weekends.'

Faye opened the door, reluctant to leave the cool interior of the car, and grimaced as the relentless heat assaulted her once again. She jammed the straw hat onto her head and slung her leather duffle bag over her shoulder. Her slim feet were encased in a pair of rubber flip-flops that quickly filled with sand as she trudged behind a suddenly energised Amma.

Amma wheeled round, seized Faye's elbow and pointed to a small group of people lounging on the sand a few feet away.

'Look!' she said excitedly. 'There's Edwin and the others. Let's go and join them.'

Wincing at the combination of heat, sand and slippery sandals, Faye dutifully stepped up her pace and was soon being scrutinised by several pairs of curious eyes. Panting slightly from the exertion of her near gallop across the sand carrying the mat and the heavy bag, Amma took a couple of deep breaths before speaking.

'Everybody, this is Faye – our friend from London.' She pointed to a tall, rather lanky man lounging on a beach mat. 'This is Edwin, my boyfriend.' He stood up, easily towering over her, and took off his sunglasses before wiping his hand on his shorts.

'Welcome to Ghana, Faye. It's nice to meet you.' He shook her hand, his grip firm and slightly damp.

Amma continued with the introductions. 'This is James Brown' – gesturing with a giggle at the man who had been sitting next to Edwin – 'well, actually his real name is Kwamena Pratt, but we all call him JB.'

James Brown – alias JB – looked around twenty-five. He was small in build and very dark and wore his hair in a full, round afro. His only clothing was a pair of black swimming shorts and a heavy gold chain around his neck. A gold signet ring sat loosely on his thin middle finger and as he smiled in greeting, a glint of gold was clearly visible in the gap between his two front teeth.

Unlike Edwin, he didn't stand up or try to shake Faye's hand. Instead, he tapped a skinny forefinger against his forehead before pointing it at Faye with a loud 'pshoo!' as if firing a gun, all the while flashing his gold tinged smile.

'How ya doin'?' His voice was high, with an accent that sounded to Faye like a cross between a Texan and a Korean.

The girl sitting next to him rolled her eyes, clearly not impressed by JB's performance. Her generous cleavage was almost spilling out of a low cut, stretchy black T-shirt that seemed to have reached the full extent of its elasticity. Even seated, her colourful wrap-around skirt could not hide what appeared to be very sizeable hips. Her hair was braided into short plaits that framed a small face with penetrating dark eyes and full pouting lips.

She smiled engagingly at Faye and reached out a languid arm encased in jingling gold bangles. 'Hello. I'm Baaba,' she said. Her voice was surprisingly deep and incredibly sexy. Faye smiled back and murmured a greeting.

Her attention was immediately diverted by the sight of a new arrival. He had clearly been swimming and his low-slung black swimming shorts highlighted a muscular abdomen and perfectly sculpted muscles. He picked up a towel from the beach mat, wiped his face and then turned to smile at Faye, displaying a dazzling set of even white teeth.

Transfixed, Faye simply could not tear her gaze away. Ghana was definitely proving to be a very attractive adventure!

Smiling broadly, Amma slapped her hand against his raised one in greeting and turned back to her friend. 'Faye, this is Sonny – Sonny, this is our friend Faye from London,' she said. She winked at Faye. 'Sonny is our local hottie – women just melt whenever he's around.'

Sonny gave Amma a gentle punch on her shoulder and after unsuccessfully trying to dry his hands on his wet shorts, held out his right hand. Slightly dazzled by the high-beam smile he was directing at her, Faye shook his hand and mumbled something unintelligible.

'Please take no notice of Amma,' Sonny said in a low husky voice that suited his handsome features perfectly. 'She just likes to tease me.'

'How long are you staying in Accra?' The silky voice so close to her ear startled her and Faye spun round in alarm. Her hat fell forward over her eyes and pushing it back, she found JB standing only inches away from her. In her flip-flops, they were almost the same height and now, up close, she could see the faded marks of old scars on his face. Faye took a step back before answering.

'I'll be here for about three weeks.' A rare gust of wind almost blew her hat off and she held it down firmly with both hands.

'Oh man, that's just *great*, man!' he said. His accent was so strange that she could barely make out what he was saying. Of greater concern was the fact that whenever she took a step back, he would take another step forward, oblivious to her efforts to create some space between them.

Seeing her discomfort, Sonny pulled JB's arm and dragged him backwards, ignoring the angry glare his friend directed at him. 'Heh, *abongoman*! Give her some space. Can't you see you're crowding her? Seriously, bro!'

He turned his back on his friend and flashed another high-wattage smile at Faye. 'Don't mind JB – he's just a bushman with no manners.'

Sonny's eyes were hooded like those of a sleepy serpent as they travelled up and down the length of Faye's long rangy legs. 'Do you want to swim?' he drawled, his tone slow and husky. 'The water feels great, especially in this heat.'

Faye looked at the sparkling water and agreed enthusiastically. Moving over to where Amma was laying out their beach mat, she quickly stepped out of her shorts and removed her shirt, conscious of Sonny's brooding gaze fixed on her as she undressed. Tossing the hat onto the straw mat, she tied her hair back and followed him down to the water's edge.

They trudged past groups of children laughing loudly and splashing each other in the shallow waters and dodged around a large black horse that galloped past, its rider holding on to the mane and balancing on the strong bare back of his mount with just the grip of his calves.

The water was warm as Faye surged forward against the deceptively powerful waves. With strong lazy strokes, she swam out into the sea, closely followed by Sonny.

Back on the beach, Baaba watched them with narrowed eyes. Slipping on her sunglasses, she turned to Amma who had wriggled onto the beach mat between her and Edwin.

'She seems nice enough,' she remarked.

Amma was leaning back against Edwin, her braided head nestled against his shoulder.

'She's really nice,' she agreed airily. Without thinking, she added with a laugh, 'and from the way he's behaving, I'm beginning to suspect Rocky rather likes her too.'

Baaba's expression froze. She smoothed out her brightly coloured skirt and kept her tone neutral. 'What makes you say that?'

Amma, now totally relaxed, had shut her eyes and didn't notice the change in her friend's demeanour. 'Well, it's hard to describe,' she murmured drowsily. 'I think it's the way he looks at her – it's, like, really intense, you know?'

When Baaba didn't reply, Amma sat bolt upright in alarm, suddenly aware of what she had said. She seized Baaba's arm, noting in panic the grim expression on her friend's face.

'Now don't go getting worked up,' she said, switching to *Fanti*, the Akan dialect that Baaba spoke. 'She's only here for a short time. Anyway, you know Rocky has just finished with Clarissa – he's not likely to get involved with someone else so soon!'

Edwin burst out laughing. 'Amma, you don't know much about men, do you?' Ignoring the angry glare Amma shot his way, he leaned back on his elbows and added, also in *Fanti*, 'Baaba, if you're wise, you'll keep a close eye on Rocky now that he's free,' he said. With a nod towards the sea, he added with a sly grin. 'It looks like she's got Sonny hooked as well.'

Amma pushed him in exasperation as Baaba's expression darkened. Taking a bottle of iced water from her bag, Amma took a long sip and offered the chilled drink to her friend.

'Baaba, don't mind him! He's just messing with you. Anyway, I've told you before; Rocky won't go out with you because you're my best friend – he says it would be too close to home,' she added diplomatically.

As her friend looked at her sceptically, Amma carried on, her breathless voice earnest as she tried to sound convincing.

'Look, I even asked him to come to the beach with us today and he refused – he used the usual work excuse to get out of it. Besides, he thinks my friends are too young for him to hang around with.' She took another long drink from her bottle.

'So if he's so *anti-so*, what's he doing here, then?' Baaba asked sweetly, gazing past Amma at a tall figure approaching their group.

Amma choked on the water she was drinking. She spun her head round and gaped at the sight of her older brother striding towards them.

Before Amma could say a word, Baaba was on her feet. Her enormous hips swaying, she walked rapidly towards Rocky, reaching him before he had taken more than a few steps. Reaching up, she kissed him on the cheeks three times in the traditional Ghanaian fashion, and grasped his arm firmly as they walked to where Amma, Edwin and JB were sitting.

Rocky greeted the two men, shaking hands with Edwin and raising a hand in salute to JB, his sunglasses barely concealing his distaste at the sight of the latter. Baaba reluctantly released Rocky's arm as he sat on the mat beside Amma and contented herself with quickly sitting down beside him and manoeuvring her curves as close to him as possible.

'Where's Faye?' Rocky asked, looking around the crowded beach. He had changed into a pair of long white shorts and a black T-shirt that emphasised his compact muscles. Despite the heat, he somehow still managed to look cool.

'She's swimming,' Amma said briefly, looking out to where Faye and Sonny were now splashing each other in the sea.

Baaba hid a sly smile as she watched Sonny in the distance playfully trying to duck Faye's head under the water. 'It looks like Faye and Sonny are getting very friendly.'

Her voice was smooth and she watched Rocky covertly from under her long curly lashes. Her large breasts strained even harder against their tight covering as she leant against him, her face the picture of wide-eyed innocence as she reverted to her native *Fanti*, 'Well, the girl's on holiday, isn't she? She should have some fun while she's here. And if *anyone* knows how to show a girl a good time, it's our gorgeous Sonny!'

Rocky stood up so abruptly that Baaba almost fell over. Shaking the sand from his leather sandals, he hitched up his shorts and smiled back impassively at the surprised faces looking up at him.

'Where are you going?' Amma asked. Shading her eyes with her hand, she looked up at her brother in bewilderment.

'I hadn't planned on staying – I just dropped by to tell

you that Stuart's having a party next weekend at his house and that you're all invited. I'll see you at home this evening.'

With a casual wave of farewell to the astonished quartet, he turned around and strode back in the direction of the car park.

Faye staggered out of the sea, with Sonny close behind her, both of them weak with laughter from their horseplay. Looking over to where Amma and the others were sitting, she stopped abruptly, causing Sonny to bump into her.

Grabbing her waist to prevent her from falling over, Sonny laughed, not releasing his hold even when she had regained her balance.

'What's the matter?' His husky voice, so close to her ear, sent a small shiver through her.

'Look! Isn't that Rocky over there – by the others?' Faye exclaimed, trying not to sound agitated.

Shrugging carelessly, Sonny wiped the lingering drops of seawater from his eyes with one hand, the other hand still on Faye's waist, and looked over to where his friends were sitting.

'Yeah, that looks like Amma's brother,' he replied.

Just as he spoke, the receding figure turned and looked in their direction. Rocky paused for a moment, his face expressionless as he watched the two of them standing immobile at the water's edge, Sonny's hand resting possessively on Faye's waist.

Turning abruptly, he walked away without looking back.

9

Cultural Contrasts

The cock crowed relentlessly, its strident cry breaking through the gentle hum of the air conditioner. Faye turned over slowly in bed, groaning as her stiff muscles protested against the movement. Squinting through her mosquito net at the clock beside her bed, she saw that it was almost six o'clock in the morning.

That bloody animal is begging to be made into chicken soup! she thought viciously, wincing again as she burrowed her head back into the warm hollow in the centre of her soft pillow. Willing her mind to go blank before a stream of conscious thoughts could enter her brain, she breathed in and out deeply for several minutes. Just as she began to float back into sleep, the cock crowed again, followed by the piercing sound of a car horn from the house next door.

Doesn't anyone sleep in this country? With a deep sigh she rolled over gently onto her back and slowly opened her eyes. Pale shafts of morning sunlight filtered through the thin curtains. Through the white mosquito net, the advancing swords of light gave her room a pale ghost-like aura.

The unaccustomed exercise of the previous day was making itself felt. She reached down to rub her aching thigh and felt a marked soreness in her shoulders and back from her swim. After Rocky's sudden departure, she and Sonny had returned to the sea, swimming and frolicking until the cooling temperature had forced them reluctantly out of the water.

The rest of the evening had been uneventful with a quiet dinner at home followed by an early night. Rocky had still not appeared by the time Faye, yawning and struggling to keep her eyes open, bade her host family good night. After a quick shower, she had fallen into the welcoming bed and slept soundly.

She stirred restlessly as the images of the previous day started to crowd into her consciousness. Unable to lie still any longer, she sat up cautiously and gently crawled out of bed. With the sound of the flowing water muffling her groans, she stood under the shower until the warmth brought some relief to her aching muscles.

Feeling more energised, she rummaged through the clothes hanging in the spacious wardrobe. After considering her options, she pulled out a straight dark-chocolate linen skirt with a high slit at the front and a multicoloured top in a mix of gold, brown and scarlet that she'd picked up from a street market in Southall. The top was cut in the style of a sari blouse and she shrugged helplessly as she realised that her belly button was exposed.

Checking her appearance in the mirror, she giggled as she thought of her father's frequently raised eyebrows at the kind of clothes she wore and her ultra-conservative brother's constant pleas to tone down her – in his words – 'seriously weird' outfits.

After one last fruitless effort to tug the blouse down, she left her room, wincing at the ache in her calves as she walked down the stairs, and headed for the kitchen.

Martha, back from her day off, was bustling around the large kitchen singing a church hymn very loudly and equally off-key. She stared dubiously at Faye's exposed midriff as she walked in and her singing faltered as her eyes wandered further down to the split skirt. Recovering quickly, she smiled at Faye and wished her a good morning.

'Would you like some breakfast, Miss Faye?'

Faye shook her head, eyeing the full coffee pot longingly. She was just about to ask for a cup when Rocky sped into the kitchen. Dressed in dark navy tailored trousers and carrying the jacket of his suit, he stopped abruptly when he saw Faye before nodding coolly in greeting.

'Good morning.' He sounded in a hurry and turned to Martha who silently handed him a cup of coffee. He gulped it down hastily, holding the cup well in front of him to avoid spilling coffee onto his pristine white shirt.

'Isn't it a bit early for the office?' Faye looked at her watch in surprise.

Rocky took a final gulp and handed the cup back to Martha, who shook her head in exasperation at his idea of breakfast. Turning to Faye, he paused before answering, his dark caramel eyes taking in the slim exposed midriff with the peeking belly button. Resisting the impulse to tug the hem of her blouse down again in the face of his naked scrutiny, Faye looked back at him coolly, waiting for an answer.

'Not really,' he said, his eyes finally coming back up to meet hers. 'In Ghana our working hours usually start at eight. You're up early for someone on holiday – do you have plans for today?'

Two short loud blasts of a car horn from outside the house cut off her response.

'Damn! Sorry, I need to go. That's my father – I parked my car behind his last night,' he said, picking up his jacket as he spoke. With a hasty farewell, he dashed out of the kitchen, the sound of screeching tyres shortly afterwards confirming his departure.

Not wanting to get in Martha's way, Faye gratefully accepted a cup of coffee and wandered off to the dining room where Auntie Amelia was sitting reading a newspaper while finishing her breakfast. She looked up in surprise as Faye entered, then smiled warmly and gestured to her to take a seat across the table from her. On the table was a plate of sliced oranges along with a teapot and two clean teacups.

'Good morning, my dear,' Auntie Amelia said cheerfully. 'I hope you slept well? I'm surprised you are up so early – you looked so exhausted last night, I thought you would have a lie-in today.'

Faye sat down and placed her coffee cup carefully on the wicker coaster she had extracted from the rack in front of her.

'I slept like a log after all the swimming I did in the afternoon,' she laughed. 'Well, that is until a cock started crowing the national anthem at the crack of dawn!'

Auntie Amelia chuckled, her beautiful eyes crinkling in amusement. She offered the plate of oranges to Faye who shook her head and continued to sip her coffee.

'I see you're a coffee drinker, not a tea person like me,' Auntie Amelia said, with a nod at Faye's cup. 'Your mother was a coffee drinker too, you know,' she mused. 'In our day, it was considered very ladylike and genteel to drink tea. But Annie, as usual, didn't care about such things. She loved her coffee and that was that!' Settling back in her chair, she sipped her tea and smiled in remembrance.

'She sounds more like William than me,' said Faye, looking wistful. She was only too aware of her talent for bending over backwards to accommodate other people. While she always wanted to be liked, William was just the opposite and had never been known to compromise about anything if he could help it. It was a quality that had helped to make him a successful barrister but also a resolutely stubborn or – in Faye's words – pig-headed older brother.

'Oh, I don't know,' Auntie Amelia said, looking at Faye over the top of her coffee cup. 'I would say you have quite a bit of your mother in you. I mean, look at that striking combination of clothes you're wearing – I noticed it as soon as you walked in. You see, that's probably the way Annie would have dressed if she were your age today. She *loved* fashion and was always designing clothes for herself and her friends. Obviously you won't remember, but she used to make most of your clothes herself, and you always looked beautiful.' She paused for a moment in thought. 'There was always something slightly *different* about the way Annie put things together.'

'Really? That's what William says about *me*,' said Faye in surprise, and a rush of pleasure flowed through her at the unexpected connection to her mother she had just discovered.

'So what work do you do in London, Faye? Are you in the fashion business?' Auntie Amelia looked at her curiously.

Faye grimaced. 'No, I'm the secretary to a partner in a law firm.'

Auntie Amelia raised her shapely eyebrows in surprise. 'Really – why is that?' she queried. 'Do you find it interesting?'

Faye shrugged awkwardly, embarrassed to admit that she didn't have the confidence or the brains to look for a better job. Auntie Amelia patted her arm and gave her a reassuring smile. 'You are still young, my dear, I'm sure you'll find out what you really want to do in time. Just make sure it's something that really interests you and pursue it with all you've got. As I'm always telling Amma, look for what you feel passionate about and then just go for it, as you young people say.'

She paused for a moment, and then shook her head in resignation. 'Unfortunately, my daughter seems to have interpreted my advice that she should focus on her passion to mean Edwin!'

Faye was still giggling as the subject of their con-versation entered the room, yawning widely as she sat at the table next to her mother.

'Good morning Mama, morning Faye.' Amma sounded tired and listless as she reached across for the plate of sliced oranges.

'Good morning, Amma.' Her mother looked at her with amusement. 'Did you sleep at all last night? You don't look to me like you've woken up yet.'

Amma shook her head and chewed slowly on a segment of the juicy fruit. Her braids were tied back with a red scarf, which matched the red shirt she wore over her jeans. 'I was up until midnight on the phone with Edwin,' she said in between bites of orange. 'He had a lot on his mind that he wanted my opinion about.'

Faye almost choked at the exaggerated 'I-told-you-so' look Auntie Amelia cast in her direction.

'Really, dear? Has he found a job yet?' Disregarding the mutinous expression that appeared on Amma's face, her mother stared back at her, her expression unwavering.

'No, Mama,' Amma muttered sulkily. 'You know, it's not his fault that he can't find a decent job that takes into account all the studying he's done. He's very clever – *and* he got a really good degree!'

She poured herself a cup of tea, frowning ferociously at the pot as if she held it personally responsible for Edwin's unemployment.

Her mother maintained a tactful silence. Her diet temporarily forgotten, Amma stirred two spoons of sugar into her cup before continuing moodily. 'He won't even hear of us getting engaged until he's got a job. And now he's talking *again* about going to America! I thought that after the last time they refused him a visa, he'd finally given up, but he's obsessed with the place. Mama, what am I supposed to do if he goes away?' She looked at her mother, her brown eyes piteous and shadowed from lack of sleep.

'Well, as I keep saying, it wouldn't hurt *you* to get a job either, my dear,' her mother retorted. 'After all, you also have a good degree and now that you've finished your National Service, you should be applying to companies and starting your own career instead of worrying about Edwin.'

Her warm smile took the sting out of her words. 'Anyway, never mind that now. Faye is here and at least this means that you are free to take her round and entertain her while she's with us.'

Amma nodded and turned to Faye. 'Has Rocky left for work?'

Gazing back steadily at the younger girl whose face had lit up with a mischievous grin as she asked the question, Fay nodded. 'Yes, he left about twenty minutes ago,' she said as casually as possible. Changing the subject before Amma could persist, she went on. 'So, tell me. As my chief tour guide, what do you have planned for us today?'

'Well, I have to collect an outfit from my dressmaker later today. That is, if she's actually finished making it – she's not the most reliable person in the world. She's always doing something or other at church. She's a big time *chrife* – sorry, Faye, that means a devout Christian – and she's so involved with her church that it's really hard to get her to finish making clothes on time. I have to tell her I need something about two weeks earlier than I really do, otherwise she just takes so *long* and—'

Auntie Amelia interrupted hastily, anxious to get her request in before Amma launched into full flow. 'Well, if you don't mind, can you take the two new ceramic flowerpots outside over to the shop for me when you're ready? I've asked Baaba to reorganise the place a bit – it's all starting to look very cluttered and uninspiring, so I'm hoping the pots will brighten it up a bit.'

After both girls refused the offer of toast and eggs, Auntie Amelia rose quickly to her feet and excused herself to see to things in the kitchen. Amma finished her tea quickly and Faye followed her outside to find the flowerpots.

Although it was not yet eight o'clock, the sun was shining brightly, casting a clean, cheerful glow on the green lawn behind the house. A profusion of well-tended colourful flowers spilled gracefully out of their beds and added to the early morning brightness. The flowerpots were on the covered veranda next to a wicker sofa and armchairs covered with plump blue and white floral cushions. The veranda was cool and shaded and, for a moment, Faye was sorely tempted to collapse into one of the basket chairs.

After shouting for Togo to come and help, Amma sighed and tested the weight of one of the pots.

'Togo always conveniently goes deaf when you need him to do something,' she grumbled as she tried to lift it. 'You'll have to help me with these, Faye.' Puffing a little, she managed to lift one of the large hand-painted pots. Faye stooped and picked up the second one, grimacing at the combination of its weight and her sore calves. The two of them staggered around the side of the house and, after much pushing and pulling, managed to get both pots safely into Amma's car.

Faye ran up the stairs to her room to collect her bag and went back down to join Amma at the car, stopping for a few seconds to pop her head around the kitchen door and say goodbye to Martha and Auntie Amelia.

Driving out of Labone towards the shop, they had to contend with considerably more traffic than on the day before. After a lengthy period of sitting in a slow moving procession of cars, Amma parked in front of a small parade of shops. Her mother's was the first in the line of stores, with the words *Unique Clothing and Gifts* painted in a dashing font on the black awning above the door. In the large glass window, a few headless pink mannequins stood locked in a pose designed to display their brightly coloured outfits. Faye slid out of the air-conditioned comfort of the car and helped Amma carry the pots into the shop. Baaba was standing at the cash desk drinking a cup of tea and flicking through a newspaper as they walked in. She wore a tight knee-length skirt in a batik fabric, that somehow managed to encompass her huge hips, and a matching fitted top that hugged her straining bosom. She greeted them coolly and watched them hump the heavy pots inside.

'And what, may I ask, are those things for?' She raised a pencilled eyebrow as she watched them collapse into a couple of chairs after their exertions.

'Mama says the shop needs to be reorganised,' Amma replied, trying to catch her breath and forgoing any effort at tact in the process. 'She says it looks really boring and cluttered.'

The shop consisted of a large room with a low ceiling. The cash register was on a counter near the door, making entry into the shop somewhat awkward. An archway at the back of the store led to a small anteroom. From the main room, a closed door concealed a small corridor leading to a tiny kitchenette and bathroom. Looking around the room at the indifferent display of traditional outfits and jewellery, gift packs, cosmetics and toiletries, Faye secretly agreed with Auntie Amelia's comment, although she had enough sense to keep her thoughts to herself.

Baaba shrugged and looked round the store without interest, clearly uninspired by the challenge. Her eyes, heavily outlined with a dark pencil, came to rest on Faye and narrowed as she took in her expressive features.

'Well, Faye, you've just come from London,' she murmured throatily. 'Why don't you show us natives how things are done in the big fashion shops over there?' Her eyes flashed with malice as she noted Faye's discomfiture.

'Ah, Baaba, leave her alone!' Amma glared at her friend with indignation. '*You're* supposed to be a designer, for goodness' sake. Can't you put some style into this place?'

Baaba shrugged again and swallowed the rest of her tea. She walked across to the front of the shop and the sway of her broad hips caused her skirt to swish against her shapely legs. With her back to the shop entrance, she looked around the room with a critical eye for a few moments and then raised her hands helplessly.

'Look, Amma, I know how to design and sew clothes, but I've never claimed to be any good at decorating. I haven't got the first idea what to do with those pots, or anything else.'

Faye stood up and walked around the large room thoughtfully, taking in the wall space, shelving and the merchandise on display. 'Well,' she said, hesitant at putting herself forward. 'If you like, I'd be happy to try and help – I love decorating rooms.'

Amma and Baaba sighed in unison. 'Good', they chorused and promptly sat down, looking at her expectantly like children at a birthday party ready to be entertained by the magician.

Faye giggled at their combined expressions of relief and anticipation. She looked around the room slowly before speaking. Her voice was suddenly brisk as she started listing the things she would need, ticking each item off with her fingers as she spoke. Baaba, clearly grateful for the help, for once made no comment as she quickly seized a piece of paper and wrote down everything Faye said. Once or twice she raised her head and looked at Faye incredulously, but thought better of interrupting her and continued to scribble hurriedly.

When Faye had finished, Amma and Baaba went into a huddle to scrutinise the list and then stood up and announced that they would be back shortly. As they left, Faye flipped around the *Open* sign before any customers could walk in, and locked the shop door.

Turning back into the room, she sighed with pleasure at the task ahead of her and began to stack all the merchandise into one corner. Folding the garments that had been displayed on the mannequins, she was impressed by the beautiful fabrics and the fine workmanship of the clothes. From the similarity they bore to Amma's dress, she guessed that they were Baaba's designs.

Wondering why Baaba didn't wear some of her own range instead of the tight-fitting numbers she seemed to like so much, Faye put the clothes to one side and gathered up the hand strung bead necklaces and matching bracelets from the window display. She put them carefully into a large empty box she had retrieved from the kitchenette, where she had also found a dustpan and brush and some cleaning materials. She had just finished clearing the shop when Amma and Baaba returned, perspiring from the heat outside and with their arms piled full.

'Well, I hope you know what you're doing, Faye,' Baaba said doubtfully, looking at the items she had just deposited on the floor. 'Amma, just make sure your mother knows that this was *not* my idea.'

Amma waved her away impatiently. 'Oh, let's give her a chance – whatever she suggests can't be worse than what you and I could do!'

Baaba shrugged and handed Faye a long shirt that had clearly seen better days. 'I couldn't find any overalls, so I hope this will do,' she said. Faye nodded, taking the shirt and slipping her arms into the sleeves. She went into the small kitchen where she had laid out sheets of old newspapers on the floor in readiness. She dragged the pink mannequins into the kitchen and swiftly repainted them jet-black using the gloss paint she had requested. She stood them outside the back door of the shop to let them dry and went back inside to find Amma and Baaba sitting comfortably chatting.

'Okay, you two need to make yourselves useful,' she ordered, and proceeded to bark instructions at them for the next few hours. By midday the blazing sun had successfully dried the paint on the mannequins left outside, and Faye had completed all the paintwork inside the shop. She hoisted the mannequins, now a glossy black, back inside the kitchen and dressed them in the clothes she had removed earlier. She picked out some of the bead necklaces from the box and draped a few around the necks of the headless dolls.

She walked back into the shop and dissolved into helpless giggles at the baleful looks directed at her from Amma and Baaba who had collapsed into chairs, exhausted from the orders they had been scurrying around to obey all morning.

'Okay, girls, one last thing,' Faye said when she could stop laughing. 'Just help me put these mannequins back in the window and then I think we're done.'

With loud groans and exaggerated sighs, Amma and Baaba reluctantly stood up to help her lift the figures into the window display and they all trooped outside to see the full effect.

'Wow, Faye – it looks fantastic!' Her tiredness forgotten, Amma clapped her hands with excitement as she took in the new window display.

Faye had draped gold netting around the sides of the large window while tiny swirls of gold paint had been sprayed at intervals along the top and bottom of the glass pane. More of the netting, draped on the floor, created the effect of a diaphanous golden carpet. One of the new flowerpots sat in the centre of the window display filled with long stemmed silk flowers, some of which had been sprayed gold to highlight the gold flecks in the terracotta pot. The now-jet-black mannequins provided a strong contrast to the brilliant colours of Baaba's designs, which were further enhanced by the contrasting tones of the bead jewellery. The overall effect was eye-catching and dramatic and as they stood outside, a few people walking past stopped to admire the display.

'Now our only problem is that people will think the shop is too posh and won't come in to buy our things,' Baaba said moodily after staring at the stunning new display in silence for a few minutes. Secretly pleased at how the display had made her designs stand out, she was still reluctant to praise Faye whom she now saw as a threat to any potential chance with Rocky.

'Don't be so ungrateful, Baaba,' Amma glared at her. 'Why can't you just admit it looks beautiful? Mama will love it!'

An hour later, the transformation inside the shop was also complete. Earlier, having instructed the girls to drag the cash register to the back of the shop where it occupied less space, Faye had them assist her as she sprayed little golden swirls around the cream walls from the front door all the way around the main room of the shop. To accent the plain white walls, she had carefully painted a thin glossy black line where the wall and the ceiling met and along the top of the skirting board. One side of the room was now dedicated to clothing and shoes, while on the other side she had arranged the toiletries and gift packs on shelves lined with the remnants of the gold netting she had used in the window.

The most dramatic change was the small anteroom, where they had painted the walls a pale gold before turning the room into a display area for the shop's entire jewellery collection. The small jewellery stands had been given a coat of the black gloss paint and now formed a dramatic backdrop for an eye catching display of bangles, chains, bead necklaces and earrings. Against the wall behind the display, the second ceramic flowerpot, also filled with gold and coloured flowers, formed a backdrop that toned beautifully against the newly painted walls.

Amma gasped in disbelief as she walked slowly around the shop, and even Baaba couldn't help but exclaim at the finished product.

'Well, I must say I would never have thought of doing anything like this,' she confessed. 'I was thinking about just tidying up and rearranging the stock.'

Amma hugged Faye in gratitude. 'Mama will *not* believe this,' she enthused. 'Why aren't you a designer? I can't believe you are a secretary when you have such talent!'

Faye squirmed with embarrassment and pleasure. Although she was regularly called on by her friends to help with decorating ideas, this was the first time she had been given a completely free hand to use her imagination.

'Well, I'm glad you like it,' she grinned. 'Let's hope Auntie Amelia does too or we're all back here tomorrow changing it back!'

Amma glanced at her watch and did a double take.

'Oh shoot!' She squealed in shock. 'Look at the time! Faye, let's go and get something to eat and go to my dressmakers before she leaves home for her bible study class or whatever it is she's doing today.'

Faye went into the bathroom and took off the paint-stained shirt. She washed her hands, scrubbing at the obstinate specks of black oil paint. As soon as she emerged, Amma bundled her off with a quick farewell to Baaba who, too tired to even walk them to the door, waved languidly at them from where she sat.

It was now almost two o'clock and the heat and humidity were intense. Amma's car, which had been parked on the street, felt like an oven. The steering wheel was so hot to the touch that she was forced to open the car windows for several minutes to let some of the stifling air escape before starting the engine.

'What do you feel like eating?' Amma asked, as she pulled out into the road, grasping the warm wheel as lightly as she dared.

'Anything,' said Faye. 'I'm starving after all that work!'

Amma drove quickly through some quiet back roads before turning into a busy single-lane road. The cars were bumper to bumper, honking furiously as they inched along slowly.

Faye pushed her hair back from her face and flapped her hand in front of her in an effort to cool down. Her skin felt sticky and she longed for a cool drink to soothe her parched throat.

She stared in fascination at the activity taking place on the street, forgetting her hunger for a moment, when a skinny beggar approached their car, which was almost stationary in the busy traffic, with outstretched hand, only to turn away sorrowfully at Amma's dismissive gesture of impatience.

A boy carrying a large metal bowl of fish walked alongside their car for several minutes, intent on making a sale and completely unperturbed at Amma's look of disgust as he lifted the dead fish up to her window.

'Madam, the fish dey very good,' he said confidently, keeping pace with their slow moving vehicle. Amma ignored him and concentrated on keeping up with the traffic. The young man ducked his head to look across at Faye.

'Madam, I say, make you buy my fish, eh?' His grin was wide as he made his cheeky plea. Unable to resist it, she smiled, giving him renewed hope of a sale, even as the strong smell from the metal bowl wafted into the hot car.

'Madam, you see de fish? I swear, it dey make good stew or you go make fry 'um well well plus kenkey.' Undaunted by Amma's glare, he kept up the patter until eventually, after several minutes of fruitless advertising, he finally conceded defeat and ran to the car behind them to relaunch his sales pitch.

'This is our famous Oxford Street,' Amma explained, blowing the horn stridently while at the same time skilfully swerving to avoid a taxi that had pulled out from a side road and almost hit the side of their car. 'This road is always busy, but there are quite a few fast food restaurants here so we can stop and get something to eat.'

Looking round, Faye was immediately struck by the contrast between the luxurious saloon cars and four wheel drive vehicles on the street and the endless stream of hawkers who appeared to have set up an alternative market along the side of the road, selling everything from dog chains to lurid wall clocks. As their car crawled along, the young entrepreneurs would tap on the car windows, grinning broadly while energetically displaying their wares. A number of women, some with children tied firmly on their backs with cloths, seemingly oblivious to the heat, walked in the dust along the side of the road with large bowls on their heads full of items for sale. Some bowls were piled high with bananas, while others were filled with yams, green plantains and even washing up sponges.

Still on Oxford Street, they drove past banks, petrol stations, small boutiques displaying designer clothes and expensive handbags, restaurants and even a large hospital. A neon sign, its lights temporarily switched off, identified a casino set back on a side road.

'This road seems to have every kind of business and every type of person,' Faye remarked, her nose almost pressed against her window.

Amma honked her horn in irritation at a street hawker who had run out in front of their car in pursuit of a white backpacker showing no desire to buy the framed photograph of three fluffy white kittens the hawker was trying to sell.

'It's madness here sometimes,' she muttered, looking around for a parking space in front of what appeared to be a very popular restaurant, judging by the number of cars crammed into the small parking lot. Luckily, a car was reversing out, allowing Amma to pull in expertly into the vacated space.

Entering the building, they climbed up a flight of stairs to the restaurant where they were shown to an empty table by the window. From there, they had a clear view of the activity taking place on the street below. A smiling waiter handed them two menus and took their order for drinks. A few minutes later, he reappeared and placed their drinks carefully on the table.

'Ah, waiter, what is this?' Amma frowned and pointed to the bottle he had just placed in front of her.'

'Please, it is Pepsi, madam,' the waiter replied, beaming widely at her with sparkling white teeth.

'I didn't order Pepsi,' Amma said, her frown deepening. 'I ordered Coca-Cola.'

The waiter's smile was, if possible, even wider.

'Yes, madam,' he agreed happily.

Amma sighed deeply and tried again.

'So, why have you brought me Pepsi if you know I ordered Coca-Cola?' She spoke slowly and with exaggerated patience.

His smile unwavering in the face of the clear hostility directed at him, the waiter replied. 'Please, madam, it is all the same.'

Faye had started sipping on her Pepsi and choked on the drink as she burst into laughter. Amma, who had been on the verge of losing her temper, suddenly saw the funny side and started laughing. The waiter joined in the general hilarity for a few moments until he received a warning glare from a fast-sobering Amma and scuttled back to the kitchen.

After their meal, they drove out of the hectic atmosphere of Oxford Street and headed off to Amma's dressmaker who, she explained, lived in an area called Ridge. The difference between Oxford Street and Ridge could not have been greater. Lined with tall leafy trees, the roads in Ridge were almost empty of traffic, with only the occasional car and a few desultory pedestrians to be seen. The houses were, without exception, very large and situated in huge plots of land. Although some appeared well tended, they passed many that seemed to be badly in need of a facelift.

'This is the area where a lot of the British officials lived during colonial times,' Amma said, as they drove along a tree-lined avenue. 'The houses look big but some of them are deceptively small inside. In the old days, many of the colonial civil servants left their families behind in Britain when they were posted to Africa.'

As she finished speaking, she came to a stop in front of a pair of brown gates and tooted the car horn twice. The gate was quickly opened by a young man of about seventeen, who saluted in greeting and stood back as they drove in. The house was fairly large but the grounds, although spacious, lacked the well-tended quality of the Asante's home.

Amma parked in the gravelled driveway and led the way up a short flight of steps leading to the front door. She gave a loud knock at the door and as they walked inside, Faye was struck by the contrast with the airy brightness of the Asante's house.

I wouldn't mind giving this place a makeover, was her first thought as she took in the dark panelled walls and drab brown paintwork. They were shown into a large living room and waited on a brown velour sofa covered in stiff clear plastic that was so old it was cracking at the corners. Most of the furniture in the room was in a matching shade of brown, while gilt-framed family photographs perched on almost every surface. Large battered legal books filled the shelves of a heavy bookcase set back against the wall, their titles stamped in gilt lettering on worn hard spines. A hefty black bible sat on a teak centre table, as did a smattering of religious pamphlets and a pile of yellowing newspapers that partially obscured from view a red glass vase filled with faded artificial flowers.

Amma, who was perched next to Faye on the uncomfortable sofa, cast a wary look around before speaking.

'My dressmaker's husband is a retired judge,' she whispered. 'He's usually drunk, so let's hope he doesn't show up.'

Faye stifled a giggle and shifted uncomfortably on the sofa. She had to sit forward to prevent her exposed back from sticking to the plastic covers. Although the room was fairly cool, the old books gave it a musty and oppressive atmosphere and she silently prayed for Amma to finish her business quickly.

Her prayer was answered by the arrival of a small middle-aged woman carrying some clothing over one arm. With greying hair and twinkling eyes behind wire bifocals, she immediately reminded Faye of Miss Campbell.

Both girls stood up and Amma quickly introduced Faye. The dressmaker stared at Faye's clothing dubiously and introduced herself as Mrs Appiah.

'Can I offer you something to drink?' she asked, her eyes travelling down to the slit in Faye's skirt in an exact replay of Martha's reaction that morning.

'No, thank you,' Amma said quickly. 'We've just had lunch.'

Mrs Appiah tore her eyes away from Faye's outfit and turning to Amma, she draped the garments she was carrying over the back of the sofa and held up each item in turn.

'I've made the adjustments on your other clothes too, Amma,' she said. 'The skirt should fit properly now.'

She retrieved a plastic bag from behind the sofa and quickly emptied the contents onto the table before folding the clothes and popping them in. Amma handed over a large wad of notes, which Mrs Appiah counted, nodding in satisfaction when she'd finished.

'Thank you very much, my dear,' she said. 'And how is your mother? Please give her my regards when you get home.'

Amma nodded with a polite smile and closed her handbag.

'I know you will look wonderful in the *boubou* at your friend's engagement ceremony.' Mrs Appiah nudged Amma gently in the ribs with a sly smile. 'And you know, my dear, with God's help it will be your turn to marry soon. You just wait and see.'

Amma sighed as she picked up the plastic bag full of clothes. 'I hope so, Auntie,' she said. 'But my boyfriend doesn't seem to be in a hurry and my mother is more interested in me getting a good job than getting married.'

Mrs Appiah shook her head vigorously, her tone earnest. 'Eh! My dear, as for this one, listen to me,' she said. 'The most important thing is that you must *pray*! Pray all the time, never stop – and the Good Lord will find you a husband. And Amma, I've told you before, come to my church! We have plenty of God-fearing young men who are looking for a wife. So, if this boyfriend of yours is not ready, you come! As for finding you a husband, it's not a problem, eh, you hear?'

She pushed the wad of notes securely into the pocket of her skirt. 'Don't make the mistake of going to chase after a career and thinking you have all the time in the world, you hear?' She wagged her finger solemnly. 'I tell you, find a good husband and settle down quickly!'

She pushed her spectacles back on her small shiny nose and frowned at her client. 'Ah Amma, listen eh? When you die, nobody will ask what you did for a *career*!' She spat the word out in disgust. 'All they will want to know is how many children and grandchildren you left behind.'

She turned to Faye who had been listening in incredulous silence.

'So, young lady,' she demanded, 'do you go to church?'

Faye nodded meekly. 'Yes, Mrs Appiah, I'm a Catholic.'

The older woman sniffed. 'Well, technically I suppose you are a Christian,' she conceded, her tone grudging. 'But all these old churches have lost their way. Until you are born again, you are still a sinner in God's eyes. You should come to my church and hear the word of God. Of course, you would need to dress modestly,' she said pointedly, looking down at Faye's skirt.

Amma took one look at Faye's outraged expression and quickly said goodbye to the older woman. Mrs Appiah walked them out to their car, talking non-stop all the way.

'Eh, Amma, that's a nice car you are driving,' she said, examining the vehicle critically as they got in. 'But be careful your young man doesn't get worried that you are too expensive to marry, eh?' She wagged her finger again at Amma who, after a swift glance at Faye, was struggling to restrain her giggles.

'Actually, it's my brother's car, Mrs Appiah,' Amma said, her voice slightly unsteady from suppressed laughter. 'His company gave him a new car so he lets me drive this one.'

The older lady nodded, mollified by the explanation. Pressing a pamphlet with a black cross on the cover into each of their palms, she finally stepped back from the car.

'Heh, Adamu!' she shouted, looking around for the watchman. The young man appeared almost immediately.

'Adamu, open the gate for madam!' As he rushed to obey, she looked at her watch, said a hasty goodbye to the girls and turned around and hurried back inside the house.

Amma drove off and unable to hold back any longer, they both burst into laughter. Amma was laughing so hard she almost hit the gatepost as she drove through the gates. Gasping with laughter, Faye wagged her finger at Amma.

'Eh, Amma, make sure you don't drive too well or your young man will think you are too clever and run away,' she mimicked Mrs Appiah's reedy voice. 'No wonder the old judge turned to drink!' she exclaimed, reverting to her normal voice and rolling her eyes in horror.

They were both exhausted and Amma headed straight back to Labone. Once at home, she fetched some cold drinks from the kitchen and they collapsed in the living room, still laughing as they took turns impersonating Mrs Appiah.

A piercing cry suddenly shattered the peaceful atmosphere. Faye and Amma sprang to their feet in panic, but before they could take a step, Auntie Amelia burst into the room. Seizing Faye, she whirled her round and round and then squeezed her in a suffocating hug while a stupefied Amma looked on.

'Mama, what is it?' she asked in alarm as her mother whooped loudly and kissed Faye soundly on each cheek.

The sound of a loud cough from the doorway caused everyone to freeze for a second. Rocky stood on the threshold looking at his mother in amazement. He had just arrived home and was still holding his briefcase.

'Ma, what's the matter?' he asked. He looked anxious but, as Faye noted while trying to disentangle herself from her excited aunt, even the worried frown on his face didn't mar his handsome features. His tie, for once, was slightly askew although his shirt was as white as untouched snow. His caramel-brown eyes narrowed with concern as he watched his mother resume her excited twirling and he moved into the room to stand beside his bemused sister.

Coming to an abrupt halt, Auntie Amelia smiled reassuringly at the three faces staring at her in stunned silence. Smoothing back her hair, she beamed at Faye before turning to her offspring, breathless in her excitement.

'I'm sorry! Don't think I've gone mad. It's just that I am so *excited* by what Faye did to my shop!' Reaching out to Faye again, she hugged her tightly before releasing her to stroke her cheek softly.

'Whatever made you think you don't have talent, my dearest child?' she said gently. 'What you have created in my shop is absolutely wonderful!'

Taken aback by the depth of sincerity in the words,

Faye's eyes misted over. Clearing her throat, she smiled a little shakily. 'I'm glad you liked it – I was worried you might think it was a bit over the top.'

'*Over the top?* No way,' Aunt Amelia said. 'It's simply beautiful.' She turned to Rocky. 'Son, you should see the place now – what she did is so simple and yet so different!'

Rocky heaved a sigh of relief at his mother's apparent return to normality, although his expression was still wary as he looked at her.

'Okay, Ma, let me understand this. Faye redecorated your shop,' he said slowly, his tone cautious. 'And you like it,' he went on. Although he didn't say so, it was clear that he would dearly have loved to add, 'and, for that, you had to scare us all to death?'

Amma gave her brother an impatient look and sat down again. Now that she was sure her mother was not heading for the local asylum, her own euphoria at Faye's transformation of the shop resurfaced.

'Rocky, you really must go and see the shop,' she enthused. 'Faye did a really good job. You wouldn't believe it was the same place.'

Rocky tossed his jacket over the back of the sofa before sitting down in one of the leather armchairs and stretching his long muscled legs out in front of him.

'It sounds too good to miss.' He smiled at Faye, who flushed with embarrassed pride. He made no attempt to break eye contact and she felt her heart pound as a rush of pure joy shot through her. Conscious of Rocky's open scrutiny of her partially exposed midriff, she sat down on the sofa next to Amma and curled her feet up under her.

'Amma, I'll definitely go and take a look,' Rocky said. 'My only problem is how to get past that man-eating friend of yours.'

Picturing Rocky's closely cropped head trapped within Baaba's menacing cleavage, Faye couldn't stop laughing. Amma glared at her brother for a moment and then, unable to help herself, also started laughing.

'Don't say rude things about my friend,' she said, trying to sound stern. 'Baaba is very fond of you, you know.'

'A feeling that is *not* mutual, I can assure you,' was the unsympathetic reply. 'She's terrifying – and as for those tight skirts and blouses...' his voice tailed away and he pulled off his tie and unbuttoned his collar as if just the thought of Baaba was causing him to suffocate.

Amma looked curiously at her brother. 'What are you doing home so early? Did someone burn the bank down?'

'Very funny. What's so strange about a man coming home after a day at the office?'

'It isn't strange for normal people. But *you*?' Amma scoffed. 'I can't remember the last time you've been home from work before dinner.' She paused and her gaze wandered thoughtfully across to Faye before coming back to rest on her brother. With her head cocked to one side, she stared at him hard with narrowed eyes.

Rocky crossed his legs and looked straight back at her. His face was inscrutable and his eyes gave nothing away as he mocked the incredulity in her voice. 'Well, *maybe* it's time for me to mend my ways – aren't you the one who's always saying there's more to life than work?'

Amma rolled her eyes. 'Okay, now you're just being

weird.' She looked so sceptical that Rocky burst into laughter, his even teeth a dazzling white against his copper-brown complexion.

Conscious that she was staring at him, Faye dropped her gaze and studied the pattern on the Persian rug intently.

'So, Faye,' Rocky's voice interrupted her reverie. 'How are you finding Ghana?'

Slightly startled, Faye paused for several moments before answering.

'Well, apart from the fact that no one seems to sleep past dawn,' she grimaced, 'I'm having a good time. It was great helping at the shop this morning and we drove around town for a while afterwards.'

She smiled at Amma and continued. 'But I'm sure my fabulous tour manager will be taking me to a few more places while I'm here.'

Rocky nodded. His brow furrowed in thought for a moment, and then he smiled. 'Well, things are pretty busy for me this week but I would be glad to take you out over the weekend,' he said.

Another jolt of happiness coursed through her and she forced herself to be calm and to focus on what he was saying. 'There's a very nice jazz club that I often go to. Maybe on Friday evening we can—'

He broke off as Martha came into the living room, wiping her hands on the apron tied around her waist.

'Oh, Miss Faye, forgive me.' Martha looked extremely guilty.

'Why?' said Faye, looking at the older woman in bewilderment. 'What's wrong, Martha?'

'I forgot to tell you earlier that you had a phone call while you were out with Amma. I wrote the message down but I put it in my apron pocket and I didn't remember until just now.'

Rocky smiled lazily, amused at the housekeeper's embarrassment. 'Don't look so worried, Martha. It's not the end of the world,' he said. 'Who phoned – her father?'

Martha looked at the note in her hand and frowned as she tried to make out what she had written.

'No, it was someone called Sonny – he said to remind you about your date on Friday.' Apologising once again, she bustled out of the room.

For a moment no one spoke. Amma glanced quickly at Rocky, a hint of anxiety in her eyes, and then turned to Faye. 'Oh, you have a date with Sonny? You didn't mention it – when did that happen?'

Faye shrugged, wondering why she suddenly felt guilty. 'I wouldn't exactly call it a date. He mentioned something when we were leaving the beach about maybe meeting up later this week. I'd actually forgotten all about it.'

She looked at Rocky as she spoke, waiting for him to finish what he had been about to say before Martha's interruption, but the lazy smile that had been on his face earlier had disappeared. Puzzled at the sudden change in his demeanour, she looked helplessly at Amma who smiled brightly, although her cheerfulness seemed a little forced.

'Well, I suppose you can trust Sonny not to waste any time when he sees an attractive woman,' she said. 'But if Friday doesn't work, maybe…?'

Faye looked back at Rocky but he made no attempt to

pick up on his sister's cue. Instead, taking a quick look at his watch, he rose to his feet and picked his jacket up from the sofa.

'Rocky, you were—' Faye started to speak and then stopped abruptly, put off by the expression of chilled politeness on his face. She looked at him in dismay. *What just happened?*

'Please excuse me, I need to make a couple of calls before dinner,' he said. His voice was expressionless, although his face looked bleak as he turned and walked out of the room.

10

Cultural Relationships

The fly in the ointment of a perfect Thursday afternoon was literally buzzing around Faye's head as she tried to take a short nap out on the cool veranda. After a heavy lunch, Amma had disappeared to her room leaving Faye to stretch out undisturbed on the chintz covered wicker lounger. Undisturbed, that is, except for a persistently friendly fly. Finally convinced that a conspiracy had been hatched by the animal and insect kingdoms to deprive her of sleep, Faye sat up in exasperation, ready for battle. Reaching for her magazine, she rolled it into a tight wad and swiped ferociously at the hapless fly as it came back to visit.

'Damn!' She cursed as the fly shot away in panic, finally accepting that it was not on friendly terrain. Unrolling the magazine, she lay back on the lounger and skimmed carelessly through the pages. Tips on how to keep your skin supple in winter and where to shop for the best bargains in boots held little attraction on a warm afternoon in the tropics. Lounging in only a pair of cotton shorts and a thin strappy top, she tried and failed to imagine the cold weather she had left behind.

It's hard to believe I've only been here for five days, she mused. She thought back over the events since her arrival in Ghana on Saturday evening, and for what must have been the hundredth time, mentally thanked Wesley for being the catalyst that had finally brought her here.

I must get William to come out to Ghana, she thought drowsily. She dropped the magazine on the side table and lay back on the lounger, closing her eyes as the cool breeze wafted over her. *I'm sure he and Rocky would get on like a house on fire.*

The thought of Rocky had the same effect on her nap as the earlier unsolicited visits by the fly. Jolted out of her semi-somnolent state, she pondered over her inexplicable reactions to him. Since Sonny's phone call, Rocky had been pleasant but distant whenever their paths happened to cross. The offer to take her out had not been repeated and it appeared that the brief glimpse she had seen of the relaxed charming host had been closed off, leaving only a polite stranger in view.

Where someone like Lucinda would have taken the initiative in this situation, two years with Michael, not to mention the memory of his predecessors, had left Faye sorely lacking in confidence when it came to the opposite sex. It didn't help that while she couldn't deny the electric effect Rocky had on her, she was not at all sure what, if anything, to do about it. It was abundantly clear that Rocky was an extremely eligible bachelor who could have his pick of the most beautiful girls in town. In the short time she had been in Accra, she had seen enough leggy beauties around to realise that even with Clarissa out of the way, there was no shortage of women available to console the handsome young banker.

She giggled as she remembered Baaba's visit to the house the previous evening, ostensibly to return a magazine Amma had lent her. After asking where Rocky was in what she thought was a casual tone, Baaba had stayed for hours, obviously hoping to bump into him. It was only after Amma had nodded off on the sofa that she had finally taken the hint that it was time to leave. Reluctantly wishing them a good night, she had swayed out of the house in tight black skinny jeans that defied all the laws of science in their ability to accommodate her hips. A scowling Togo, who had been taking a nap outside the gate, had stomped off grumbling under his breath at being forced to wake up and find her a taxi. Still muttering angrily on his return, he barely allowed the vehicle to drive out through the gates before slamming them shut. Rocky had appeared ten minutes later; but aside from a brief hello, he had little to say to anyone and went up to his room shortly afterwards.

But if Rocky was proving to be Mr Elusive, Sonny, on the other hand, was in serious contention for a medal in the field of persistence. He had phoned every day since the beach trip and made no secret of his attraction to her. While she dismissed his increasingly passionate claims to have fallen madly in love with her, she had to admit that his sense of humour and charming good looks were a pretty potent combination. After Michael's serious approach to everything in life, it was fun to talk to Sonny, who took nothing seriously and whose idea of literature was the cartoon strip in the national daily.

As Rocky had said nothing more about the jazz club, she had finally agreed to go out with Sonny on Friday, although she had insisted on lunch rather than dinner.

'That's fine with me,' was his reaction. 'I'll take you to a proper Ghanaian chop bar – they're our local restaurants – so you can eat real Ghanaian food. Not like those expensive bourgeois restaurants Amma always goes to!'

JB had also phoned several times since the afternoon on the beach. Although he always called Amma's mobile, he would then insist on speaking to Faye. Each time they spoke, his accent seemed even more incomprehensible and she was forced to ask him to repeat almost everything. Peppering every sentence with 'You know what I'm sayin'?' when she truly didn't, made phone conversations with him almost as undesirable as having him nose to nose in front of her.

In reality, the whole experience of being pursued by men was something of a novelty. The seven years she had spent at a Hampstead girls' school for the elite had offered precious few opportunities to meet men of her ethnic background, and working at an old-fashioned family firm like Fiske, Fiske & Partners made it even less likely that she would come into contact with African or Caribbean men. While the few black men she had come across were more than happy to date white girls, the type of middle and upper class white men she usually ended up meeting were rarely in the market for a black girlfriend. With them, she was usually treated more as one of the boys or the channel to approach one of her girlfriends rather than as a potential mate. The few exceptions she had come across to this rule had been looking for what she had once described to Caroline as 'an exotic rebellion' and *only* asked her out because she was black. Finding Michael had been like stumbling across an oasis when she had given up hope of seeing anything more than miles of endless desert.

Having Michael as a boyfriend had been the proof that she so badly needed that she was indeed attractive – which made it particularly ironic that his constant criticisms of her clothes, her hair or what he termed as her cultural inadequacies, had ultimately only deepened her lack of self-esteem.

Now back in her cultural home and with two suitors within five days – even if, she conceded, one *did* sound like a strangled canary – she was beginning to feel more confident about herself than she had for years.

She pushed the puzzle of Rocky's attitude to the back of her mind and wandered off to the kitchen in search of a cold drink. Martha was sitting at the table chopping the fresh spinach leaves she had bought from the market that morning, and looked up as Faye bounded in.

'Can I get something for you, Miss Faye?' she asked. Although normally soft spoken, Faye knew from the exchanges she had overheard between Martha and Togo from her bedroom window that Martha's voice could be extremely loud when she chose. Today her soft curves were encased in a straight dark blue polyester dress with a frilled white collar. The warmth in her dark eyes diluted the severity of the hospital matron look.

'Martha, please can I get some cold water?' Faye pleaded, flapping the hem of her tiny top to cool herself down. She flopped down at the table directly under the whirring ceiling fan while Martha wiped her hands on a clean cloth and placed a glass and a large bottle of iced water on the table, chuckling as Faye speedily gulped down three full glasses of water.

'You remind me of my son.' Martha shook her head in amusement. 'He also drinks water like a tortoise that has sat in the sun for too long.'

Faye almost choked on her last gulp, never having been compared to a sun-drenched tortoise before. Wiping her mouth unceremoniously with the back of her hand, she looked at Martha curiously.

'I didn't realise you had a son, Martha. Where is he?'

The older woman picked up the glass and the almost empty bottle and carried them over to the sink.

'Oh, he lives in my village with my mother and his three sisters,' Martha replied as she washed the used glass. The humour left her voice and a note of sadness crept in to take its place.

'You must miss them very much,' Faye said sympathetically. 'What about your husband – where is he?'

Martha gave no reply and for a moment Faye was afraid that she had offended her. Martha turned round with a sigh and came back to the table. She pulled out her chair and sat down, her face sombre and without her usual smile.

'He's dead, Miss Faye,' she said quietly. 'It will be fifteen years at Christmas time since he was killed in a road accident.'

She shook her head as Faye tried to apologise for raising the subject. 'No, no, Miss Faye, it all happened a long time ago. These things are the will of God and we must accept them,' she said with a resigned shrug.

After a brief silence, Faye spoke again. 'So how old is your water-swigging son?'

Martha chuckled. 'He is now twenty-four – at the time his father passed away he was only nine years old. He is my oldest, but I also have three daughters. When Paa Kwesi died, the girls were seven, five and two years old.'

Faye was horrified. 'No!' she exclaimed. 'How awful for you! How on earth did you cope all alone with four children?'

Martha shrugged her plump shoulders philosophically. 'Sometimes I wonder myself. But with help of my family and some good friends, I was able to survive.'

Faye continued to eye her curiously and Martha laughed good-humouredly.

'My husband, Paa Kwesi, and I came from neighbouring villages and our fathers knew each other well,' she said. 'I finished school when I was fifteen but Paa Kwesi continued until he completed his secondary education. His family was quite rich – at least compared to most of the people in our village – so he was lucky to be able to go to school for so long. Most of the time, children were not allowed to stay in school because they had to help their families on their farms. Many also ran away to the cities to find work.'

Picking up her knife, she continued to chop the spinach into thin strips as she spoke. Faye listened intently, not interrupting once.

'Paa Kwesi's family liked me because I was humble and very hard working,' she went on. 'So when he finished his training to be a mechanic, his people came to ask my parents for me. Of course my family agreed and, at eighteen years old, we were finally married.

'My mother was one of those women who wanted to make sure that all her daughters had some skills and so after I left school, she arranged for me to work with the village dressmaker and learn how to sew. My dream was to be able to buy a sewing machine and set up my own dressmaking business one day. After Paa Kwesi and I married, his family helped him to start on his own as a mechanic and he was soon doing well. As our tradition demanded, I moved into his family house and helped his mother and his sisters with the household chores. But I still carried on working at the local dressmaker's shop, sewing for other people on her old machine. I knew that in time, if I worked hard, I would earn enough money to buy my own sewing machine.

'Eh, Miss Faye, if I were to tell you how I worked, you wouldn't believe me! Even when my children started coming, I didn't stop sewing until the day I gave birth. As soon as I was strong enough after each child, I would start my sewing again. Because I had to add most of the little money I made to the chop money Paa Kwesi gave me, it took a good few years before I had enough money to make my dream come true.

'At last the day came when I had saved enough money to buy my sewing machine. I was so excited that for the whole night before, I did not sleep! I remember the day when I went into town to buy the machine like it was yesterday. I brought it back to the house and, I tell you, almost everyone in the village came to admire it. It was so shiny and beautiful and new. I was so proud of that machine – no one was allowed to even touch it!

'But it was after my machine came that our problems started. My mother-in-law began to complain to my husband that I was no longer respectful towards her and that now that I had my own machine, I had become too proud. At the time my husband's business was not doing well and he had started spending more and more time at the village drinking spot. The more his mother complained, the more he became angry with me. Soon every time he came home he would start abusing me for the smallest thing.'

She stopped chopping for several moments and then shook her head with a small sigh and went on.

'Ah well, it was not all his fault, Miss Faye. It's true, I *was* very proud and I suppose it was not too comfortable for him to see me busy with my customers and my new machine when he was struggling to keep his business. His other brothers had left the village. One went to Agege – that is what we called Nigeria – and the others left to go and find work in the city. So Paa Kwesi was the only man left to take care of all of us. But I won't lie to you – his mother was very difficult to live with. She would shout at him as though he were a child and not a grown man. Then she was always accusing him of neglecting her and his sisters and caring only for his wife and children. As for me, even though I was working night and day to make some money for the household, she just hated me more and more.

'One morning as I was finishing a dress for one of my customers, one of Paa Kwesi's friends came running to the house. He was weeping and as soon as I saw his face, I knew something terrible had happened! He told us that my husband had been killed by a timber driver, who had lost control of his overloaded truck and driven straight into him. Eh, Miss Faye, I tell you, the shock was so great I nearly collapsed! As for Paa Kwesi's mother, she did not stop crying for ten solid days! His brothers returned home immediately to bury him and my family also came from our village for the funeral. In fact, the whole village came to mourn with us and for many weeks afterwards, in accordance with our custom, we had to provide refreshment and shelter for the visitors.

'When my family eventually returned to our home town, Paa Kwesi's mother and his sisters began to make my life hell. Soon they were even blaming me for his death, telling me that if I had not made him feel so angry because of my wicked pride, he would not have been drinking and would have been able to jump out of the way of the timber truck. No matter how I tried to calm them, the abuse just become worse.

'One afternoon as I was sewing at the back of the house, my mother-in-law appeared and once again began to insult me. When I refused to respond, she rushed to my room and gathered all my clothes and my children's clothes together. I begged her on my knees but she just threw the things at me and pushed my sewing machine to the ground, screaming at me to leave her house and that I was a murderer. His sisters, who had come running to see what had happened, soon joined her in attacking me.

'I tell you, Miss Faye, I was so afraid I didn't know what to do! I quickly collected the children and our remaining belongings. But, before I could stop them, they seized the heavy stick we used to pound fufu and destroyed my precious sewing machine!

'Fearing for my life and the safety of my children, we fled from that house and by God's grace we found a kind lorry driver who took us back to my village. I was so sick about the loss of my machine that I couldn't eat for several days. Finally, I realised that I had to look for work since my mother and father could not afford to feed all of us. One of Paa Kwesi's friends who had heard about what happened came to visit me in my mother's house about a week after we returned. He was very kind and told me that he would contact his brother who was a priest in Accra to see if he could help me find work there – you see, without my machine I could no longer stay at home to work. His brother happened to be the priest at Mrs Asante's church. Hearing of my situation, she told the priest that she needed someone to help look after the house and her children and asked him to send me to her. So I came here and I have been here now for fourteen good years! So, you see, Miss Faye, I do not have to complain about anything; this family has taken care of me and allowed me to provide for my children. Now they have all grown up and are in good health, thanks to Mrs Asante – God bless her.'

With that, she scooped the chopped spinach into

plastic freezer bags and put them into the huge deep freezer. For several minutes Faye sat watching Martha as she deftly went about her business. Hearing about the housekeeper's experiences had sobered her and she wondered if she would have had the strength to cope in such circumstances. Her own worries now seemed petty in comparison to what Martha must have gone through.

Her thoughts were interrupted by the arrival of Amma, freshly showered and dressed in a long flowered skirt with a matching short-sleeved top.

'Oh, there you are Faye,' she said in breathless relief. 'I've been looking everywhere for you! We're going out to dinner with my parents at their friends' house and Mama said to tell you that we will leave at six o'clock.'

She glanced at the clock on the kitchen wall before eyeing Faye's shorts and top critically. 'I'm guessing you will want to change before we go – and it's almost quarter past five,' she said.

Barely suppressing a smile at Amma's attempt at tact, Faye thanked Martha for the water and went upstairs to her room to take a shower and change her clothes. By the time she had finished, it was just before six.

Uncle Fred grinned as she walked into the living room where he and Amma were waiting. 'Ah, it's our superstar interior designer,' he teased as she sat down carefully, trying not to crease the knee length lilac linen skirt she was wearing. 'Although I must say you are looking more like a supermodel this evening – isn't that right, Amma?'

Amma studied Faye's outfit appreciatively. The sleeveless silky white Mulberry top with a draped cowl neckline tucked into the fitted skirt showed off Faye's slender shape.

'I think Daddy is right, Faye,' she said. 'That skirt really suits you. It's just as well you're much thinner than me or you would have to leave half your wardrobe behind when you go back to England.'

Pleased and a little embarrassed by the attention, Faye smoothed out the skirt that was already threatening to crease.

'I hear we're off to dinner at your friends' house, Uncle Fred. Do they live nearby?'

'They live further to the west of the city,' Uncle Fred replied. 'It's a part of town that has historically been an industrial area. But, more recently, there has been a huge expansion in residential housing developments and—'

He broke off and stood up as Auntie Amelia came into the room. She looked stunning in a beautiful outfit made from a dark pink and navy blue traditional print. A piece of the fabric had been twisted into an elaborate turban style headdress that accentuated her high cheekbones and almond shaped eyes.

Kissing his wife gently on the cheek, Uncle Fred twirled her round slowly, letting out an exaggerated wolf whistle as he did so. With an impatient tut, although clearly pleased at her husband's show of admiration, Auntie Amelia went through to the kitchen to tell Martha they were leaving.

Sitting in almost immobile traffic twenty minutes later, Faye stared out of the window, both fascinated and horrified at the antics of the bus and taxi drivers. One driver in particular, driving a minibus with the words *Only*

God Knows painted on the back, was clearly not enchanted by the idea of being a part of the slow moving line of cars and was suddenly inspired to create a third lane of traffic along the verge of the dual carriageway. Ignoring the outraged protests of his terrified passengers and the startled cries of the weary pedestrians walking home from work, he suddenly swerved onto the dusty track along the side of the tarmac road and sped off, grinning cheerily at his ingenuity.

Uncle Fred shook his head in disgust as an impatient taxi driver, impressed by the manoeuvre, followed his new role model and sped off in the wake of the van. Another bus, this one christened *In God We Trust*, hooted furiously and took off in hot pursuit of the taxi. The faint shouts of its alarmed occupants could be heard, echoed by vigorous cursing from the almost stationary queue of drivers, the sides of whose cars barely escaped being scraped.

Ten minutes later, they reached the junction of a huge six-exit roundabout. Uncle Fred burst into laughter, unable to restrain himself at the sight of the intrepid bus driver and his followers trying to pacify an angry policeman. An overturned police motorcycle at the side of the road told its own story while the jeering passengers, still trapped inside the two buses, hurled abuse at the sheepish drivers.

Faye joined in the general laughter at the drivers' comeuppance.

'You can just imagine *that* conversation,' she chuckled. 'When the policeman asks the driver "why were you driving like that?" what are the chances he'll reply "Only God Knows!"'

Uncle Fred drove carefully along the busy road, neatly dodging potholes. 'One can only hope that they take their driving licences away.'

'In God We Trust,' Amma said solemnly, throwing them all into another fit of giggles.

Darkness was falling as they turned into a wide road that led to a pair of high wide gates manned by three security men. Stopping his car at the barrier in front of the gates, Uncle Fred waved at one of the men, who smiled broadly, raised the metal barrier and waved him through.

'Faye, now I think of it, our friends Mr and Mrs Debrah are also old friends of your father.' Uncle Fred turned his head slightly towards the back seat where Faye was attempting to smooth out the creases forming in her skirt.

She looked up in surprise, momentarily distracted from her task. 'Oh, really?' She frowned doubtfully. 'I don't think I remember hearing their names before.'

Auntie Amelia turned back to look at Faye, nodding her head in emphasis as she spoke. 'Oh yes, my dear, they used to be very close friends when your father lived in Ghana. In fact, Akosua Debrah comes from the same home town as your mother.'

Faye absorbed this new piece of information, marvelling at how little she knew about her father and his life in Ghana with her mother. It was as though the death of his wife had caused him to seal off the first part of his life. Although he had made a point of trying to educate his children about their ancestry, he rarely made reference to specific events or friends from his earlier life in Ghana, as though it was all too painful to relate. Since her mother's death, despite the fact that he was an attractive and highly sought after widower, her father had showed no interest in finding romance again and had never brought another woman home. Instead, he focused his considerable energy on his work and, when he was at home, on his children.

The housing development they were now driving through reminded Faye of the new-build developments in England. Unlike the walled-off detached houses she had grown used to seeing in Accra, these houses were of a uniform design and set back at regular intervals from straight paved roads. Pristine, well-maintained green lawns fronted each dwelling and gleaming luxury vehicles could be seen parked in driveways.

Uncle Fred stopped in front of a particularly large house and they piled out of the car and walked up the paved pathway to the front door. Auntie Amelia rang the doorbell and straightened her headdress, while Faye made a last attempt to smooth out the creases in her skirt. A few moments later the door was opened by a short, cheerful looking man who stood back and welcomed them in.

Amma and Faye hung back as the older couple entered first and hugged their friend warmly. Coming into the house, they walked through into a large living room. Faye looked around curiously, her eyes widening at the sight of several carved wooden stools placed along one side of the room. Hearing her name, she turned to find her host smiling, one hand extended towards her.

She hastily shook hands and smiled shyly as Auntie Amelia introduced her. The next moment she was seized in a suffocating embrace as the older man realised who she was.

'Ey, ey, ey! But this is wonderful!' he exclaimed. He released her from his grip and scrutinised her face.

'My goodness, she looks like Annie, eh?' He addressed his question to the Asantes, who smiled indulgently at Faye like the proud parents of a child prodigy. Auntie Amelia introduced their host as Mr Charles Debrah, but whom everybody called 'Uncle Charlie'.

'Well I know Faye is the novelty today, but I'm also here, Uncle Charlie!' Amma laughed and stepped forward to be hugged in turn. With one arm around her, he motioned them all into the living area and invited them to take a seat. They had barely sat down when his wife hurried in and they rose again to exchange hugs. Auntie Akosua was the same height as her husband and had a broad face with an equally cheerful expression. Her short, naturally styled hair was liberally sprinkled with grey and her wide smile displayed strong white teeth.

She had clearly been expecting Faye, for after greeting the Asantes she took Faye's hands in hers and subjected her to a few moments of intense scrutiny. Apparently satisfied with what she saw, she released Faye's hands and folded her into a warm hug that seemed to last for ever.

'I am so happy that you have come home again, Faye,' she said as she reluctantly let her go. 'I was afraid that you had completely forgotten about us.'

Faye's smile held more than a tinge of guilt since that was a pretty fair reflection of the truth. Luckily, Auntie Akosua didn't wait for an answer and instead urged her back into her seat and bustled round organising drinks for her guests.

Faye gazed appreciatively around the cool living room and sipped on a cold fruit punch. She had finally given up on her skirt, which had now creased into horizontal pleats and risen up above her knees. At each corner of the room, six-feet-high chrome lamps cast a pale golden glow against the walls. The stools along the wall ranged in size; the smallest being so small that it could be held in the palm of a hand. The long curtains were of translucent white linen and hung from black metal curtain rods, the ends of which twisted into metal knots.

'So what do you think of the design then, Ms. Faye?' Uncle Fred had been watching her survey the living room and his eyes twinkled with unconcealed amusement. She squirmed in embarrassment as everyone waited for her to speak. Taking pity on her, Uncle Fred turned to his friends.

'This young lady is very talented, you know. She's turned Amelia's shop into a very trendy boutique – you should see it now.'

Auntie Akosua, who was perched on one of the stools, exclaimed in delight.

'Why, that's wonderful! Is that what you do in London, Faye?'

Faye shook her head in denial. 'No, I'm afraid I'm just a secretary. I enjoy doing up places, that's all.'

Auntie Akosua studied her thoughtfully and then nodded her head slowly. She turned to Auntie Amelia who met her gaze and smiled ruefully in silent acknowledgement.

'You know, Faye, your mother was also very talented in design,' Auntie Akosua said slowly. 'We come from the same home town and went to school together. When we were young, Annie often used to make our clothes when we were going out, and some of her designs were really unusual.'

She smiled broadly, displaying her sparkling white teeth. 'I remember one particular time when we were about seventeen. We had been invited to a party – Amelia, do you remember Esi Brew?'

Auntie Amelia nodded but didn't interrupt and Auntie Akosua continued. 'Esi was at our school and had very rich parents. For her seventeenth birthday, they arranged to have a huge party for her at one of the big hotels in Kumasi. It was to be a really grand affair with a live band. Well, Annie and I were invited and she was determined to make her own outfit for the party. Her father – your grandfather – was very strict and was always complaining about the way she dressed.

'Anyway, the night of the party came. My father had offered to take the two of us to the hotel and pick us up again at the end of the evening. When we arrived at your grandfather's house to collect her, Annie was still getting ready. I remember I was wearing a white dress with long sleeves and a full skirt – very ladylike, for once!' She chuckled softly before returning to her story.

'So here we are, waiting in the sitting room when Annie comes downstairs. She floated into the room looking like a movie star. She had made the most incredible dress – I remember it like it was yesterday. It was made from a sheer silver chiffon fabric wrapped around a fitted cream satin sheath and had tiny straps and a small fishtail. She had found some high-heeled silver sandals from goodness knows where and her hair was piled high on top of her head. She looked breathtaking!

'I remember your grandfather's face as she walked into the room. He had just been congratulating me on my nice modest dress when his own daughter walks in looking like a cross between a mermaid and a Hollywood movie star! He was so appalled he nearly choked with anger and shouted at her to go and change immediately. Annie, of course, was outraged and refused to give in. If my father had not intervened, she would have been banned from going at all! Luckily we were able to calm your grandfather down and persuade him that Annie would come to no harm.'

Auntie Akosua paused and smiled at Faye. Her head crooked to one side, she took in the lilac skirt and the multiple multicoloured bracelets Faye was wearing on her bare arms.

'From the little I see and from what I've heard from Fred and Amelia, I think Annie's talent did not die with her,' she added gently. She rose to her feet and clapped her hands together lightly.

'Now, you must all be very hungry, so let me go and see to dinner.' Just before she left the room, she turned back to Faye. A smile of pure mischief was on her face as she spoke.

'By the way, we *did* make sure Annie came to no harm at the party. That was the night she met your father – he took one look at her and fell head over heels in love!'

Never having heard the story of how her parents had met, Faye sat deep in thought, picturing her mother as a beautiful and defiant seventeen-year-old girl and her father as a young medical student losing his heart in an instant, and it was several minutes before she tuned back into the conversation going on around her.

Shortly afterwards Auntie Akosua returned to announce that dinner was served and they all moved into the adjoining dining room and took their places around a long metal-framed dining table. Faye sniffed the spicy aromas appreciatively as dish after dish was laid down on white linen tablemats. She loved the way meals in Ghana often combined so many different dishes. Lottie had learned to cook a number of Ghanaian dishes and had made sure that Faye and William had the opportunity to eat their traditional food as much as possible. But, nice as they were, they did not compare with the truly home-cooked meals she had come to enjoy so much at the Asante's.

She helped herself to some of the rich *jollof* rice made from tender rice cooked with vegetables in a spicy tomato stew. After adding some crisp yam chips, seasoned meatballs and a sweet vegetable salad to her plate, she ate hungrily. Amma, who had abandoned her diet yet again, was for once silent as she gave the food her total attention.

When everyone had eaten to their fill, they leaned back into the comfortably cushioned dining chairs; the men drinking ice cold beer while the women savoured the chilled white wine Auntie Akosua had served. The conversation was lively and centred mostly on politics – a subject that Faye had quickly learned was very dear to the hearts of most Ghanaians.

Auntie Akosua broke off in the middle of a heated debate with Uncle Fred on the merits of the government in power and turned to Auntie Amelia.

'Before I forget, I'm afraid I won't be able to come to our Old Girl's Association meeting next week. I have to go to Ntriso for my uncle's funeral,' she explained in apology.

Faye looked up sharply, the reference to her mother's home town distracting her from the remains of the chicken drumstick she was trying to dissect. Seeing Faye's reaction, Auntie Amelia made a suggestion.

'Why don't you take Faye along with you? It will give her a chance to see where her mother was born and meet some of her extended family.'

'What a wonderful idea!' Auntie Akosua beamed at her friend and then at a startled Faye who reluctantly abandoned the drumstick and wiped her fingers on her linen napkin.

'The funeral will start on Wednesday with the wake-keeping, and the burial is scheduled for the next day,' Auntie Akosua went on thoughtfully. 'Unfortunately I won't be able to go to Ntriso until Friday. But at least we will still be in time for the funeral on Saturday.'

Faye was puzzled. 'How can they have a funeral if they've already buried your uncle?'

Uncle Charlie chuckled. 'When we talk about a funeral, we are usually referring to the funeral rites, which are performed after the deceased has been buried,' he explained patiently. 'It involves drumming and dancing and other rites that are traditionally performed by the family elders.'

249

Faye still looked confused, so he went on. 'Funerals in Ghana are a process rather than just a one-off event, like you have in England. This is particularly true for the Akan people because, for us, death leads to a prolonged period of mourning and we have a series of rituals that mark the transition of a living member of the community to a revered ancestral spirit.'

Auntie Amelia nodded in agreement. 'You'll find as you stay here longer, my dear, that funerals are given as much – if not more – attention as weddings and christenings. In the daily newspapers you'll often see funeral announcements published with the names of the deceased's family members and close friends, who are referred to as the chief mourners. The more people who attend, the more successful the funeral is considered to have been – unless, of course, there weren't enough refreshments for the mourners!' she added with a laugh.

Amma repressed a shudder. 'Frankly, I think the worst part is when you have to file past the dead body. It's really awful to see someone you've known lying there looking so different.'

'But the dancing is so wonderful to watch,' Auntie Akosua said with a smile. Turning to Faye, she explained further. 'At funerals, the idea is that dancing helps the bereaved to express their grief and console themselves. The drummers have to entice the mourners to dance and the skilful way in which they do that is absolutely marvellous to see.'

Faye listened in fascination. It seemed that there was no end to the lessons she had to learn about her people and their traditions. Finishing her wine, she put down her glass carefully.

'It sounds amazing, Auntie Akosua,' she said with enthusiasm. 'I can't wait to see it all in action.' Suddenly aware of how it might have sounded, she added hastily, 'I mean, I'm really sorry about your uncle dying...'

Auntie Akosua interrupted her with a smile, patting her hand gently. 'It's all right. I know what you meant, and I'm also looking forward to the chance to show you our town.'

Uncle Charlie set his empty beer glass on the table and sighed in satisfaction.

'So, Amma, what's the latest with you and your young man? Should I be preparing my speech as the favourite uncle of the bride?' He chuckled as Amma pouted at his teasing.

'Uncle Charlie, seriously, all Edwin talks about now is America this and America that,' she said flatly. 'Honestly, the way he talks you'd think there was absolutely nothing he could do in this country!'

'Well, let's hope he finds a good job soon,' Auntie Akosua remarked. 'But you know, maybe it wouldn't be such a bad idea if he did work overseas for a little while – it would probably give him some valuable experience.'

Amma sighed. 'Auntie, now you sound like Rocky. All he thinks about is making his international career move as soon as possible.'

Auntie Akosua turned to her friend and asked with a smile, 'Amelia, how is your gorgeous son – has he finally popped the question to that pretty girlfriend of his? I saw her on television the other day advertising some new hair care product. If I were younger, I would definitely have been persuaded to buy it.'

Auntie Amelia laughed and shook her head. 'I'm starting to think I have to give up on Rocky,' she said ruefully. 'He is *so* obsessed with his career he won't give any woman a chance. As for proposing, according to my sources,' she glanced slyly at Amma, 'the pretty girlfriend is no longer on the scene. So it looks like we are back to square one.'

'Well, I wouldn't give up hope yet, Mama, some strange things have been known to happen,' Amma murmured, gazing into her half-empty wine glass. She didn't elaborate on her cryptic comment and refused to be drawn any further on the subject.

With dinner over, they staggered back to the living room where the conversation continued until Uncle Fred exclaimed at the time.

'Some of us have to go to work tomorrow,' he retorted, when the girls protested that it was too early to leave. After prolonged farewells, they climbed back into the car and headed back to Labone.

It was after ten o'clock and there was relatively little traffic on the roads as they drove back. It was still hot and humid as Faye rolled down her window and peered out. 'It's so dark, Uncle Fred, how can you make out where you're going? And why are so few of the streetlights on?'

'That's a good question,' he sighed, shaking his head in resignation. 'I wish I knew the answer. Particularly since when I get my electricity bill, there's always a charge for street lighting!'

He drove slowly and carefully through the capital and about twenty minutes later they were home.

Rocky's car was parked in the driveway and Faye felt a dart of excitement shoot through her. But when they went into the house, it was clear from the darkened living room that he had already gone up to bed.

Quashing her disappointment, Faye wished everyone a good night and headed up to her bedroom where she showered quickly before lying down. Pleasantly tired, she replayed the events of the day until her thoughts became one big jumble and she drifted off to sleep.

11

Down Home Culture

The wake-up call came in the form of a loud clap of thunder followed by rumbling. Faye shot up in bed, rudely awakened from a fascinating, if bizarre, dream in which Rocky was rescuing her from a charging crowd of bus and taxi drivers wearing T-shirts printed with the words *In God We Trust*.

She slid out of bed and walked towards the window. Despite the fact that it was morning, the sky was almost black and it was clear that it was going to rain heavily. Her mouth felt dry after the wine she had drunk at dinner the night before and she was suddenly desperate for a cup of coffee.

She took a quick shower and went back into her room to dress, slipping into a pair of narrow black trousers. She rummaged through the wardrobe and pulled out a long sleeveless white top she had bought on sale from Topshop and jazzed up by sewing rows of multicoloured glass beads along the round neckline, giving it the appearance of a jewelled collar.

She jumped nervously as another loud clap of thunder reverberated around the room. The sound of heavy rain followed and she watched in fascination through the window as a tropical storm began to rage outside. Occasional flashes of lightning lit up the dark sky as the thunder continued to boom and rumble. The rain was so heavy that the trees in the garden were bowed over, as if to protect themselves from the onslaught. The sound of the heavy raindrops on the roof could have been a stable full of horses pounding furiously on the pretty pink tiles. Peering through the louvre blades, she could see huge pools of water forming on the ground and over the paved area to the side of the lawn. Rainwater poured off the roof through a drainage pipe in a strong steady stream, further soaking the already sodden ground.

Faye looked out in awe at the power unleashed by nature and shivered at the thought of being caught outside during such a storm. Suddenly, a clap of thunder sounded so loudly that she squealed and jumped away from the window in panic. Closing the slats, she slipped on a pair of sandals and ran downstairs in search of company.

She rushed into the kitchen hoping to find Martha. Instead, Rocky was at the kitchen table, engrossed in the business section of the daily newspaper and drinking a cup of coffee. He looked up as she came in and she felt her heart thud as he gave her a slow smile that softened the hard angles of his face.

Walking more sedately, she murmured 'Good morning' in reply to his greeting and moved over to the kitchen cabinets where the cups were kept. She took out a mug and walked back to the table to fill it with coffee from the pot on the table. Sitting down opposite Rocky, she took a few sips of the black unsweetened liquid, sighed with satisfaction and leant back in her chair. She looked across at Rocky, who had lowered his newspaper and was watching her through his smoky brown eyes, clearly amused by what he saw.

'What?' she demanded, sounding defensive as he continued to stare at her. He was dressed for work and his jacket and briefcase were on the chair next to him. His closely cropped dark hair had a slight sheen, which caught the light when he moved, and in a pristine pale blue shirt and dark navy tie, he looked every inch the successful young executive.

'Nothing,' he laughed. 'It's just the way you drank the coffee – as though you wanted it more than anything in the world.'

No, that would be you! For one horrified moment she thought she had spoken the words aloud but as he was still smiling and not staring at her as if she had lost her mind, she took a deep, calming breath.

The effect was wasted as a loud clap of thunder reverberated around the silent kitchen. Startled by the noise, she jumped and gripped her cup even tighter between her hands. The rain thundered down outside and, cocooned in what suddenly felt like their own world, Faye looked across at Rocky, mesmerised by the sheer beauty of his chiselled features and unable for the life of her to tear her eyes away. His eyes met and held her gaze and then without warning the lights flickered out, throwing them into momentary darkness. Neither of them made a move and the only sound in the room came from the heavy downpour taking place outside.

Just as suddenly as it had gone out, the kitchen light came back on. Faye put her cup down carefully and, feeling unaccountably shy, ducked her head to avoid his eyes and instead focused her gaze on his mouth. Rocky, meanwhile, seemed to have lost any interest in the business news and had carelessly pushed the newspaper aside. His attention was fully engaged on her and his eyes dropped down to her blouse and rested on the profusion of jewelled beads around her neck.

'That's a stunning top,' he murmured, his eyes dropping lower still and lingering on the curves revealed by the thin fabric of the garment. She looked up and flushed as she followed his gaze, the sudden surge of heat in her body rising up into her face. She could feel her heart racing and when he didn't look away, desperate to break the tension, she took a quick gulp of coffee and scrambled around in her mind for something to say.

All her years in England did not fail her as a clap of thunder gave her an opening to talk about every Englishman's favourite subject.

'Lovely weather for ducks, isn't it?' she remarked, and watched bemused as he burst into unrestrained laughter. After a few moments, he wiped his eyes and stared at her again, as if seeing her for the first time.

'You know, you're pretty funny,' he said, still chuckling softly. 'Quite the talented guest, aren't you Faye? You've managed to transform Ma's shop into the trendiest boutique in town and capture more than one heart in the short time you've been here, from what I hear. What's your secret?'

Although he was still smiling, the teasing look in his eyes also held a challenge, as if daring her to deny the truth of his words. Refusing to rise to the bait, Faye shrugged and sipped her coffee, and her eyes flashed with mischief.

'What can I say? I'm just devastating, that's all.' She had expected him to laugh, and was caught off guard when he simply nodded.

'Yes, you are.' He spoke softly and, this time, there was no teasing laughter in his voice. As she stared back at him, her heart pounding, he smiled slowly and raising a hand, softly traced the curve of her cheek with his forefinger. She sat frozen, her mind in a whirl of confusion; the sensation of his touch making her mouth feel drier than two full bottles of wine could have accomplished.

He dropped his hand but before either of them could speak, the door opened and Amma wandered in. She paused doubtfully when she saw the two of them at the table, as if sensing the simmering tension between them.

'Good morning, people,' she said, and went in search of a clean coffee cup before joining them at the table. 'The storm was so loud I couldn't sleep,' she complained, spooning two heaped teaspoons of sugar into her mug. Stirring the contents moodily, she shook back her braids and took a sip of the drink.

'I'm just waiting out the storm before I leave for the office,' her brother said easily, going back to his newspaper. 'It's madness to try and drive while it's like this out there.'

He lowered the paper again and looked across at Faye who was gazing pensively into her almost empty cup.

'Faye, I seem to remember that I promised you a trip to Cape Coast,' he said casually. 'Amma mentioned that you're going with her to Frieda Ansah's engagement ceremony tomorrow. What about next weekend – do you have anything planned?'

Faye opened her mouth but, before she could get a word out, Amma shook her head. 'Sorry, she's busy then too. Auntie Akosua is taking her to Ntriso for a family funeral and to show her the village.'

She grinned at her brother. 'But I have a better idea. I think you should take a day off work after she gets back from Ntriso and take her then – and Edwin and I can come along to keep you company,' she added wickedly.

Rocky shrugged in agreement. 'If it's okay with Faye, I should probably be able to take a day off later that week.' He ignored Amma's look of stunned surprise at his ready agreement to her suggestion and went on, sounding rather more dubious. 'Although I'm not so sure I want you and your unemployed other half along for the ride.'

He ducked out of the way as his incensed sister aimed a blow at his head.

'*Rocky*, that's not fair!' she protested. 'You know how hard he's trying to find a good job.'

Totally unmoved by her defence, Rocky folded over another page of his newspaper and scanned the headlines. 'Well, he's not likely to get very far with his job hunting if he spends all his time stalking the American Embassy officers to see if they'll help him get a visa, is he?'

'Okay, calm down Amma,' Faye said, trying hard not to laugh at the indignant expression on the younger girl's face. 'Cape Coast sounds like a great idea and of course you and Edwin should come along.'

Rocky looked up at her, one eyebrow raised questioningly and she looked back at him helplessly. Shrugging slightly, he sighed and said with exaggerated courtesy, 'Okay, okay, I give in. Amma, you and your delightful boyfriend are invited and will be most welcome.'

Somewhat mollified, Amma scrutinised Faye's outfit approvingly. 'I love that top, by the way; it's really striking. So, what are your plans for today?'

Faye groaned inwardly, desperate to keep Sonny's name out of the conversation while Rocky was there. She stalled for time by getting up to rinse out her coffee cup. The sound of the rain had lessened considerably and the sky had lightened to a pale blue. With her nose pressed against the window slats, she could see that the trees were standing upright again and a few birds were hopping around on the wet grass.

Rocky put down his newspaper and for a moment his eyes rested on Faye as she stood looking out of the window. Then, with a sigh, he picked up his jacket and briefcase.

'Okay, ladies, I'd better get going before the traffic starts to build up,' he said, his voice reverting to a brisk business-like tone. With a brief wave, he left the kitchen and they heard the familiar screech of his car driving out of the front gate soon afterwards.

'Okay, Faye, so what *are* you up to today?' Amma's clear gaze fixed on her made it obvious that she knew exactly why Faye had not answered her earlier. Faye shrugged and cleared her throat, wondering why she suddenly felt so guilty.

'Well, Sonny asked me out to lunch today,' she said, trying not to sound defensive. 'What about you? What do you have planned?' she asked, hoping to change the subject.

Amma hesitated, clearly in a dilemma. Then she plunged on. 'Faye, Sonny's very nice and one of my best friends, but he's not the most reliable man...' She hesitated, not quite sure how to phrase what she wanted to say.

Faye took pity on her. 'Amma, it's okay, you don't have to worry about me,' she said, trying to set her friend's mind at rest. 'I know Sonny's really laying on the charm at the moment, but I'm a big girl and not about to fall for his tactics. I'm only here for a short time, he's fun to talk to and *all* we're doing is going to lunch. Okay?'

Amma stared back at her doubtfully but thought better of saying any more. With a sigh, she stood up and smoothed down her dress before taking her cup over to the kitchen sink.

'Well, as it's stopped raining, I'm going over to the shop for a couple of hours,' she said. 'Mama has given Baaba the day off today and I promised I would cover for her this morning. Do you want to come along?'

Faye shook her head. 'If you don't mind, I'd rather just stay in this morning. I want to write some postcards for the folks at home and sort out some clothes for washing. Besides,' she added with a teasing smile, 'I don't know what time Sonny's coming over, so I should probably stay close to home.'

Martha walked into the kitchen, her arms full of damp clothing destined for the clothes line now that the storm was over. Faye quickly relieved her of the pile and followed her outside to where the damp clothes line was swaying gently in the balmy breeze.

The garden looked fresh and clean, as though the storm had carried off every speck of dust and dirt from the grass and trees. The multicoloured bushes of pink and yellow hibiscus, creamy white frangipani, orange carnations and delicate green ferns sparkled in the sunlight while the pools of water lying on the ground had already begun to evaporate in the rapidly increasingly heat.

Faye held the bundle of clothes while Martha swiftly pegged them onto the line. Handing over a pair of navy boxer shirts, she flushed as she realised that they probably belonged to Rocky. She thought back to the scene in the kitchen and was so engrossed in reliving the moment he had touched her that she didn't realise for several moments that she was holding out arms that were empty of clothes and that Martha was staring at her in amusement.

Excusing herself, she went back up to her room to collect the postcards she had bought earlier in the week and headed for her favourite lounger on the veranda.

She scribbled Caroline's address on the first postcard and pondered what to write. *Wish you were here* was definitely not the case for this particular holiday. She was well aware that she was still almost clueless about her country of birth but she saw this trip as a personal journey, and one that she needed to make by herself. Much as she loved Caroline, Faye thought, she simply could not imagine doing this with her. Dashing off some bland lines about what a wonderful time she was having, she signed her name and turned to the next card.

The picture on the front was of a nubile young girl in traditional African dress standing in front of a flowering hibiscus bush. Chuckling quietly, she addressed the card to Dermot. She scribbled a short message and then added *PS: Hope you like the new me. Thought you'd like to see how well I've adapted – not a bowl of pasta in sight!*

She wrote William's card, sobering up as she attempted to explain to him within eight square inches how wonderful the experience was proving to be and how much she was learning. After short loving messages to her father and Lottie, she stacked the postcards together and lay back on the lounger.

The sun was now high in the sky and there was little to show for the storm that had taken place earlier. Faye looked out over the green lawn and sighed in contentment. She was still not sure what the morning's exchange with Rocky really meant but it was the first time that he had reached out to her and she felt a thrill every time she remembered the moment.

She was starting to drift into sleep when Martha appeared at the door to the veranda, holding out the house phone.

'Miss Faye, it's your friend calling for you.' She handed over the receiver and went back inside.

'Hello? Is that you, Faye?' Sonny's smooth voice sounded like liquid chocolate flowing through the phone.

'Hi, Sonny, how are you?' Faye tried to keep her tone

brisk and impersonal but, as usual, Sonny soon had her giggling. After a short chat, he rang off telling her to expect him at midday.

It was still only eleven o'clock and she decided to stay on the veranda for another half an hour before going up to get ready. Unfortunately, the combination of the heat and a boring article in the magazine she was reading sent her to sleep and she woke up to find Martha shaking her shoulder and telling her that Sonny was waiting for her in the living room.

'Oh no!' Faye groaned in panic and ran her hands through her dishevelled hair. 'Martha, tell him I'll be five minutes, okay, and keep him in the living room – don't let him out until I come down!'

As Martha turned back to corral the visitor, Faye gathered her belongings and tiptoed in through the kitchen and up the staircase to her room. After washing her face, she quickly applied some make-up and ran a comb through her hair. She exchanged her sandals for a pair of denim canvas shoes and sprayed some perfume liberally around her neck and arms. She deftly wound a multicoloured beaded necklace around her wrist before seizing her trusty leather duffle bag, and then dashed down the stairs, her postcards clutched in one hand.

Sonny was still imprisoned in the living room and he looked up in relief as she came in.

'There you are,' he said. He smiled and, moving towards her purposefully, said, 'I was beginning to wonder if you still existed.'

Faye suppressed a sudden sense of panic as he advanced

towards her. She quickly held out her right hand but instead of shaking it, he raised it to his lips and kissed it softly, all the while keeping his hooded eyes fixed on hers.

Oo-kay, then... This is not quite going to plan, Faye thought nervously as she gently pulled her hand away, wondering if Amma had not been right after all. This was no Michael with cerebral intentions and a desire only to teach her the history of hip hop. Sonny, the funny, teasing joker who had been so easy to talk to on the phone was now a real flesh and blood, albeit very handsome, man with his own intentions, none of which, she suspected, included any reference to black music. He was dressed in a pair of black trousers with a fitted white shirt that showed off his muscular physique. His hair was short and gleamed with what looked suspiciously like salon-inspired waves and his wolfish smile revealed a set of sparkling white teeth.

'Would you mind if we go to a post office first?' She raised the sheaf of cards in her hand for him to see. 'I need to post these cards today or I'll be home before they arrive.'

'That's no problem,' he said easily. 'I don't have a car like your rich friends but I've got a taxi outside that we can hold on to for as long as we need.' Gesturing to her to take the lead, he followed her out of the living room and waited in the hall while she ran to tell Martha she was leaving and wouldn't be back for lunch. She led the way outside and then stood back as he walked up to a somewhat rickety-looking white car parked in the driveway with bold squares of yellow paint on the hood and boot indicating its status as a taxi. The driver, a scrawny looking man with

265

bloodshot eyes and a sulky expression, saluted briefly in greeting when she reached the car and ignored her thereafter.

Togo stood just inside the gate and, with his arms folded aggressively, watched the taxi driver like a hawk. Sonny gave the driver some instructions and then opened the door for Faye. He walked around the car, slid smoothly into the seat behind the driver and sidled over to her, his muscular leg pressing against hers. The scent of a strong, spicy aftershave wafted over her and she tried to shift away from the somewhat overpowering aroma; an impossible task as she was now effectively wedged against the door.

Togo opened the gate slowly and smiled at Faye for a brief second before scowling at the other occupants of the taxi as they drove out of the grounds. Faye looked around for a seat belt and soon realised that if the taxi had ever had any, it certainly didn't possess them today. She gripped the strap above the door instead and braced herself against the shock of the car's poor suspension on the uneven roads.

'We'll stop at the post office first,' Sonny said in explanation as the driver darted off down the dual carriageway that was fast becoming familiar to her. She nodded and concentrated on gripping the handle as they careened along, the small car shaking with shock every time they hit a pothole and Sonny's warm body pressing against her with each jolt.

Being in such close proximity to her handsome suitor wasn't having quite the effect that Faye had hoped. Her eyes were almost watering from the strength of

Sonny's aftershave, and in the stifling atmosphere of the ramshackle taxi, the only feelings aroused by his body pressing against her were those of acute discomfort.

They swung around Danquah Circle, narrowly missing another taxi that was reluctant to wait until its exit was clear, and carried on down the busy road. Pausing at a set of traffic lights, they drew up alongside a sleek red convertible driven by an attractive woman in her mid-thirties who turned her head in their direction. Faye glanced at Sonny just in time to see him give off one of his high-beam smiles at the woman. She returned his smile, her eyes sparkling with delight, before shooting off as soon as the lights changed.

Conscious of Faye's scrutiny, Sonny shrugged. 'Ghanaians are very friendly. It's one of the things we are best known for.'

There's friendly and there's *friendly*, Faye thought sceptically, but decided to say nothing. The last thing she wanted to do was give him the impression that she was jealous of him paying attention to other women. But, despite herself, she couldn't help feeling a faint sense of disappointment.

'Hey, relax Faye,' Sonny said. His brooding eyes were fixed on her expressive features as he reached out for her hand. 'I was just being nice, it didn't mean anything.'

He held her hand between his own and declared in the husky tone that was so disturbing, 'From now on, you get my undivided attention and I refuse to be friendly or even nice to any other woman!'

Faye giggled at his melodramatic declaration and

gently extricated her hand, pretending to sort through the postcards on her lap. They drove up into a crowded car park where the taxi driver managed to squeeze the car into a small recently vacated space. Sonny climbed carefully out of the car and, as the inside door handle on Faye's side was missing, came round to let her out.

The post office was made up of two or three buildings, in front of which stood a few stalls with people selling greetings cards, stationery and an assortment of souvenirs. Sonny led the way into the biggest of the three buildings where they joined a short queue. After paying for the postage and dropping the cards into the post box, they left the building and headed back to the taxi.

Faye stopped in front of a stall displaying a selection of wooden sculptures and painted canvases of African women. The stallholder perked up at the sign of a potential customer and rose quickly from the wooden bench where he had been dozing. Picking up a cloth, he made a great show of dusting one or two of the carvings, enthusiastically pushing them under her nose.

'Lady, check these out,' he said. His accent sounded uncannily like JB's.

Faye took one of the carved figurines from him and was considering whether to buy it when Sonny plucked it out of her hands.

'You don't want to buy this kind of stuff here,' he said dismissively, returning it to its owner. 'You should go to the Arts Centre: there's a lot more choice and the prices are better.'

The stallholder glared at him in outrage. Faye shrugged

and smiled a silent apology but the offended salesman was having none of it and muttering under his breath in disgust, he slouched back to his bench.

On the short walk back to the car, she noticed rows of numbered metal boxes to one side of the car park. As she watched, an elderly gentleman took out some envelopes from a box and locked it again with a key.

'What are those – safe deposit boxes?' she asked curiously.

Sonny shook his head as he ushered her back into the waiting taxi.

'No, they're postboxes. In Ghana, we don't get our mail delivered to our houses like you do abroad. It's delivered to your post office box and you have to collect your mail yourself.'

The taxi driver inched his way out of the car park and set off at a pace that had Faye clinging tightly to the strap above her door. As they drove, an oncoming driver would occasionally spot Sonny and flash their car headlights in acknowledgement. Each time it happened, Sonny would wave enthusiastically and call out a greeting.

'Do you know *everyone* in this city?' Faye asked in amusement.

Sonny grinned at her disarmingly. 'I told you before, Ghanaians are very friendly. We always look out for old friends when we're driving – new friends too,' he added meaningfully, reaching for her hand again.

She quickly moved it away to clutch her duffle bag while she held on grimly to the door strap with the other. Sonny was fun to be with, she thought ruefully, but in spite of his drop-dead gorgeous features and athletic body, she was struggling to feel anything resembling the feelings he claimed to have developed for her. What made it worse was that the more she tried to keep her distance – a near impossibility given the confined space in the taxi – the closer he would slide towards her. Trying not to feel like she was under siege, Faye smiled at him and asked where they were going.

The frown that had appeared on his face when she pulled her hand away faded and he explained that they were heading towards a part of Accra called Abeka.

'It's not a posh area like those places that I bet Amma's been taking you,' he warned. 'This is a strictly working class area. I promised you a look at the real Accra, so don't expect too much.'

Faye's response was cut off as their taxi swerved suddenly to avoid a minibus whose driver had unexpectedly pulled out into the main road. The taxi driver and Sonny cursed in unison and Sonny was thrown back before ricocheting forward and almost falling into Faye's lap. Not about to miss an earth-sent opportunity, he continued leaning heavily against her as they drove on.

Faye, still holding onto her makeshift seat belt, was now well and truly wedged into the corner. After a few minutes of trying to hug the door, she gave up the struggle and relaxed against Sonny's muscular frame, resigned to the suffocating aroma of his cologne.

'You've probably realised by now that the taxi drivers and tro-tro drivers are the worst road users here,' he said, his husky voice close to her ear.

'What are tro-tro drivers?' Faye asked curiously.

'That's the name we give to the minibuses here. It comes from the word "tro" which means three pence. In the old days, that was what it cost for a ride.'

The sun blazed high in the sky and any sign of the morning's rain had been completely obliterated. Without air conditioning, the heat in the taxi was becoming oppressive and, combined with the heat radiating from Sonny's hard chest, Faye was feeling extremely uncomfortable. Suddenly her stomach rumbled loudly and she glanced at him, wondering if he had heard.

He smiled briefly at her and said reassuringly, 'Don't worry, we're almost there. This is Abeka and the chop bar is about five minutes from here.'

Staring out at the bustle of people, taxis, tro-tros and the inevitable herd or two of goats, Faye marvelled again at the contrasts between the different parts of Accra. They drove past what looked like a small market, with the vendors shouting good-natured banter across stalls to each other. The number of shops on either side of the highway was a clear sign that this was a busy commercial area. The road was pitted with potholes and, as with many parts of the city, there was no pavement, leaving the pedestrians to make do with a dusty verge.

Much to Faye's relief, Sonny leaned forward and gave the driver instructions on where to go. Shortly afterwards, he pulled off the high road and they came to a stop in front of a large building. Sonny stepped out of the car and came round to let her out. Pulling out a rather worn leather wallet, he extracted some notes and handed them over to the taxi driver, who perked up slightly as he counted them.

With a grunt and a final salute, he then revved his engine and rattled off.

Faye looked across at the building they were about to enter. It was an old two-storey house painted blue and yellow and covered with posters and stickers advertising the local beers and a popular mobile phone network. A faded signboard bearing the words *Maggie's Chop Bar and Grill* hung above the entrance, with the specials for the day written in chalk on a blackboard propped up against the wall by the door.

Sonny ushered her inside, his hand resting possessively against the small of her back. Holding her duffle bag firmly, she walked into an open courtyard where a number of wooden tables and chairs had been set up on an uneven concrete floor. Faded umbrellas stuck through each table offered a degree of shade for the diners and most of the tables were occupied by people concentrating silently on the plates and bowls of food in front of them.

Sonny steered her to an empty table alongside the wall encircling the compound. The wooden table was basic and had uneven legs that caused it to wobble slightly. The tabletop had been wiped clean but faded stains steeped deep into the wood bore evidence of the many meals that had been served on it.

A painfully slim girl dressed in a well-worn black skirt walked over to their table, dangling an empty tray by her side. Her oversized white blouse had a frayed lace-edged collar and hung loosely on her thin frame. After muttering a cursory 'Good afternoon', she stood silently waiting for them to speak.

'Is there a menu?' Faye looked helpless, wondering what was expected of her.

'Yes, that was it outside,' Sonny grinned. 'Don't worry about the food for a moment; what would you like to drink – beer?'

Faye shook her head and asked for a Coke. As far as she was concerned, alcohol and Sonny definitely did not mix. He, on the other hand, had no such inhibitions and promptly ordered a large bottle of chilled beer. The girl vanished to get the drinks and Sonny leant forward.

'Like I said before, the food here is all local dishes – so don't expect to find Lobster à la French people or Spaghetti Bolognaise or anything like that.'

Remembering Dermot's warning not to go around ordering pasta, Faye tried not to giggle. 'I didn't get a chance to look at the blackboard outside; what was on the menu?'

Before he could reply, the waitress returned with their drinks, opened the bottles and stood waiting silently again. Deciding that there must be some telepathic chop bar communication she wasn't privy to, Faye also kept silent. After a moment or two, Sonny smiled at the waitress, telling her that they would go up to the counter themselves. The girl stared blankly back at him, unimpressed by his high-beam smile, and shrugged, slipping away as silently as she had arrived.

'Come on, let's go and see what they have!' Sonny took a sip of his beer and scraped his chair back, holding out a hand for Faye to join him. She stood up and followed him to the back of the courtyard where the kitchen was located. It was a wooden structure with an open hatch where three women were standing guard over a row of black cauldrons that bubbled with various soups and stews giving off spicy aromas. The women passed steaming plates of food through the hatch to the waitresses who came to collect the orders for their tables. A couple of men had lined up at the hatch; obviously diners like themselves wanting to inspect what was available and place their orders. Faye and Sonny stood in line behind them and Faye watched with interest as the men joked and cajoled the women behind the counter to serve them extra large portions. Although what they were saying was in one of the local languages, their crude gestures and raucous laughter made it obvious what the nature of the banter was.

Sonny walked around the men and took a quick look at the steaming pots of food.

'Right, they have fufu and palm nut soup, fufu and groundnut soup, mixed grill, snail and kontomire soup, yam and plantain with kontomire stew, banku with okro stew or with tilapia fish and light soup with pigfoot.' He reeled off the names of the dishes swiftly and looked expectantly at her.

Faye looked at him blankly, trying to process what he had just said.

'Okay, I quite like kontomire stew – that's spinach stew, right? I don't mind fufu and I like banku,' she said, referring to the popular Ghanaian dishes her father had made for them on occasion. Fufu, a dumpling made from pounded yams, cassava and green plantain, was difficult to make the authentic way in England and her father usually compromised by using potato flour and processed potato flakes. His fufu was always tasty and served in large bowls surrounded by lashings of hot peppery soup. Banku, cornmeal dumplings that were usually served with okro stew or pepper, was another favourite. Faye was clear about one thing, however.

'A big N-O to the soup with pigfoot,' she shuddered. 'I don't think I can ever face that again.' At his curious expression, she shook her head and said, 'I'll explain some other time.'

She gestured towards the cook waiting impatiently behind the counter, 'I think we'd better go ahead and order.'

She settled for what sounded like the easy option. 'I think I'll have the mixed grill. What does that include – steak and sausages and stuff?'

Sonny gave her an odd look and then burst out laughing. He laughed so hard that even the harried cooks had to smile at the handsome young man who was obviously finding something very funny indeed. Faye watched him, completely perplexed.

Eventually he stopped laughing and wiped his eyes, a broad grin still on his face. 'I'm sorry, I shouldn't have laughed,' he apologised. 'I keep forgetting you haven't lived here.'

As she raised one eyebrow in enquiry, he went on, still chuckling as he spoke.

'It isn't a mixed grill of the posh stuff you'd get in a hotel restaurant,' he said. 'This one's a local soup. It's called a mixed grill because it's made with a load of different types of meat and fish – beef, goat, sea fish, river fish, grasscutter – that kind of thing. You have it with fufu.'

'Oh.' Faye laughed at her mistake and then conscious of the other diners lining up behind them, she quickly ordered banku and tilapia while Sonny chose the fufu and groundnut soup.

They went back to their table and soon the silent waitress arrived with their food, swiftly depositing the plates and bowls on the bare tabletop before gesturing towards a ceramic sink in the corner where they could wash their hands. They returned to their table to find a large pitcher of iced water and two plastic cups deposited by their plates.

Faye was ravenous and the seasoned grilled tilapia fish garnished with sliced onions and tomatoes and freshly ground pepper sauce accompanied by a huge steaming ball of banku looked delicious. She gingerly broke off a portion of the banku, blowing on it gently as the heat almost burned her fingers. She dipped it into the pepper sauce before eating it. The sauce was hot but not unbearable and she tucked into the food without further ado.

Sonny watched her for a couple of minutes and when he was satisfied that she needed no further instruction from him, ate his own food with undisguised enthusiasm. After a few mouthfuls he paused and looked up, his forehead covered in a thin sheen of sweat from the heat of the food.

'So, isn't this better than all those bourgeois places Amma Asante takes you to?' His hooded eyes probed her flushed face and she shrugged uncomfortably.

'Well, it's delicious but it's also nice for me to see as many different places as possible since I'm only here for a short time,' she replied, trying to be diplomatic.

'When are you leaving?' he demanded, wiping his forehead with a crumpled white handkerchief.

'I've got just over two weeks left now,' she said, before popping a piece of the delectable soft white fish into her mouth. 'Why?' she asked when she could speak.

'Because you will spend every moment you have left with me,' he said grandly. The sheer arrogance of his statement left her speechless and she decided to concentrate on her food rather than say anything that would spark a quarrel.

Sonny finished eating quickly, skilfully scooping up all the soup with his fingers. After grazing over a piece of bone marrow for a few minutes he stood up and with a muttered 'Excuse me', went over to the sink to wash his hands. Faye looked regretfully at the rest of her banku but now feeling too full to eat any more, she followed him to the sink. A well-used square of hard yellow soap was perched on the large utility sink and she scrubbed her hands vigorously with it before rinsing them under the single tap. She took one look at the tired-looking towel hanging by the sink and instead shook her hands in the air to dry them.

Sonny had relaxed in his seat and was drinking his beer when she came back to the table. She picked up her cup and gulped down the contents. After the spiciness of the pepper sauce, the carbonated drink burned her tongue and then soothed her throat as it went down.

'Thanks for the meal, Sonny,' she sighed with satisfaction. He smiled at her and took her hands in both of his before she could protest.

'You have nice hands,' he said huskily, stroking them with the ball of his thumb. Holding them firmly to prevent her from pulling away, he looked deep into her eyes.

'You hold my heart in between these beautiful hands of yours. Don't crush it, please.'

Feeling very uncomfortable at this unwarranted display of affection in the middle of a busy chop bar, and conscious of the curious eyes watching their little drama, Faye wrenched her hands away in embarrassment. 'Sonny, I don't think this is the right place for this conversation. Can we go now, please?'

If he was offended by her response, he didn't show it. He simply shrugged and finished off his beer in one gulp before standing up and pulling his wallet out from the back pocket of his jeans. Their waitress came back to their table and proceeded to stack the used dishes onto her empty tray. Sonny removed some worn notes and handed them over to her. She swiftly counted the money and nodded before putting the notes inside her apron pocket and moving off with her tray.

Faye reached for her bag, which had been hanging on the back of her chair, and stood up, following Sonny out of the chop bar and onto the pavement which was teeming with pedestrians. After walking for a few minutes, dodging in and out of the impatient human traffic, Sonny flagged down a taxi and they climbed in.

This vehicle was in considerably better shape than the one they had travelled in earlier and the driver had his radio tuned to one of the popular FM stations where a lively phone-in show was taking place. Faye listened in amusement as caller after caller phoned in to make a contribution to the show, most of which involved rants against the government or one of the country's political parties.

With her handbag rammed firmly between her and Sonny and with one ear on the radio programme, Faye enjoyed the journey back to Labone and smiled at Sonny with genuine warmth when the taxi stopped outside the Asantes' house.

'Sonny, thanks so much for lunch,' she said, relief at making it safely home infusing even more enthusiasm into her words. He followed her out of the car and stood directly in front of her, his eyes fixed thoughtfully on her face.

'So when do I see you again, Faye? I had a great time today.' His hand, ever mobile, rose and tugged gently at a lock of her hair. Unlike Rocky's touch earlier, Sonny's made her feel uncomfortable and as though she had unwittingly released a tiger that now refused to go back into its cage.

She stepped back awkwardly. 'If you're going to Stuart's party tomorrow night, we can meet up there.'

'But there'll be a lot of people around and I want to be alone with you,' he said, his expression mournful.

Faye was saved by Togo pushing open the gate to see what was going on. She gave Sonny a quick peck on the cheek and waved goodbye, calling out a final thank you before he could react. As soon as she had scampered inside the gates, Togo promptly slammed them shut. With a conspiratorial wink, he whistled happily and sauntered off.

Cultural Ties

'Just wear something comfortable, Miss Faye,' Martha said, checking her list for the market a final time.

Faye had to laugh as she left the kitchen and headed for her room. *'Something comfortable' in Martha-speak means don't wear one of your weird combinations of clothing and show me up*, she thought in amusement. However, as Martha had agreed to take her along to the market this Saturday morning, she willingly changed into a plain navy shirt-dress.

Not even Martha could have a problem with this dress, she thought wryly, giving her appearance a final check before she left her room. *I could probably enter a convent with this one.*

She stopped by Amma's room before going downstairs and found her sitting on her bed, sewing a button onto a beautiful pale blue fabric.

'I'm just leaving now for the market with Martha.' Faye stood in the doorway and surveyed Amma's room. It was about the same size as hers but far more cluttered. Clothes were draped over open wardrobe doors and several pairs of shoes were scattered on the floor by the bed.

Amma glanced quickly at the small black clock on her bedside table and nodded.

'You won't be long, will you?' She winced as she pricked her finger with the needle. She sucked hard on the puncture and checked to make sure there was no risk of bloodstains on her outfit. 'We need to leave here by ten o'clock for the engagement.'

Faye hastened to reassure her. 'It's only seven-thirty. Martha says we'll be about an hour at the most.'

'What are you going to wear, by the way?' Amma asked. She finished with her task and bit off the cotton thread. 'Do you have any traditional outfits?'

Faye's blank expression gave Amma her answer. Carefully laying the fabric she was holding onto the bed, Amma walked over to one of the wardrobes and waved Faye over.

'We usually wear something traditional for engagement ceremonies rather than Western clothes,' she said. 'I've got heaps of traditional cloths and *boubous* here – you can borrow one, if you like.'

Faye walked over to the wardrobe and quickly scanned through the clothes draped on wooden hangers. She decided to wear a loosely cut *boubou* since the traditional cloths were obviously made to fit Amma's figure, and she settled on one in a pale grey fabric with beautiful silver embroidery at the neck and around the hem of the long wrap-around skirt. A matching embroidered strip of cloth for a headdress completed the ensemble.

'Thanks a million, Amma, this is beautiful!' she said, lightly stroking the pretty fabric. 'I'll take it downstairs now and iron it when I get back. I'd better go before Martha goes off without me.'

Amma grinned. 'Sooner you than me. I really don't know why you're so keen to go to the market; it's so crowded and noisy, not to mention the smell!'

Faye laughed. 'Actually, I've got a lovely painting in my room in London of a Ghanaian market scene and I really want to see the real thing.'

With a final wave, she ran down to the kitchen where she deposited the *boubou* on the ironing board and then went outside to the gate where the housekeeper was waiting.

Martha nodded approvingly at Faye's appearance and commented on how nice she looked. Faye suppressed a grimace and relieved Martha of one of the two baskets she was holding. Togo was standing outside the gate and flagged down a taxi for them. Martha briefly exchanged words with the driver and then gestured to Faye to get in.

Once in the car, she read through her list yet again, frowning in concentration as she reviewed the items. 'I don't need to buy too many things today, Miss Faye, so we'll go to the market in Osu. Normally, if I have a lot of shopping to do, I prefer to go to Makola. That is a very big market and you can find almost anything there.'

The taxi rattled along the main road and down Oxford Street. As it was still early, the shops were shut and the street was relatively quiet. Some roadside vendors had started to set up their stalls and without the usual traffic to contend with, the women reached their destination in less than fifteen minutes. Faye stepped out of the car and looked around, slightly disappointed by the size of the market. Stalls were laid out in tight rows and despite the hour, most of the stall keepers were ready for business. A few were still arranging their wares, stacking dark smoked fish, perfumed spices and freshly washed seasonal vegetables in carefully measured quantities on the wide wooden pallets or table tops that served as stalls.

Faye fell in behind Martha, who moved purposefully towards a stall halfway down the first row. Recalling Amma's comment about the smell, she had to admit that all the foodstuffs in such close proximity did give rise to a lot of pungent aromas. Martha stopped in front of a large stall with its pallets groaning from the weight of the produce stacked on them. She greeted the stall keeper, a plump woman wearing a dark pink blouse tucked into a traditional cloth that was wrapped tightly around her ample waist and hips. Martha introduced Faye and the woman grinned widely at her, revealing a row of white teeth with a wide gap in the middle, and greeted Faye in broken English.

Martha skimmed through her list and called out item after item. Despite her bulk, the stall keeper swiftly packed up fresh garden eggs, ripe red tomatoes, some green okro, a large bunch of bulbous onions, long red chilli peppers and fat round green peppers, as well as the strong-smelling dried salt fish that Martha used for seasoning soups and stews. When the woman did not have a particular item on her stall, she would shout across to another stall keeper who would quickly pack up the requested amount of the missing item and bring it over to them.

Now that's *what I call service*, Faye thought, highly impressed by the collaboration taking place as she witnessed one stall keeper after another bring forth their produce. *Wele*, the long brown curled tubes of cow hide so popular with Ghanaians, corn dough, with its distinctive sharp smell, used for making banku, small fresh crabs, chopped pink pigfoot and fresh spinach leaves were all neatly packaged in black polythene bags and stacked into Martha's shopping basket.

When she had exhausted the items needed from that area, Martha paid the stall keeper and thanked her for her assistance. The older woman nodded and shouted to one of the young girls playing nearby to carry the heavy basket. The girl, who looked about fourteen, quickly rolled up a short piece of cloth and placed it on top of her head. She hefted the basket up with surprisingly strong arms and placed it on top of the rolled cloth. Once she had the basket perfectly balanced on her head, she looked expectantly at Martha.

Martha again led the way, her plump hips swaying as she moved further into the market. The market was bigger than Faye had initially realised and she looked with interest at the profusion of foodstuffs, provisions and other items for sale. One stall keeper was noisily refilling a huge basket with ripe red palm nuts, used to make the rich palm nut soup Faye enjoyed so much. As they passed another stall, a basket toppled over and several children shrieked and rushed forward to recover the feisty little crabs that had been held captive inside. A peek inside another container revealed some fresh snails moving around in slow circles.

Almost tripping over a stray chicken, Faye followed Martha to where she was busy examining some large yams before selecting two for her basket. From the same stall, she bought a handful of small green unripened plantains, which she usually boiled and served with spinach stew, as well as some ripe yellow plantains that were delicious when fried.

Martha took the second basket from Faye and deposited it beside a fruit and vegetable stall. There she bought some oranges, explaining tartly to a protesting Faye that the round green and yellow fruit were indeed oranges and probably far sweeter than the oranges she was used to in England! She motioned to the young girl selling the fruit to add some green runner beans, carrots, cabbage, lettuce and cucumber to the basket.

Once she had crossed all the items off her list, they retraced their steps back to the front entrance of the market. Wrinkling her nose at the sharp, acrid smell coming from the open gutter, Faye navigated her way through the narrow gaps between the stalls, followed by their young porter with the basket still balanced securely on her head.

The sun was now high in the sky and the heat was becoming more intense. Almost as soon as they emerged from the market, Martha stopped a taxi that was cruising past and Faye climbed in, relieved to be out of the sun. The young girl dumped the basket into the boot of the car, gratefully snatched the note Martha gave her and ran off triumphantly, waving her booty under the noses of her envious friends.

They were soon back in Labone and Togo, his skinny arms evidently much stronger than they appeared, lifted the two heavy baskets out of the boot before sending the taxi on its way. Faye gave Martha a quick hug of thanks for including her in the shopping trip and rushed off to find Amma.

Her friend was in the living room painting her nails when Faye burst in. She looked up briefly from her task and looked meaningfully at Faye's unusually sober dress.

'I see Martha's got you dressing like a good Christian girl already,' she remarked, blowing on the coat of paint she had just applied. 'Well, I'm glad you're back because you need to start getting ready.'

She eyed Faye's dishevelled hair with a critical eye. 'You should have gone to the hairdressers instead of the market,' she said, and then added more charitably, 'I suppose the head scarf will cover most of your hair, anyway, so you should be okay.'

'Thanks a lot,' Faye retorted. Before Amma could say anything else, she added casually, 'Where is everyone? Are your parents coming to the engagement with us?'

Amma took a break from blowing on her nails and nodded. 'Yes, they're upstairs getting ready. They are real sticklers for being punctual at these things. I don't know why they bother; Ghanaians are always late for every function and you end up just sitting around for hours if you arrive on time!'

She giggled as she told Faye about how one of her friends

had printed the time on her wedding invitation cards for an hour earlier than the service was really due to start.

'And the church was *still* only half full when she arrived,' she added with a resigned sigh. 'By the way, I've ironed the *boubou* for you; it's on your bed.'

Ecstatic at having been spared her pet hate of ironing, Faye gave her a warm hug, ignoring the squeals to mind her wet nails.

'Okay, I'm going up to change. You'll need to do the head-scarf part for me so I'll come to your room when I'm ready.'

She flew up the stairs, surreptitiously blowing a kiss at Rocky's picture, and went into her bathroom for a quick wash before getting dressed.

A few minutes later, she stood admiring herself in the mirror, amazed at her transformation from Western city girl to traditional African woman. The grey *boubou* had a long wrap-around skirt, with edges scalloped in a delicate silver design reminiscent of a rolling wave. The loose top was cut with a deep square neck and long wide sleeves, with elaborate designs embroidered around the neck and bodice in the same silver thread. The same rolling wave design was embroidered around the edge of the top, which fell loosely around her slim hips.

She slipped on the strappy black and silver sandals she had brought with her from London and thrust a cotton hanky and a tube of lipstick into the sparkly silver bag she had made from a sequinned stole she'd discovered on one of her flea market expeditions. After a final check in the mirror, she picked up the headscarf and headed for Amma's room.

A muffled 'Come in' was the response to her knock and she walked in to find Amma in the process of getting into her own *boubou*. Faye looked appreciatively at the pretty pale blue outfit. It had a round neck with little insets of lacy white fabric interspersed around the bodice. The embroidery on the fitted skirt was of a matching white thread and she watched admiringly while Amma deftly twisted the fabric for the headdress to tie back her long braids.

'Wow, you look gorgeous! It's a shame Edwin can't see you now; he'd propose on the spot.'

'If only,' Amma said dryly, tweaking the ends of her head tie upwards with a flourish. 'Okay, now let's see to yours.'

She reached for a newspaper lying on the bed and deftly folded it lengthwise into a strip about three inches wide. She laid the headscarf on the bed and placing the newspaper strip in the centre, she wrapped the fabric around it. Standing behind Faye, she carefully positioned the scarf around the crown of her head and tied the ends at the back. The sculpted headscarf accentuated Faye's soft high cheekbones and Amma nodded in satisfaction.

'Great, you look fabulous! Now, we'd better get going before my father has a fit.'

Faye admired Amma's handiwork in the mirror, then picked up her handbag and followed her out of her room.

As she turned to close the door behind her, she asked, 'Is Rocky coming to the engagement?'

'No, he is not,' said a deep voice behind her, causing her to start violently. She turned around to find herself almost up against the subject of her question. He was wearing shorts and a rather damp T-shirt and held a sports bag in one hand. He stepped back to take a long, hard look at her and she flushed as his eyes raked over her from head to toe.

'Definitely full of surprises, Faye,' he said appreciatively. 'You look like you've worn traditional dress all your life. You look stunning.' He turned to his sister. 'Amma, you look great too. I take it you're off to Frieda's engagement? Well, have a good time.'

'You're not coming?' Still slightly unnerved by his sudden appearance, Faye asked the question in what she hoped was a casual tone. He shook his head with a laugh.

'No, I've just finished a two-hour squash game and I don't have the energy to watch some poor sucker get a noose tied around his neck.'

Faye bridled. 'Well, I'm sure no-one's *forcing* him to get engaged' she said in indignation. 'I think it's wonderful to see two people who have chosen to make a real commitment to each other.'

Amma tugged at Faye's arm impatiently. 'Come on, let's go,' she said. 'Don't even bother trying to get Rocky to understand about commitment; he's impossible.' She glared at her unrepentant brother and set off downstairs.

Faye followed her lead, taking the stairs slowly in her heels and fully aware that Rocky was watching. She felt a wave of despondency flow over her and shook herself mentally, refusing to let his words get to her.

Waiting in the living room for Auntie Amelia and Uncle Fred to come down, Faye sat carefully on the edge of the sofa, hoping her outfit wouldn't crease. Elegant as it was, she was fast learning the limitations the wrap-around skirt placed on moving freely. Amma, more accustomed to the demands of wearing a *boubou*, relaxed in the armchair checking over her nails critically to make sure the varnish was still intact.

'Don't let Rocky upset you,' she said suddenly, looking across at Faye. 'He's not as hard as he makes himself out to be.'

Faye sighed, not bothering to pretend she didn't know what Amma was referring to.

'Why is he so anti-commitment, anyway? Is it because of what happened with Clarissa?'

Amma shook her head vehemently and her long braids swung from side to side.

'No! I don't think Rocky was ever in love with Clarissa,' she scoffed. 'Actually, although he's never spoken very much about it, I think he fell for someone when he was in America doing his Masters a few years ago.'

Faye was surprised. 'Oh, I didn't know he used to live in the States. So you think someone out there let him down?' She made no effort to hide her curiosity.

'That's what Mama and I think, anyway,' Amma said sagely. 'He used to talk a lot about this American girl he was seeing – her name was Celine. But by the time he finished his MBA, instead of staying on in the States for a year or two to work as he had planned, he wrote and said he was coming home. When we asked him about Celine, he just said he wasn't seeing her anymore and didn't want to talk about it. He didn't date anyone for ages and then, about a year ago, he started seeing Clarissa.'

Faye digested the information in silence. The arrival

of the older Asantes put an end to her introspection. They were wearing matching milky-coffee-coloured *boubous* and looked magnificent. Uncle Fred's outfit was made up of a long embroidered tunic over loose trousers with a round embroidered cap perched on his grey locks. Auntie Amelia's *boubou* had a wrap-around skirt similar to Faye's with tiny glass beads highlighting the delicate stitching of the embroidery around the neck and sleeves of the matching top.

She exclaimed at the sight of the two girls. 'Faye, your father would be thrilled to see how beautiful you look in traditional dress. Fred, quickly, bring the camera and let's take a picture of her for Kwame!'

She pushed her husband gently towards the door. Uncle Fred went off and came back a few minutes later holding an expensive-looking camera.

'Amelia, I couldn't find our camera and we don't have time to look for it, so I've borrowed Rocky's,' he said, fiddling with the settings. 'Ah, there we are,' he said finally. 'Okay, everybody, stand together and smile!'

After taking a couple of shots, he looked up.

'Now, let me take a special one of our supermodel here.' He winked solemnly at Faye.

She was still laughing when he took the shot, her head thrown back and her long lashes almost covering her almond-shaped eyes.

'All right, let's go before we arrive late,' Auntie Amelia fussed, picking up her handbag and shooing them all out of the room. Uncle Fred left the camera on the table in the hallway and picked up the car keys.

The Ansah family lived close to the airport in a part of Accra that housed many of the city's wealthier citizens. As it was a Saturday morning, there was relatively little traffic and they arrived at the house about twenty minutes later.

The long line of cars parked outside the Ansahs' gate made it clear that something special was taking place. Uncle Fred let the women out of the car and drove further down the road to find a parking spot. While they stood waiting for him, Faye looked admiringly at the sleek saloon cars and luxury vehicles lined up along the street.

'I can't get over the contrasts in this country. One minute it's open gutters and desperately poor people and the next, it's shopping malls, fast food restaurants, big houses and expensive cars like these!'

Auntie Amelia sighed in agreement. 'You're quite right. But Faye, this country is so blessed with natural resources that quite honestly no one should be poor. You know we are one of the biggest producers of cocoa and gold in the world and we produce some very valuable and sought-after minerals. Unfortunately, we have had a series of unstable governments, which has led to terrible corruption and mismanagement of our assets. And because we rely so much on our main exports, we are also vulnerable when the world prices for these commodities drop. You should talk to Auntie Akosua about it next weekend when you go to Ntriso. She's a professor of History and Political Science at the University.'

Uncle Fred joined them and led the way inside. The house was an elegant white building with stately columns; pink and white ribbons and balloons decorated the front of the house and the double front doors were wide open. The grounds were spacious and the lawn in front of the house looked freshly mown.

They went through the open doors and walked straight into a large hall where multiple rows of white chairs had been arranged on both sides of the space. The chairs on one side of the room were empty while most of the chairs arranged across the other side of the hall were occupied by guests dressed in a colourful array of traditional clothing.

'You have to go round and greet everyone individually,' Amma hissed in her ear as Faye stood smiling vaguely at no one in particular. 'You should always start greeting people from the side of the room that's to your right and then work your way round. Follow me,' she instructed. Dutifully tailing Amma, Faye shook hands with the guests seated in the front row, murmuring 'Good morning' to each one in turn. Mr and Mrs Ansah, dressed in matching blue and white *boubous*, were already seated and they stood and welcomed Faye warmly. One or two of the other guests, having been told who she was by a beaming Auntie Amelia, looked at her curiously. Without warning, one woman jumped up excitedly from her seat and crushed Faye in a warm, scented hug against a very generous bosom.

Having completed the greeting ritual, Faye took a seat between Amma and Auntie Amelia. 'So where are the couple who are getting engaged?' she asked quietly, looking around the room.

Auntie Amelia smiled. 'They won't come in until the ceremony is almost over. In fact, traditionally, it's quite possible for a couple to not even be present when an engagement takes place.'

Faye looked at her blankly. Seeing her confusion, her aunt explained. 'What we refer to as an engagement is, strictly speaking, a customary marriage. Now, although Frieda and her partner will also get married under civil law either in church or at a registry office, in terms of our own culture, it's not really necessary for them to do so. Once this ceremony today has taken place, they are deemed to be married.'

Uncle Fred, sitting next to his wife, had been listening and chipped in. 'You see Faye, what you need to realise is that in our traditional culture, a marriage contract is not between two individuals, but actually between two families, which is why the couple themselves are not an essential part of the actual ceremony. According to our tradition, this ceremony is where the negotiations take place between the two families to secure the marriage contract. When they finally agree on the terms, which usually means providing gifts and token sums of money for the bride's family, the marriage contract is sealed by the groom's family giving drinks – which are called the *tiri nsa* – to the bride's family.'

He stopped speaking as the sound of car horns blaring loudly outside carried into the room. This was soon followed by singing that grew ever louder in volume. A group of women dressed in matching traditional wear burst into the room waving white handkerchiefs and singing lustily. In full voice and with broad smiles on their faces, they filed round the chairs greeting the seated guests. Finally, with a last chorus they took their seats in the previously empty rows opposite Frieda's parents.

'They're the representatives of the groom's family,' Amma explained quietly. 'They usually come as a group.'

A tall man dressed in a majestic white *boubou* who had been sitting next to Mr and Mrs Ansah stood up and announced that, as a senior member of the bride's family, he would be acting as the *okyeame* – or spokesman – for the Ansah family.

Speaking in flawless *Twi*, which Auntie Amelia swiftly translated for Faye's benefit, he invited the Ansah family and their friends and supporters to welcome the new arrivals to their home. Immediately everyone on Faye's side of the room stood up and filed round to shake hands with the newcomers before resuming their seats.

When everyone was settled, the *okyeame* rose again and formally welcomed them before enquiring about the reason for the visit.

That's a bit coy given all the ribbons and balloons hanging outside, Faye thought in amusement.

The *okyeame* for the groom's family, a pleasantly plump middle-aged woman, launched into a long and colourful explanation to the effect that they meant no offence by their visit. She went on to explain that their son had come to them to tell them that he had seen a particular young woman and that he was of a mind to make her his wife.

This was greeted by loud cheering and further singing from her family members and supporters; the African Chorus, as Faye mentally dubbed them. Waving them down, the *okyeame* continued. After making enquiries, she said, they discovered that the girl in question came from a good family and so had come to see her people and to ask for her hand in marriage to their son.

When the African Chorus had died down again, the Ansah family's *okyeame* rose. Clearing his throat apologetically, he explained that while his family were happy to welcome them as guests to their home, they had spent many years caring for their daughter and were not keen on losing her. However, having consulted the parents, he was agreeable to hearing what they had to say.

The drama continued with what was essentially good-natured haggling as one side stressed the value of their daughter while the other side hinted at what they could offer to alleviate the family's pain at losing such a jewel.

'They're laying it on a bit thick, aren't they?' Faye whispered to Amma at this point.

'I'll say,' Amma hissed back. 'Frieda's mother has been on at her for ages to get married!'

Eventually, some of the Chorus members left the house and returned a few minutes later in full voice. Between them, they carried a large aluminium bowl, which they laid on the ground while some young men followed carting several crates of drinks. The *okyeame* rose to her feet again. She earnestly described the very modest contribution they could offer to the Ansahs to salve the pain of losing their cherished daughter. Apart from copious drinks, including a bottle of aromatic schnapps, the 'modest contribution' included several pieces of beautiful fabric, a set of gold jewellery consisting of a delicate necklace, earrings and a bracelet, rolls of printed dress fabric for the mother of the bride and a white bible for the bride. Last, but definitely not least, she proffered a small red box containing a magnificent diamond engagement ring.

The African Chorus could not contain itself at this point and the women burst into song for several minutes before being hushed to hear the Ansah family's reaction. The Ansahs' *okyeame* took a few moments to confer with Frieda's parents before standing up. He acknowledged the gifts on offer with gratitude but warned them that their daughter was not for sale. However, he added, given the enthusiasm and sincerity with which they had come for her, he was happy to report that the girl's parents had given their consent to the marriage.

The African Chorus lost all restraint at this stage and launched into a medley of songs that went on for a good ten minutes. When they were eventually calmed down by their *okyeame*, they sat shifting in their seats, smiling happily. One of the leading Choristers leaned over and whispered something to the *okyeame*, who nodded vigorously.

Rising to her feet, she thanked the Ansah family for their generosity in agreeing to the marriage and promised that they would take good care of their daughter and treat her as one of their own. Faye's thoughts suddenly flashed back to her conversation with Martha and her troubled relationship with her late husband's family, and she could only hope that it was something that Frieda would never experience.

The *okyeame* then asked to see the girl they had come for, to assure themselves that they were all speaking about the same person. After a token show of indignation that there could be any doubt about the matter, the Ansahs' spokesman directed that the bride should be brought in to meet her new family.

'This is like watching a play,' Faye whispered to Amma, enjoying herself hugely at this ages-old enactment of her people's customs.

'Wait and see what happens now,' Amma giggled. 'Frieda has two sisters and they're going to send them in one after the other before she finally appears.'

As Amma had predicted, the first girl that came in was greeted by disappointed shouts from the African Chorus.

'No. No! This is not the girl we came for,' they cried indignantly. Giggling shyly, Frieda's sister left the room and another young woman was brought in, a cloth covering her face. When she was 'unveiled', the African Chorus broke into a fresh round of 'No. No. No!' until she was also led away.

At that point, a few of the women on the bride's side of the room stood up and hastened out of the hall. They returned shortly afterwards, singing loudly and ushering in a pretty girl in her twenties dressed in a beautiful snow-white *boubou* embroidered with gold thread. As they approached, the African Chorus exploded into an ecstatic burst of very loud singing, clapping and cheering. Auntie Amelia and Uncle Fred were also on their feet clapping and Faye and Amma joined in enthusiastically.

When everyone eventually calmed down, the bride was led over to stand by her parents. Her mother's face was wet with tears of joy and the *okyeame* called for silence and stood up again. His voice grew sober as he explained to Frieda that the Koranteng family had come to ask for her and that, despite her family's sorrow at the prospect of losing her – he pointedly avoided looking at the ecstatic expression on Mrs Ansah's face – her family had agreed to let her go. However, he wanted to be sure that she was agreeable to the marriage and it was now up to her to say whether or not she wished to go with them.

The African Chorus held their collective breath as he finished speaking and all eyes in the room were trained on Frieda. For a moment she could only giggle nervously before finding her voice and saying 'Yes' very softly. The Chorus was up and running again in full unrestrained voice.

After peace was restored, the *okyeame* consulted with Frieda's parents and stood up again, this time with a smile on his face. He explained that, in all fairness, they could not let their daughter go without seeing the man who had become her husband. After offering some half-hearted objections, a section of the Chorus filed out of the house, chattering happily. Shortly afterwards, their voices raised again in song, they marched back in. This time they were accompanied by a tall, solidly built man wearing glasses and dressed in a white *boubou*.

'That's Ken, Frieda's boyfriend,' Amma said above the din.

'You mean her husband.' Her mother corrected her with a smile.

Ken was guided over to the centre of the negotiation forum and stood next to Frieda. The Ansah's *okyeame* cleared his throat again and then launched into a speech about the importance of what had just taken place. After offering them detailed and unsolicited advice on how to deal with the storms of married life, he advised them to remember that their families were always there to help them and that they should never hesitate to seek their advice if it were needed.

'Frieda's mother would just send her right back to Ken if she ever came back home to complain about him,' Amma whispered tartly, unimpressed with the reconciliation option on offer.

Mr Ansah gave a short speech of thanks and immediately afterwards crates of chilled drinks were brought in and the refreshments served. Hand in hand and with broad smiles that held more than a tinge of relief that the formalities were over, the happy couple went around the room greeting their guests. When they reached the Asantes, Auntie Amelia hugged them both and wished them a long and happy marriage. Uncle Fred pumped Ken's hand furiously and with a knowing wink, congratulated him on joining the club.

After kissing both Frieda and Ken warmly, Amma introduced them to Faye, who shook hands and congratulated them on their marriage.

Frieda smiled her thanks before turning to Amma. 'So when are you and Edwin going to take the plunge?' she teased. 'You should have brought him along with you.'

'I don't want to terrify him even more than he is already. By the way, Rocky sends his congratulations. He's sorry he couldn't come today, but—'

Frieda saved Amma from perjuring herself any further.

'But, knowing Rocky, he's probably at the office!' she laughed. She looked across the room, distracted by the sight of her mother vigorously waving at her to come and greet another relative. Pulling on Ken's hand,

Frieda nodded towards her excited parent and sighed in resignation.

'Ken, we'd better go and say hello before Mama knocks herself out with all that waving!' Making their excuses, the couple moved off in Mrs Ansah's direction.

About an hour later, Auntie Amelia came over to find them chatting with a group of Amma's friends. 'Ladies, we need to leave now,' she said apologetically. 'Please say your goodbyes to the family. Your father—' She broke off as she glanced across the room in search of her husband. Biting her lip to hide a smile, she hastened across the hall to rescue him from the attentions of an elderly lady who was obviously quite hard of hearing. He made his excuses with undisguised relief and led the way as they walked down the road to their car.

Faye admired the pretty matchbox and bookmarker she had been given as a souvenir of the day. Ken and Frieda's names were engraved on the lid of the matchbox along with the date of their engagement ceremony.

'I'll have to show these to William and the others when I get back. I really enjoyed that ceremony, even if it was a bit over the top at times.'

Auntie Amelia smiled in agreement. 'Faye, I hope you have an engagement ceremony like this when you have chosen your future husband. It's something to remember forever.'

Trying to suppress the picture of a pair of caramel-coloured eyes that suddenly popped into her mind, Faye answered softly, 'I hope so, too.'

13

Cultural Recreation

Martha knocked twice on Faye's door before going in to deposit the dress she had been cajoled into ironing for her. Faye was singing loudly in the shower, unaware of her audience. Chuckling at the tuneless sounds emerging from the bathroom, Martha returned to the sanctuary of her kitchen.

Ten minutes later, wafting a cloud of Miss Dior shower gel in her wake, Faye padded into the bedroom, her towel wrapped securely around her slim body. She stopped short as she spotted the expertly ironed dress laid out on the bed and silently blessed Martha. Sitting on the edge of her bed, she stroked lavish amounts of the expensive perfumed cream she had brought from London all over her body, pausing to admire her beautifully manicured nails.

Earlier that afternoon, after Faye had asked to borrow some shampoo, Amma had dragged her protesting to the local hairdressers, insisting that *no one* washed their own hair in Ghana. Faye, still smarting from *Sharice of Streatham's* sadistic experiments on her hair, had been pleasantly surprised by the hairdresser, who skilfully trimmed and styled her hair, leaving it looking full and glossy.

While at the salon, Amma had further insisted that she treated herself to a manicure and pedicure and her feet now felt as smooth as silk.

With the air conditioner on at full blast, Faye sat down to apply her make-up. Slapping on layers of mascara to build up her long but fine eyelashes, she was forced to admit that her hectic social life in Ghana was a million miles away from the monotonous routine she had allowed her life in London to become. Because she had always wanted to please Michael, or at least avoid his epic sulks, she had missed out on films, shows and even parties that he had considered culturally bankrupt. Every year, she had listened wistfully to Caroline's descriptions of her fabulous holidays with Marcus and scrolled through hundreds of photographs of William and Lucinda riding on the backs of camels in Egypt or skiing down the slopes of Aspen. Michael's usual response to the suggestion of a holiday together was she needed to work on eliminating her desire to buy into the neo-colonialist economic trap being set by greedy travel agents and tour operators. Now, she realised, with Michael out of her life, it was time for a different view of life and to take responsibility for her own happiness.

She outlined her lips with a dark-ruby pencil before carefully applying the matching glossy lipstick. From an angled side parting, her hair fell in a glossy curtain down the side of her face, just reaching her shoulders. She gave it a last flick with the hairbrush, impressed by its new fullness and shine.

She slipped slowly into the silky black dress Martha had ironed, easing it up over her bottom before sliding her arms through the thin straps. From the v-shaped ruched neckline cut low in the front down to the silver-edged hem, which rested a few inches above her knees, the soft fabric clung seductively to her slim shape. She wriggled her newly manicured feet into the silver sandals and stood, striking a pose like the supermodel Uncle Fred insisted she was.

Engrossed in admiring her reflection, she jumped at the loud knock at her door as in walked Amma. She took one look at Faye and her eyes widened in shock.

'*Oh. My. God*!' She enunciated each word slowly and clearly, her tone ominous. 'You are in *big* trouble tonight, my friend – you look seriously sexy. I'll have to put Edwin on guard duty, assuming I can trust him to keep his own hands off. You look amazing in that dress!'

Faye laughed and twirled in front of the mirror. 'It *is* pretty wicked, isn't it? It certainly cost me enough! I'm surprised Martha was able to bring herself to iron it – she probably had to cross herself every time she put the iron down.'

She stopped pirouetting and looked at Amma in admiration. 'I don't think you need to worry about Edwin tonight – have you looked in a mirror? You look gorgeous! You have such nice legs; you should wear shorter skirts more often.'

Amma looked pleased although she tugged gently at

the hem of the ruby-red skirt she was wearing. She had teamed it with an almost-transparent chiffon shirt in a matching red over a deep ruby bustier. A chunky statement necklace served to emphasise her generous cleavage. She had twisted her braids up into an elaborate chignon and finished her outfit off with a pair of pale-gold stilettos.

She glanced at her watch and raised her eyebrows. 'Come on, supermodel. It's almost ten; we'd better get going.'

Faye sprayed one last burst of perfume, then picked up her silver bag and turned off the air conditioner and the lights on her way out. Rocky had left the house much earlier, having promised to help Stuart set up at the house for the party.

As she carefully manoeuvred her way down the stairs in her spiky heels, she heard voices from the living room and walked in to see Auntie Amelia standing with her hands on her hips gazing open-mouthed at her daughter. She turned and blinked in shock when she saw Faye.

'Well, all I can say is thank goodness Rocky and Edwin will be at the party! The two of you are going to be in need of protection wearing those outfits.'

She took a quick look around the hallway and returned hastily. 'Amma, if you want to get out of here alive, you had better go now, before your father comes downstairs!'

Taking the hint, Amma and Faye said goodnight and left the older woman to return to the film she had been watching. Martha had gone off to bed, which was probably for the best if Auntie Amelia's reaction was anything to go by, Faye thought.

Once in the car, Amma slipped off her heels, preferring

to drive barefoot, and set off in the direction of Stuart's house, which, she explained, was in an area close to Labone known as East Cantonments. Stuart had been posted to Ghana six years earlier and had systematically turned down any job promotions that would have meant he had to leave, she laughed. As a fun-loving bachelor in Accra, Stuart had a frenetic social life and had developed an insatiable passion for Ghanaian women.

A few minutes later, Amma slowed in front of a house from which they could hear loud music blaring. The long line of cars parked on the roadside, including more than a few luxury models and convertibles, indicated that a very lively party was in full swing.

Amma found a parking space quite a way down from the house and they walked slowly back up the street, treading warily on the rough tarmac in their delicately heeled sandals. A security guard ushered them through the front gate to Stuart's house and, as they walked up the gravel path, Faye looked around the grounds in amazement. Party lights had been strung through the trees that lined the driveway and multicoloured lights twinkled across the front of the house – a sprawling two-storey structure with a Swiss chalet style façade. White plastic tables and chairs, tilting slightly on the springy grass, were dotted around the lawn. Under an awning, a long table covered in a white linen cloth and loaded with piles of plates and gleaming silver cutlery had been set up to the side of the garden and two huge pigs on metal spits rotated slowly over a flaming charcoal pit.

The music grew louder as they approached the open

front door and walked in. People were crammed into a large hall and living room that had been almost completely emptied of furniture. Most of the crowd, a cosmopolitan mix of Africans, Europeans and Asians, were gyrating wildly, and not always in rhythm, to the pulsating music blaring from huge speakers. The few guests trying to carry on a conversation shrieked at each other, their faces barely inches apart.

Amma seized Faye's hand and pointed in the direction of the bar – an extended dining table covered with a huge array of drinks. On the floor next to the table were several huge plastic containers filled with blocks of ice competing for space with fizzy drinks and beer bottles. Pushing their way through the mass of people, the girls headed for the bar. The waiter deftly pulled a bottle of white wine out of one of the iceboxes and poured the chilled contents into two huge wine glasses. He handed over their drinks and turned his attention to a tall red-faced man wearing a tartan kilt.

A frantic tug on her sleeve made Amma spin round and almost spill her wine onto Baaba. Her friend was wearing a short hot-pink Lycra dress with a matching lipstick, and new glossy hair extensions reached down her back. Baaba hugged Amma in relief and then stepped back quickly, eyeing the full wine glass warily.

'You're late!' she shrieked above the din. 'I've been trying to call you – didn't you see my missed calls?' She nodded at Faye and smiled before turning back to Amma.

'We're all out there,' she mouthed, pointing towards the veranda. Shielding their drinks from the exuberant movers on the dance floor, they followed Baaba out to the terrace. As Baaba led the way, her hips tightly wrapped in the pink dress, Faye stared in amazement at the size of the curves confidently swaying a path through the crowd.

A cool breeze was blowing through the veranda as they stepped outside. Edwin sat on the veranda wall, a small bottle of beer dangling from his fingers. As soon as he spotted Faye, JB jumped down from the wall where he had also been perched. He wore a black shirt and dark trousers and his gold tooth was very much in evidence as he grinned widely at his newfound prey.

'Hey, girl! How ya doing?' He swaggered up to her and delivered his trademark greeting with gusto. A small gold mask dangled from his heavy gold neck chain and his open shirt revealed a skinny, hairless chest.

Faye smiled in greeting and moved over quickly to hug Edwin who gave an appreciative whistle when he saw them. With his arm draped possessively around Amma, Edwin stared in admiration at Faye, who struck an exaggerated pose that showed off her long legs to perfection.

'You look gorgeous,' said a husky voice behind her and she whirled around, almost falling into Sonny's arms. A leather waistcoat over his bare chest showed off his muscular physique, as did the tight denims he was wearing. Faye stepped back and almost bumped into JB who was hurrying towards her in a bid to head Sonny off from his prospective pitch.

'Hey, Faye, you wanna dance?' JB asked in his grating high-pitched voice, scowling at Sonny who had calmly put an arm across Faye's shoulders.

'No, she doesn't, bro. She's quite comfortable here.' Sonny interjected before Faye could speak. Ignoring the venomous glare his friend shot at him, Sonny gently pulled Faye back against his chest.

Baaba had been watching them through narrowed eyes and she smiled wickedly. 'Now, now, boys, let's keep it friendly, shall we? Well, Faye, it looks like you are, quite literally, spoken for these days, eh?' Giggling in great amusement at her own joke, she reached behind Edwin for her drink, a tall glass filled with a sparkling red concoction. Raising it high, she said loudly, 'Here's to all of us. May we all get what we are looking for tonight!'

'Now, there's a toast I can agree with!' Rocky walked towards them looking relaxed and handsome in a white linen shirt and black trousers. His gaze travelled over the group and his eyebrows rose briefly at his sister's almost transparent shirt before coming to rest on Faye, who was trying to wriggle out of the unwanted shelter of Sonny's arm.

'You look beautiful,' he said, looking straight into her eyes. She gazed back wordlessly, her heart thumping even louder than the music blaring out over the speakers. For a moment everyone stood frozen, caught up in the electricity between them. Baaba watched them and her heavily lined eyes narrowed almost to a slit, while JB looked on helplessly and Sonny's expression darkened in anger.

The tableau moved back into play as a tall rangy man with curly brown hair came out onto the veranda and walked towards them, clutching a large bottle of beer in one hand.

'Why aren't you all dancing?' He spoke with a broad

accent straight from Liverpool and emphasised his question by wiggling his straight hips in what he imagined was a sexy move. 'Come on, Rock, let's show them how it's done!'

Rocky laughed and introduced Stuart, his boss and the host of the party. His palms moist from clutching his drink, Stuart shook hands with each of them and his jaw dropped as Baaba turned around to put down her glass before turning back to shake his hand.

'Okay now,' he said, 'we'll be serving food outside in a short while, so just drink all you want and dance, dance, dance!' He gave another wiggle of his hips and extended a hand of invitation towards Baaba, who took it without a second's hesitation and swayed off into the room where she could soon be seen bobbing up and down in the crowd of dancers.

Rocky reached for Faye's hand and tugged her gently towards him. She almost fell against his chest and looked up at him, her heart racing.

'Let's dance,' he said softly. She nodded and moved off with him, oblivious to the sulky expression on Sonny's face and JB's obvious frustration.

Rocky pushed his way through the crowd and turned to face her. Suddenly the frenetic music stopped and a soft ballad wafted through the speakers.

'Oh!' was all Faye could say as Rocky smoothly pulled her against his hard chest, encircling her waist with one arm. Praying her make-up wouldn't rub off onto his white shirt, she tried to lean in and move along with him.

'Relax, I won't bite', he murmured, causing her to promptly tense up even more. Pulling back slightly, he looked down at her in the semi-darkness and raised an eyebrow enquiringly.

'Or would you prefer to go back to Sonny?' For the first time she detected a slight hint of anxiety in Rocky's usually impenetrable features. Suddenly relaxing, Faye shook her head and smiled.

'No, let's dance.' She moved back into his arms and rested her head against his chest, oblivious to anything going on around her.

The change in tempo had clearly found no favour among the guests for as soon as the song ended it was followed by a raucous club number and, with a roar of approval, the partygoers who had wandered off headed back to the dance floor. Taking her hand, Rocky led Faye back to the veranda where Amma, Sonny and JB were laughing at one of Edwin's jokes.

The laughter stopped abruptly as Faye and Rocky appeared hand in hand in the doorway, silhouetted against the faint light from inside the living room. Then, without warning, a squealing flash of purple whirred across the veranda from the direction of the garden and hurled itself at Rocky, almost toppling him over. Releasing Faye's hand, he quickly steadied the girl who had thrown her arms around him so forcefully.

'Hello, Clarissa,' he said dryly, trying to disentangle her arms from around his neck. Sonny and JB's faces immediately lightened up as they recognised Rocky's former girlfriend, although there was nothing former about the way she continued to cling to him or the plum-coloured lipstick imprint she had left on his chin.

Clarissa was even taller than Faye and was undeniably beautiful. Her flawless skin was a warm chocolate-brown and her long slim legs were shown to their best advantage by the very short purple dress she was wearing – or *almost wearing*, Faye thought cattily. Her hair cascaded down her bare back in a profusion of waves arranged in carefully styled carelessness.

'Sweetie!' she gazed up at Rocky with heavily lashed deep brown eyes and pouted. 'I've missed you so much! Why haven't you called me?'

'You're looking very well, Clarissa,' Rocky said evenly and discreetly tried to disengage himself as she clung possessively onto him. Amma took pity on her brother and moved forward to give Clarissa a hug, forcing her to release her hold. Taking advantage of his freedom, Rocky quickly put an arm behind Faye who had been standing awkwardly to the side and propelled her forward.

'Clarissa, let me introduce you to a family friend of ours who's over here on holiday from England,' he said smoothly. 'Faye, this is Clarissa Martinson, an old friend of mine.'

'I'm not sure I like being called *old*,' Clarissa retorted, shooting him an annoyed glance before turning her attention to Faye. 'Well, I suppose I ought to say 'Welcome to Ghana' or something.' Her tone was dismissive. 'How long are you here for?' she added, taking note of the fact that an extremely attractive girl in a very sexy dress was standing rather closer to Rocky than she would have liked.

Faye shrugged carelessly. 'Another couple of weeks or so.' She noted with irritation the gleam of satisfaction in the other girl's eyes.

Just then Baaba appeared, fanning herself with one hand and adjusting the top of her dress, which had slipped while she was dancing. She stopped short when she saw Clarissa, and then advanced slowly, a malicious glint in her eye.

'Well, well, what do we have here?' she drawled. Her voice sounded even deeper than usual. 'Clarissa – are you still in town? I thought you said you were leaving for some exciting international modelling assignment not too long ago,' she asked in feigned surprise.

Clarissa glared back at her. 'Why, Baaba, how nice to see you too!' She made no effort to disguise her sarcasm. 'You're looking even,' she paused as she eyed the other girl appraisingly, '*fuller* than I remember,' she said sweetly. 'Have we added a teeny bit of weight to our hips?'

Baaba's eyes spat fire and Amma moved in hastily. 'Baaba, let's go and get a drink. How about you, Faye? Would you like another?'

Sonny jumped in quickly. 'I'll get her a drink. What were you drinking, Faye, white wine?'

Conscious of everyone's eyes upon her, Faye nodded quickly and the three of them left, Amma practically dragging a bristling Baaba along with her. JB quickly seized his opportunity and sidled up to Faye. Grinning at her wolfishly, he jerked his head towards the dance floor.

'What do you say to a dance?' His expression suggested that much more than a dance was on offer. Faye looked desperately at Rocky but Clarissa had seized his arm again and was expertly steering him away to the side of the veranda, while talking ten to the dozen.

Turning back to JB, Faye nodded reluctantly and

followed him into the darkened dance room. Thankfully the music was still uptempo and Faye was able to keep a few inches between them as they danced, which was just as well as JB clearly fancied himself as Ghana's answer to Michael Jackson and would squeal and spin round without warning, forcing her to step back quickly whenever it happened, or risk bodily harm.

Through the crowd, Faye spotted Sonny dancing with a pretty girl wearing a suede mini and a matching cropped top with long fringes that swayed as she danced. He smiled down at her as they moved rhythmically to the beat, his arm encircling her slender waist. The girl placed her hand on his shoulder and Faye watched with interest as she reached up and whispered something in his ear. He threw his head back in laughter before bending down to answer her.

The tempo changed to a slow reggae beat, but before Faye could leave the dance floor, JB had gathered her into his skinny arms, bending and swaying her to the rhythm of the music. To add insult to injury, he then started to sing – badly – against her ear. Moments later she gasped with relief when a pair of strong arms prised her out of JB's suffocating embrace.

She turned to see Rocky trying without much success to keep a straight face. Unmoved by JB's obvious irritation, he invited them to make their way out to the garden where dinner was about to be served. JB draped an arm around Faye who promptly pushed him away and went in search of Amma who was out in the garden trying to calm an irate Baaba.

'Oh, there you are!' Faye was relieved to see that no blood had been shed. 'Let's go and find a table. Where's Edwin?'

Amma was equally relieved to abandon her role of mediator and she linked her arm through Baaba's and propelled her onto the lawn towards an empty table. Spotting Edwin coming out of the house, she waved him over to where they sat. Sonny had been deep in conversation with the girl in the suede skirt and he gallantly escorted her to another table before turning back to join his friends.

Pausing briefly at the bar, Sonny strode over and took the empty seat next to Faye, handing her a full glass of wine.

Baaba, who was sitting next to Amma, sniggered. 'I suppose we'd better get another chair ready so JB can also sit next to Faye.'

Edwin laughed while Sonny's lips tightened in annoyance. 'Where is the LAFA boy anyway?' Still looking amused, Edwin scoured the stream of people flooding out of the house into the garden.

'What does LAFA mean?' Faye asked curiously as Amma and Baaba dissolved into giggles. Amma shook her head reproachfully at her partner.

'Edwin, don't be so mean!' She bit her lip and tried to stop giggling. 'It stands for 'locally acquired foreign accent'. Basically it's someone who fakes an accent from a country they've never even visited.'

She stopped speaking as JB strode towards them. He dragged over a chair from the table next to them and planted himself squarely between Faye and Edwin, ignoring the empty chair on the other side of Sonny.

315

Baaba and Edwin promptly burst out laughing, causing JB to look at them in bewilderment. Amma glared at them and they slowly sobered, trying to avoid eye contact in case one set the other off again.

Rocky came over to stand behind Amma and rested his hands on his sister's shoulders. 'Okay, you folks can go up to the buffet table now.' He nodded in the direction of the food and then moved on to the next table.

Amma stood up and tugged Edwin's hand, pulling him out of his chair. 'Come on, I'm hungry – and don't make any comments about my diet!' The others followed, with Faye taking the lead and keeping Amma firmly in her sights.

There were a number of people ahead of them waiting in line to reach the buffet table. They took their place at the end of the queue behind a group of expats who, judging from their accents, were British. They seemed friendly and as Faye watched them chatter excitedly, it dawned on her that for the first time in a very long time, she was not the one who stood out as a minority. She was so deep in thought about the unaccustomed role reversal and how good it felt to be an accepted part of her home country that she failed to register what was happening in front of her.

'You don't mind if I slip in here, do you?' Clarissa squeezed into the line between Amma and Faye, turning her back on the latter as she directed her words at Amma. 'The line is *so* long and we're practically family anyway, aren't we?' she smiled sweetly at Amma, who shot her an irritated glare.

'How about apologising to Faye for just pushing her out of the way? And you know as well as I do that you and

316

Rocky are not together any more.'

With a sulky pout, Clarissa turned to Faye and muttered an insincere 'Sorry' under her breath. Smiling at Amma with perfectly outlined plum-coloured lips, she slipped her arm inside hers.

'Okay, I've apologised, sweetie, so don't be angry with me. And, as for Rocky,' her smile slipped for a moment as she glanced at Faye briefly with a hard expression in her eyes, 'don't you worry. He'll forgive me – he knows I was only kidding around with Stuart. I hardly even *speak* to the man, you know.'

Oblivious to the contradiction between her words and her presence at Stuart's party, Clarissa babbled on. 'So, have you seen my new TV commercial yet? The company wants me to film another ad for a new fragrance they're launching. Apparently, I looked *really* hot in the beach scene and their sales have been rocketing. Isn't it *amazing*?'

Clarissa continued to chatter away as they moved towards the food. Baaba decided to ignore her and instead chatted quietly to JB. When she reached the buffet table, Amma picked up a couple of plates from the stack at the side and passed one each to Clarissa and Faye, while admiring the sumptuous spread of local and European dishes.

'Wow, this looks fantastic. I'm *so* hungry!' Amma exclaimed. She reached for another plate and sighed happily. Several waiters were stationed behind the table ready to assist but she waved them away, serving herself generous portions of her favourite dishes.

Clarissa tipped a few grains of plain white rice onto her plate and scooped up some green salad. She waved away the salad dressing offered by the waiter and patted her enviably flat stomach gravely.

'Those of us in the public eye have to be *so* careful what we eat,' she said to no one in particular. Looking over at Baaba, who had started to serve herself, she said thoughtfully, 'Baaba, you're so lucky to be able to eat all you want. I would *love* to make a pig of myself too, but since my figure is my fortune, what can I do?'

Baaba paused and studied her plate for a long moment, torn between the desire to eat what was on it and the joy of tipping it over Clarissa's head. Amma watched her nervously, but just then Stuart appeared and slipped an arm around Baaba's waist.

'You know you have the most *incredible* figure,' he said in admiration, his face flushed from a combination of dancing and the contents of the now empty beer bottle in his left hand. 'Are you having a good time? Let me know if there's anything you need, eh?' He patted her generous behind before moving off to check on some other guests.

Baaba smiled smugly at Clarissa and went back to filling her plate. 'Well, Clarissa, while you're busy impersonating a stick insect, the rest of us real human beings – especially those of us with *incredible* figures,' she paused to rub in Stuart's words, 'will enjoy the food on your behalf.'

Clarissa glared at her furiously and tossed her curly mane in indignation. Unable to think of a good comeback, she turned on Faye who was trying without much success to repress a giggle.

'Do you know how to eat our local food, Faye – is it?'

Not fooled for a moment by the saccharine sweet

tone, Faye stared at her, wondering what was coming. She resisted the temptation to reply 'you put it in your mouth and chew it, don't you?' and simply said 'Yes'.

She turned and selected a slice of delectable looking seasoned fish and added some rice and salad. Moving down the table, she added a piece of barbecued chicken to her plate and some delicious roast pork fresh off the spit. A number of traditional dishes had been laid out further down the table and, peering into a large bowl, she spotted *kontomire,* with large chunks of pink pigfoot nestling in the spicy green spinach stew. Although she liked spinach stew, her mild distaste for pigfoot had assumed mammoth proportions after the Pigfoot Etcetera saga and she couldn't help the grimace that crossed her face.

Unfortunately for her, Clarissa noticed the change in her expression and moved in swiftly. 'What is it, Faye?' She looked at her with exaggerated concern. 'Does our food upset you? You just looked like you were going to be ill.'

The others looked over at Faye in surprise.

'Are you feeling all right, Faye?' Amma asked with an anxious frown. Embarrassed by the attention, Faye shook her head, restraining the urge to strangle Clarissa. 'I'm feeling perfectly well,' she said evenly. 'The food looks delicious.' She moved on and had started to serve herself a spoonful of the rich tomato gravy that was to be found in almost every Ghanaian buffet when Clarissa dumped a heaped serving spoon of the spinach and pigfoot stew on her plate.

'I'm sure you'll love this, Faye; it's one of our most popular dishes.' Her lips were curved into a malicious smile as she waited to see Faye's reaction.

Faye stared with dismay at the pink pieces of pork lying on her plate. Instantly, the memories of Jasmine and the humiliation she had suffered at Pigfoot Etcetera came flooding back. With one spiteful gesture, Clarissa had hit her weak spot, and Faye could feel her hard-won self-confidence starting to ebb. Her friends were now staring at her curiously and instead of the cosy glow of cultural acceptance she had just been basking in, she suddenly feared that the chill of alienation was going to envelop her once again.

Amma took in the distressed expression on Faye's face and the triumphant look on Clarissa's and acted swiftly. Gently removing Faye's plate from her hands, she transferred the spinach stew onto a clean side plate before handing it back.

'You know Clarissa,' she said mildly, 'if you're not planning to eat anything else, you should go and sit down. You're holding up the people behind us.'

With a sulky pout, the other girl stalked off and the others went back to their table.

Faye touched Amma's arm. 'Thanks,' she whispered gratefully, not sure how to explain what had just happened.

'Take no notice of that girl,' Amma said, shaking her head in exasperation. 'She just likes to get attention and she scratches like a cat if she sees anyone around Rocky.' She giggled and added in a whisper, 'I warned you that dress would get you into trouble, didn't I?'

They strolled back to their table, eager to tuck into their food. Waiters circulated between the tables with trays of drinks and one in particular seemed very taken by Faye's long legs. After his fourth attempt to refill her glass, after she had barely taken a sip from it, Sonny glared at him and he scurried off.

Edwin finished eating first and sat back in his chair. Looking around the table, he cleared his throat noisily. 'Okay, everybody, I've got some news.' He glanced at Amma nervously and she took a last bite from her plate and looked at him enquiringly.

'What news?' She wiped her mouth carefully to avoid smudging her lipstick.

'I got my American visa yesterday,' he replied slowly, avoiding her eyes. She sat in silence while Baaba hugged him excitedly and the two men slapped his back in congratulations. JB was practically hopping up and down with joy. In his excitement, he dropped his guard and his accent reverted to a normal Ghanaian intonation.

'Yes, my brother!' he chuckled, his gold dentistry flashing in the dusk. 'You are lucky, eh! I tell you. The way they keep refusing me a visa, unless I find a chick with a foreign passport, I'm stuck in this place!'

Everyone fell silent and he suddenly realised what he had said. He glanced nervously over at Faye. She struggled to keep a straight face and chewed delicately on the remains of her chicken, pretending she hadn't heard anything untoward.

Amma hadn't said a word since his announcement and Edwin turned to her, trying to disguise the anxiety in his voice.

'Aren't you going to congratulate me?' He injected a

note of bravado into what sounded more like a plea than a question. She stared at him, expressionless.

'Congratulations,' she said coolly. 'I'm glad you got what you wanted.'

Sonny, clearly eager to avoid any conflict, excused himself and moved off in the direction of the suede miniskirt. Baaba, on the other hand, put down her cutlery and watched the interchange with interest.

Edwin had taken Amma's hand and was pleading with her. 'It's not that I want to leave you, but you know how hard it's been for me to get a good job here. Look, if I can work for a year or two over there and maybe do a postgraduate course, it will make all the difference when I come back.'

'Come on, Amma! It won't be forever,' Baaba chipped in helpfully.

'How do you know?' Amma glared at her, her eyes flashing in anger. '*How* do you know it won't be forever?' Her voice broke, and with a sob she leaped out of her chair and rushed into the house.

There was silence around the table. Dropping her napkin onto the table, Faye stood up. 'I'll go and find her.' She smiled sympathetically at Edwin who now looked completely miserable. Baaba shrugged, for once at a loss for words, while JB kept his eyes down, still unable to look at Faye.

She walked back into the house; the living area now deserted with all the partygoers still outside eating. The music echoed around the empty dance room as she walked across the hall and headed for the veranda. Rocky, on his way out of one of the side rooms, came to a halt when he saw her and she walked over to him.

'Have you seen Amma?'

He shook his head. Struck by her anxious expression, he asked curiously, 'Why, what's the matter? Isn't she feeling well?'

Faye sighed. 'She's a bit upset, that's all. Edwin has just told her he's got his visa to go to America.'

Rocky chuckled, ignoring her frown of disapproval. 'Well, well, so the man finally got someone to take pity on him. Oh well, it's probably a good thing – he'll have to knuckle down and do some real work for a change,' he added heartlessly.

He steered her gently towards the veranda. 'Let's take a look out there,' he suggested. The record had finished playing and it was quiet as they headed for the double doors leading out to the veranda. Just as they approached the doorway, a deep male voice could be heard from the other side of the partially open door and they both automatically froze.

'You have beautiful hands,' said the husky disembodied voice; the words drifted over the silence to where they stood. 'You hold my heart in between these beautiful hands of yours. Don't crush it, please.'

From where Faye stood, Sonny was not visible but she could dimly make out the outline of the girl in the suede miniskirt. The girl tugged at Sonny's hands and led him out into the garden, where they disappeared into the darkness.

Embarrassed at witnessing the scene, Faye turned

around swiftly and bumped into Rocky's hard chest. He held her firmly for a long moment before lifting her chin gently with his hand and looking anxiously into her eyes.

'Are you okay?' His voice was gentle and his eyes were narrowed in concern.

He has *incredibly* sexy eyes, she thought staring up at him. She nodded dumbly.

'I wanted to tell you what a dog that guy is, but I didn't think you would believe me,' Rocky sighed, his thumb gently caressing her chin. 'I'm sorry you had to hear that.'

'Don't be sorry,' Faye said softly. 'I'm not.'

Rocky looked at her quizzically for a moment. Without saying another word, he bent his head and softly kissed her mouth. She moved into his arms with a small sigh, her lips parting under his.

Holding her tightly against him, he wrapped his hand inside her silky hair and held her head firmly as he kissed her over and over again. Her senses swimming, she kissed him back, oblivious to the sound of footsteps entering the room.

'Er, Rock, old chap...' Stuart cleared his throat loudly. 'The people want some music,' he said, shrugging in silent apology.

Rocky lifted his head slowly, his eyes fixed on Faye's bemused face.

'No problem,' he answered calmly. 'I'll put another DVD on in a minute.'

'Okay, mate. See you outside, eh?' Stuart said awkwardly before hastily leaving the room.

The spell broken, Faye moved out of Rocky's hold and smoothed down her hair with shaking fingers. He, on the other hand, looked completely unperturbed.

'Do you want me to say I'm sorry?' he asked gently. She shook her head slowly and he nodded thoughtfully.

'Good, because I would be lying if I did. I've wanted to do that for a long time.'

She smiled tremulously at him and her heart literally skipped with joy.

He sighed. 'Having said that, I'm not the dog that Sonny is and I don't think I should be abusing my parents' hospitality by fooling around with their guest.'

Faye looked at him speechlessly. 'Well, thanks a lot!' Her voice was high with indignation when she could finally get the words out and she glared at him furiously. 'I'm going to look for Amma, so you can continue with your DJ duties without worrying about abusing anybody's hospitality!'

'Faye, hold on a minute...' he started. Ignoring his outstretched hand, she turned away before he could see the hurt in her eyes and stormed back outside.

She almost ran into Amma as she reached the front door. Amma was clearly distraught and her eyes were wet with tears. Forcing back her own emotions, Faye put a comforting arm around her friend.

'Come on,' she sighed. 'Let's go home.'

14

Cultural Tensions

Faye sat on her favourite wicker lounger, her long legs folded beneath her, and flicked moodily through one of Amma's magazines. A cool morning breeze blew across the veranda and in the distance Togo could be seen watering the grass, his skinny legs wet with the spray from the hosepipe.

She still burned with indignation at Rocky's casual dismissal of a moment she thought had meant something and for three days now since the eventful party, she had managed to avoid being alone with him and evaded his attempts to talk to her privately. Amma was being equally cool with Edwin, who phoned several times a day pleading with her to hear him out.

Sonny had also called a few times, puzzled at Faye's unusually curt responses to his usual teasing banter. One positive outcome of the party, from Faye's perspective, was the disappearance of JB from the scene. Since his unguarded outburst at the party, he had made no effort to call her. Pratt by name and prat by nature, Faye thought in exasperation, wondering how on earth Edwin and Baaba tolerated him.

Baaba, in stark contrast to her girlfriends, had been in a state of uncontrolled excitement since the party. Stuart was clearly smitten with her and had already taken her out twice. The previous evening, after instructing him to drop her off at the Asantes' house, Baaba had spent almost an hour filling them in on every detail of their evening.

'Oh come on, you two, you're depressing me!' she said grumpily. Polite interest was not a good enough response to her state of romantic euphoria.

'Amma, I know what's wrong with you – although I still think you're overreacting – but Faye...' She looked at her through narrowed eyes. 'What's your problem?'

Faye shrugged and said nothing. With the exception of Clarissa, Baaba was probably the last person she would have chosen to talk to about her mixed-up feelings for Rocky. But when it came to men, the other girl was as sharp as a razor.

'Well, I doubt if our Sonny could make you look so miserable.' Baaba eyed Faye appraisingly. 'So I suppose it's Rocky.'

Still Faye said nothing, and Baaba gave a loud sigh. 'Oh well, I suppose it was bound to happen,' she conceded, feeling magnanimous now that her love life was clearly superior to both of theirs. 'I don't know what happened, but I know from experience that Rocky can be very difficult to pin down. If I were you, I'd concentrate on Sonny – after all, you're here for what, another week and a half? Two weeks? Just have some fun and don't go looking to get your heart broken,' she added helpfully.

'Oh, Baaba just shut up!' Amma said in irritation as Faye winced visibly. Baaba's words, although not exactly diplomatic, hit home as the truth. Even more miserable than she had felt before, Faye had remained silent until Baaba had taken her leave, completely exasperated by their long faces.

As she sat staring out at the back garden, Faye tried to put the events of the other evening into perspective. If she was honest, she thought guiltily, a tiny part of her did appreciate Rocky's respect for her as a guest of his parents. Given the same situation, she was fairly sure that such a sentiment would never have occurred to someone like Sonny. But what had hurt far more was that he had labelled what had happened between them in such an offhand way. The complicated mess of feelings she had when it came to Rocky, she thought resentfully, could not simply be described as 'fooling around'.

Her feelings about Sonny were far less complicated. Although she was still shocked at his ability to chase two women at the same time and at the same party, she recognised that what she had really been attracted to was the light-hearted and, at least so she had believed, uncomplicated attention he had showered on her. Although she was still irritated by his behaviour, she knew she didn't care enough about him to stay angry with him.

Her thoughts were disturbed as Amma walked out onto the patio with her bag slung over one shoulder. She still looked downcast and Faye dismissed her own troubles and smiled affectionately at her.

'Where are you off to?' She eyed the handbag with curiosity. Amma had hardly left the house since the weekend, keeping to her bedroom or lying on the sofa in the living room listening to mournful love songs.

Amma replied with a wan smile. 'Mama's asked me to go to the bank to deposit a cheque for her. Why don't you come with me? I haven't been a very good tour guide lately.'

Faye shrugged and tossed the magazine onto the table. 'Okay, why not? Just give me a minute to freshen up.'

Up in her room, she ran a comb through her hair, noting with satisfaction that the hairdresser's handiwork had held up. Her jeans, although faded, were clean, emphasising her long legs. She changed quickly into a long-sleeved white blouse in soft Indian cotton with leather laces at the neckline and tiny glass beads dotted around the bodice. Slipping on a pair of flat brown leather sandals, she dug her small brown leather purse out from the drawer before going back downstairs.

Auntie Amelia was in the living room writing out a cheque for Amma and smiled at Faye as she walked into the room.

'Are you going with Amma?' Faye nodded and her aunt smiled in satisfaction.

'Good. It's about time she left the house and cheered up a bit.' Ignoring her daughter's frown, she signed the cheque and handed it over to her. 'And tell Rocky that I haven't yet received my statement for last month,' she added.

'Mama, he doesn't work on the banking operations side,' Amma said patiently, in the tone of one who had made the same statement a hundred times. 'He's in the investment banking division.'

'Well, whatever,' her mother said absently, waving her off. 'He can talk to the right person and get them to sort it out, can't he? See you both later.'

Faye frowned. 'Are we going to *Rocky's* bank?' The outing was swiftly beginning to take on stressful implications.

'Yes,' Amma said, as they reached the car. 'Why, is something wrong?' Pausing for a moment, she looked at Faye over the top of the car. For the first time she noted small shadows under Faye's eyes and the absence of her usual exuberance.

'I've been so busy worrying about my own problems that I haven't even asked you what happened at the party.' Amma cocked her head to one side. 'You were also upset when we left; I remember now. Was it something to do with Rocky?'

Faye smiled, embarrassed. 'Oh, it's nothing really. We just had a slight disagreement, that's all.'

Amma started to speak and then stopped herself. She unlocked the door and said cheerily, 'Come on, let's go and deposit Mama's cheque and then we'll go somewhere nice for lunch to cheer ourselves up.'

The traffic was unusually heavy as they drove through Danquah Circle, where two vehicles had been involved in an accident on the roundabout. Amma had been speeding along the main road and slowed down after passing the crumpled vehicles.

Faye glanced sideways at her friend. She had tied her braids back into a ponytail, with one or two of the plaits trailing loosely at the sides.

'I think you've lost a couple of pounds, you know.' She peered closely at Amma. 'That's one good thing, isn't it?'

Amma laughed out loud for the first time in days. 'You're right,' she grinned. 'Maybe I should stay miserable for a bit longer – what do you think?'

They stopped at a set of traffic lights and were immediately besieged by a posse of young boys armed with wet sponges. Despite Amma's frown, they rushed forward to clean the windscreen, enthusiastically smearing dirty water across the glass. Amma tooted her horn crossly, causing them to stop and look enquiringly at her. She waved them away and flicked on the car wipers. For a few seconds, the boys stared mournfully as the greasy streaks on the glass were swiftly cleaned away, then they quickly moved on to try their luck with the car behind.

After a few minutes drive, they stopped at another set of lights and Faye looked with interest at a large building, shaped a little like an oversized boat, at the corner of the junction.

'What's that building over there?'

'It's the National Theatre. It's quite a large complex that's used for plays, exhibitions and private functions. A friend of my parents had his sixtieth birthday party there last year – Mama said it was really grand.'

The lights changed to green but before she could even put the car into gear, the taxi behind her was hooting impatiently. Sucking her teeth in irritation, she turned right and drove up a busy dual carriageway. A few moments later, she turned into a gravelled entrance with a barrier armed by security guards. After a quick glance into their car, the guards raised the barrier and waved her through to a large car park.

'Wow, I've never seen such a beautiful bank!' Faye looked with admiration at the elegant white building in front of them. From the pretty plum-coloured roof tiles to the elegant columns, the building was an unusual combination of ultra-modern glass and chrome windows and fittings and some of the more traditional Ghanaian buildings she had seen in Accra. A profusion of colourful plants and beautifully landscaped green lawns gave the grounds an atmosphere of serenity not usually associated with the hectic world of finance.

Faye followed Amma up the wide shallow steps leading up to the entrance and past more uniformed guards, one of whom was sitting on a stool, holding a long rifle across his lap. A smiling receptionist wished them a good morning and directed them through to the banking hall.

'They don't really have a lot of walk-in traffic here because they deal with mostly corporate customers,' Amma explained, as they joined a short queue to pay in her mother's cheque. At the counter, the teller swiftly examined the cheque, stamping it and the pay-in book briskly before handing back the book with a polite smile.

'I'll just call Rocky from reception and give him Mama's message before we go,' Amma said.

They walked back to the reception desk where the receptionist obligingly put the call through. Amma took the receiver from her, smiling her thanks, while Faye took a seat and flicked through a newspaper.

'Rocky? Hi, it's me,' Amma said. 'I'm here with Faye – Mama asked us to deposit a cheque for her.' She paused for a moment as he spoke, before continuing.

'Oh, and she said to let you know that she hasn't received her statement this month, so can you chase it up for her?' Another lengthy pause ensued during which Amma listened intently.

'That sounds like a good idea; we were going to go out for lunch anyway. Okay, we'll wait for you here.'

With a smile of pure mischief, she handed the receiver back to the receptionist and went over to sit beside her friend. Faye put down the copy of the *Financial Times* that she had been scanning with little interest and looked at Amma suspiciously.

'What have you been up to? You look like the cat that swallowed the cream.'

'The what...? Oh never mind!' Amma spoke quickly before Faye could interrupt. 'Listen, Rocky said he was on his way out to lunch with Stuart and asked us to join them.' She smiled at Faye slyly. 'I said yes. I hope you don't mind?'

Faye *did* mind but, at the same time, she was so relieved to see Amma looking like her old self again that she didn't have the heart to say so. Besides, a nagging little voice in her head said, *you have to face him sometime so you might as well do it on neutral territory with other people around.*

While they waited for Rocky and Stuart, Faye watched curiously as the bank staff came in and out of the reception area to pick up clients. The female employees were smartly dressed; some wore tailored suits while a number of them were dressed in dark navy skirts and crisp white tops. All the men were in suits and murmured 'good afternoon' as they walked past, one or two of them smiling at Amma and asking after her mother.

'Every time Mama comes here, you should see the way some of the men rush over to help her,' Amma whispered.

'I'm not surprised – she's gorgeous! Uncle Fred is very lucky.'

Just as Faye finished speaking, Rocky and Stuart strode into the reception area, laughing at something Stuart had said. Faye's heart wobbled as she watched Rocky walk towards them, tall and handsome in a charcoal grey suit. *He's so beautiful*, she thought with longing, while schooling her features to appear uninterested. Stuart reached them first and shook hands with her warmly.

'Well, hello Faye,' he said, his eyes twinkling. 'It's nice to see you again.' Turning to Amma, he kissed her on the cheek three times, complimenting her extravagantly on her pretty linen dress. Amma laughed, well used to Stuart's flirtatious ways.

Rocky held out his hand towards Faye. Despite his smile, his expression was wary. 'Peace?' he asked gently, holding onto the hand she reluctantly extended. Mesmerised by his long-lashed eyes, she nodded, and then gave a wry smile.

'Peace,' she said, gently reclaiming her hand.

Amma watched them in satisfaction and then punched her brother lightly on the arm. 'So where are you two taking us, then? We're very hungry, so don't think you can get away with offering us KFC.'

'I think we can do better than that,' Stuart laughed, and gestured to the ladies to lead the way. Conscious of

Rocky's eyes on her tight denim-clad bottom, Faye walked quickly down the steps to the car park.

A sleek Mercedes drew up and a smartly dressed driver stepped out to open the door for them. Faye, Amma and Stuart climbed into the back while Rocky took the front seat.

'This is a seriously cool car,' Faye said, totally blown away by the array of gadgets in the vehicle. She sat back and enjoyed the smooth air-conditioned drive and the chance to see the city through the tinted windows of the luxury car. After about twenty minutes, they drove into the car park of a large hotel with four gold stars emblazoned above the entrance. A uniformed doorman pulled open one of the heavy glass doors as they approached and saluted in welcome.

Feeling a little self-conscious about wearing denims in such a luxurious hotel, Faye unconsciously slowed down causing Rocky, who was walking behind her, to almost run into her. He held her shoulders briefly to steady her and she mumbled a garbled 'Sorry' before shooting off to catch up with Amma. They walked into the hotel restaurant and Faye was struck by the number of smartly dressed men and elegantly attired women occupying the tables. With a pang, she thought of the contrast they presented to the many young people she had seen on the roadside hawking dog chains, batteries and other merchandise.

A waiter showed them to a table and took their order for drinks. Faye asked for a glass of wine, while the others opted for soft drinks and, in Stuart's case, a beer. From where she was sitting, Faye could see the hotel swimming pool and brightly coloured sun loungers and canopies.

'Amma, we should have brought our swimsuits and gone swimming after lunch,' she teased.

'Sooner you than me!' Amma sipped her ginger ale and gave a sigh of contentment. 'If you want to swim, go ahead; I'm quite happy to relax on a lounger and leave the energetic stuff to you.'

Stuart took a long drink of his beer and sighed in satisfaction. 'I just love Ghanaian beer!' He looked at his glass appreciatively before he set it down.

'You just love anything Ghanaian,' Rocky said dryly, causing his boss to chuckle in agreement.

'So, Faye,' Stuart said. 'How are you enjoying your holiday? Baaba tells me you're breaking hearts all over the city.'

Faye choked on her wine. She cleared her throat delicately before trying to speak. 'Baaba is talking rubbish!' she protested. 'I don't know where she got that idea from.'

She didn't dare to look at Rocky. Stuart, on the other hand, showed no such inhibitions. 'Is that not right, Rock old man?' he asked innocently. 'Well, then, I must have got it wrong.'

Amma had cheered up remarkably since leaving the house and was enjoying herself hugely. She waved at an attractive young woman who had finished her meal and was leaving with an older well-dressed man.

'That's Patricia Wilberforce,' she said in a low voice. 'Rocky, do you know her? She was a couple of years ahead of me at University.'

Rocky looked discreetly at the woman in question while Stuart turned himself around to see who Amma was talking about.

'No,' he said finally, 'I don't think I know her – although the man she's with looks familiar.' He turned to Stuart, a crease furrowing his forehead. 'Isn't he one of the guys from that plastics company we were trying to raise finance for last year?'

Stuart peered at the man and shrugged helplessly. 'He could be, Rocky, but I can't remember, to be honest – you know I'm hopeless with faces.'

He winked at the ladies, taking another sip of his drink. 'Not a very good quality for a banker, I can assure you,' he said cheerily. 'That's why Rock here is going places, unlike some of us who are just happy to have a good job, a nice house, a great woman and lots of cold beer!'

He turned to Amma. 'Talking of great women, how's Baaba today? Isn't she just terrific?'

Rocky rolled his eyes in exasperation before suggesting that they walk over to the lunch buffet. The food was set up on a large circular table in the middle of the room and included a wide array of cold meats and salads, as well as a variety of continental and local dishes. Stuart, to no-one's surprise, headed directly for the Ghanaian food and heaped his plate with fluffy white rice and a hot beef and vegetable stew. Amma's appetite had returned with her spirits and she filled her plate happily. Faye, on the other hand, was still feeling jittery around Rocky and settled for some cold cuts and salad before returning to the table. The others were already seated and as soon as she had taken her place, they started to eat.

A loud drawl cut through the contented silence like a knife.

'Rocky, darling, there you are!' Clarissa towered over their table, her long legs shown to their full advantage by a short white lace skirt. Her glossy hair hung straight and cascaded down her bare shoulders and over a fitted pink cropped top with a thin halter strap. Her lips, carefully made up in a matching shade of pink, were curved into a smile, which quickly faded when she recognised Faye.

'Oh, hello,' she said shortly. She flashed a pearly smile at Amma and Stuart, who simply nodded back, his smile disappearing for the first time since they had left the office.

'Darling, I called your office and your secretary said that you and Stuart were on your way here for lunch. Of course, I didn't know that you had company,' she shot a venomous look at Faye, 'so I thought I'd join you.'

Rocky took a sip of his drink before standing up. 'Well, you can see it's not convenient since we're here with Faye and Amma,' he said politely. 'I'll walk you back to your car and maybe we can have lunch another time.'

Clarissa's eyes narrowed angrily and she glared at the other occupants of the table, as if expecting them to protest on her behalf. But Amma, after a brief smile of greeting, had turned her attention back to her food, while Stuart had suddenly taken a great interest in the activities of the people swimming in the hotel pool. Faye simply kept her head down, hoping the other girl would leave.

Ignoring Rocky, who was waiting to see her off, Clarissa looked down at Faye's plate. 'I see you're still having trouble eating our local food,' she commented spitefully. 'Well, it's just as well you live abroad, isn't it? From the looks of things, you wouldn't be able to handle cooking for our men here.' She patted Rocky's cheek affectionately. He stared back at her impassively for a moment before steering her firmly out of the restaurant.

'Poor Rock,' Stuart chuckled, the smile back on his face. 'I wouldn't let her bother you, love,' he said to Faye, his voice suddenly serious. 'She just likes to make a nuisance of herself and muck people about, that's all.'

Suddenly, his face was suffused with colour as he bit into a hot chilli pepper in the stew.

'Bloody hell!' He reached for his beer and took several swallows before loosening his collar and leaning back in his chair, his breathing heavy. Faye and Amma, who had been watching him anxiously, relaxed as his natural colour slowly returned, along with his cheeky grin.

'That was a close call, eh?' he said, clearing his throat loudly. He gestured to a shapely waitress who came over instantly.

'Let me have another beer, love.' His eyes followed her generous backside appreciatively as she walked off to fetch his order.

Baaba's got her hands full with this one, Faye thought, biting back a smile. *Mind you, if anyone could handle him, it would be her.*

Rocky returned and took his seat, calmly finishing his meal before asking the ladies what their plans were for the rest of the day.

'I've got to go to Auntie Amelia's dressmaker's this afternoon to collect the funeral outfit she's making me to take to Ntriso. Apparently, she's more reliable than the lady Amma uses,' Faye said. 'Amma, where does this one live again?'

Amma put down her cutlery and wiped her mouth delicately in satisfaction.

'Hmm? Oh, she lives in Dansoman but her workshop is in Lartebiokoshie. You remember we had to drive through that really busy roundabout when I took you to have your measurements taken?'

Faye shuddered at the memory. 'How can I forget? It was so scary going round that roundabout that I had to keep my eyes closed! To be honest, I can't believe how anyone can drive here.' She tilted her glass and let the last drops of wine fall onto her tongue.

'Tell me about it, love,' Stuart grimaced. 'That's one thing I don't love about Ghana. I crashed two cars before the bank insisted on me using the driver!' He shook his head regretfully for a moment before turning back to Faye.

'Are you looking forward to getting back home again?'

Faye blinked for a moment, unsure of what he meant, until it dawned on her that he was referring to London and not Labone. She sat thoughtfully for a moment and the others looked at her curiously.

Stuart coughed, still suffering from the after-effects of the chilli pepper, and the sound brought her back into the moment.

'Oh, I'm sorry, Stuart,' she smiled in apology. 'I didn't mean to go off into a daydream. It's just that I was trying to think where home was, and for the first time I didn't automatically think of London.'

Stuart nodded sagely. 'I know what you mean, love. When I was in Liverpool last year on a visit, I kept saying 'back home' when I was talking about Ghana. My family didn't have a clue what I was going on about!

'This place can get you like that. My brother came out here earlier this year for a visit and now he's got the bug too,' he chuckled. 'He keeps going on at his company to send him out as their representative in Ghana – it doesn't seem to matter to him that they sell central heating radiators!'

They were still laughing as they left the restaurant and headed back to the car. Once they were back at the bank, Stuart said goodbye and left to prepare for a meeting. Rocky walked them over to Amma's car and held the passenger door open for Faye.

'Since you've forgiven me, how about coming out with me for a drink this evening?' he murmured as she slid as gracefully as she could into the car.

Faye smiled up at him, her eyes sparkling. 'That would be very nice,' she said primly. He laughed and closed her door before leaning through the window.

Looking at his sister, he went on, 'and, before you ask, you and your boyfriend are *not* invited!' She stuck out her tongue at him, then smiled and thanked him for lunch. He waved and stood watching as she manoeuvred her way out of the car park and drove away.

Faye settled back in her seat with a deep, contented sigh. Amma glanced across at her and smiled, amused at the expression of pure bliss on her friend's face.

'*Now* who looks like the cat that got the cat food?' she laughed.

'Cream,' Faye said automatically.

'What?' Amma asked, baffled.

'The cat that got the cream, not cat food – oh never

mind,' Faye said, laughing at the expression of complete incomprehension on Amma's face.

Amma shook her head in resignation. 'I think I'll just stick to the expressions I know. Changing the subject, you're the only person who hasn't given me advice about Edwin and his travel plans. Do *you* also think I'm overreacting?'

'No-o,' Faye said slowly, trying to imagine how she would feel in Amma's shoes. 'I don't think you are. The two of you have been together for a while and you're obviously crazy about each other.' She paused for a moment before continuing. 'But I do think that you need to give him a chance to tell you what he plans to do now and where you fit into it.'

She turned to face Amma. 'That means *talking* to him and not cutting him off when he calls you.'

Amma sighed. She turned into the infamous Obetsebi-Lamptey Circle that took them to Lartebiokoshie and deftly negotiated the stream of tro-tro vans and taxis that sped around the busy roundabout with scant regard for other vehicles.

'I suppose you're right,' she said reluctantly. 'I'll call him when we get home. As you're going out with Rocky tonight, maybe Edwin and I can go for a drink and talk things through.' Having reached a decision, she cheered up again and they spent the rest of the drive laughing at Stuart's antics during lunch.

Miraculously, the dressmaker had actually finished making the funeral cloth and had it ready waiting for collection. Faye quickly tried on the long black skirt and fitted top, twirling round in front of a long mirror with a deep crack running across it. The top was simply tailored and had short puffed sleeves and round black buttons down the front. After satisfying herself that everything fitted properly, the dressmaker folded up the garments and walked with them out to their car.

Back at home, Faye put her new outfit away and wandered down to the living room where Auntie Amelia was sitting on the sofa. Her aunt was engrossed in one of Amma's magazines and she looked up as Faye walked in.

'Hello, my dear. Now just listen to the advice this silly magazine is giving to a young woman who's wondering if she should go to college. "College is a great place to meet men, not to mention picking up a degree."' She threw the magazine aside in outrage. 'No wonder Amma thinks the way she does about Edwin if she reads this kind of nonsense!'

Faye sat cross-legged in the leather armchair and smiled at the expression on the other woman's face.

'I wouldn't worry about Amma, you know. She may be young but she has a lot more sense than many girls I know.' She paused and then added thoughtfully. 'She really loves Edwin, Auntie Amelia, and maybe we should all be a bit more supportive.'

The older woman stared at her for a moment and then shook her head.

'You are so much like Annie,' she said. She sighed deeply with a shrug of resignation. 'You may be right, Faye. After all, I wasn't much older than she is now when I knew Fred was the man I wanted to marry.'

She glanced at Faye mischievously. 'So what about you then, Missy? Do you know who you want to marry or are you still searching for the right man?'

Faye laughed at the skilful way the subject of the conversation had been twisted.

'Now you sound just like Mrs Debrah! No, I'm still looking,' she added firmly.

Auntie Amelia looked sceptical for a moment, but held her peace. Standing up, she handed the offending magazine back to Faye.

'I need to go and see to dinner, so I'll leave this for you,' she said. 'Are you girls in tonight or is it just us old people?'

'Rocky is taking me out for a drink and I think Amma's out with Edwin. I wouldn't bother with dinner for us; we both had a big lunch.'

It was almost seven o'clock when Rocky returned from the office. He strolled through to the living room, loosening his tie. Amma was upstairs getting ready to meet Edwin while Faye was still on the sofa, engrossed in the glossy magazine.

She looked up with a guilty smile. Not wanting to be caught reading the 'How Compatible are You and Your Man?' quiz, she quickly clasped the magazine to her chest.

'Hi,' she said brightly. He smiled back, gently extracting the magazine from her hands. Scanning the title, he looked down at her.

'So, what do you think?' A mischievous smile crooked his lips. 'Are we?'

Confused and feeling at a disadvantage as he towered above her, Faye uncrossed her legs and stood up.

'What time do you want us to leave?' She ignored his question and tried to sound casual. He didn't press the point, although his smile showed that he was well aware of her attempt to duck the question.

'I'd like to take a shower first.' He glanced at his watch. 'Why don't we meet down here in an hour – is that okay?'

'That's fine,' she said. Seizing the magazine, she brushed past him and ran upstairs before he could ask any more awkward questions. Walking down the corridor, she stopped as Amma came out of her room. Dressed in black trousers and a fitted royal blue top with a ruffle running diagonally down the front, she had tied her long braids back and had a silver clutch purse clamped under her arm.

'You look very nice.' Faye nodded in approval. 'Now remember, just give him a chance to speak, okay?'

'Yes, mother,' she replied dutifully and with a weak smile. 'I can't believe I'm nervous about meeting *Edwin*. I'd better get going. Have a nice evening – and tell me everything tomorrow.'

Faye left her and went to her room where she had a leisurely shower before padding through her depleted wardrobe in search of something to wear. After trying on countless different combinations, she settled on her narrow black cropped trousers and a short-sleeved, pale-gold mandarin-style jacket.

Realising with a shock that it was already ten to eight, she quickly applied some eyeliner and dusted her eyelids with translucent gold eye shadow. After carefully applying some bronze lipstick, she thrust the tube into her purse and brushed her hair vigorously before going downstairs.

Rocky was waiting in the living room and stood up as soon as she came through the door. His parents were watching a current affairs debate on TV and looked up as she walked in.

'That's a beautiful outfit, Faye,' Auntie Amelia exclaimed. 'I must say, I wish I was a young girl again. There are so many nice fashions around today.'

Rocky leant over and kissed his mother affectionately on her cheek. 'Ma, you always look beautiful, no matter what you wear. The guys at work seem to lose the power of speech whenever you go there.'

'You see, my dear?' his father interjected innocently. 'That's why I don't talk much – one look at you and I'm struck dumb.'

Auntie Amelia slapped her husband's arm in protest while Faye and Rocky laughed at Uncle Fred's attempts to look serious. He winked at his son and gestured towards Faye. 'I don't think you will say much this evening either, son, from the look of our own supermodel here.'

'No, Dad,' Rocky agreed in a solemn voice. 'I have a strong feeling I'm about to be struck dumb.'

As his father chuckled appreciatively, Rocky gently steered Faye out of the room, calling goodnight to his parents. Grabbing his car keys from the table in the hallway, he led the way out to his car. He opened the passenger door for Faye and she snuggled into the luxurious leather seat, sliding the seat belt smoothly into the chrome holder. Even the click of the seatbelt sounds rich, she thought dreamily.

Rocky headed the powerful car down the dual carriageway and Faye sighed with satisfaction, comparing the drive in this sleek, high-suspension machine with the bumpy rides in the rickety taxis she had been using over the past few days.

Rocky glanced across at her in the shadowy light of the car and grinned at the wide smile on her face.

'What are you thinking about?' he asked in amusement.

She looked at his handsome profile and laughed self-consciously. 'I was just thinking that this makes such a nice change from the taxis I've been travelling around in.'

He smiled at her candour. 'Well, it's nice to have you in it at last. I thought we might go to one of my favourite places,' he went on. 'It's a private jazz club not too far from here.'

A few minutes later he drove into a large courtyard where a number of cars were parked. Switching off the engine, he climbed out and came round to open her door. Faye smiled inwardly as she remembered Michael's lectures on how opening a door for women was an affront to their struggle to attain their rights. Smiling in gratitude for the affront, she slid out of the car and walked with Rocky into the club.

As they went in, a tall, slim woman wearing a long black dress and with a black turban wound around her head glided over.

'Rocky! We haven't seen you for a while.' Her voice was warm and husky; she kissed him lightly on both cheeks and then turned to Faye with a wide smile.

'Welcome! I'm Marcia – the manager of the Jazz Hut.' Her accent was unmistakably American and Faye returned the smile and introduced herself.

Marcia ushered them over to a small table in an alcove where they had a good view of the band playing on the small stage. After making sure they were comfortably seated, she gestured to one of the waiters to come and serve them before wishing them a pleasant evening and gliding off to greet some new arrivals.

When the waiter arrived, Faye ordered a glass of white wine while Rocky opted for a beer. She looked around the club admiring the 1930s Harlem jazz joint décor. Framed black and white prints of black jazz musicians and singers adorned the walls. The bar extended across an entire wall of the club and was manned by three waiters. A few patrons perched on leather and chrome bar stools and sipped on their drinks while they listened to the band play.

The waiter had just served their drinks when a tall lanky man in his thirties with an untidy goatee beard came up to their table. He stared at Faye in open admiration and patted Rocky's shoulder in greeting.

'Long time, no see, my man!'

Rocky leaned back in his chair and looked up at him, a resigned smile on his face. 'Hello Nii, how are you?'

If the man noticed the lack of warmth in Rocky's greeting, it didn't appear to bother him. He looked around, seized a chair from an adjoining table and sat down next to Faye before anyone could speak.

'So who is this beautiful woman?' he asked with a wolfish smile as he set his drink down on their table. Rocky frowned for a moment before introducing her. 'Faye, this is Nii. He's married to my cousin, Serwah, for her sins.'

She smiled and shook Nii's hand, tugging her own

away when he appeared unwilling to release it.

'Hey, Rocky, you always seem to find the pretty ones,' Nii remarked, stroking his goatee. 'What happened to that model I used to see you around with?'

'How are Serwah and the boys?' Rocky countered, taking a long swallow of his beer. 'I haven't seen them for a while.'

'They're all fine,' Nii said airily with an indifferent shrug. Turning to Faye again, he grinned broadly, baring strong white teeth.

'So where are you from, pretty lady?' he asked. Rocky sighed with a mixture of impatience and irritation and was about to speak when a young girl marched up to their table, a sulky expression marring her pretty features.

'Nii, you just walked off and left me by myself!' She glared angrily at him and Faye's lips twitched with suppressed laughter. Rocky, on the other hand, looked thunderous.

Nii sighed. He stood up and put a placatory arm around the young girl's slim shoulders. He took one look at Rocky's face and prudently made no attempt at introductions. Instead, he contented himself with a weak smile at Faye and a casual farewell before steering the girl away.

Rocky exhaled loudly, shaking his head more in sorrow than anger as he watched Nii walking off, his head close to the girl's ear and talking swiftly as he tried to pacify her.

'The longer you stay in this town, the more you'll come across characters like him.' Rocky's eyes were still on Nii. 'He has a beautiful wife and two sons and yet he spends most of his time hanging around nightclubs or the university campus preying on young impressionable girls.'

'She doesn't look too impressionable to me,' Faye laughed, looking pointedly over to where the girl was clearly haranguing a sheepish Nii.

Rocky laughed reluctantly. 'Serves him right,' he said. Turning back to Faye, he leaned forward and took her hand.

'Forget about him. Let's talk about you,' he said. She gazed back at him happily, feeling as though she had just stepped into a warm perfumed bath after coming in from the cold.

True to his word, Rocky did nothing but listen to her, prompting her with questions from time to time, as though determined to learn everything there was to know about her. They talked late into the evening, oblivious to the comings and goings of club members, the occasional intrusion by the waiter and curious glances from Marcia.

'Okay, now I've told you everything about me except my shoe size,' she said. 'It's your turn to answer my questions.'

Rocky laughed and nodded slowly. 'Okay. That sounds fair. Although I warn you, you might not like the answers,' he teased.

'Okay, first question. What do you want right now, more than anything?' She asked the question with a part of her hoping that he would give the answer she wanted.

He replied without hesitation. 'The international promotion I've been working for.'

It wasn't the answer she had hoped for, but she carried on gamely.

'Apart from your promotion, what do you really want?' she persisted.

This time he paused and thought for a long moment. 'I think I have everything I want,' he said slowly. 'Except maybe the new squash racquet I saw in town last week.' He looked at the downcast expression on her face and burst into laughter.

'Faye, you are so—' He broke off in the middle of his sentence, groaning as he saw Nii approaching their table. Now relieved of his teenaged burden, he was heading towards them, his eyes fixed purposefully on Faye.

'I don't think I can stand another minute of that guy,' Rocky said softly. 'Let's go.'

Faye, who had been feeling increasingly uneasy with each step Nii took towards her, nodded in agreement and quickly picked up her evening bag. She stood up just as he reached them.

'Oh, pretty lady, are you off so soon?' His face fell in disappointment as she smiled and bid him a brief farewell before walking quickly in the direction of the door. Rocky walked alongside her, stopping at the bar to pay their bill before guiding her out into the warm night.

Safely inside the car, they burst into laughter as he gunned the car engine and drove rapidly out of the car park.

'Did you see his face?' Faye gasped with laughter. 'He looked like someone had snatched his food away just as he was about to eat!'

Rocky glanced across at her, smiling at her amusement. 'Talking of food, are you hungry? You haven't eaten anything since lunch.'

Touched by his concern, she nodded. 'Actually, I wouldn't

mind something to eat – oh, Rocky, look!' She pointed excitedly through the window at a woman sitting in front of a coal pot heaped with burning coals. On top of the fire was a huge frying pan. Rocky, who had automatically slowed down, pulled over to the side of the road.

'I was about to offer you a decent meal and you want *kelewele*?' He shook his head in mock sorrow.

'Please, I *love* it!' Sighing in defeat, Rocky slipped off his seat belt and walked across to where the woman was stationed. A few minutes later he was back with a newspaper-wrapped parcel giving off the sweet spicy aroma of hot fried plantain. Faye beamed at him and held onto the parcel as he drove them home, inhaling the appetising scent of ginger, spices and hot chilli.

As soon as they drove through the gates, she jumped out of the car and raced into the kitchen. Emptying the contents of the parcel onto a plate, she sat down at the kitchen table, contentedly munching the delicious pieces of sweet plantain. Rocky came in and sat at the table watching in disbelief as she steadily ate her way through the large portion of food.

When she finally stopped eating, he leaned across and gently brushed an errant crumb from the corner of her mouth. 'I wouldn't have believed it if I hadn't seen it with my own eyes,' he said looking at her in fascination.

Feeling more than a little ashamed at her display of greed, Faye gave a sheepish smile. 'Sorry, I didn't even ask if you wanted some.' She bit her lower lip and looked at him apologetically.

Reaching for a lock of her hair, he pulled her face close

to his. 'Don't worry about it, this is what I want,' he said in a low voice. Brushing her lips softly with his own, he kissed her lightly. Tugging gently, he pulled her even closer as the kiss deepened. She reached for him, caressing his strong jaw with her hand as she felt a passion she had never experienced before flood through her. Rocky kicked his chair away and slid his hand behind her waist, standing up with her in one fluid movement. She gasped but didn't break away as she felt his warm hand stroking her bare back.

The sound of the front door slamming caused them both to freeze for a split second before jumping apart. Faye was breathing so hard she could have been running and Rocky, for once, had lost his composure and looked dazed. They jumped again as the kitchen door burst open. Amma stood in the doorway; she looked tearful but had a broad grin on her face.

Faye moved forward in concern but Amma held up her hand to stop her. Her voice was shaking and more breathless than ever.

'Edwin's just asked me to marry him!'

15

Spiritual Culture

The bus bounced along the tarmac road, speeding through miles of green bush and forest. The air conditioning didn't quite succeed in masking the scent of the dried fish the woman in the seat behind her had packed tightly into the basket on her lap and Faye shifted slightly in her seat, hoping to move out of the path of the strong aroma. When that didn't work, she adjusted the knob above her head that directed the flow of the cold air and sighed with relief as the fishy vapours cleared.

Auntie Akosua, seated beside her, smiled sympathetically. Although not directly in the line of fire, she had picked up the occasional whiff from the basket and could well imagine Faye's discomfort.

'We've only got about another hour to go before we reach Kumasi,' she whispered consolingly.

The bus swerved violently as a car that had been overtaking them was forced to cut in front of them when another vehicle unexpectedly appeared in the oncoming lane. The passengers exclaimed loudly while Faye saw her life flashing before her eyes.

After shouting insinuations about the other driver's mother through the window, the bus driver calmed down and went back to listening to his radio, muttering quietly to himself.

'Honestly, the driving in this country is crazy,' Faye said in exasperation. 'Why can't people just follow the rules?'

Auntie Akosua, who had been crossing herself vigorously at their narrow escape, shook her head in resignation. 'Too many people get behind the wheel without learning how to drive properly,' she said. 'Unfortunately, our police force is so under-equipped, they can rarely enforce traffic rules, and some of them are only too happy to look the other way in return for a quick bribe.'

'We've driven past two car crashes so far on this journey alone,' Faye shuddered. 'It makes you wonder how many people are getting hurt all the time.'

'Unfortunately, road accidents are all too common.' She leant back into the cushioned seat and smiled at Faye. 'But let's talk about more pleasant things, my dear. How is Amma? Amelia told me her news when we spoke on the phone yesterday. She must be very excited.'

Faye sighed, remembering how impossible Amma had been to live with since Wednesday night. '*Excited* is not the word, Auntie Akosua,' she grimaced. 'She's completely lost her mind. You can't get a sensible word out of the girl. She's either dancing around hugging and kissing everyone or she's crying her eyes out because she can't stand the thought of a whole year without Edwin!'

The older woman laughed heartily. 'Well, that's love for you! I must say it's nice to see you young ones starting out on your lives together – it reminds me of how exciting it once was for us oldies.'

'You're not old,' Faye protested, looking at the still-unlined attractive face beside her. She tried, and failed, to contain her curiosity. 'How did you and Uncle Charlie meet?'

'Oh my goodness,' Auntie Akosua exclaimed. 'It all seems so long ago. Let me see – we were at University together and both of us were passionate about politics. We were members of the Debating Society and ended up having heated arguments every time we attended meetings.'

She paused, her eyes half closed as she cast her mind back. She smiled and went on.

'On one occasion, the President of the Debating Society was so fed up with our constant arguing that he ordered us to go to the students' cafeteria and stay there until we had finished. I think we even argued about which table to sit at to finish arguing!'

'I used to suffer terribly from migraines, which was probably not surprising given how much time I spent getting fired up about politics. Anyway, that day as we were talking, I felt a migraine coming on. Charlie was busy making his point about something or other when he noticed that I had gone quiet and looked unwell. I think he was so shocked that I was actually human that he didn't quite know how to react! He walked me back to my hall of residence and made sure there was someone to take care of me before he left. When he came back later that evening, I was still feeling weak, so for once we actually talked instead of arguing – and that was how our friendship began.'

'That's a beautiful story,' Faye sighed wistfully. 'I love happy endings.'

She sniffed and quickly adjusted the air vent above her head before settling back into her seat.

They had been on the road for over three hours and Faye was beginning to feel the effects of her early start. For once she had beaten the neighbourhood rooster to the punch, setting her alarm to go off at four-thirty. Auntie Akosua had arrived at five-thirty to collect her, with Uncle Charlie looking distinctly drowsy in the driver's seat. After dropping them at the State Transport terminal where they were to board the six o'clock bus to Kumasi, he had driven back home to catch up on his interrupted sleep.

Despite the early hour, the Transport yard was busy with anxious travellers milling around the departure areas. Huge sacks of foodstuffs and heavy bags were strewn around the bus terminal, many with their owners perched on top, waiting for the buses to start loading. Their bus, which had left only slightly late, was clean and comfortable except, of course, for the aroma of dried fish wafting over her seat.

After a couple of hours on the road, they had stopped at a wayside cafe in the town of Nkawkaw where most of the passengers had rushed off in search of the washrooms and facilities. A quick glance at the food in the cafe – anaemic-looking egg and sardine sandwiches and huge meat pies encased in dense pastry – was enough for Faye, and she settled for a soft drink and a sweet bread roll.

After a short break they had set off again, driving through miles and miles of unspoiled virgin land and forest. The road undulated through the hilly landscape like a curling ribbon of tarmac peppered with huge potholes, causing cars to swerve without warning into the oncoming lane. Impatient drivers, anxious to reach their destination, would often overtake slower vehicles in their paths, careless of the dangers of oncoming vehicles. Faye kept her focus on the passing landscape, fascinated by the many small villages they drove through.

Now, with less than an hour before they were due to arrive in Kumasi, where they would be met and driven to Ntriso, Faye felt her lack of sleep catching up with her. She glanced across at Auntie Akosua whose closed eyes and steady breathing indicated that she had nodded off. Faye burrowed into her seat and drifted off to sleep, oblivious even to the aroma of smoked fish.

Auntie Akosua's hand shaking her shoulder roused her from a dreamless sleep. Rubbing her eyes, she peered out of the window. Instead of green bush and tall trees, the landscape was now distinctly urban. Large buildings covered in a layer of red dust lined the dual carriageway on which they drove. The signboards welcomed them to Kumasi and pedestrians dodged in and out of the heavy traffic.

'So this is the famous Garden City,' Faye murmured, looking at the drooping vegetation lining the highway.

'It's certainly not looking its best these days,' Auntie Akosua said. 'It's a pity because, as the capital of the Ashanti region, Kumasi is a city that is rich in ancient history, culture and tradition.'

She gestured to their left. 'If you follow that road, it takes you to Manhyia Palace, the residence of the Asantehene, the King of the Ashantis. Kumasi used to be such a beautiful city; when we were younger, it was always an adventure to come here. These days, people seem to just build anywhere they wish, the traffic is terrible and so much of the city's infrastructure is a mess. Look over there.' Leaning across Faye, she pointed towards a group of people walking slowly down the main road. They were all clad in traditional cloths of black and red and the women wore black headscarves.

'Funerals are quite commonplace at the weekend in Kumasi,' Auntie Akosua said. 'You're likely to see a good number of people dressed in mourning clothes.'

She glanced at her watch. 'My younger brother, Kodjo, will meet us at the transport yard in Kumasi and drive us on to Ntriso. It's about another forty minutes drive – once we get out of the Kumasi traffic, that is.'

They drove through the slow moving traffic, eventually arriving at the bus terminus. The passengers piled off, elbowing each other in a bid to retrieve their luggage first from the cavernous hold of the dusty bus. Auntie Akosua held her ground and soon returned to where Faye was standing, clutching both their bags triumphantly.

'Sister Akosua, I'm here!' Both women turned around at the sound of a male voice behind them. Faye looked on as Auntie Akosua gave a loud cry and embraced the short, wiry man who had just appeared. He hugged her warmly before stepping away and smiling at Faye, his teeth as strong and white as his sister's.

'Kodjo, meet Faye Bonsu.' Auntie Akosua smiled as she watched him look at Faye appraisingly. 'Does she remind you of anyone?'

Faye stood awkwardly as the older man scrutinised her features for a few moments and nodded slowly. 'She reminds me very much of Sister Asantewaa,' he said finally. 'Is this her child?'

Faye nodded, feeling a sudden lump in her throat. It felt so strange to hear someone referring so casually to her mother, as if Annie Asantewaa Boateng had not died almost twenty years before.

Auntie Akosua hugged her gently before turning to her brother and handing over their bags. 'Kodjo, it's been a long journey. Let's get going so we can reach Ntriso quickly and get some rest.'

Her brother nodded in understanding and quickly relieved her of the bags. Leading the way, he walked quickly to a dusty double-cabin pick-up truck parked outside the bus terminus. After stowing the bags inside, he helped Faye into the back seat before giving his sister a gentle push up into the front seat beside him. He then climbed into the driver's seat, which, Faye noted with amusement had been padded with a cushion to give him a few critical inches of visibility, and gunned the engine into life.

They drove out of Kumasi with their sturdy pick-up rattling comfortably along the bumpy roads. Once out of the city, they passed through small villages, many appearing to be no bigger than a scattering of houses on either side of the road. Uncle Kodjo waved and shouted greetings several times, honking amiably at young children playing near the roadside and, less patiently, at the goats and chickens that seemed bent on crossing the road just as they approached.

'Many of these villagers are artisans who weave traditional cloths and make handicrafts and wooden carvings,' Uncle Kodjo said, looking over his shoulder to where Faye sat behind him. 'I work with some of them to market their crafts and help them with selling their products into the larger cities and tourist areas.'

Faye watched the passing scenery, fascinated at the difference between this side of Ghana and the slick sophistication she had grown used to experiencing in the city. Uncle Kodjo explained that some of the villages had not yet been connected to the national grid and did not have electricity. For these people, he said, life had changed very little over the years and modern inventions and labour-saving devices had yet to make their mark.

Almost an hour later, they drove past a signboard bearing the single word 'Ntriso' and Faye sat up in excitement. What had just been a name to her, up until now, was about to become a reality.

'Are we there yet?' she asked, as Uncle Kodjo carefully navigated the truck up a long winding hilly road. She had barely finished uttering the words when several houses came into view. As they reached the crest of the hill, she could see brightly painted houses and shops in what was clearly a busy town. They drove down the main street to a small roundabout where they branched left and down a narrow road that led to a large house with dusty blue walls. Uncle Kodjo parked the truck and jumped down to open the back door for Faye before hoisting out their travel bags.

To one side of the house was a large strip of land, which, he explained, was the neighbourhood football pitch. Today, however, rows of plastic chairs sheltering under large green canopies had taken over the space normally used by the local Michael Essien wannabes. Some of the seats were occupied by elderly people clad in funereal black and red cloth, chatting quietly among themselves. A few children ran around, weaving in and out of the chairs and calling out to each other in excitement.

'Faye, welcome to our family house,' Auntie Akosua said. 'It's been a long day; let's go in and freshen up.' She walked into the house and Faye followed, barely able to contain her rising excitement at finally seeing her home town.

Inside, the house was dark with a slightly musty smell. The living room furniture was of solid brown mahogany, with faded white lace antimacassars draped over brown velvet cushions. Dark-brown curtains contributed to the somewhat oppressive atmosphere.

Auntie Akosua grimaced at she looked around the room and wrinkled her nose in distaste. 'You can tell Kodjo is hardly ever around; this place looks barely lived in.'

'Who else lives here?' Faye walked over to an ancient-looking wooden cabinet sitting on squat curved legs, to take a closer look at the faded black and white framed photograph perched on top. The picture was of a couple on their wedding day. The woman stared straight into the camera with a forced smile that didn't quite reach her eyes, while her groom, slightly shorter, held her hand possessively and beamed with pride.

'That picture of my parents was taken on their wedding day,' Auntie Akosua said, looking over Faye's shoulder. 'I've always thought that my mother looked like a very reluctant bride, although she always denied that was the case. Kodjo lives here with his son, Solomon, a couple of our elderly aunts, and the uncle who just passed away. But as they tend to stay in their rooms or sit outside, much of the house is unused. My parents died many years ago and these are our closest remaining relatives.'

Faye gently replaced the photograph and followed Auntie Akosua up a flight of wide, slightly creaky stairs into a huge bedroom.

'This will be your room,' the older woman said, pulling back a pair of heavy dark green curtains from the windows. 'It was my parents' room but we keep it for visitors now.'

Faye's bag had already been deposited by the bed. Auntie Akosua walked her through to a small adjoining bathroom. 'I'm afraid that these days we rarely have running water like we used to in the past.' She smiled apologetically. 'Solomon will fetch some more water for you from the reservoir outside when you're ready for a bath. There's enough here for you to freshen up, so I'll leave you in peace to rest for a while.'

Left to her own devices, Faye sat on the bed for a few minutes, gazing around the almost cavernous room. A larger version of the wedding picture she had seen downstairs hung on the wall opposite the bed. Auntie Akosua's mother's smile looked even more pained than in the smaller print and Faye felt a pang of sympathy for her.

How awful to get married when you feel like that about it, she thought. Surely you shouldn't have to force a smile on your wedding day of all days. Lying back on the bed, she drifted off to sleep. Lost in her dreams, she pictured herself smiling widely and waving to friends and family as she floated down the aisle in a beautiful white dress. She saw herself turning towards her soon-to-be husband and seeing Rocky smiling back at her.

She woke abruptly and lay still for a few minutes trying to remember where she was and to forget what she had been dreaming about. Shaking herself abruptly, she jumped off the bed and went into the bathroom to wash her face and hands, shivering slightly as the cool water cascaded over her heated skin.

You must be crazy, Faye! She scrubbed her cheeks vigorously with a soft perfumed soap. *A couple of kisses and you're already planning the wedding!*

Returning to the bedroom, she decided that her jeans were still clean enough to pass but changed her top for a black T-shirt before heading downstairs. The house was quiet and her footsteps echoed on the wooden stairs as she walked down. Anxious to leave the rather oppressive atmosphere of the old house, she walked out into the sunlight, almost tripping over a barefoot toddler wearing nothing but an extremely dirty pair of shorts. She walked towards Uncle Kodjo who was sitting on one of the chairs chatting to an elderly man in a black and red funeral cloth.

They both looked up as she approached and the younger man patted the empty seat beside him.

'Come and sit down, Faye,' he said with a warm smile.

He turned to the older man. 'This is our friend, Faye,' he said by way of introduction. 'She came today with Akosua to help us mourn Uncle Ofosu.'

The older man said something in his own language and Uncle Kodjo shook his head before replying in English. 'No, she was brought up in England and I don't think she speaks *Twi*.' He raised an eyebrow enquiringly at Faye as he spoke and she shook her head in apology.

The elderly man looked hard at Faye; his dark eyes twinkled beneath bushy grey brows. Then he spoke in perfect English. 'Welcome to Ntriso.' His voice was strong and surprisingly deep. 'On behalf of the Obeng family, let me thank you for coming to mourn with them.'

Faye smiled at him, a little unsure how to deal with such formality. Then, finding her voice, she answered shyly. 'I wanted to come very much. This is where my mother was born and grew up and it means a great deal to me to be able to visit and see it for myself.'

The man looked at Faye for a long time before turning to Uncle Kodjo, a questioning look on his face. The other man smiled broadly, his strong teeth sparkling white against his dark skin.

'You see the resemblance now?'

Without responding to the question, the old man raised his right hand slowly and touched Faye's cheek. Murmuring quietly to himself in his language, he shook his head in wonder.

'Asantewaa's girl,' he said finally. 'Asantewaa's girl has come back to us, God be praised!'

Faye looked at him in amazement. Auntie Akosua,

she knew, had been a close friend of her mother's, which would account for how Uncle Kodjo had recognised her. Even though Ntriso was a small town, she was completely baffled as to how this man would know who she was.

Her confusion was clear and Uncle Kodjo intervened. 'He is your great-uncle, Faye,' he said softly, gesturing towards the older man whose eyes had suddenly become moist. 'He's your grandfather's younger brother.'

He looked sheepish as the older man glared at him. 'I wanted him to see you before I told him who you were. I should have known he wouldn't be fooled.'

Faye stared at her newly discovered relative with interest. 'What do I call you?' she asked finally. He smiled and rearranged his cloth before answering.

'I am your *nana*,' he said firmly. 'Your grandfather, in effect, as he has now passed away.'

'Wow, I didn't know I still have a grandfather. William will never believe this. That's my brother,' she added disjointedly. 'He's in London.'

Nana nodded, a wry smile appearing on his face. 'Now I have seen one of my absent grandchildren, I hope he will also come to Ntriso so that I can know him before I die. Kodjo will bring you to our family house so you can greet your relatives before you leave.'

Faye nodded and the old man stood up to take his leave. 'We'll come over soon, Nana,' she assured him. Standing up, she watched him walk away, his tall frame stooping slightly. Uncle Kodjo accompanied him a little way down the road and returned after a few minutes, rubbing his hands cheerfully.

'That was wonderful!' he said with a cheeky and completely unrepentant smile. 'Now, let's go inside and see what we can offer you to eat.'

His cheerfulness was contagious and she grinned and followed him back into the house. He went directly to a spacious kitchen where an ancient gas cooker dominated one end of the room. Several saucepans were ranged on the hob.

'What do we have here? Ah, fried fish, and here some jollof rice and here some kontomire.' As he ran through his commentary, he raised the lid of each pot. 'And here we have some nicely boiled yam. What do you fancy?'

Just then Auntie Akosua walked into the kitchen. She stifled a yawn and headed to one of the cupboards to take out some plates.

'Kodjo, have the old ladies eaten yet?' She looked enquiringly at her brother before closing the cupboard.

Uncle Kodjo nodded in amusement. 'They said they were too distraught by Uncle Ofosu's death to eat, so they only managed to get through two helpings each of fried fish and *kenkey*.'

Auntie Akosua laughed and set three plates out on the wooden kitchen table, adding some rather worn silver cutlery.

'Faye, what would you like to eat?' she asked, moving towards the cooker. 'Will you have some kontomire? It's been made with some very nice fish and pigfoot.'

Faye instinctively shook her head. Although she was hungry, she would have preferred starvation to the rubbery pink meat.

'I'd prefer the jollof rice, if that's okay.' At Auntie

Akosua's urging, she sat down and tucked into the spicy rice cooked with tender vegetables and the delicately flavoured fried fish that accompanied it.

'So is there anything planned for this evening?' Faye looked around the gloomy kitchen doubtfully. Auntie Akosua and Uncle Kodjo exchanged looks and Uncle Kodjo spoke first. 'Why don't we go over to your family house so you can greet your Nana and meet your family?'

Her face lit up. 'That sounds great. I can't wait to see what they're like.'

Auntie Akosua stood up and stacked the dirty plates. She carried them over to a large enamel sink and washed them quickly using a wiry sponge. Rinsing the plates with water from a large jug, she stacked them in the draining tray and wiped her hands on a tea towel.

'I'll take you there.' She threw her brother a mischievous look. 'Kodjo can stay and greet the mourners who come over this evening.'

Dusk was falling as they walked down the road towards the roundabout. Arms linked, they headed east in the direction of the Boateng family house. As they walked, Auntie Akosua described the local sights.

'Over there is the primary school.' She pointed in the direction of a large building with a concrete roof. 'In our day it was run by the Catholic Church and the teachers were very strict.'

'And over there, just behind the school, is the church,' she went on. 'That building over there is the post office – awful isn't it?' For a few minutes they walked along past shops that were now closed, large padlocks securing their front doors. Occasionally they would pass a group of mourners returning from a funeral or see people sitting outside their houses listening to the radio or engaged in intense debate. The sound of a crying child drifted over to them as they strolled along, and a frisky dog sniffed around them, in search of food or a friendly pat.

Auntie Akosua stopped and pointed down a side road. 'You see that house over there – the one with the white roof?'

Dusk was falling but Faye was still able to make out the house in question. 'Yes, is it another famous landmark?'

Auntie Akosua grinned cheekily and Faye could imagine just how she must have looked when she was a schoolgirl. 'I suppose you could call it that. That's where Paul Adjaye lived. He was your mother's first love; she had a huge crush on him when we were growing up and she used to make me walk with her past that house every day after school just to catch a glimpse of him going inside.'

'Did he like her too?' Faye was tickled at this new perspective on her mother.

'Paul?' Auntie Akosua collapsed into giggles. 'He was absolutely terrified of Annie; he was quite shy and she, on the other hand, was completely fearless and terribly outspoken, not to mention the crazy clothes she liked to wear! The nuns were always chastising her for the way she dressed.'

Faye laughed as she pictured her determined mother stalking the terrified object of her affection. Auntie Akosua stopped in front of a big two-storey house. The house was painted a pale shade of pink and colourful potted plants poked out through the railings of the first floor veranda.

'Here we are,' Auntie Akosua announced. 'Welcome home.'

Faye stood for a moment gazing up at the house, trying to comprehend that this was where her mother had been born and had grown up. A figure leaned over the balcony and called out something in *Twi*.

'Paapa, it is me, Akosua,' the older woman said loudly. 'I have brought your granddaughter to visit you.'

'Oh, good!' This time it was Nana's voice that came wafting down. 'You are welcome. Come up, come up!'

Auntie Akosua propelled Faye forward with a gentle nudge and they walked round to the side of the house and climbed the steps leading up to the veranda.

'*Akwaaba*, my granddaughter. Welcome to your home.' Nana stood up and walked across to meet them, taking Faye's hand between his own rather frail ones. 'I am very happy that you have been able to come home.'

He turned to the older woman and shook her hand. 'Akosua, welcome home,' he said. 'I came to pay my respects earlier but Kodjo told me you were resting. Please, be seated.' He gestured towards a wooden bench covered with faded brown cushions. A tall figure had been standing in the shadows by the railings and he came forward to greet them.

'Good evening, Auntie Akosua.' The man was in his early thirties and Faye gaped at him, wondering for one incredible moment what William was doing here in Ntriso.

He turned to shake her hand and she realised that although his build and even the tone of his voice was almost exactly like her brother's, this man had a full head of hair and a closely cropped beard.

'Sister Faye, welcome to Ntriso.'

If I closed my eyes, I could swear that it was William speaking, Faye thought. Nana made the introductions. 'This is your cousin Joshua. He's also called Nana Osei and he's my oldest grandson,' he said. 'I say "cousin" because we are speaking in English, but you know that in *Twi*, there is no such word. In our language, the only word for your relationship is "brother". So, meet your brother. Nana Osei, greet your sister.'

Joshua had taken a seat next to them as his grandfather was speaking. Following his instructions, he stood up again and shook Faye's hand a second time, his smile warm and friendly.

'I am very glad to meet you, my sister.'

'I am glad to meet you too, Nana Osei.' Faye grinned at him. 'You really are my brother – you look *exactly* like my older brother William. It's amazing!'

The ice broken, Nana called out for refreshments for the women. A few minutes later a teenage girl with short hair walked out onto the veranda carrying a tray of glasses and a large bottle of iced water. She smiled shyly at Faye and Auntie Akosua and greeted them before putting the tray down and pouring out two tall glasses of cold water. She held the tray out in front of them and they each took a glass.

Nana Osei beckoned her over and she moved to stand by his side. 'Faye, this is my youngest sister, Yaa. She came with me so we could spend a few days with our grandfather while she is on her school break.' Turning to his sister, he pushed her gently in Faye's direction.

'Yaa, greet your big sister from London,' he said encouragingly. Yaa walked across to Faye and shook her hand, accompanying the gesture with a little bob.

'Nana Osei, how many brothers and sisters do you have?' Faye was curious to know more about her newly discovered extended family. Having relatively few surviving relatives himself, her father had been notoriously vague on the subject of his wife's family.

'I have three sisters and a brother,' her cousin answered with a grin. 'They all live with my parents in Koforidua, which is in the Eastern Region of Ghana. I teach at a secondary school in Winneba.'

'Yaa, go to my room and bring me the photo albums on my table,' Nana said. 'Let your sister see what the rest of the family looks like.'

The younger girl scurried off and quickly returned with several well-thumbed photo albums that she handed over to her grandfather. He flipped through the first one before gesturing to Faye to come over. She sat beside him as he leafed through the album, pointing out his children and grandchildren.

While the other family members didn't bear the same striking resemblance to the Bonsu branch as Nana Osei, most of them seemed to share the same tall lean frame of Faye and her brother. Before he opened the last album, Nana looked at her appraisingly and a small smile hovered on his lips.

'I think you will find this album very interesting,' he said. The first picture was an old black and white print of a chubby baby sprawled on a white cloth and wearing nothing but a smile. Instead of his usual commentary, Nana was silent. Faye looked at him enquiringly.

'Whose baby is this?'

'Your grandfather's,' Nana replied simply. For a moment Faye was confused and as the meaning of his answer dawned on her, all she could say was 'Oh!' She stared in amazement at the first picture she had ever seen of her mother as a baby. After a few moments, Nana turned the page and she gasped again. This time, the identity of the young girl posing beside a flowering bush was in no doubt. The almond-shaped eyes and high cheekbones could have been hers, as could the long slim legs encased in a pair of fitted slacks.

'Wow, I really do look like her!' Faye stared in wonder. 'How old was she when this picture was taken?'

Nana studied the photo, his forehead creased in concentration. 'I think this was taken when they came home for my son Akwasi – Joshua's father's – wedding. Akwasi was a few years older than Asantewaa, so she would have been around nineteen or twenty at that time.'

Faye sat spellbound as Nana leafed through the rest of the album, marvelling at the many pictures of her mother. One picture in particular held her attention.

'Auntie Akosua, you were right about my mother's taste in clothes,' she giggled. 'Take a look at this picture of the two of you.'

Auntie Akosua wriggled into the space on the sofa next to Faye and burst into laughter at the exaggerated poses she and her best friend had struck for the camera.

'Oh my goodness – I remember that dress! Annie had

seen the style in a magazine my auntie brought me from America and decided to make one herself. Look at those lapels – they look like daggers!'

Nana shook his head and his lips curved into a wry smile as he reminisced fondly about his late niece. 'That child always had to be different from everyone else,' he said. 'She was so stubborn, but also such a kind-hearted person.'

Just as Faye turned the last page of the photo album, a loud clap of thunder sounded, followed by an ominous rumble. The air suddenly grew cooler and Auntie Akosua sat up in alarm.

'Come on, Faye,' she said. 'It looks like it's going to rain. We'd better get going before we get caught in it!'

Remembering the tropical storm she had witnessed in Accra, Faye jumped hastily to her feet. 'Nana, thank you so much for showing me the photographs,' she said hurriedly. 'Will you be at the funeral tomorrow?'

Nana nodded and walked with them to the top of the steps. 'Yes, we shall all be there tomorrow to pay our final respects.'

He glanced up at the dark sky and shooed them off. 'Akosua, don't lose any time,' he said anxiously. 'You must go quickly before the rain starts.'

Waving a final farewell to Yaa and Nana Osei, the two women scampered down the steps and down the road, laughing and gasping for breath as they rushed back home. The first fat drops of rain started to fall just as Auntie Akosua's home was in sight and they raced the final few metres into the old house.

A flash of lightning was followed by another loud clap

of thunder before the heavens opened and heavy rain cascaded down onto the parched ground. Sighing in relief at their narrow escape, Auntie Akosua led the way up the stairs and to Faye's room.

Suddenly they were plunged into darkness as the dim lights inside the house went out altogether. For a moment no one spoke and the only noise to be heard was of the deluge of rain on the rooftops. Faye's eyes were slowly adjusting to the darkness when she realised that the older woman had somehow acquired a torch.

'We keep several of these here in the drawer in case of power failures,' Auntie Akosua said, guiding Faye through to her room. 'It's quite possible that the storm has damaged an electrical cable or something, but don't worry, they usually repair these faults quite promptly.'

Having satisfied herself that her young guest had everything she needed, she left her with the torch and wished her a good night.

'We have to wear our funeral clothes tomorrow,' she reminded her. 'After breakfast, we'll go to the venue and sit down with the rest of the family to greet those coming to mourn with us. It will be a long day, so sleep well, my dear.'

Wishing her a good night in turn, Faye yawned and flicked the torch up and down in search of her travel bag. Rummaging inside, she found a cotton vest and changed quickly. She switched off the torch and burrowed down inside the enormous bed, grateful that the darkness had also blotted out the gloomy portrait of Auntie Akosua's parents.

'I'm in Ntriso,' she whispered sleepily to herself before falling asleep.

16

Cultural Rites

The storm raged on until the early hours of the morning. The breeze blowing through the louvre windows in the spacious bedroom was cool and Faye wrapped herself tightly in the thin bedcovers to keep warm. As daylight struggled through the dark sky, she thought back over the tumultuous events of the previous day and her first encounter with her mother's relatives.

Accra seemed light years away from the quiet darkness of this house and she thought of Rocky with a pang before turning her mind back to Ntriso. Although Amma had warned her that Ghanaian funerals entailed a lot of 'sitting around and doing nothing', as she had described it, she was looking forward to seeing first-hand how this traditional event was conducted.

Glancing at her watch, she decided that six o'clock was a decent enough hour to wake up. It was still quite dark in the room and she walked over to switch on the light. Nothing happened, and it took a minute for her to remember the power failure of the night before.

She padded through to the adjoining bathroom, the rusty fittings and old-fashioned bath looking even more pitiful in the morning half-light. A second bucket, full to the brim with water, had been placed alongside the bath. Faye dipped her finger into the bucket, shivering as the cold water surrounded it.

Debating on how to warm up the water without disturbing any of the other inhabitants, she decided to brave the situation and take a cold shower.

After all, lots of people do it every day, she reasoned. She walked back into the bedroom to retrieve her wash bag and stripped quickly before climbing into the antique bath. A small bowl had been placed on the side of the bath to scoop up the water in the bucket and she filled it and gingerly poured a little over her feet to test her resolve. Gritting her teeth, she poured another bowlful over her body, gasping with shock as the cold water coursed over her.

Five minutes later, she was rubbing her body vigorously with a thick towel, determined to wake the whole house if necessary, rather than try a cold bath again.

She slipped into her funeral cloth and tried without success to tie a knot with the slippery black fabric used for the headscarf. Slipping her feet into the low-heeled black sandals she had brought with her, she went downstairs in search of her hosts.

The sun had risen and light streamed into the old house, giving it a more cheerful appeal than it had possessed the previous night. She walked into the kitchen and stopped short at the sight of two old ladies in unrelieved black cloth sitting at the kitchen table drinking tea from white enamel mugs. They looked at her curiously as she walked in, feeling slightly self-conscious in her new cloth, and greeted her in *Twi*. Murmuring 'Good morning' in response, Faye stood awkwardly for a moment until one of them, the taller of the two, gestured to the chair next to her, indicating that she should be seated.

The smaller lady continued to stare at Faye, although a gentle smile robbed the action of any hostility. The taller lady, obviously the more proactive, poured weak milky tea from a flask into an empty cup and offered it to Faye. She grimaced inwardly, but accepted the cup meekly.

'We did not see you yesterday when you arrived. Akosua was supposed to bring you to greet us, but Kodjo said you had gone to see your relatives?' Her voice was stern and her English heavily accented. She stared at Faye doubtfully as though waiting for her to deny the charge.

Faye nodded and took a sip of the tasteless white tea, willing herself not to shudder. 'Yes, my mother's family is from Ntriso and I had wanted to go and greet them,' she explained.

'That's very nice, my dear.' The smaller woman spoke up eagerly, now that the ice had been broken. 'Welcome to our home. My name is Serwah and this is my sister Dufie.'

Dufie interrupted her sister impatiently. 'You said your mother's family is from here? What is their name?' Her eyes raked Faye's features as she shot out the questions. Forcing herself to take another sip of the tepid, tasteless tea, Faye answered calmly.

'My mother's name was Annie Asantewaa Boateng,' she said. 'She was Auntie Akosua's classmate and best friend.'

The reaction from the two women was instantaneous. Serwah dropped her cup on the table with a clatter and cooed with pleasure, leaning forward to pat Faye's shoulder happily. Dufie, on the other hand, sniffed loudly and looked thoroughly put out, as though she had been mortally offended. Faye stared at her for a moment, puzzled by the frosty attitude.

'Don't mind Dufie,' Serwah whispered as her sister rose to wash her cup in the old enamel sink. 'She has a very unforgiving nature and never forgets anything. Your mother once hid snails in her favourite shoes because she shouted at Akosua for coming home late.' Serwah giggled mischievously. 'You should have seen the look on Dufie's face when she put her feet inside the shoes and felt the snails crawling inside!'

Faye's lips twitched dangerously as she tried not to laugh. Dufie was approaching the table again and Serwah was now tittering openly. The situation was saved by Auntie Akosua's entrance into the kitchen.

'Oh, there you are Faye,' she said. 'I just went to your room to see if you were up. I hope you slept well and the storm didn't disturb you too much?'

Faye swallowed the giggles threatening to erupt and returned the greeting.

'Good morning, Auntie Akosua. I slept very well, thank you.'

'I see you've already met my aunts,' the older woman

said dryly. 'The power is back on now, so perhaps I can make you a fresh cup of coffee?' She looked dubiously at the half-full cup of milky liquid Faye was clutching.

'Yes, please,' Faye replied gratefully. 'Is Uncle Kodjo up yet?'

'Oh, yes,' Serwah piped up. 'He went to oversee the arrangement of the chairs and canopies at the school grounds and to make sure that all the preparations have been made for the day.'

Dufie sniffed. 'Hmm! I still think we should have used the land the chief offered us for the funeral,' she said to no one in particular.

'Auntie Dufie, we discussed it at length,' Auntie Akosua answered patiently. 'The grounds are not big enough for the numbers that will be coming. You know there will be a lot of members of staff from Uncle Ofosu's old company coming today, as well as all his Lodge brothers and friends. The chief understood and has even promised to come himself and pay his respects today.'

Her aunt merely sniffed again, rising from the table and rearranging the piece of black cloth tied around her waist.

'Well, don't worry about what I think,' she said with a pained expression. 'I shall just go along with what has been decided – after all, who listens to old people anymore?' With that she swept majestically out of the kitchen, leaving Auntie Akosua staring after her in exasperation.

'Akosua, drink your coffee,' Serwah said placidly. 'Don't mind her – that's what comes of not having children,' she added in a self-righteous tone.

Faye stared at the old woman, puzzled. She was sure she had been told that both ladies were spinsters who had never left the family house.

Auntie Akosua gestured to Faye to come over and take the cup of steaming coffee she held in her hand.

'Auntie Serwah never married but she does have two children,' she murmured quietly. 'Although she hardly ever sees them since they went to live abroad some years ago, she's always holding it over Auntie Dufie's head that she was at least able to have children. The two of them can be quite something when they get going.'

After they finished their coffee, Auntie Akosua fixed Faye's headscarf and she went upstairs to fetch her bag and pick up some handkerchiefs. Uncle Kodjo, who had arrived just as they left the kitchen, went up to change and came back down wearing a pair of dark shorts and with a magnificent black cloth with a glossy sheen draped over his shoulder. Despite his lack of height, he still managed to look dignified in his attire.

The women were assembled in the front hall and he took the lead as they made their way to the dark blue car parked outside. Auntie Dufie suddenly turned round and stared at Faye with disapproval.

'Asantewaa's girl, you are wearing earrings.' She pointed accusingly at Faye's small gold hoops. 'Even if they do so in the big towns, we Ashantis do not wear jewellery when we are mourning our close relatives.'

Faye meekly removed her earrings and slipped them into her black clutch bag before following the older people out to the car. Uncle Kodjo helped settle the older ladies in the back and opened the front passenger door for Faye.

Pools of water lay in patches on the hilly ground as they drove the short distance to the school. The sun was climbing in the sky and it promised to be another hot day. Driving along, they passed people dressed in the traditional mourning colours of black, brown and red walking in the direction of the school.

As they drew up to the school where the funeral rites would take place, Faye noticed several large posters of the late Uncle Ofosu nailed to the front gates. Inside, the school grounds, a huge expanse of grass, still damp from the morning rain, had been converted into an open amphitheatre with hundreds of chairs arranged in circular rows. Canopies had been set up over the chairs to protect the guests from the glare of the sun. Quite a few people had already taken their seats and it was clear from the number of chairs that this was expected to be a well-attended event.

Uncle Kodjo parked the car in a cordoned off area, helped his aunts out and then led the way to the seats that had been reserved for the family. Looking around, Faye spotted printed signs designating reserved areas for the staff of the rural bank where Uncle Ofosu had worked before his retirement, for members of his Masonic Lodge, and for the church society of which he had apparently been an active member.

She sat down next to Auntie Akosua and, as the morning wore on, she watched as cars and minibuses arrived and discharged groups of dark-clad mourners, until eventually most of the seats were occupied. As each group arrived, the guests would come over to where they sat and offer their condolences to the elderly sisters, Auntie Akosua and other members of their family.

Music blared loudly from huge speakers set up at one end of the field and a group of drummers played vigorously, gyrating and moving their well-muscled bodies in time to the rhythm. Whenever a distinguished guest arrived, the drums would quicken in intensity and the MC would announce the new arrival through the PA system.

It was almost midday when the sound of a loud cheer brought the music to a sudden halt. Faye looked over to where a slow procession was making its way onto the field. Sitting on a *palanquin* carried by a number of black clad young men was a middle-aged man wearing a magnificent black and white *kente* cloth and literally covered in gold ornaments. Solid gold chains were draped over his ample torso and he wore chunky gold rings on almost every finger. The drummers went into a frenzy of beating and the crowd surged around the procession.

'That's the chief of Ntriso,' said Auntie Akosua, raising her voice above the din. 'He was a good friend of Uncle Ofosu and promised to come today.'

The chief's procession had reached the seats occupied by the family and the *palanquin* was gently lowered. The chief stepped down and one of his entourage immediately opened an intricately carved golden umbrella and held it high over his head to shield him from the sun. He was stocky and not particularly tall, but he seemed to radiate majesty and, seen up close, the sheer quantity and richness of the gold paraphernalia he wore further underlined his royal status. Moving slowly, the traditional ruler walked over to the family members who all stood to greet him. Uncle Kodjo was the first to shake the chief's hand. He bowed deeply and thanked him for doing them the honour of coming.

When it was Faye's turn, she shook his hand nervously, bobbed her knees in an awkward curtsey and ducked her head shyly. She looked up and was slightly shocked to find him still looking at her. After a moment he smiled and patted her hand gently with his heavily ringed fingers and moved on to greet Auntie Akosua.

When the chief had moved further way, Auntie Akosua smiled mischievously at Faye.

'You look so much like your mother that I'm sure he knows who you are. I probably should have told you that before he was enstooled as Chief Kwame Karikari II, his name was Paul Adjaye.'

The sun was now high in the sky and, despite the canopy over their heads, it had grown very hot. A number of men, dressed in dark T-shirts and trousers, moved around the field offering drinks to the thirsty mourners and Faye gratefully seized a bottle of water and gulped it down thirstily.

'What happens now?' she asked Auntie Akosua in a low voice. After sitting for such a long time and shaking hands with countless strangers, she was beginning to appreciate Amma's earlier description of funerals.

'There will be tributes read shortly to Uncle Ofosu and then there will be some traditional dancing,' her aunt replied. 'Be prepared – you will have to dance with the family.'

Faye looked horrified. 'I don't know how!' she exclaimed, alarmed at the prospect of a field of people watching her efforts at traditional dancing.

Auntie Akosua laughed at her terrified expression. 'Don't worry. Just shake your body and go with the music. Everyone will be happy that you tried.'

'It doesn't seem very solemn to be dancing when someone has died,' Faye frowned as she looked around. 'This is supposed to be a funeral and yet people are laughing and chatting and drinking rather than looking sad.'

'Oh Faye, you still have a lot to learn! Death is very much a part of life for us here in Ghana and, truth be told, funerals are one of the most important of our social functions. Look.' Auntie Akosua gestured towards a table manned by two harassed-looking men who were busy scribbling on little chits of paper and handing them out to the line of people queued up in front of them.

'Because funerals are so important, not to mention expensive, friends and well-wishers contribute to the cost. Those people lined up there are giving donations – we call it *nsa* – to help our family pay for all this.' As they watched, one of the men seated at the table scribbled out a receipt and handed it to a donor in exchange for an envelope filled with cash and then announced the donation in *Twi* over the PA system.

'As for the dancing; well, you should know we have dances for every occasion; whether we are happy or sad,' Auntie Akosua went on. Changing the subject, she gestured towards the field. 'You see that man who is walking over to the public address system – he came over to greet us earlier?'

Faye looked across to where her aunt was pointing but couldn't distinguish the man from what seemed like the hundreds of people who had greeted the family that day. She shook her head in apology.

'He was my late uncle's best friend,' Auntie Akosua continued. 'He's now going to read the first tribute, which will be my uncle's biography.'

The elderly man adjusted his black cloth, tossing it over his shoulder with ease, and straightened out a sheet of paper he had retrieved from his shorts. He slipped on a pair of glasses and in a surprisingly strong voice, read out a long biography of the late Mr Ofosu Obeng. Faye listened in fascination to the life history of the deceased, which was followed by other tributes given by his friends, former work colleagues and relatives.

After the tributes had been concluded, the family headed back home to have lunch and to give the older aunties a chance to rest before returning to the funeral ground. Back at the house, they had a simple meal of hot *kenkey* with fried fish and pepper sauce and about an hour later, set off back to the school for the remainder of the funeral rites.

They returned to their seats, accompanied by loud drumming as the MC announced their presence. The drummers had tied their cloths around their waists and their lean dark torsos gleamed with sweat as they played.

Nana Osei and his grandfather walked over to greet the family and sat down to chat with them. Nana Osei sat in the empty seat next to Faye and gave her an impromptu lesson on the drums being played. The large drums with inverted metal bowls were called *ntumpane* drums, he explained, while the other drums that looked to Faye rather like elongated wooden barrels with tightly stretched hide across the top were called *fontomfrom* drums. Beating the *fontomfrom* with sticks with a right-angled hook at the ends, the drummers skilfully stirred the crowd of mourners into action.

Before long a number of women had taken to the field, dancing rhythmically to the sound of the drums. Waving their handkerchiefs, they danced towards the family, beckoning to them to come and join them.

The old aunts rose stiffly to their feet and moved onto the field. Auntie Dufie was surprisingly agile as she waved her arms in time to the drums and swayed towards the other dancers. Auntie Serwah gyrated her hips and moved along with Uncle Kodjo, who managed to dance a series of convoluted steps while still keeping his cloth draped over his shoulder. The other family members stood up to dance and Auntie Akosua pushed a nervous Faye forward onto the field.

Although she was initially appalled at the thought of all the eyes upon her, once she was on her feet and felt the throb of the drums, she lost any sense of self-consciousness and began to sway in time to the beat. Soon she was waving and gyrating sinuously with the others, lost in the rhythmic beat of the drums. A group of women danced over to her and raised their hands over her, two fingers extended as though in victory, in salute to her dancing. Eventually, the drums died down and they returned to their seats, invigorated by the experience.

A couple of hours later, the old aunts were visibly wilting. After a quick word from Uncle Kodjo, the announcement was made over the speakers by the MC that the family were leaving. Shaking hands with their relatives and other well-wishers as they left the grounds, they made their way to the car and were soon back at the house.

Faye collapsed onto the aged sofa as soon as they arrived home, the elderly ladies having immediately headed off to their rooms to lie down.

'Whew! What a day.' She pulled off her black headscarf with a sigh of relief. 'It's amazing how tiring just sitting down can be.'

Auntie Akosua sat on a chair, stretched her legs out in front of her and gently kneaded her temples.

'These events are exhausting,' she said with a deep sigh. 'Although we're leaving tomorrow, the tradition is that the family has to go round and visit those who came or helped with the funeral and thank them. Then, they've got to sit down and go through all the expenses connected with the funeral – *ayi asi'ka*, as we say in *Twi*, and to see whether the *nsa* that was donated by family members and friends will cover the cost.'

'What happens if it doesn't?' Faye asked curiously. The older woman laughed and shrugged. 'Well, then the family must make up the difference, which usually means that the cost will be shared out amongst us, the blood relations.'

Faye dragged herself off the sofa. 'Well, I know it doesn't sound like me, but I'm so tired I don't think I've got the energy to stay awake for supper. Is it okay if I go up to bed now?'

Auntie Akosua nodded. 'That's fine, my dear. Go up and rest.' She smiled as Faye yawned widely, unable to disguise her fatigue. 'We'll leave after breakfast tomorrow. Kodjo will drive us back to Kumasi and we'll get the midday bus to Accra.'

Faye waved goodnight and trudged up the stairs, barely managing to remove her funeral cloth and wash her face before collapsing into bed and sleeping dreamlessly.

The following morning, after a warm bath this time, and a hearty breakfast, Auntie Akosua and Faye bid farewell to the elderly aunts. Auntie Serwah hugged Faye warmly, insisting that she come back to visit them. Auntie Dufie unbent slightly and thanked her grudgingly for coming to support them in their grief. Trying not to smile at Auntie Serwah's broad wink as she stood safely behind her sister, Faye thanked them both gravely for their hospitality before heading towards the pick-up and clambering into the back seat.

'We'll stop at your grandfather's first so you can say goodbye,' Uncle Kodjo said cheerily as he climbed up onto his cushion and started the truck. He gave his aunts a farewell wave and drove up the road and around the small roundabout, following the same route past the church that Faye and Auntie Akosua had taken two days earlier.

Parking in front of the Boateng house, he gave two short blasts of his horn and waited. Shortly afterwards, Nana's stooped figure appeared and he walked slowly towards them.

Smiling at Faye who waved at him from the back seat, he greeted the older couple first.

'Kodjo, I don't want to delay you but I think my granddaughter has one last very important visit to make,' he said. The two men exchanged a look and Kodjo turned enquiringly to his sister.

She nodded and climbed down from her seat to assist the old man to climb up and take her place, and then joined Faye in the back of the pick-up.

'Are we going to visit another relative?' Faye was curious about the silent interplay that had just taken place. For a moment no one spoke. Auntie Akosua took Faye's hand between her own and spoke gently.

'We're going to the cemetery where Annie is buried. You know that she was brought back here after she passed away, don't you?'

Faye sat for a moment in stunned silence. 'Dad never said anything about it, and I guess we never asked him because it was all so painful.'

Auntie Akosua stroked her hand gently. 'I think you'll be glad you had a chance to see where she is laid to rest.'

They drove in silence for about ten minutes and came to a stop at the side of the main road leading out of the town. Uncle Kodjo climbed down and walked round to help the older man out, while the two women stepped down from the back.

Faye looked around apprehensively, noting a signboard that bore the simple words 'Ntriso Cemetery'. There was scarcely a sound to be heard except for the loud chirping of birds and the odd car driving by. She followed the old man and Uncle Kodjo for a few minutes through thick grass and past marble headstones, with Auntie Akosua close by her side.

The men came to a sudden stop and stood back, beckoning to Faye to come forward. Her heart pounding in her chest, she moved to join them and stared transfixed at the tombstone before them. It was made of white marble and the words 'Annabel Asantewaa Bonsu' were carved in gold along with the dates of her birth and death. Inset into the headstone was a picture of a smiling woman with high cheekbones and striking almond-shaped eyes.

Faye's eyes misted over as she stared at the serene expression on the woman's face. She had never seen this particular picture of her mother before but, as she took in the features so like her own, she knew now without any doubt that she had inherited more from her mother than she had ever realised.

'Nana, she was beautiful, wasn't she?' She turned to the old man who had been watching her sadly. He nodded slowly, suddenly looking older than he had just moments before.

'Asantewaa had a natural beauty that drew everyone to her,' he said heavily. He patted her gently on the shoulder. 'You have the same quality, my dear,' he added, his dark eyes twinkling at her. 'Come, we should leave now so you can take this old man back to his house before you set off.'

They walked back to the pick-up and Faye stayed silent during the drive, still caught up in the whirlwind of emotions brought on by what she had just witnessed. Back at his house, Nana hugged her warmly, waved goodbye and watched them as they drove off.

On the drive back to Kumasi, Auntie Akosua and her brother chatted quietly about the follow-up arrangements for the funeral while Faye sat quietly in the back seat. As they drove through the small rural settlements along the main road to Kumasi, she could see women pounding fufu and cooking with charred coal pots, while little children chased after chickens and played in the dust.

Uncle Kodjo glanced over his shoulder and took in her expression as she watched them.

'Yes,' he said soberly, in answer to her unspoken question. 'I'm sure it's quite different from the parts of Accra that you've seen. When you spend as much time as I do meeting and doing business with people from these small villages, you sometimes cannot believe that you are all part of the same country.'

'We have so much to do to improve the lives of the people in the rural areas that sometimes the task seems impossible,' Auntie Akosua interjected. 'With all the modern conveniences we are used to in the city, it's easy to forget that out in these areas, very little has changed.'

Uncle Kodjo nodded in agreement. 'Our contact with the West has had a very uneven impact on our culture here in Africa. As a result, you will see a major contrast between a very Westernised society – the educated people in the urban centres – and the traditional rural people whose beliefs and way of life are in many ways not very different from what they have always been.'

He slowed the truck down to allow a young boy in tattered shorts to herd some goats across the road. He grinned at them as he ran after the last of his animals and waved cheerfully before continuing on his way.

'You take that young man,' Uncle Kodjo said. 'Now

he could be a potential doctor or engineer and yet it is unlikely that he will even finish school.'

Faye pondered on this for a few minutes. 'Dad is always saying that at least in Ghana people have been able to avoid the wars that some of the other countries in Africa have experienced.'

Uncle Kodjo nodded. 'That's true, but until we start taking more control of our economy, we are always going to struggle to catch up with the rest of the world.' He glanced round at her and grinned. 'But I also think that sometimes we are given a poor deal in how the developed world sees us. It's funny that when there's fighting in Europe it's called "ethnic conflict" but when it happens in Africa, they call it "tribal warfare".'

Auntie Akosua chipped in. 'Oh yes, we in Africa have villages but in the West they have "rural communities".'

Faye laughed ruefully. 'I know what you mean. You wouldn't believe the number of times in this day and age – despite the internet and everything – that I still have to explain to some people that Africans don't live in trees or run around spearing each other to death!'

The rest of the journey went by swiftly and soon they were at the transport yard saying goodbye to Uncle Kodjo. He waited until they were safely aboard the bus bound for Accra before waving farewell and returning to his truck.

There were fewer people on the bus during the return trip. This time they made the journey without the accompanying aroma of dried fish and Auntie Akosua kept Faye entertained with stories about her mother and their adventures as teenagers.

It was late afternoon by the time they arrived at the busy state transport yard in Accra. Retrieving their bags from the hold, they walked out into the hot sunshine in search of a taxi.

'I'll drop you off at Labone and then carry on to my house, Faye,' Auntie Akosua said, as a taxi pulled up at her signal. When they arrived at Labone, Faye gave the older woman a warm hug before stepping out of the car.

'Don't bother getting out, Auntie Akosua. You must be exhausted.'

'I am rather tired, my dear. Give my regards to the family and tell Amelia that I will call her later this evening.'

The driver revved his engine noisily at the delay, earning an irritated glare from Auntie Akosua. 'Take care, Faye, and thank you for coming with me. I hope you enjoyed the trip?'

'I had a wonderful trip, Auntie Akosua,' Faye replied, the sincerity in her voice unmistakable. 'Thank you for taking me home.'

17

Cultural Pains

'Oh no, it's raining!' Faye wailed in dismay at the fat drops of water splashing against the windows of her bedroom. True to his word, Rocky was taking the day off to take them to Cape Coast and now the weather looked set to put their plans in jeopardy.

A loud knock at the door was followed by Amma's entrance into the room. Still in her nightshirt, she looked thoroughly disgusted as she marched in.

'Just look at that rain,' she said crossly. 'I was really looking forward to going out of town today – I've hardly had any time with Edwin over the last few days!'

Faye tactfully refrained from pointing out that Edwin had been over to Labone for at least three hours every day since her return from Ntriso two days earlier. With his flight to America scheduled for that weekend, he was making every effort to spend as much time with Amma as he could.

'Well, why don't we get dressed and see if the weather

improves,' Faye said, trying to sound practical. She had really been looking forward to spending the day with Rocky and to their planned visit to the old castles in Cape Coast. Painfully aware that she had only a week left in Ghana, she could relate only too well to Amma's frustration.

With another heavy sigh, Amma stomped out of the room, leaving Faye staring out gloomily at the weather.

It looks just like London out there, she thought moodily before taking her own advice and heading for the bathroom. Ten minutes later, feeling fresh from a bracing shower, she was back to pressing her nose against the glass panes.

The rain had subsided considerably although it was still drizzling lightly. Feeling a bit cheerier, she rummaged through the chest of drawers for something to wear. Settling on a pair of black jeans and a pink Mickey Mouse T-shirt, which always managed to make her bust look a bit bigger, she dressed quickly and slipped on a pair of black canvas shoes. She brushed her hair vigorously and spent a few minutes carefully applying some make-up. After a final check in the mirror, she left her room and walked down the corridor to tap on Amma's door.

A muffled shriek was the only response and she pushed the door open in alarm to find Amma and her braids tangled in a long dress she had been trying to pull over her head. Stifling her laughter, Faye walked over and after much pulling and tugging, managed to get the straight shift down over the girl's curvy hips. Breathing heavily from her exertions, Amma adjusted the dress and tied her braids back firmly with a bright red scarf.

'I'm going to call Edwin to see if he's on his way,' she said breathlessly, spraying two quick bursts of perfume on her wrists. Faye followed her downstairs and headed straight for the kitchen, leaving Amma to make her phone call in the living room. Martha, who had her back to the kitchen door, was singing one of her favourite church hymns so loudly she didn't hear the door open. Turning around to pick up a dishcloth she jumped, exclaiming in shock as she clutched her ample bosom.

'Good morning, Miss Faye! I didn't hear you coming in.' She took two deep breaths before continuing. 'Can I serve you some coffee?'

Faye nodded and waited while the housekeeper filled a large mug with the fresh brew. Taking the cup, Faye added a splash of milk from the milk jug in the fridge and had a sip.

'This tastes wonderful, Martha,' she said happily. 'Where is everyone?' she asked artlessly. Martha looked sceptical, not fooled for one moment by the apparently casual question.

'Master Rocky is in the dining room with his mother,' she replied dryly, turning back to her washing up and hiding a grin.

Faye stared doubtfully at the older woman's back, then turned and headed to the dining room.

'Good morning, Faye,' Auntie Amelia said warmly as she walked in. 'I was just telling Rocky that you people should set off soon so you have enough time to see all the sights at Cape Coast.'

'The rain has stopped now so we can leave as soon as

Edwin gets here,' Rocky said lazily. He leaned back in his chair, his eyes on Faye. She smiled at him, feeling the now familiar wave of excitement coursing through her. Rocky looked relaxed in a stone-coloured denim shirt with the sleeves partially rolled up to reveal his strong forearms.

Taking a seat next to his mother, Faye sipped slowly on her coffee and tried her best not to look at him. Rocky, on the other hand, made no effort to look away, keeping his eyes on her expressive features all the while.

Amma came in, clutching her phone.

'Good morning, Mama; hi Rocky,' she said absently, sitting down in the chair next to her brother. 'Edwin should be here in a few minutes.' She paused for a moment, and then went on. 'I can't believe he's leaving in only three days!'

Auntie Amelia stirred in alarm and stood up to leave before her daughter started on the same theme she had been forced to listen to every day since the now famous marriage proposal.

'I'll be in the kitchen with Martha,' she said hastily as she snatched her empty teacup from the table. 'Let me know when you are leaving.' With that, she swept out of the room, leaving Amma staring after her in surprise.

Trying not to laugh, Faye took refuge in her coffee mug while Rocky rubbed his chin slowly, amused at his mother's less than subtle flight and Amma's clearly perplexed face. The sound of the gate opening distracted her attention and she rushed off to open the front door.

As soon as Amma had left the room, Faye couldn't contain herself any longer and burst into laughter.

'Poor Auntie Amelia,' she choked. 'Did you see the

hunted expression on her face when Amma mentioned Edwin?'

Rocky laughed. 'You can't blame her – she must have heard his name about a thousand times in the last week. It's enough to drive anyone crazy!'

'Who's crazy?' Amma demanded as she walked back into the room, dragging a damp-looking Edwin behind her.

'You are,' Rocky answered coolly before turning to shake hands with his future brother-in-law. 'Is it still raining out there?' he asked, taking in the drops of moisture clinging to Edwin's short hair.

Edwin gave Faye a hug and shrugged carelessly. 'It's not too bad now. It will probably stop soon, so we can get started if you are all ready.' He looked enquiringly at them and Faye immediately jumped to her feet.

'I'll just get my bag. I'll be down in a minute,' she said. Amma followed her up the stairs and ten minutes later, they were in Rocky's luxurious car driving down the dual carriageway out of Labone.

Amma and Edwin had dived straight into the back seat, leaving Faye quite happy to be in front with Rocky. It had stopped raining and a cool breeze wafted through the half-open car windows. Faye sat back and listened to the soulful songs on the radio.

'Rocky, can you change the station to something more lively,' Edwin piped up from the back. 'That music will put you to sleep.'

'You're so unromantic!' Amma grumbled. 'Listen to the words of the song – they're a lot better than that awful hip hop stuff you keep forcing me to listen to.'

'You said you *liked* rap!' Edwin protested. 'You even came with me to the Nas concert last year, remember?'

'How quickly they forget. You'd better get used to it, man,' Rocky chuckled. 'That's what happens when you mention the word *marriage*, my brother.'

Incensed at Rocky's attitude, Faye sniffed in disgust and turned in her seat to gaze stonily at the passing scenery.

'Oh wow!' She sat upright, completely forgetting her irritation at Rocky, and pointed. 'What is *that*?'

To their right, rising majestically out of the green bush and scrubland was a huge hill dotted with large, white-roofed houses.

'It's beautiful isn't it?' Amma sighed. 'That's McCarthy Hill. One of my friends lives up there and the view from her house is breathtaking.'

Edwin looked sceptical. 'It's beautiful if you're not worried about earthquakes. That hill is right in the centre of earthquake country. It's like the San Andreas fault of Ghana.'

Faye bit her lip to stop the giggle threatening to erupt as Rocky glanced at her and rolled his eyes upwards in exasperation. Between Amma who only talked about Edwin, and Edwin who only talked about America, he was beginning to question the wisdom of his invitation.

They drove along a dual carriageway that eventually gave way to a single-lane main road. Rocky navigated its uneven surface carefully, slowing down from time to time to avoid potholes. Faye watched the passing scenery in fascination. Clusters of tall green trees interrupted a series of industrial buildings, warehouses, shacks and tiling factories, their coloured tiles prominently displayed by the roadside. Straggly coconut and palm trees hung desolately, struggling to survive in the face of the industrial encroachment onto their land.

Rocky slowed the car down and they stopped just before a road barrier manned by a couple of bored looking policemen, one of whom was carrying a rifle.

'What's going on?' Faye whispered in apprehension, her eyes fixed on the weapon slung casually over the policeman's shoulder.

Rocky gave her a reassuring smile. 'Don't worry, it's just a checkpoint barrier – it's supposed to be for surveillance against smugglers.'

'*That* wouldn't deter any decent smuggler.' Faye looked incredulous as she took in the makeshift barrier, which consisted of a rusty gate attached to a concrete pillar.

'It's unmanned half the time anyway,' Edwin scoffed. 'If we had passed here earlier when it was raining, you wouldn't have seen a soul.'

Saluting the policeman who waved him on, Rocky pressed down on the accelerator and the car shot forward again. The road was still wet and puddles had formed in the potholes dotted haphazardly along their route.

'We'll be in Kasoa soon, Faye,' Amma piped up from the rear. 'I tutored some secondary school students in ICT there a couple of years ago.'

They drove into Kasoa, where both sides of the road suddenly turned into an impromptu market. Faye craned her neck to see the wares being displayed by cheerful stall keepers, literally within arms reach of the car.

Now this looks more like I imagined a market to be than the one I went to with Martha, she thought, *and much closer to the picture on my bedroom wall.*

Rocky honked in warning as two boys rolling a tyre along the road with a stick almost ran into the path of the car. He drove slowly until they had passed through the densely populated market area.

'Kasoa is a very important trade centre for the farmers in this region,' Amma explained to Faye. 'They do everything here from selling their foodstuffs at the market to buying their spare parts. They even do their banking here – Rocky's bank has a branch in the centre of town.'

'They also do their praying here,' Rocky added with a grin, pointing out several signboards bearing the names of different churches.

Faye read the names out loud. '*Church of God, Divine Believers' Society, Holy Divinity Worshippers...* Who thinks up these names?'

Amma announced that she was thirsty and Rocky pulled into a petrol station, parking in front of the small supermarket on the forecourt. Edwin and Amma went in and returned a few minutes later armed with bottles of cold water and a large bag of popcorn. Ignoring Rocky's exasperated expression when he saw the popcorn that was about to enter his precious car, Amma slid into the back seat and cuddled up to Edwin as they resumed their journey.

They drove out of Kasoa and for several miles the scenery was once again green forests and bush. The music was lively and Faye and Amma sang along tunelessly to the radio, taking no notice of the pleas from the men to stop. Amma passed the bag of popcorn to Faye who munched happily on the sweet buttery snack, giggling as she succeeded in cramming a few handfuls into Rocky's protesting mouth.

Taking a quick swallow from the bottle of water Faye held out to him, he drove fast past coconut trees and palm trees with their branches spread out against the sky. The road curved through bushes, shrubs and thick green vegetation. Occasionally they would pass small groups of men and women trudging along from their farms or sitting behind vegetable stalls set up alongside the busy road.

'Most of the people in these parts are farmers,' Rocky said, nodding in the direction of a woman who was busy replenishing a large basket on her stall. 'They grow pineapples and a wide variety of vegetables. They sell them along the road and in the major markets like Kasoa, Accra and other parts of the region.'

'Oh, look, that signboard said we are 83 kilometres away from Cape Coast!' Faye pointed at the board as they sped past.

'We'll go through Winneba first, and then it's not too far to Cape Coast,' Rocky said, smiling at her enthusiasm. He swerved to avoid a burnt out vehicle; the remains of the destroyed car had been stripped by scavengers of any spare parts that could be sold.

Faye shivered. 'It reminds me of what Auntie Akosua said about car accidents being one of the main causes of death in the country. Why can't people just drive more carefully?'

Faye stared out of the window, marvelling at the African

landscape. Tall eucalyptus trees rose out of the seemingly endless miles of bush. Towering pylons carrying cords of power across the countryside to the urban areas hovered over the clusters of small hamlets and villages like an army of angry housewives, their giant arms crooked onto metallic hips.

Ironically, many of the communities nestling in the embrace of these iron arms were yet to receive their share of the national grid's largesse and coal pots and kerosene lamps were the chief sources of power and light for many of them.

The eucalyptus trees gave way to coconut trees clustered together in groves and Faye leant across Rocky, trying to see the horizon.

'Is that the sea?' she asked impatiently, her eyes darting round.

'No,' Amma replied. 'But we'll soon be driving along the coastline and you can see it then.' She leant forward and tapped Faye's shoulder. 'Look over there, quick!'

Faye turned back to look through her window and squealed in shock as they drove past a group of young men dressed in ragged shorts standing by the roadside. 'What were they holding? They looked like giant rats!'

'They're grasscutters.' Amma laughed at Faye's reaction to the large furry animals the boys had been dangling by their tails. 'They're grass eating rodents and a very popular bush meat in the local soups. Sometimes they sell them smoked and flattened on frames. They are pretty tasty.'

Her friend shuddered. 'I'll stick to basic beef, chicken and fish, thank you.'

Rocky laughed and pointed to a road sign that indicated that Cape Coast was now 36 kilometres away. They drove quickly through Mankessim, another market town, but this time the goods on sale appeared to be almost exclusively timber and related products.

Then, finally, through the swaying coconut trees, Faye saw a strip of blue.

'Oh, look, it's the sea!' She turned to look at the flashes of seawater, visible between the trees and shrubs that separated the road from the beach.

They drove through a few more villages and rural hamlets that reminded Faye of the communities they had passed on the long drive to Kumasi the previous weekend. As they headed towards Cape Coast, they passed an ancient fort perched on top of a hill, its reddy-brown walls decaying in the salty breeze. The sparkling blue sea was now clearly visible, as were numerous signboards dotted along the road inviting visitors to any number of hostels, hotels and churches.

They drove through the small town of Anomabo before reaching Biriwa. Here, empty kiosks with rusted corrugated-iron roofs lined the streets. The town was silent and the streets almost empty, as though all the energy has been sucked out.

'You see children and older people, but there hardly seem to be any young men or women walking around,' Faye observed, her gaze fixed on the passing scenery.

Edwin, whose mother had been born in Anomabo, explained that most of the younger generation had left for the larger towns and cities such as Cape Coast, Takoradi and Accra in search of better opportunities.

'There's so little to do in these small towns now that no one wants to stay,' he said. 'They just send their children back for the grandparents to look after and go and look for jobs in the hotels or tourist areas in the bigger towns and cities.'

The state of the road suddenly improved dramatically and the potholed highway was transformed into a smooth dual carriageway along the side of which they could see food stalls manned by young girls selling the Fanti version of *kenkey*, the popular fermented maize, wrapped in dark leaves and stacked like bricks on the tables.

Rocky slowed the car down as they drove into Cape Coast. The road wound uphill past run-down buildings with peeling green and yellow walls. Kids called out to each other as they scampered along the edge of the road playing football, and took little notice of the vehicles driving past them on the narrow roads.

'So what's special about Cape Coast – apart from the pineapples?' Faye asked, tapping Rocky's knee.

'Well, Cape Coast does have an important history. It was once the capital of the Gold Coast – as Ghana was called before independence from the British – and it's now the capital city of the Central Region of Ghana.' He lowered his voice dramatically. 'It's also the home of 99 little gods.'

She looked askance at him but before she could speak, he gestured to his right.

'Cape Coast is also famous for its church spires and steeples. Just look over there.' Faye stared, astonished, at the sheer number of spires that appeared in quick succession as they drove along.

Then, as they drove further up the hill, Cape Coast Castle came into view. She gasped at the sight of the huge white edifice and the rusting black cannon visible from the road.

Rocky drove up to the castle and parked the car on the grass verge and clambered out onto the soft earth, still moist from the morning showers. He came round to open the passenger door and held out his hand. Faye automatically slipped hers inside his, looking upwards in awe at the Castle as they walked towards the entrance.

Rocky took care of the tickets and they passed through into a large paved courtyard in the centre of the Castle. Looking up, they could see roughly hewn stairs leading up to balconies with black railings and windows screened by blue wooden shutters. Black rusting metal lampposts converted to use electric light bulbs were planted around the courtyard.

Edwin had gone to make enquiries and came back shortly afterwards to join the others. 'There's a tour starting soon, but the guide says we have time to take a look at the museum first.'

The four of them climbed up a stone staircase and entered through the door marked 'Museum'. They moved past a darkened side room where a group of tourists stood engrossed as they watched a short video about Ghana, went through into the main hall, and walked slowly around the museum exhibits.

Faye paused beside the first display and read the information on the card with interest.

'The Gold Coast was an important trading centre with

flourishing towns and city states and it existed long before the first Europeans ever arrived. Oh, and listen to this... "By the 1480s the Portuguese had reached the coast and started the gold rush. Ghana's subsequent history has been one of interaction between Africans and Europeans trading in gold, ivory, pepper and eventually, slaves."'

She gave a hollow laugh. 'No wonder they say we are such a welcoming people – we welcomed the traders for years, even after they started selling us!'

Rocky stood beside her, a brooding expression on his handsome face as he read the notes below the display. He shook his head in disgust at the more gory aspects of the castle's history. 'Most of these fortresses and castles that the Europeans built have fallen into decay, although some of them were refurbished into schools and government offices. This castle and the one in Elmina are registered as World Heritage Monuments, which is just as well. They are a reminder to us to never forget what was done to our people – by others and by ourselves.'

They moved from one exhibit to the next, fascinated by the unfolding story of the continent and the slave trade, described there as one of the most tragic chapters in the history of Africa and the Americas. In one exhibit, beautiful photography highlighted the story of gold, and how raw gold starred in abundance in Ghana's history; being used over the centuries for sculpture, for currency, for regalia, jewellery and ornaments.

'Edwin, do you realise where the word *cedi* comes from?' Amma asked, pulling Edwin away from the metal gold weights he'd been scrutinising. Without waiting for an answer, she gestured towards the exhibit she had been examining.

'It says that when the European traders arrived in 1470, they came in search of gold. But, as trade developed into more than bartering, gold dust was used as currency along with iron bars and cowrie shells. The name of our currency today, the *cedi*, comes from *sedee*, the Akan word for cowrie shell.' She smiled affectionately at him. 'You see? You learn something new every day.'

Edwin was still reading the information below the exhibit. 'Well, we were certainly popular,' he remarked. 'First came the Portuguese, then the Dutch, before we were handed over to the British in 1872 to be part of their empire. I wonder how much the "notional sum" the British paid for Elmina Castle was,' he added speculatively.

They moved on to an exhibit about the castles at Elmina and Cape Coast, which as the two largest outposts had been the regional headquarters for the development of trade in the region. Manned by soldiers, merchants, doctors and other officials, they had served also to protect the local population in times of war.

Edwin grinned and pointed to a line in the text. 'It looks like Christopher Columbus "discovered" Ghana before America. It says here that he visited one of the forts – Sao Jorge de Mina – ten years before he set off on his famous voyages to the Americas.'

On hearing Edwin say the word 'America', Rocky quickly dragged Faye off to the next exhibit, which was a pictorial history of Cape Coast Castle.

'Rocky, you were right about Cape Coast once being

the capital. According to this, it was the seat of English administration in the Gold Coast until 1877 when the capital was relocated to Accra.'

They walked slowly through the exhibition hall, looking at black and white pictures of colonial Ghana and reading out titbits from the historical accounts accompanying the pictures. Standing in front of a series of pictures depicting scenes from a nineteenth century Fanti market, Faye and Amma gave voice to the same thought.

'It looks pretty similar to the market I went to last week! It doesn't seem like we've made much progress in almost two hundred years.'

'I know what you mean,' Amma replied, peering at the cooking utensils in another picture. 'Look at that black grinding bowl. It looks just like the ones you'll see in Ghanaian homes today.'

The next exhibit stopped them cold; it told the story of slavery. Torn between horror and fascination, they silently read the account of the beginnings of the Atlantic slave trade in the 1500s and how, by the 1600s, the slave trade had become firmly established.

Amma was the first to speak. 'It's hard to believe that the slave trade lasted for four centuries – that's *four hundred years!* It says that between twelve and twenty-five million Africans were forced into the trade during that time.'

Faye shook her head slowly in amazement. 'One third of the slaves went to Brazil, one third to the Caribbean and one third were scattered throughout North and South America.' She turned to look for Rocky, who had moved onto the next exhibit, and walked over to him.

'Do you know what that is?' he asked her softly, gesturing to the glass case in front of him. She looked at the metal artefacts in the case and shook her head.

'It's a branding iron,' he said slowly. 'They would heat it in an open fire and use it to brand the slaves.'

Faye's eyes welled with tears as she looked at the short metal stick with a flattened wedge and imagined it heated to a hot red temperature before being pressed against human flesh.

He pointed to the circular metal objects on the shelf below. 'Those are the shackles they used. They would chain the captured slaves at the neck and wrists and ankle.'

'Ladies and gentleman, the tour of the Castle is about to begin downstairs!' The announcement rang out loudly in the quiet hall. Reluctantly, they broke away from the exhibits and headed down the stone steps to join the small group that had gathered at the far end of the courtyard.

The tour guide, a tall, very dark man with a loud booming voice, waited for them to take their place before he started speaking. The passion in his voice was undimmed by years of repetition as he took his riveted audience through the voyage of the Africans torn from the bosom of their homes and transported as slave labour to a foreign land from which they would never return.

In lyrical accented English, he explained that as the home of the British Governors, the Castle served as the seat of government in colonial times.

'The British traded in gold, ivory and in slaves,' he said. 'Captured from neighbouring countries and from the deep recesses of the Gold Coast – tragically, often with the connivance of their own chiefs – they were exchanged for iron rods and jewellery.' He paused and began to walk. 'Follow me, please.'

The group walked along the courtyard and stopped outside a door marked 'Palaver Hall'. The guide entered the room and waited until the group had assembled inside the long bare hall.

'This is Palaver Hall, where the exchange of slaves took place,' he announced, gesturing grandly around the room.

Amma shivered. 'You can almost picture what it must have been like,' she whispered.

Faye nodded and turned to follow the guide who was striding out of the room. They walked across the uneven paving stones of the courtyard, stopping in front of a wooden door with a plaque identifying it as the Male Slave Dungeon.

'When the slaves were brought to the Castle,' the guide went on, 'the men were separated from the women and both groups were locked into slave dungeons,' he said. 'Follow me.'

Faye instinctively reached out for Rocky's hand and he held onto hers tightly as their guide led the way down a slope into the darkened dungeons. The male dungeons were made up of four interconnecting underground rooms with a few tiny windows carved out of the rough stone walls providing the only light and ventilation.

The guide pointed to a large gap near the top of one wall. 'That window up there was designed, not to give the slaves air, but to provide an avenue for eavesdroppers to listen to the slaves and report anything seditious to their masters,' he explained.

They stooped to pass between the interconnecting rooms in the wake of their guide. Suddenly he stopped and waited for them to surround him again. Neither his voice nor his face betrayed emotion as he spoke.

'If you feel that our small group has almost filled this room, you should know that one thousand men were kept in here at any one time.' He nodded to emphasise his point. 'When they were captured, the Africans were forced to walk barefoot for days from the Northern villages, from the east, the west and across borders. Many died during those long walks, while some were eaten by wild animals.'

He paused for a moment as an elderly woman at the front of the group removed a handkerchief from her bag and dabbed at her eyes.

'Unfortunately, trapped as they were in these dungeons, many did not survive the overcrowded, unhygienic conditions and the tropical diseases. And, although they were all black men and all sons of Africa, they were mostly unable to communicate with each other as they had no common language.'

The guide moved through to a side room and again waited for the group to enter. 'This room was reserved for the slaves who resisted their masters. They were chained to the walls here or sent to the cells where, with no light and no air as the airtight doors ensured, they died a slow and painful death in the hot overcrowded dark rooms. When they died, they were buried together or thrown unceremoniously into the sea.'

He paused for a long moment while the group looked around the warm, dark room, a faint dripping of water on the stone walls the only sound to be heard. After a moment, he gestured to them to follow him and led them back up into the open courtyard. Faye, her hand still in Rocky's, was silent as they followed the other tourists past the rusted black cannon balls placed around the paved courtyard. They came to a halt outside the Female Slaves Dungeon, edging past the underground water tank that the guide explained used to be filled with captured rainwater and used for cooking and washing.

They walked into the women's dungeons and looked expectantly at the guide. He cleared his throat and gestured broadly around the confined quarters.

'These dungeons held three hundred women slaves.' His voice echoed loudly in the chamber. 'Although the women slaves were not as valuable as the men for manual labour, they served more than one purpose for the slave masters.' He paused meaningfully for them to understand what he was inferring and then continued. 'Evidence of this can be seen from the number of *mulattos* – mixed race children – in the area at the time.'

He walked out of the chamber into the courtyard and raised his voice dramatically, a note of emotion creeping into his narration for the first time. He pointed to a huge wooden door further down the paved walkway.

'When the time came, the men would take their final walk down the tunnels and join their wives and sisters here.' He moved forward until they stood directly in front of the door marked with a small plaque.

'Ladies and gentlemen...' He paused momentarily before continuing. 'They would then walk through this door, the "Door of No Return", leaving behind the land of their birth, their families, their parents and their children.' He paused for a moment and continued softly while the group strained forward to catch his words.

'Shackled to each other, they would walk down the cobbled walkway behind the Door and down a flight of stone steps into the ships waiting on the waters to receive them as cheap labour in the rice and cotton plantations of the slave masters.'

After another period of silence during which the tour guide bowed his head, he looked up with a sombre expression on his face and informed them that the tour was finished. Slightly dazed, the group broke up slowly, its members drifting off to inspect other parts of the Castle.

Faye broke the silence first. 'It's so incredibly hard to believe, even after hearing everything and seeing those shackles upstairs in the museum, that this all happened,' she said soberly. 'The thought that people were sold as though they were rice or coffee or flour is horrific.'

Amma, who had been uncharacteristically silent through-out the tour, nodded in agreement. 'Rocky's right, these castles should be preserved. You know, they are actual proof that it *did* happen, that slavery was real.' She looked so upset that Edwin put a comforting arm around her shoulders.

'I don't know about you guys but I think we've seen enough here.' He turned to Rocky. 'Why don't we drive out to Elmina now? We can take a look around the castle and then get some lunch.'

Cheering up at the mention of food, the girls led the way out of the castle grounds. There were few signs left of the rain that had fallen earlier in the day and the sun, now blazing high in the sky, warmed their chilled bones as they strolled back to the car. Rocky drove out of the winding streets and onto a major road running parallel with the beach and adorned with signboards advertising resorts and hotel complexes.

A short time later, they arrived at Elmina and were soon driving along a busy market road. They drove past boat builders hammering together their latest creations, past old salt-beaten houses and groves of coconut trees swaying in the marshy wetlands. Leaving a narrow road sandwiched between market stalls, they saw Elmina Castle sitting perched on a low hill.

Rocky parked the car, ignoring the plaintive begging for coins by some young boys hanging around the parking area. He took Faye's hand and led the way across a drawbridge with huge rusted hinges, into the castle. Having already agreed in the car to take a quick look around and then go on to lunch, they avoided the guided tour that was about to start, choosing instead to take a walk around the ancient fort.

They were immediately struck by its similarity to Cape Coast Castle, although the courtyard here was much smaller. A visit to the exhibition room revealed that the Portuguese had built the Sao Jorge Fort–Castle at Elmina in 1482.

Unwilling to revisit the overpowering emotions they had experienced at Cape Coast Castle, they contented themselves with a peek into the slave dungeons before climbing upstairs to explore the bedchamber and living quarters of the Governor.

Amma's stomach rumbled loudly, breaking the tension that gripped them as they walked through the room that had once been occupied by the colonial master.

'Okay, we get the message.' Edwin smiled and gave her a quick hug. 'Let's go.' Relieved to be able to do what their ancestors never could, the four of them made their escape and headed back to the car.

After a brief stop for lunch at a small hotel, they set off back to Accra in high spirits. The journey back took less time as Rocky concentrated on getting them back to town before the traffic started to build up in the late afternoon. Within two hours, they were back in the heart of Accra and heading towards Labone.

Amma and Edwin, after a hasty whispered conversation in the back, asked Rocky to drop them off in Osu.

'I'll see you back at home later, Faye,' Amma said as she slid out of the car. 'Thanks for taking us along, Rocky. Now we'll leave you two in peace.' With a wicked smile, she reached out for Edwin's hand and dragged him off down Oxford Street.

With the engine still purring, Rocky turned to Faye, an eyebrow raised enquiringly. 'Well, it's only five o'clock,' he said mildly. 'Do you want to go back home or shall we go somewhere for a drink?'

Faye smiled, more than happy at the thought of prolonging the time they had together. 'A drink sounds like a great idea.'

Pulling back onto the main road, Rocky drove down Oxford Street and turned into a narrow side street.

'There's a quiet pub at the end of the road where they serve some incredible grilled kebabs, if you feel like something to eat'. He drove slowly, careful to avoid a large open hole in the road, and parked in the forecourt of a large walled off house.

He came round to open her door before locking the car and leading her through a pair of dark-brown gates. A number of tables had been set up in the courtyard outside the pub and potted palms and miniature lamps between the tables allowed its patrons a degree of privacy.

They spied a table and Rocky beckoned to a waiter to take their order. A few minutes later, Faye took a long sip of chilled white wine and leant back in her seat.

'Mmmm, this is delicious!' She sighed happily. 'Thanks so much for today, Rocky,' she looked straight into his warm caramel-coloured eyes.

'It was my pleasure,' he answered. He put down his glass of beer and reached for her hand. He gently stroked her thumb with his finger and smiled.

'I'm glad we finally got to spend some time together,' he said softly. 'Even if it meant we had to have my little sister and her boyfriend along for the ride.'

Faye laughed. 'Come on, you must admit that they were very well-behaved. In any case, you have to be nice to Amma – she's going to miss Edwin terribly when he leaves this weekend.'

Rocky looked at her quizzically. 'And I'm going to miss *you* terribly when you leave next week.'

Lost for words, Faye took a hasty sip of her wine and looked around the bar, her mind in a whirl of confusion.

'Faye?' His voice was insistent as he tugged gently on her hand. She turned back to look at him, horrified to realise that she was close to tears.

'I know,' she whispered, her churning emotions clearly visible on her expressive face. 'I'm going to miss you, too.'

'Rocky!' Engrossed in each other, they both jumped as the shout came from the bar area across the courtyard. Rocky looked up sharply and groaned in exasperation.

'Damn it!' he muttered, sitting up straight as Nii strolled over to their table, his arm around a plump young girl who looked like she was barely out of school.

Rocky glared at the other man, who merely stroked his goatee as he took in the scene at their table.

'Hey man, what's up?' He was obviously in a jovial mood and when it became clear that Rocky had no intention of responding, he turned to Faye.

'It's Fiona, isn't it?' He bared his white teeth in a wolfish grin.

'Actually, it's Faye.' Unable to resist it, her gaze moved to the young girl, who simpered at them both and nestled into the arm cradling her.

'This is Gloria,' Nii said blithely, nudging the girl forward. 'She's a very good friend of mine, aren't you sweetheart?' He laughed loudly as she giggled in appreciation.

'Nice to meet you, Gloria,' Faye said quickly, looking apprehensively at Rocky, who continued to glare coldly and silently at Nii. Finally taking the hint, the other man gave a slight shrug and turned to the young girl.

'Hey, Gloria, I think we're interrupting a *tête-à-tête*. Let's leave these lovebirds alone, eh?' With a brief wave and salute, he propelled her away to the other side of the bar.

Rocky shook his head in resignation and took a long swallow from his glass.

'I don't know how Serwah puts up with that man. She really doesn't deserve the kind of humiliation he puts her through.'

Faye remained silent for a few moments, sipping her wine thoughtfully. 'Why does she stay with him?' she asked curiously. 'He certainly doesn't appear to be particularly discreet – that's the second girl I've seen him with in less than a week!'

Rocky shrugged helplessly, clearly at a loss to explain his cousin's tolerance. 'All I know is that if you can't be faithful to someone, there's no point in staying together,' he said flatly.

Faye looked at him, wondering if she dared to ask the question that had been preying on her mind ever since Amma's revelations about Rocky's time in America. Before she could reconsider her decision, she took a deep breath and blurted out the words. 'Rocky, what happened with Celine?'

For an instant he froze, his glass lifted halfway to his lips. Carefully putting the glass back down on the wooden tabletop, he looked at her, his face expressionless.

'Who told you about Celine?' he asked. Before she could speak, he cut in. 'Amma, obviously.'

He took a sip of his drink and stared hard at the table for a minute. Looking up, the warmth had left his eyes and he stared ahead blankly. 'Celine is history and there's nothing to discuss.' Swallowing the last of his beer, he shrugged.

'All she taught me was that the only thing you can count on is working hard and making a success of yourself.'

Before Faye could say another word, he called the waiter over and dropped a pile of notes on the table in payment for their drinks. Completely unprepared for the abrupt change in him that her question had brought about, she stood up reluctantly, digging her fingernails into her hand to stop the threatening tears.

As she followed him back to the car, Auntie Akosua's description of her son sounded clearly in her head. *He is so obsessed with his career, he won't give any woman a chance.*

18

Arts and Culture

'Faye, are you ready?' Amma's breathless tones floated through the closed bedroom door, rousing Faye from her brooding. Sitting up on her bed where she had flopped after a tiring afternoon of sightseeing, she called back loudly.

'Almost. Just give me five minutes,' she added optimistically. She hastened into the shower and ten minutes later, having hastily donned her favourite black trousers and a cool sleeveless linen shirt, she ran a comb through her hair and rushed downstairs to where an impatient Amma was quite literally pacing the floor.

'Oh good, you're ready,' she said with relief. 'Edwin's flight is at nine o'clock and he's got to check in by six-thirty.'

She scrabbled in her handbag and retrieved her car keys before hastening across to the living room where her parents were watching TV.

'Mama, we're off to the airport now,' she said, her long braids swinging as she put her head around the door. Blowing a kiss at her parents, she scooted out of the hallway and into the car, Faye following close behind.

Taking another anxious look at her watch, Amma gunned the car into action and almost knocked down Togo, giving him barely enough time to open the gate before she shot through.

'Erm, Amma, you need to calm down.' Faye said hesitantly, casting a nervous glance at her friend. Amma was hunched over the wheel; her eyes stared intently forward in fierce concentration and she drove as though she was in competition with the crazy taxi drivers. She glanced across at Faye and burst into laughter at the look of apprehension on her face.

'I'm sorry,' she said. She slowed the car down and sat back trying to relax. 'It's just that I want to make sure we don't miss Edwin at the airport.'

Her smile faded and her face clouded over. 'I can't believe I'm not going to see him again for a whole year,' she said, sounding so disconsolate that Faye's heart ached for her. She tooted half-heartedly at a bus driver who looked set to leap into the road in front of her.

Faye nodded in sympathy. 'I know, but it will give you a chance to sort out a job for yourself and take the project management course you've been talking about without Edwin to distract you. Besides, you're going to need the time to plan your engagement ceremony – hopefully, even Mrs Ofori can manage to get your outfit ready in a year!'

Amma smiled as she took the turning towards the airport. 'You're right, as usual. When you put it like that, it's not so very long until next December to plan the engagement. I'll have to choose the fabrics I'd like his family to present to mine, find a ring I like, and everything.' Despite herself, a note of excitement crept into her voice.

Still smiling, she drove into the airport car park and slid neatly into a parking space. It was now almost quarter past six and they rushed round to the check-in area, pushing their way through groups of people congregating around departing travellers, and craning their necks in search of Edwin. The line of people waiting to check in for the flight to New York was now quite short and a quick scan of the queue confirmed that he was not among them.

Just then, Amma squealed and Faye turned to see Edwin with one arm wrapped around his fiancée and a small holdall in the other. He greeted Faye with a smile.

'I've finished checking in,' he said, his eyes back on Amma. 'You just missed my parents – they dropped me off earlier.'

Amma nodded and brushed the lapel of his dark jacket, then linked her arm through his.

'Are you sure you've packed everything?' She looked up at him, her expression solicitous, and Faye bit her lip, trying not to smile at her wifely tone.

Edwin smiled affectionately down at her. 'Everything, except for you,' he said quietly.

'Okay, you two, break it up and give me a chance to say goodbye,' said a deep voice from behind Faye.

'Hey, Rocky!' Edwin looked up and a broad smile crossed his face. Her heart thumping, Faye turned slowly to see Rocky standing directly behind her, his hand outstretched towards Edwin.

The two men shook hands vigorously and hugged

briefly before Rocky stepped back to stand beside Faye. 'Have a good trip.' He said. He paused while a muffled announcement reverberated around the terminal. 'You'd better make a move to the departure lounge,' he added.

Amma's hold tightened on Edwin's arm and her determined smile wobbled. Rocky put an arm lightly around Faye's shoulders. 'We'll leave you two alone to say your goodbyes,' he said.

Faye moved forward to hug Edwin. 'Have a safe journey,' she said softly, and kissed him on the cheek in the Ghanaian fashion that now came to her so naturally.

'Make sure you come back to Ghana for our engagement ceremony next Christmas,' Edwin warned.

'I wouldn't miss it for the world,' Faye said. With a final wave, she turned and followed Rocky.

Once outside, they stood to one side of the entrance where they would be able to see Amma when she came out. Neither of them spoke and Faye kept her attention firmly focused on the people streaming in and out of the airport.

'Are you still upset with me?' Rocky asked softly, looking straight ahead. For a moment Faye was tempted to pretend otherwise. But three days of fretting over his abrupt change in attitude could not be so easily glossed over and she nodded slowly.

'Yes, I am,' she said, her voice hesitant. 'I don't understand why you reacted the way you did. It really hurt my feelings.'

Rocky sighed and rubbed his head wearily. After a long pause, he turned to face her.

'Look, Faye, I'm sorry I was so abrupt,' he said, his voice level. She noticed tiny lines of tiredness around his eyes. 'I'm just not very rational when it comes to the subject of Celine.'

She started to speak and he held up his hand. 'No, I still don't want to discuss her, but I do want to apologise for hurting you,' he said. 'I hope you know that I would never do that on purpose.' There was no doubting the sincerity in his voice and she gave a tiny nod.

'Okay. I can't pretend I don't want an answer to my original question but if you don't want to talk about it, we'll stay off the subject.'

'Thank you for being so understanding,' he said, and an impish smile suddenly lit up his tired features. Before she could react, he bent down and swiftly kissed her before straightening up again.

She looked up at him wordlessly, her hand automatically rising to touch her lips. Grinning even more broadly, he asked suddenly. 'What have you got planned for tomorrow?'

She shrugged helplessly, trying to remember what she had in mind for the day.

'Well, as I'm leaving on Tuesday, I thought I'd get some souvenirs for my family and friends. Amma mentioned a couple of places I could try.'

'Okay, let me suggest something,' Rocky said. 'To make up for wasting the last few days when we could have spent some time together, I'll take you to the Arts Centre tomorrow. It's a huge market and you can get all kinds of souvenirs from carvings to jewellery. Deal?'

Faye smiled back at him and nodded her head in agreement. 'Okay, deal.'

She looked past him to Amma who was slowly making her way over to them, her eyes suspiciously wet. Faye walked over to meet her and put a comforting arm around her friend's shoulders.

'Don't worry,' she said, trying to sound reassuring. 'He'll be back soon. Come on, let's get out of here.'

Rocky hugged his tearful sister and took his leave, explaining that he and Stuart had dinner plans with some clients. Despite Faye's best efforts to cheer her up, Amma remained quiet throughout the journey home and went straight up to her room when they arrived.

Faye wandered into the living room to find Auntie Amelia curled up on the sofa watching a Ghanaian play on TV. She looked up and smiled as Faye walked in, patting the space next to her on the couch. Sitting down next to her, Faye looked over with affection at the woman she had come to love in the short time she had known her.

'How are you, my dear?' Auntie Akosua said, touching Faye's hand gently. 'You look a little lost. Where's Amma?'

'She's gone up to bed,' Faye sighed. 'It's going to take her some time to get used to the fact that Edwin's gone – but at least she's got the engagement to look forward to.'

Auntie Amelia chuckled. 'Don't worry. If I know my daughter, she'll start planning the whole ceremony as soon as she wakes up tomorrow morning!'

She glanced quickly at Faye. 'You look a little sad yourself – is everything all right?'

Faye shook her head. 'Oh no, I'm fine. I was just

thinking about having to leave for London and how I'm going to miss all of you so much.'

Auntie Amelia smiled and took her hand between hers. 'We will miss you too, Faye. To tell you the truth, I've become so used to you being with us, I have been trying not to think about you going back. I do hope you will come back and see us again very, very soon.'

'I'll be back before you know it. I've already promised Amma that I'll be here for her engagement.' She paused thoughtfully. 'Maybe I can get William to come for a visit too,' she said. 'He would love it, I'm sure.'

Auntie Amelia smiled. 'I can't imagine what William looks like today. He was such a sweet little thing when I last saw him – he was always following Rocky around, not that either of them will remember that!'

Faye laughed and her face lit up at the mention of Rocky's name. 'Isn't that amazing? I've always thought that they would probably get along really well.'

In her excitement she missed the speculative look that appeared on Auntie Amelia's face.

'Did you see Rocky at the airport?' her aunt asked casually. 'He phoned earlier to find out what time Edwin's flight was leaving.'

'Yes, he arrived just in time to say goodbye to him.' She fell quiet, reliving the kiss at the airport, and failed to see the satisfied smile that crept over her aunt's face. Uncle Fred's arrival changed the topic of conversation and Faye watched the rest of the drama with the older couple before pleading tiredness and heading up to bed.

The next morning, after a long shower, she dressed

quickly and walked down the corridor to Amma's room. Knocking on the door, she entered to find Amma still in bed, her eyes red-rimmed and puffy. She smiled as Faye walked over to sit on the edge of her dishevelled bed.

'Good morning, Faye.' Amma sounded tired and her voice was hoarse. 'I'm sorry I disappeared last night but I knew I was going to cry and I just wanted to be alone.'

Faye crossed her long legs, rumpling the bedclothes even further. 'Hey, it's okay, I understand. I had a chat with your mother and then we watched a really bad play on TV. You'd have died laughing – the camera kept showing the microphones dangling from the ceiling and, at one point, you could see the other camera in the shot.'

Amma chuckled softly. 'It can be quite painful sometimes watching those low budget dramas. Well, I suppose I had better get up and stop moping.'

Faye smiled at her in encouragement. 'You'll be fine. What are you up to today?'

Amma grimaced before replying. 'I told Baaba I'd help her with the fashion show she's taking part in.'

She laughed as Faye raised an incredulous eyebrow. 'No, she's not modelling – although I think Clarissa is. Some of Baaba's clothes are being featured and as it's a pretty big annual event and the first time she's been invited to take part, she's quite excited about it.'

Amma slid off the bed and tied her braids back with a large band before slipping into her dressing gown.

'I have to be there to keep an eye on Baaba,' she said with a resigned sigh. 'If she gets within three feet of Clarissa, there will definitely be trouble!' She looked at

Faye hopefully. 'The show starts at three o'clock. You *will* come, won't you?'

Faye stood up and shuddered in mock horror. 'I think I'll leave that particular pleasure to you,' she said. 'I don't think I could cope with another Baaba and Clarissa showdown. Besides, Rocky's taking me to the Arts Centre to buy some souvenirs later today.'

Amma had been heading towards her bathroom and she stopped and turned back. 'Well, I'm glad you two are getting on again,' she said bluntly. 'I don't think I've seen you exchange more than five words since we got back from Cape Coast.'

Faye beamed at her happily. 'Well, we've made up now and we're friends again,' she declared.

'Just friends?' Amma queried, a sly smile curving her lips. She laughed aloud as Faye came as close to blushing as her chocolate skin would allow.

'Amma, I'm leaving here in three days!' she protested defensively. 'Besides which, it's not as if Rocky is interested in a relationship with anyone – he's made *that* perfectly clear.'

Amma sniffed and turned back towards the bathroom. 'Three days can be long enough,' she said enigmatically and shut the door firmly behind her.

Faye headed down the stairs to the kitchen for her morning coffee ritual. She made a cup of the brew and moved out to her favourite spot on the veranda, from where she could see Togo watering the flower bushes, his baggy shorts flapping loosely around his thin legs.

He smiled and waved in greeting when he saw her,

and she waved back. Suddenly conscious of how dear to her the Asante family had become, a wave of desolation swept over her as she thought of her return to London and the short, dark October nights she had to look forward to. Pushing the depressing thought aside, she settled herself on the wicker lounger and sipped her coffee slowly.

'So, is this where the supermodels relax?' Faye looked up to see Uncle Fred, dressed in white shorts and a white polo shirt, standing just inside the French doors leading to the veranda.

'Why, yes,' she replied, throwing her arm in the air disdainfully and adopting an affected drawl. 'We get *so* tired of walking up and down catwalks.'

He chuckled appreciatively and she sat up and smiled at him. 'You're looking very sporty, Uncle Fred!' She took in the spotless white trainers on his feet. 'Where are you off to?'

He pretended to shadow box for a few seconds, his generous stomach wobbling slightly as he lurched from foot to foot, then stopped, panting slightly as he answered.

'Just keeping fit, my dear,' he said breathlessly. 'I'm off to play tennis with an old friend of mine – we get together once in a while.' He winked at her broadly and dropped his voice into a conspiratorial whisper. 'Actually, it's more of an excuse to have a few beers together and catch up, but it makes your Aunt feel better if she thinks I'm exercising!'

Faye giggled at the mischievous expression on his face. With a brief wave, he disappeared back inside, leaving her to finish the dregs of her now cool coffee. She took the empty cup back to the kitchen and had just deposited it by the sink when Rocky sauntered in. Dressed in a pair of jeans and a faded denim shirt, he looked ridiculously handsome. The tiny lines of tiredness she had noted before seemed to have vanished, and he radiated energy as he walked towards her, hugging her briefly before stepping back.

'Hey.' His wide smile displayed his even white teeth. 'You look good enough to eat,' he added, taking in her slender figure shown off to advantage in the fitted midi dress she was wearing. The tiny buttons down the front were unbuttoned from just above her slim knees down to her shapely calves.

For the second time that morning, she felt the heat of a blush along her cheekbones and ducked her head self-consciously at his open scrutiny.

'Good morning to you too,' she muttered, pushing away from him hastily before Martha walked in. 'Do you want some coffee – I think there's still some left in the pot?' she asked.

'I'd rather have you,' he answered slowly, then laughed at the confusion that flooded her features. Taking pity on her, he moved over to the table and poured himself a huge mug of coffee before turning back to her.

'What time do you want to leave for the Arts Centre?' she asked, desperate to change the subject and bring her emotions under control. He sipped thoughtfully for a moment and then shrugged lightly.

'Whenever you like,' he said equably. 'I'm all yours, so just say the word.'

If only, she sighed inwardly, staring hungrily at his lean handsome features. Conscious of his eyes upon her, she turned back to the sink and slowly washed her used coffee cup.

'Well, I'm ready, so we can go when you've finished your coffee,' she said, her back still turned to him. His only reply was to walk up to where she stood and to slide his arms around her waist. For a moment, she leaned back against his broad chest, breathing in the faint lemon scent of his aftershave.

'Are you sure you have to go on Tuesday?' he murmured, resting his chin on the top of her head. 'Why can't you stay longer?'

With a sigh, she placed the coffee cup in the draining tray and turned around slowly to face him. His arms continued to hold her possessively and his smile disappeared as he looked down at her, his eyes serious for once as they took in her troubled features.

'You haven't answered me,' he said softly, bending to gently kiss her full lips. She kissed him back, leaning further into him as his arms tightened around her. After a few mindless moments, she pulled back. Shaking her head slightly, she reached up her hand and outlined his firm lips with her forefinger.

'I have to go back,' she said, her smile tremulous. 'I've used up all my holidays and my boss has probably driven the temp mad by now,' she added with a shaky laugh. Hearing Martha's voice in the corridor, she pushed Rocky away, smoothing down her hair self-consciously.

'Well, what about me? *I* might go mad if you leave,' he asked sulkily. Faye smiled at the look of frustration on his face; the disappointed frown marring his perfect features gave her a glimpse of what he might have looked like as a little boy.

'Come on,' she said as Martha bustled into the kitchen. 'Let's go. We'll talk about it later.'

He gulped down the rest of his coffee and followed her out of the kitchen. She ran upstairs to retrieve her shopping list and tidy her hair before heading out to the car. Rocky had already started the engine and he turned on the air conditioner as soon as they set off.

The traffic was light and they quickly sped down the dual carriageway that ran parallel to the beach. Fifteen minutes later, Rocky turned off the main road and drove slowly down the bumpy track leading to the Arts Centre car park. It was clearly a tourist haven as, despite the early hour, the place was already buzzing with visitors. Tourists and backpackers milled around the open grounds and wandered between the stalls, hotly pursued by salesmen peddling carvings and copper bracelets.

Faye stepped out of the car and was immediately besieged by two young men, one waving a small highly polished wooden elephant under her nose, while the other dangled several twisted copper bracelets in front of her, punctuating each shake of the bracelet with 'Very cheap, very cheap'.

Rocky locked the car and walked around to her side. He waved the two salesmen away and led Faye into a large covered pavilion packed with stalls selling all manner of jewellery, fabrics and carvings. A few of the stalls sold a wide array of merchandise made from the traditional Ghanaian *kente* cloth and Faye looked around, completely overwhelmed by the sheer number of merchants calling her to patronise their stalls.

Rocky bent to whisper in her ear. 'When you see something you like, just let me know discreetly and I'll do the bargaining for you. Otherwise, you'll get ripped off and end up paying a fortune.'

She nodded, and then stepped back hastily as a plump saleswoman hastened forward to pin a highly embroidered pink *boubou* against her shoulders. Shaking her head, Faye pushed the garment back towards its owner and moved on quickly to the next stall. A profusion of copper-coloured jewellery was arranged on a dark tablecloth and she bent over to inspect the different designs.

'Oh Rocky, look.' She held up a delicately twisted bracelet with tiny copper balls at each end. 'Caroline would love this!'

The stall keeper leapt into action and quickly named a price that had Rocky exploding into laughter. Faye watched in fascination as Rocky haggled relentlessly with the merchant, at one point even walking away as though uninterested. Eventually, after complaining piteously that they were taking the bread from the mouth of his children, the stall keeper relented and grudgingly accepted the wad of notes Rocky instructed Faye to hand over. Immediately after pocketing the money, the stallholder winked cheerfully at them and moved on to a European tourist who had been examining the jewellery and was enquiring about a similar bracelet. As she moved away, Faye shook her head in disbelief when she heard the stall keeper glibly add half as much again to the original price he had offered her.

They walked past one stall after another, stopping occasionally for a closer look at the more unusual items. As he had promised, Rocky took over the negotiations whenever she found something she wanted until finally, almost two hours later, she had managed to buy presents for almost everyone on her list.

'I still haven't seen anything yet that will be right for Lottie,' Faye said, frowning in concentration as she looked back at the stalls they had already visited. She clutched the rolled-up painting she had just bought for her father securely under one arm and looked in mounting frustration at the last uncrossed name on her list.

'Let's go outside and see what's available there,' Rocky suggested patiently. He steered her through a wide doorway and they stepped outside into the bright sunlight. In a smaller open area, a number of tradesmen had set up stalls, most of which were filled with assorted items carved from teak, mahogany and other hardwoods.

Faye stopped abruptly as they passed the second stall, ignoring the calls from the owner of the first stand. 'What do think about this?' she asked, pointing to a small jewellery box made from polished mahogany. It was shaped like a miniature travel trunk and held together by four tiny gold hinges. The lid had been engraved with a delicately carved rose, while the box itself was lined with cherry red felt.

Rocky picked it up and examined it carefully, turning it over in his strong hands to examine the finish before handing it over to Faye. 'It's beautifully made,' he said appreciatively. 'I'm sure she would love it.'

Faye nodded in agreement and Rocky turned to the stall keeper who immediately launched into a long speech about the unique design of the box. After fifteen minutes of heated debate between the two men, the vendor wiped his brow with a large soiled handkerchief and conceded defeat. Rocky took out his wallet and handed him a clutch of notes and then passed the carved box to Faye.

'Tell Lottie this one's from me,' he said with a grin, pushing away the notes Faye tried to hand him. 'Now, if you've finished with your list, let's go.'

Smiling happily, Faye strode alongside him as they headed back to the car and stowed her belongings safely in the boot.

'Where to, now?' she asked, as she settled herself into the front passenger seat. Rocky started the engine and opened the car windows for a few minutes to allow the hot air to escape.

'I'm sure you don't want to hear this since you said you'd turned down Amma's offer earlier on, but I forgot I'd promised to drive Stuart over to the fashion show this afternoon,' Rocky confessed.

'Oh.' Faye stared at him in dismay.

'His driver is away this weekend and the truth is that Stuart's been banned from driving any of the bank's cars.' Taking in her disappointment, he added quickly. 'Look, why don't you come with me? We'll drop him off at the show and leave him in Baaba's hands and then we can carry on and do whatever you want.'

Faye shrugged in resignation. 'Okay, then. Look, it's not that I don't want to go to the fashion show – I just don't want to get caught in the usual crossfire between Baaba and Clarissa.'

The sun was high in the sky as they drove away and Faye looked around, basking in the now familiar sights and sounds of Accra. She smiled inwardly as she realised how quickly she had come to accept the manic driving and even the occasional herd of goats ambling across busy highways. Only too aware that she would be leaving in three days, she drank in the passing scenery and tried to capture it all to remember when she returned to England.

They were soon at Stuart's house and he came out to meet them as soon as the gates had closed behind the car. In the afternoon sunlight, the grounds of the house looked even more extensive than they had on the night of the party, and Faye looked round appreciatively at the beautifully landscaped garden.

'You have a lovely house, Stuart,' she said, reaching up to kiss his cheek in greeting. 'But don't you find it a bit big for just you?'

Ushering them inside into a large open plan living area, he chuckled in response to her question. 'Yep, it's huge,' he agreed cheerfully. 'When they brought me to take a look at the house when I first got to Ghana, I thought I'd be living here with a few other people. I couldn't believe it when they said it was just for me!'

A steward boy entered the room and smiled at the visitors, raising his right hand in a brief salute. 'You are welcome, Mr Rocky, and madam. Please, what can I offer you?'

'Have a drink, you two.' Stuart set off in the direction of

the stairs. 'I'll change quickly and then we can go.'

Faye settled for an ice-cold Coke while Rocky quickly finished a small bottle of cold beer. She had just finished her drink when Stuart walked back in. He was wearing a pair of coffee-coloured linen trousers and a long loose linen shirt in the same fabric.

'You look really nice!' Faye exclaimed, astonished at the transformation from the scruffy shorts and vest he had been wearing when they arrived.

Stuart winked at her knowingly. 'Well, I've got to make an effort, eh, since Baaba's worked so hard for this show. Shall we go?'

They went out to the car and before long they were at the exhibition centre where the fashion show was taking place. Huge banners outside the centre advertised it as the show of the year and billboards displayed the bright logos of the event sponsors. After circling around the parking area a couple of times, Rocky eventually found a space and they stepped out of the cool air-conditioned vehicle into the hot sunshine.

Rocky's arm rested casually across Faye's shoulders as he steered her up a flight of wide shallow steps leading to the entrance of the exhibition hall. Stuart followed slowly, trying not to sweat into his linen shirt in the intense heat. After paying the entrance fee, the three of them walked into a huge pavilion where a number of designers had set up stands. They quickly spotted Amma and Baaba standing in front of a small exhibition stand that displayed a range of clothes similar to those on the mannequins in Auntie Amelia's shop. Amma saw them first and waved vigorously.

'Hi, you guys,' she exclaimed, clearly excited to see them. 'Faye, I'm so glad you decided to come! You've missed the first show but the second one will start in about an hour.'

Stuart reached out to hug Baaba. 'Is that the one where they'll be modelling your clothes?'

Her voluptuous figure was moulded in a long figure-hugging black dress with dramatic slits on both sides rising up to mid-thigh. Her full bosom looked in danger of spilling out of the front of the dress as she returned Stuart's hug.

'Yes – and I've managed to sell eight dresses already!'

Pausing in her jubilation, she looked over Stuart's shoulder and honed in on Rocky's arm resting possessively on Faye's shoulders.

'Well, I see that you've been keeping busy, Faye,' she said with a sly smile. There was no malice in her tone and Faye was forced to laugh at the exaggeratedly knowing look Baaba was casting at her. From behind, a familiar shrill voice caused both her and Rocky to turn round sharply.

'Rocky! You made it!' Tottering in impossibly high heels and wearing a very short, fitted metallic tunic, Clarissa launched herself at Rocky, who was forced to move his arm away from Faye to avoid toppling over. After a prolonged and suffocating hug, she finally released him and stepped back a few inches.

'I'm so glad you're here! You *are* staying to see me in the next show, aren't you?' She tossed her hair and pouted prettily.

'Actually, Faye and I just came to drop Stuart off and take a quick look at Baaba's designs,' Rocky said. He stepped back to put more space between them. 'But I'm sure you'll be fantastic, as usual,' he said with a smile. Clarissa glanced at Faye and gave her a perfunctory nod in greeting before turning back to her preferred target.

'What do you think of my make-up?' she asked, angling her neck upward to give him a closer look. 'We're supposed to be space age robots,' she giggled.

More like spaced out, was Faye's immediate thought, and she watched in irritation as Clarissa continued to grip Rocky's arm tightly while talking ten to the dozen. Her attention was momentarily distracted by a tall man approaching them. As he drew nearer, she realised it was Sonny.

He sauntered up to them, greeting Amma and Baaba before turning to Faye and kissing her warmly on both cheeks.

'Hello, stranger.' His smile was so cheeky that she couldn't help but smile back. He looked over to where Clarissa had dragged Rocky to greet a slim older woman wearing a fitted red trouser suit.

'It looks like Clarissa and her mother have got Rocky cornered over there,' he said, looking at Faye through narrowed eyes. She refused to take the bait and stared back at him steadily.

'How have you been, Sonny?'

He shrugged carelessly, taking one of her hands in his strong grip before she could protest. 'I've really missed you, you know.' He stroked her hand and resisted her efforts to pull it away. 'I don't understand why you suddenly became so distant. I thought we were friends.'

'Faye, are you ready to go?' Rocky said sharply, suddenly appearing at her side, with Clarissa right behind him. The expression on his face was cold as he took in the sight of her hand in Sonny's. Tugging her hand away from Sonny's unrepentant grip, Faye turned to Rocky and nodded. She felt a sudden rush of annoyance at his attitude, especially after his display of tolerant affection towards Clarissa, who now smiled maliciously at her, and she turned back to Sonny with a warm smile.

'I'm leaving in a couple of days; so if I don't see you before I go, I suppose this is goodbye.'

Paying no heed to the glower on Rocky's face, Sonny smiled back, his expression mischievous. 'Don't worry,' he said. 'You'll see me before you go.'

Clarissa had been watching the interchange through narrowed eyes and she suddenly excused herself on the pretext that she needed to freshen up her make-up before the next show.

Rocky's arm propelled Faye forward and cut short any further conversation with Sonny. With a brief wave of farewell to Amma and Baaba, she turned to follow Rocky. Stuart had been admiring Baaba's designs and as Faye and Rocky walked away, he cursed quietly, slapped his forehead and called Rocky back.

'Hey, Rock old man, I completely forgot,' he said, his tone apologetic. At Rocky's enquiring look, he went on quickly. 'Günter and Manfred have changed their flight and are leaving tomorrow. They want to meet with us tonight to tie up the details on the financing deal.'

Rocky's face clouded over in irritation as he stared at

Stuart. His boss looked back at him with a bland smile, undaunted by the mutinous look on the other man's face.

'Since Amidu's not around, can you pick me up from the house at seven o'clock?' Stuart turned his attention back to the clothes stand and looked admiringly at a batik shirt from Baaba's collection.

Rocky sighed deeply, glancing down at Faye in obvious frustration at the latest turn of events. He tried again. 'Stuart, I have other plans for this evening. Can't we do this tomorrow morning?'

'Nothing doing, old chap,' his boss answered cheerily. 'They're leaving on the morning flight back to Hamburg. Look, I'm sorry about the short notice, but I think you will be very happy if we can close this deal tonight.'

Rocky looked at him, puzzled, but it was clear that Stuart had no intention of elaborating further.

He shrugged and turned back to Faye. 'I'm really sorry,' he sighed and shook his head in resignation. 'I wanted to take you out tonight, but it looks like that's going to be impossible now.'

Acutely disappointed at missing the opportunity of spending the evening with him, Faye forced herself to smile. 'It's okay.' She looked up into his troubled features. 'There's nothing you can do about it, so don't worry.'

They left the exhibition hall without any further discussion and were soon back in the car. For a few minutes, the only sound was the music blaring from the car radio as they drove back in the direction of Labone.

'Shall we get something to eat? You must be hungry,' Rocky said eventually. As if on cue, her stomach gave an audible rumble. They looked at each other and laughed, dissipating the tension that had been building up since they left the hall. Rocky turned in the direction of Osu and before long they were sitting in a quiet restaurant enjoying a late and very welcome lunch. Refuelled by the meal, Faye chattered blithely, sharing her experiences in Ntriso with Rocky who listened intently, his eyes widening at her account of the visit to the cemetery.

'That must have been really emotional. I don't think I would have been able to handle it so well.'

'Why? Are you that afraid of losing control of your emotions?' Faye asked lightly, pleating the white cotton napkin she had used between her fingers.

'Isn't everybody?'

Faye looked at him closely, but his expression gave no clue as to what he was thinking. 'No, I don't think so,' she said carefully. 'I used to want to suppress my emotions and just keep other people happy, but I've realised now that it really doesn't work.'

He looked at her enquiringly and she continued slowly. 'You remember I told you about my ex-boyfriend Michael?'

Rocky nodded.

'Well, most of the time I was with him, I was really anxious about whether I was good enough or culturally acceptable.' She paused for a moment, trying to find the right words. 'It's taken some time but I realise that I was trying to be good enough for him at the expense of how I felt about myself. I put up with a lot of stuff because I was avoiding the need to deal with my feelings about who I really was and what I want for myself.'

Rocky extricated the crumpled napkin from between her fingers and held her hand lightly.

'So now you give in to your emotions without any fear?' He looked at her curiously. Faye looked down at her hand cupped between his and felt the familiar frisson that ran through her whenever he touched her.

'Well, I think I *am* more honest with myself about how I feel than I used to be.' She shrugged lightly. 'But it's going to take a lot longer for me to undo my old habits completely.'

'And where does Sonny fit into your emotional honesty?' Rocky asked suddenly. Faye stared at him blankly, completely thrown by the change of subject.

'What do you mean?' she asked, bewildered.

Rocky released her hand and leaned back in his seat, not taking his eyes off her face. 'From what I saw earlier today, there definitely seems to be some emotional connection between you and him,' he said evenly.

Faye shook her head in exasperation. 'Sonny is nothing more than an acquaintance. He took me out once, but that's it.'

'So why would he think there's more to your relationship than that?' Rocky continued relentlessly. 'According to Clarissa, he's crazy about you.'

Faye snorted inelegantly, unable to believe that Rocky would pay any attention to observations from Clarissa, of all people.

'Sonny's crazy about any girl he hasn't been through yet,' she replied bluntly. 'You saw him at the party – did *that* tell you he was crazy about me?'

'Faye, I think you've been around long enough to know that a man can flirt with someone else and still want you.' Rocky still sounded unconvinced.

'Well, all I know is that *he* doesn't mean anything to *me*,' she retorted.

The waiter approached with the bill and Rocky paid it quickly before helping her from her chair. The weather was cooler and they walked around Osu, peering into shop windows and laughing at some of the outrageous designs on show. They wandered into a tiny boutique, almost hidden away from the main road and, at Faye's insistence, Rocky bought a stylish silk tie in a black geometric design. As he was about to hand over the money, he spotted a delicate gold and bead bracelet in the display case at the counter and asked the assistant to add it to his purchase.

When they eventually made it back to the car, he started the engine to cool the heated interior and then turned towards her. Removing the bracelet from its tiny gift box, he reached for her hand and solemnly clasped the pretty trinket around her slender wrist.

'This is to say thank you for spending today with me.' He looked at the bracelet in satisfaction, before adding softly. 'And to say I'm sorry I can't spend tonight with you.' Leaning forward, he kissed her gently before releasing her hand.

Faye gazed at her wrist, her eyes misting over as she tried to focus on the bracelet.

'It's beautiful, Rocky,' she said softly. 'Thank you.'

He nodded silently before putting the car into gear and heading for home.

19

Cultural Closure

'Faye, telephone!'

Faye scrambled to her feet from the lounger where she had been enjoying the warm afternoon breeze on the veranda, and dashed inside. Auntie Amelia was in the hallway holding out the house phone and she smiled indulgently as Faye rushed in barefoot, her long slim legs exposed by her tiny shorts.

'It's your father,' she said, as she passed her the handset.

'Dad?' Faye seized the phone in excitement. 'Dad, is that you?' She moved to the nearby armchair and sat down. After a few minutes of conversation, she said goodbye and replaced the receiver before walking through to the living room in search of her aunt. She found her lying on the couch engrossed in a thick book that she put down when she heard Faye walk in.

'Have you finished your call already?' She gestured to Faye to sit down next to her.

'Yes, I've given him my flight details for tomorrow

night so he can meet me at the airport in the morning,' she replied. 'It was so good to hear his voice! I love it here, but it will be great to see Dad and William again.'

Auntie Amelia took off her reading glasses and looked at Faye closely, her expression amused.

'You know, my dear, correct me if you think I'm wrong, but you seem so much more...' she paused, searching for the word she wanted. 'So much more *confident* than when you first arrived.'

Faye sat thoughtfully for a few moments and then nodded.

'Yes, I think you're right. I've only been in Ghana for three weeks, but it feels so much longer. And I *am* much more confident now that I know more about my country and my culture.'

'And about yourself?'

The question was asked gently and Faye smiled ruefully and nodded again. 'Yes, and about myself.'

Auntie Amelia's eyes were still fixed on Faye. 'What are your plans when you get back to London, Faye?' she asked, fingering her glasses thoughtfully.

'Well, I'm due back at work on Thursday.' Faye looked slightly puzzled by the question.

'Yes, but what are your *real* plans for yourself?' the older woman said insistently. 'Do you want to continue working forever as a secretary?'

Faye shrugged helplessly. 'Now you sound like Dad,' she grimaced. 'I know I don't want to carry on doing the same job for ever, but I've never really been sure that I can do anything else particularly well.' She shrugged again. 'I suppose I've just been marking time with my job – and probably did the same with my ex-boyfriend – because I don't have the guts to try for something better. I guess it's been a case of living down to my own expectations.'

Auntie Amelia folded her glasses carefully and laid them on the side table by her book.

'You remember what I once told you about finding your passion?'

Faye nodded and she continued. 'Well, if I remember correctly, I was talking about Amma at the time. You are like another daughter to me, so I will give you the same advice. First, look for what you love, for what excites you. Don't worry about whether or not you can do it perfectly; just start doing it and your passion will take over.'

Faye sat in silence, trying to absorb what she had heard and to make sense of it in her own mind. Impulsively she scooted over to the older woman and hugged her, resting her head against her for a moment. Auntie Amelia held her closely for a short while before raising her chin with gentle fingers and looking into her eyes.

'Your mother would have been very proud of you, my dear' she said gently. 'I know I am.'

'Thank you – I'll try and justify your confidence in me. Now as I'm leaving tomorrow, I'm going back to the veranda for my last afternoon of doing nothing,' she added mischievously. Straightening the tiny cropped T-shirt she was wearing, she blew a kiss at Auntie Amelia and headed straight back to her favourite spot.

Stretched out on the wicker lounger with her eyes closed, she was dreaming of all the things she could do with her life when she heard the door to the veranda slide open. She squealed with shock as a pair of hands suddenly seized her bare midriff, tickling her heated flesh mercilessly.

Her eyes flew open and she gazed up in disbelief at Sonny, who stood grinning down at her, his hands still resting on her stomach.

'What the *hell* do you think you're doing?' she asked furiously, trying fruitlessly to sit up. Pushing his hands away, she finally managed to get herself upright before asking the question again.

Sonny shrugged and sat down uninvited next to her. She shuffled along the lounger, trying to put some space between them.

'Well, you said you were leaving tomorrow, so I thought I'd come by and see you.' He looked sheepish as she continued to glare coldly at him. Having recovered her composure, she relaxed a little and gave him a small smile.

'Well, you didn't have to scare the life out of me, did you?' she asked mildly, not stirred in the least by his hangdog expression.

'I'm sorry,' he said, trying to sound contrite. Then he looked into her eyes suggestively. 'But I just couldn't resist it when I saw you lying there looking so inviting.' She made no comment except to glare at him again and he hastily changed the subject.

'You missed a good show the other day,' he remarked, fingering the medallion dangling from his chain. 'Clarissa was actually pretty impressive.'

He laughed at her look of scepticism. 'Okay, so I know

she's not exactly your best friend, but she *is* a good model. And,' he added more seriously, 'she's also tough – she usually gets what she wants.'

'Is that a warning?' Faye asked lightly, trying to dismiss the small knot of dread that had started to form in her stomach.

Sonny hesitated for a moment. 'No, it's the truth.' She looked at him, eyebrows raised, and for a moment he remained silent. Then shrugging as if he had no other choice, he looked across at Faye.

'Where do you think Rocky was two nights ago, and last night?' he asked. Faye stared back at him in bewilderment.

'He and Stuart took some clients to dinner on Saturday night, and he was working late at the office last night. He had to finish a report for work that he needed to send off this morning,' she said.

'So, I suppose he didn't tell you that the dinner was at Clarissa's mother's restaurant, did he?' Sonny asked, his expression challenging.

Faye paused for a moment, the knot of dread growing bigger and pulling tighter. Taking a deep breath, she turned to face Sonny. 'So what if that's where they went? What difference does it make? It was a *business* dinner.'

'So why was Clarissa with them, then?' Sonny countered swiftly. 'And why was Rocky with her last night?'

Faye looked back at him silently, her expressive features betraying her uncertainty in the face of the bombshell he had dropped. Her mind raced as she tried to think of all the possible reasons why Rocky hadn't told her about taking Clarissa to dinner on the night of the fashion show. She remembered his apparent regret at having to cancel his proposed outing with her and she shook her head doubtfully as she tried to reconcile the two things. Rocky had spent most of the previous day at the office, finishing the paperwork for the deal he and Stuart had been working on, and she had seen him only briefly when he came by the house late in the afternoon to pick up some documents he had left in his room.

Now, as she looked at Sonny smiling at her in undisguised triumph, she felt her new-found confidence waver and her old insecurities start to rear their ugly heads. Sensing her distress, he moved closer to her, putting his arm around her comfortingly and pressing her head gently on to his shoulder. Fighting back the tears, she was too distraught to pay attention to his hand rubbing her shoulder and continuing down slowly to stroke her skin where the tiny T-shirt had left her back exposed.

'Faye! Where are you? I've got some news for—' The deep voice coming from within the house came to an abrupt stop as Rocky appeared in the doorway of the veranda. Faye looked up in bemusement to see Rocky standing stock still, an expression of frozen disbelief on his face as he took in the sight of her, barely dressed and in Sonny's arms. As she watched in horror, his expression changed to one of utter contempt and without uttering another word, he turned on his heel and strode back inside.

'Rocky!' Her heart pounding, Faye pushed Sonny away and rushed into the house. She ran frantically from room to room in search of him and then outside when she heard the familiar sound of his car's powerful engine. As she raced out to the driveway, she saw the car turning out of the gate onto the main road, leaving only loose chippings of gravel in its wake.

Faye watched the back of the car disappear down the road and promptly burst into tears. She was sobbing so hard that she didn't hear Sonny coming up behind her.

'Faye?' He raised his hand tentatively to comfort her and she slapped it away furiously.

'Haven't you done enough already?' she cried angrily, hot tears coursing down her face. 'Just go, *please*!'

With that, she turned around and rushed back inside the house and up to her room. Every time she calmed herself down, she remembered the expression on Rocky's face and dissolved into tears yet again.

A loud knock at the door made her sit up sharply, hoping against hope that Rocky had come back.

'Come in,' she said, her voice hoarse from crying. Wiping her swollen eyes, she swung her legs down from the bed, ready to get up. But before she could move, Amma burst in, whooping loudly and barely able to contain herself. Too excited to notice Faye's condition, she jumped onto the bed, her long braids flying.

'Have you heard? Mama's just told me about Rocky,' she said. 'Isn't it just too amazing?' Unable to sit still, she jumped up again and twirled around the room.

'I'll miss him terribly, but I'm so glad for him!'

She turned to Faye, who was sitting dumbfounded on the edge of the bed and grinned with excitement. 'I told you a lot can happen in three days, didn't I? You must be thrilled!'

As Faye continued to stare at her in complete bewilderment, Amma stopped her dancing and peered closely at her friend. Her smile faded as she took in the tear stains on Faye's cheeks and the eyes clearly swollen from crying. Exclaiming in concern, she sat down on the bed next to her.

'What's wrong?' She stared at her in consternation. 'Oh Faye, what's happened?' Amma's sympathy brought forth a fresh flood of tears and it was a few minutes before Faye was able to haltingly explain what had happened on the veranda.

Amma listened in silence, putting a sympathetic arm around Faye after she had finished speaking. With a deep sigh, the younger girl shook her head slowly before sitting back to look at Faye.

'Oh dear, what a mess,' she said soberly. 'But Faye, don't pay any attention to what Sonny said. Clarissa overhead Stuart telling Baaba that they would be at her mother's restaurant that evening and she just showed up there. Rocky told me about it yesterday – he asked her to leave and she stormed off, really upset at him.'

'But why didn't he say anything to me about it?' Faye wailed, resorting to wiping her eyes with the back of her hand as her handkerchief was now totally soaked.

Amma hesitated for a moment before answering. 'I don't know, but since he made such a fuss about Sonny chasing after you, he probably didn't want you to think he had any interest in Clarissa. He's been really patient with her because he felt guilty about ending things and he's not the type to humiliate anyone. But he's had enough of her antics and he went to see her last night to warn her that she needed to accept that their relationship is over and that he's tired of her attempts to try and get him back.'

Faye stared at her in despair, another wave of tears welling up in her eyes. 'Oh Amma, I can't believe this – what am I going to do?'

Amma sighed again. 'Look, don't worry.' She tried to inject some conviction into her voice. 'Just give him some time to calm down and then you can explain what happened. I'm sure he'll understand.'

Faye shook her head in misery. Then a thought struck her and she looked up at her friend. 'What did you mean just now about you'll miss him and I must be so thrilled? What's happened?'

Amma squirmed uncomfortably before running her hands through her braids helplessly. 'Well, I suppose it's quite ironic really, given what's just happened, but Rocky found out today that he's being promoted to a Managing Director position.'

Faye still looked puzzled. 'Well, that's great news; he's worked really hard for this. But why does that mean you'll miss him?'

Amma grinned. 'We-ell... the new job is based in London.'

Faye sat bolt upright in shock. 'What!' Her voice was so hoarse, she could barely get the word out. Clearing her throat, she stared in disbelief as Amma hugged herself with glee. 'You're kidding, right?'

The younger girl shook her head and Faye ran her hands through her hair, her brain spinning as she took in the import of the words she had just heard. The extent of the damage caused by the scene on the veranda hit her afresh and she stared at Amma in horror.

'Oh my God,' she whispered. '*That's* what he came back to tell me. And to find Sonny of all people sitting there pawing me...' She jumped off the bed and started pacing up and down the room in agitation.

'Amma, you've got to do something!' Literally wringing her hands, she turned to her friend in desperation. 'Promise me, talk to him and tell him what happened – he'll believe you. *Please!*'

Feeling desperately sorry for Faye, Amma nodded helplessly. 'Okay, calm down,' she said, trying to sound soothing. 'I promise I'll speak to him as soon as he gets home, okay?'

Faye nodded, her expression bleak. Amma stood up and hovered hesitantly by the door. 'Why don't you wash your face and come down for a drink? Mama is in her room and it will give you time to pull yourself together before dinner.'

Faye nodded again and headed for the bathroom to repair some of the damage caused by her tears. She washed her face with cold water and looked into the mirror above the sink. Her eyes were pink rimmed and watery and her hair was sticking out in all directions. She went back into the bedroom and brushed her hair vigorously, applying a little lipstick and spraying some perfume to lift her spirits.

All the while, Amma's words, 'The new job is based in London...' were reverberating around her brain. Piercing shafts of joy alternated with bursts of despair as she thought through dozens of scenarios of how she could convince Rocky that he could trust her.

A few minutes later, determined to sort things out come what may, she ran downstairs to find Amma in the living room on her phone, scrolling down through a text message that Edwin had just sent.

'He seems to be having a good time,' she remarked, glancing up as Faye came in. 'I hope he finds that job quickly – I was looking in the jewellers this afternoon, and the kind of ring I'd like is not exactly cheap.'

She looked closely at Faye and breathed a sigh of relief. 'Well, you look a lot better now, thank goodness; you had me really worried upstairs. Oh, wait, there's a message here for you.' She scrolled down and read aloud. '"Give my love to Faye and tell her to keep a tight hold on Rocky...."' Her voice trailed off and she looked at Faye apologetically.

'You can always trust Edwin to say the wrong thing at the wrong time!' She tossed her phone onto the side table. 'Come on, there's a bottle of wine in the fridge – let's get some glasses.'

Faye laughed for the first time in hours as she followed Amma to the kitchen.

'I hope Martha's not there or she'll be totally scandalised. Do you know her church says that alcohol is the devil's brew?'

Amma peered around the kitchen door and turned back with a grin. 'The coast is clear. Quick – you get the glasses and I'll bring the bottle!'

A few minutes later, the two of them were sprawled on the rug on the living room floor, wine glasses in hand. Faye had changed earlier into a sleeveless maxi dress and she lay stretched out on her back, staring reflectively at the high ceiling.

'This time tomorrow, I'll be heading for the airport,' she sighed. 'I'm really going to miss Ghana.' Turning her head, she smiled at Amma who was sitting propped up against the sofa. 'I'm going to miss you, too. It's been just like having a sister over the last three weeks.'

Amma nodded, suddenly subdued. 'I know what you mean. It's bad enough with Edwin gone; now you're going and Rocky is supposed to start work in London next month... *I'm* the one who should be getting upset.'

'Okay, I'll stop complaining if you will. Now, where's the bottle?' Laughing, they refilled their glasses and played some of Amma's CDs until Auntie Amelia came in to tell them that dinner was ready.

There was still no sign of Rocky as the rest of the family went into the dining room, although Martha had laid a place for him at the table. Feeling very relaxed and more than a little tipsy from the wine, Faye kept them entertained during dinner with stories of Mr Fiske (Junior) and some of his more famous exploits at the office. It wasn't until she had finished telling a long story about the time her boss had unwittingly sent the cheque from the sale of a client's property to a national charity, that she realised what she had done.

Staring at her empty plate, she looked at Amma in astonishment. 'Amma, do you realise that I've just eaten a plate of *kontomire* with pigfoot and I didn't even notice?'

Amma smiled in amusement at the incredulity on Faye's

face. 'Well, I guess you've really adapted now,' she said. 'I wondered when you would realise what you were eating!'

Uncle Fred, who had been enjoying listening to Faye's office anecdotes, patted his round stomach in satisfaction. 'Listen here, pigfoot is my favourite meat and I won't hear a rude word said about it.'

He picked up the unused fork from the cutlery laid out for Rocky and tapped it against his glass, calling for silence.

'Ladies, I was hoping my son would be here for dinner but doubtless, due to his recent news, he is working harder than ever at his office. Nevertheless, I have a few words I want to say.' He paused and looked around the table, paying no attention to his wife's twitching lips and Amma's open smile.

Smiling at Faye, he raised his glass and continued. 'Three weeks ago, this delightful young lady arrived here to grace us with her presence and to renew her ties to her homeland. We have all been privileged to have her here as part of our family.'

He turned to Faye and his voice softened. 'Faye, my dear, since this is our last night together before you leave tomorrow, I just want to let you know that you have another family right here with us. We love you and wish you all the best on your return to London.'

With that he raised his glass to a chorus of 'hear, hear' from Auntie Amelia and Amma. Faye looked around at them, her eyes misting over again at the love and affection that surrounded her. Clinking his glass against hers, Uncle Fred added cheerfully, 'Make sure you come back as soon as your lawyers give you some more time off.'

With dinner over, they moved to the living room to chat and watch TV. Amma had offered to take her out for a drink, but Faye was now intent on waiting for Rocky to come home. It was after ten o'clock when the rest of the family said goodnight and went up to their rooms, leaving her downstairs on her own. As she left to follow her parents upstairs, Amma turned to Faye.

'Good luck,' she hissed. 'Tell me what happens tomorrow.'

Alone in the living room, Faye curled up on the sofa in front of the TV. She turned down the volume, her mind a million miles away from the drama taking place on the small screen. Twice she thought she heard the gate opening and ran to the front door, only to find that there was no one there.

It was close to midnight when the creaking sound of the metal gate and the powerful roar of Rocky's car confirmed that he had returned home. Her heart pounding, Faye rushed to the door of the living room and waited for him to come into the house.

He walked in a few moments later, his jacket slung over one arm, and headed straight for the staircase. She stepped forward out of the shadow of the doorway and called his name hesitantly just as he reached the foot of the stairs.

He stopped at the sound of her voice, not moving for several seconds. Then, with an audible sigh, he turned around to look at her. His eyes were as hard as pebbles and her lips trembled as she took in the look of impatient irritation on his face.

'Well?' His tone was not encouraging and she cleared her suddenly constricted throat nervously before she spoke.

'Rocky, we've got to talk,' she said, her voice husky with nerves. 'Please, you have to listen to me. What happened earlier wasn't—'

He cut her off abruptly. 'Faye, it's late and I really don't have time for this. You don't owe me any explanations. You're our guest and a free agent, and you're perfectly entitled to see whomever you wish.'

As he started to climb up the stairs, she called his name again. He stopped for a moment then turned around and came back down, walking right up to her until his face was literally inches from hers. She stared up at him, her expression one of naked pleading and for a second she saw uncertainty in his eyes. The next moment, however, his expression had hardened again and he took a step backwards.

'Rocky, please, don't do this,' she whispered, her expression agonised as she watched him literally retreating. 'Don't pretend that everything that happened meant nothing to you.'

He shook his head violently, backing away slowly away from her.

'What *did* it mean, Faye?' His expression was unreadable as he continued brutally. 'I think you've been around long enough not to read too much into what men say and do, haven't you?'

She flinched as though he had struck her, but his expression did not waver.

'It's like I've always said, Faye.' He spoke slowly and distinctly. 'The only thing one should count on in this world is working hard and getting ahead. *Everything* else,' he paused meaningfully, 'is just a waste of time.'

The tears streamed unchecked down her face as she watched him turn around and walk swiftly up the stairs without a backward glance. Sobbing quietly, she went back into the living room and burrowed into the armchair, crying as though her heart would break.

It was almost an hour later that she forced herself to leave her refuge and go up to bed where she tossed and turned for hours, unable to sleep until dawn. Exhausted, she slept through the loud crowing of the neighbourhood rooster and the usual morning noises of the city, only waking up when Amma's insistent knocking intruded into her dreamless slumber.

She sat up groggily, mumbling 'Come in' before rolling round and burrowing back under the sheet. Amma marched in purposefully and without saying a word, unhooked the mosquito net and flung it up over the frame before sitting down on the edge of the rumpled bed.

'Okay, so what happened?' she demanded. 'I saw Rocky this morning before he left for work, and he told me to mind my own business before I could even open my mouth!'

Faye groaned into her pillow, shaking her head to avoid remembering the awful scene from the previous evening. Amma was not prepared to take no for an answer and pulled the pillow away impatiently.

'Okay, okay,' Faye mumbled indistinctly. She sat up and rubbed her swollen eyes gently, seizing the pillow back from Amma to prop herself upright.

'Wow, Faye, your eyes look awful!' Amma said in alarm, peering closely at her.

'That's the least of my worries,' Faye said bitterly, leaning back against the pillow. 'What happened? I tried to talk to your stubborn brother and he didn't want to know.'

She sighed and shook her head in despair. 'I tried *everything* to get him to listen, but he was so cold...' Her voice trailed off as the memory of the events from the night before flooded back.

Amma sighed and raked her hands through her long braids. 'Unfortunately, I know what you mean. Rocky can be so difficult sometimes.'

She sat up straight and said firmly. 'Look, Faye, just give him some time. After all, you're leaving this evening and he's not going to just let you go.' She smiled confidently despite the sceptical look Faye gave her. 'Come on, get up and get dressed. Try and finish your packing so we can go and check you in early – that way, we can come back and relax at home before the flight.'

It was almost ten o'clock when Faye dragged herself out of bed and headed for the bathroom where she stood under the shower for several minutes before coming back to the bedroom. She looked around the room sadly, conscious of how much she had come to consider this *her* room.

She dressed quickly in a pair of cream shorts and a sleeveless linen blouse that tied at the waist, only too aware that she was returning to weather that was definitely not suitable for the summer clothes she was now accustomed to wearing. She smudged some eyeliner on to her swollen lids to disguise the puffiness and brushed her hair, leaving it to swing loosely around her face.

She walked downstairs and, following her usual routine, walked into the kitchen to fetch a cup of coffee. Greeting Martha, who smiled at her fondly and then frowned as she took in the brevity of the shorts, she filled her cup and sat down at the kitchen table.

'Can you believe I won't be here tomorrow morning drinking coffee with you, Martha?' she asked, looking wistful as her gaze wandered around the large familiar kitchen. The older woman, dressed in her usual navy dress with a white collar, stopped her activities and smiled cheerfully at the younger girl.

'Don't worry, Miss Faye,' she said with confidence, 'you will come home again soon, I know.'

It *is* home, Faye thought, suddenly realising why she was feeling so wretched about leaving. She savoured the thought and it felt right. She stayed with Martha until she had finished her coffee, reluctant to go out to the veranda, which now held only bitter memories from the previous day.

Returning upstairs, she emptied the wardrobe and all the drawers in her room and slowly packed her things, tucking the fragile gifts between her clothes for protection. She held Lottie's jewellery box against her chest for a long moment, remembering the laughter in Rocky's eyes when he had handed it to her. Looking down at her wrist, she stroked the gold and bead bracelet he'd bought her and wished desperately that she could turn the clock back twenty-four hours.

With a frustrated sigh, she hung the trousers and top

she intended to wear for the flight in the wardrobe and closed and locked her suitcase. After dragging the heavy case downstairs, she went into the living room where Amma and her mother were in the middle of a heated debate. They broke off abruptly as Faye entered.

'Good morning, my dear,' Auntie Amelia smiled at Faye. 'You are just in time to tell my stubborn daughter that she will *not* get married until she has found herself a decent job and started her career.'

Amma glared at her mother. 'Mama, I did not say I am not looking for a job. I *said* that when people put too much emphasis on jobs, they can lose sight of what is really important.' She glanced at Faye. 'And I *know* Faye will agree with me on that one,' she added meaningfully.

Faye raised her hands in mock surrender, laughing affectionately at the irate expression on Amma's face and the look of complete exasperation on her mother's. 'It's good to know that some things don't change,' she said. 'Amma, I've finished packing and my suitcase is in the hall. What time are we going to the airport to check in?'

Amma looked at her watch before turning to her mother. 'Mama, do you think we should go now or is it too early?'

Before her mother could speak, the sound of a car driving through the gate came through the open windows. Amma left to see who it was and came running back into the living room, a broad smile on her face.

'Faye, guess who's here?' she asked. Her heart pounding, Faye dashed out of the living room and almost collided with Auntie Akosua and Uncle Charlie, who had just entered the house.

'Whoa, hold on there, young lady,' Uncle Charlie said, reaching out to steady her. 'It's been a long time since anyone came running out to greet me,' he chuckled.

Trying desperately to hide her disappointment, Faye reached up and kissed the older man before turning to hug Auntie Akosua. The latter stepped back to take a close look at her, noting the shadows beneath her eyes that the make-up could not hide.

'Is everything all right with you, my child?' she asked quietly. Dredging up a smile, Faye nodded and ushered them forward into the living room. After exchanging greetings with Auntie Amelia and Amma, the Debrahs sat down but declined the tea on offer.

'We can't stay, Amelia,' Auntie Akosua said apologetically. 'We have to go to Tema to visit Charlie's brother in hospital. We just wanted to see Faye and say goodbye before she left.'

She turned to Faye who had perched on the sofa beside her, and patted her arm. 'I spoke to your *nana* yesterday and he sends his regards. Joshua was with him and he said to tell you to have a safe journey back,' she added.

Faye nodded, feeling a lump in her throat at the thought of leaving all these people behind. Smiling brightly, she thanked them for coming and walked with them back to their car. After exchanging hugs and kisses, the Debrahs took their leave and Amma and Faye followed Auntie Amelia back inside.

'Okay, I think we should go and check in your luggage,' Amma said. 'It's best to do it early and avoid the queues that form later in the day.'

'That's a good idea, Amma,' her mother agreed. 'Why

don't you girls go now and we'll have a late lunch when you get back.'

Togo was summoned and he shuffled inside to pick up the suitcase, hoisting it high on his shoulders before trotting out to Amma's car. After depositing the luggage in the car boot, he held the gate open for them to drive through, and gave a brief wave before he closed it behind them.

'I don't know how you managed to get Togo to be so friendly,' Amma commented, as she drove down the busy dual carriageway. 'He's normally horribly cantankerous and he drives Martha crazy.' She stopped at a set of traffic lights, tutting in disgust as the driver in the adjacent lane sped through the red light and narrowly missed hitting a car coming from the other direction.

'Well, I suppose you can't win them all,' Faye said dryly. 'I lose Rocky and win Togo instead.'

Amma giggled at the absurdity of the statement. 'I will miss your sense of humour. Even Baaba was saying the other day that it felt like you have been here for ages.'

'Knowing Baaba, I don't think she meant it as a compliment,' Faye said, her voice bubbling with laughter.

'Oh, I don't know,' Amma said. 'Now that she's with Stuart, she's over her crush on Rocky, so you're no longer a threat to her.'

'I'm no longer a threat to anyone,' Faye said gloomily, looking through the window at the passing scenery.

Amma maintained a prudent silence until they reached the airport. Parking the car under the shade of a spreading mango tree, they stepped out into the midday heat and were immediately besieged by two porters offering to carry the suitcase through to the check-in area.

'Oh it's too hot to argue, Faye; just let one of them take it,' Amma said resignedly, pointing to one of the young men to come forward. He approached them eagerly, swung the suitcase from the boot of the car as though it were as light as a feather and marched steadily ahead of them up the stairs to the airport terminal.

There was only a short queue at the check-in counter and within thirty minutes of their arrival, all the formalities had been completed.

'Thank goodness for that.' Amma heaved a sigh of relief as they left the airport building. 'Sometimes flying can be such a nightmare, especially when the airline has overbooked.'

They drove back to Labone, stopping briefly in Osu to buy some ice cream to take back for dessert. Martha served lunch as soon as they arrived home, having prepared Faye's favourite *jollof* rice and herb-coated chicken for her farewell meal.

After lunch, before the older couple retired upstairs for a brief siesta, Uncle Fred reminded everyone that they would be leaving for the airport in two hours.

Just then, a car horn sounded and was followed soon after by the creak of the gate. Amma glanced at Faye quickly and went out to see who it was. Rigid with tension, Faye stood in the hall praying that it was Rocky. When the front door opened again, Stuart walked in, closely followed by Baaba and Amma.

Faye swallowed the lump in her throat and forced a smile as she walked towards the couple. Stuart hugged her warmly while Baaba, dressed in a clinging denim dress with a low-cut bodice, kissed her in greeting.

'You look like you've been crying,' she announced, as usual making no effort at diplomacy. 'So either you're really going to miss us or someone has been upsetting you.'

Amma nudged her friend hard and hissed at her to shut up, while Stuart tactfully pretended not to have heard.

'I can't stay long, love,' he said to Faye, looking meaningfully at Baaba who had settled herself comfortably on the couch. 'We've just been out for lunch and I've got to get back to the office for a meeting. And Baaba's got to get back to the shop, haven't you, love?'

Taking no notice of the pout his girlfriend gave in response to the question, he smiled at Faye. 'We wanted to come and say goodbye and wish you a safe journey.'

Genuinely touched by the warmth in his eyes, Faye hugged him again before walking with them back to the luxury car parked in the drive. Amidu, Stuart's driver, had been chatting to Togo and he hastily climbed back into the driver's seat when he saw them coming.

With a final wave, Stuart got into the back seat of the car, tucking his long legs into the space behind his driver. Baaba swayed forward languidly and gave Faye a brief hug before saying goodbye. She paused before getting into the car and looked at Faye, her heavily made-up eyes serious. Her voice was without the usual sarcastic tone when she spoke.

'You know, I don't know what's going on but you've clearly been crying even though Rocky is moving to London. Obviously something is not going according to plan.' Ignoring Amma's warning glare, she looked squarely at Faye.

'Rocky's not perfect, but he's as close to it as most of the men I've met – *and* he's gorgeous. If you want him, don't let your pride get in the way. Fight for him.' With a final nod and a brief 'Safe journey', she climbed into the car, imperiously ordering the hapless Amidu to drive off.

'Now I know things are desperate – I'm even getting advice about Rocky from Baaba, of all people!' Faye exclaimed in despair. 'Who's next – Clarissa?'

'God forbid!' Amma shuddered. 'Let's go back in. It's too hot out here.'

The next hour passed swiftly, but with no word from Rocky, and it was with a heavy heart that Faye trudged upstairs to change into her travel clothes. She packed her shorts and shirt into a small carrier bag and tucked it into the corner of her leather rucksack. Blowing a kiss to the silent room, she walked out slowly, closing the door behind her.

Auntie Amelia was finishing a call as Faye came down the stairs and she looked up in apology.

'Oh, Faye. That was Rocky's secretary on the phone. He's in a meeting but asked her to call to wish you a safe journey home.'

She took in the sadness of Faye's expression and put an arm around the younger woman's shoulders, hugging her gently. 'I don't know what's going on between the two of you, but I really hope you can put it right.'

Faye flushed with embarrassment. 'What do you mean?'

'My dear, I may be old but I'm not senile,' Auntie Amelia said dryly. 'I have seen more of my son over the last three weeks than I have for the past three months. And for Rocky to take a day off work for *anybody* is unheard of!'

'It's all my fault.' Faye looked miserable. 'He's been so kind to me and I messed everything up.'

'I sincerely doubt that – there are always two sides to every story. I think you two need to talk and sort things out.'

Uncle Fred came bounding down the stairs before she could say any more. Exclaiming at the time, he shooed them all out. Faye rushed into the kitchen where Martha was cooking, and gave her a warm hug before speeding back out to the car. Togo smiled broadly at her as she climbed into the car, saluting her in farewell as they drove out of the gate for the final time.

Heading to the airport for the second time that day, Faye looked out of the window, drinking in the sights and sounds of the city that had come to feel like home. Dusk was falling and the evening traffic was heavy as they inched along the dual carriageway leading to the airport.

A number of cars had slowed down in front of the departure lounge to discharge passengers and they had to wait for a few minutes before they could get out of the car safely. Uncle Fred dropped them off, then drove off to park before joining them in the forecourt of the departure area. The impression of heat and noise was compounded by groups of people around the departure area saying noisy farewells to friends and family and shouting out greetings to other people they recognised.

'As you've already checked in, you can go straight through to the departure lounge,' Uncle Fred said, after a quick look at his watch. 'You should probably go through now before the rush starts,' he warned.

Faye looked around the busy forecourt one more time, hoping against hope to see the familiar close-cropped head before she went into the airport. Swallowing the overwhelming sense of disappointment that flooded over her, she turned to the three people beside her and hugged them hard. Auntie Amelia held her for a long moment before releasing her.

Her eyes were moist as she kissed Faye gently on both cheeks. 'Have a safe journey, my darling girl, and give our love to your father and William. Tell them we look forward to seeing them here soon.'

Amma hugged Faye one last time, whispering in her ear as she did so.

'Don't worry, it will work out; you'll see.' Stepping back, she smiled tearfully at her friend. 'Don't forget to email me when you get back.'

Faye nodded, sniffing back her tears, and slung her leather duffle bag over her shoulder. She walked towards the departure lounge and after taking a few steps, turned to blow a final kiss in their direction. Turning back, she moved purposefully towards the lounge and was quickly swallowed up in the noisy crowd.

She passed swiftly through the various checkpoints, reaching the final boarding area without incident and sat quietly, lost in thought, until the flight was called.

Even as she walked up the metal staircase to enter

the plane, she cast her eyes around, still praying that she would see the man with whom she had fallen so hopelessly in love.

I guess it's only in movies and books that the hero appears at the last minute to claim his lover, she thought sadly as she reached the top of the stairs. A gentle nudge from the passenger behind her brought her back to earth and she walked inside the aircraft.

The plane was only half full and she slid into the window seat she had been allocated, hoping that the seat next to her would remain empty for the duration of the flight. She vaguely heard the pilot's announcement over the whine of the engines and watched with unseeing eyes while the safety video was played.

It was only when the lights in the plane were dimmed and the plane started to buck gently before moving purposefully towards the runway, that she finally faced that fact that Rocky would not change his mind. Amma's words from long ago suddenly came flooding back: 'If you know my brother, you know he's as stubborn as a mule and never goes back on what he's said.'

As the plane rose into the sky, Faye fingered the bracelet on her wrist, her eyes filling with tears in the darkness. 'Goodbye, Rocky,' she whispered.

Part Three

DESSERT?

They can conquer, who believe they can

John Dryden

20

Cultural Triumphs

The cold November wind stung Faye's exposed face, bringing tears to her eyes as she ducked her head to avoid the impact of another gust. She thrust her gloved hands into her pockets and trudged up the short hill leading to Caroline's flat. Although it was only seven o'clock, the short day had given way to darkness and the streetlights provided the only lighting on the gloomy street.

The chilly winter evening made the short distance from the tube station to her friend's house seem like miles, and once again she cursed her car for leaving her at the mercy of public transport and the elements. As though in retribution for her absence, her Fiesta had refused point blank to cooperate when she tried to start the engine on her return home and she had finally given up in disgust, phoning the AA to have it towed to the local garage.

Arriving at Caroline's block, she pressed the buzzer. A few seconds later, the door opened and Caroline charged her with a loud shriek.

'Oh, Faye! I've missed you *so* much!' She hugged Faye so hard she almost knocked her over. Grinning at her friend's euphoric reception, Faye detached herself gently, pushing Caroline back inside the building to escape the cold.

'I've missed you too, Caro,' she said. She slipped out of her bulky winter coat and, after hugging her friend excitedly, stepped back and rubbed her cold hands together.

'Quick, give me a drink. It's freezing out there!' She turned and scooted up the steep flight of stairs leading to Caroline and Marcus's flat. Once inside the warm flat, she looked around the familiar living room in bemusement.

'I can't believe it's only four weeks since I was last in here. It feels like a lifetime ago!'

Caroline tossed Faye's coat onto the coat rack before walking over to the sideboard where the drinks were kept. Her face was pink with excitement and strands of her red hair, which had been tucked up into a bun, now stuck out in all directions. Faye watched her best friend affectionately as she poured red wine into a huge wine glass.

'You're not driving tonight, so you might as well drink all you want,' Caroline said, handing the glass to Faye. 'Marcus will be home shortly and we can have dinner as soon as he gets here.'

Faye took a large gulp of the wine and closed her eyes in bliss.

'Oh, and Dermot will probably stop by since I told him you'd be here tonight,' Caroline added as she headed for the kitchen. 'Let me just check quickly that I haven't burned the salmon. Sit down and get ready to tell me *everything*!'

Faye slipped off her short winter boots and stretched

out on the coffee-coloured leather sofa before taking another sip of her wine. Putting the glass down carefully, she stared at the ceiling, trying to stop her mind from turning back to the thoughts of Rocky that, try as she might, she had not succeeded in banishing since her arrival back in London. Although she had talked at length about her trip and answered the multitude of questions her father, William and Lottie had posed, apart from the occasional casual reference to Amma's brother, she had managed to avoid mentioning Rocky's name. It had been less easy to banish his face from her mind, however, or the crushing pain of his rejection.

'So, who is he?' Caroline asked with unerring accuracy. Walking back quietly into the room, she was immediately struck by the sad expression on her friend's face as Faye, unaware that she was being observed, lay motionless on the sofa.

'Who's who?' Faye parried, unwilling to revisit the raw emotions that discussing Rocky was going to involve. For that evening, all she wanted to do was to bask in the love and comfort of her friends and try to forget her broken heart.

For a moment Caroline looked as though she was going to press the point, but one look at Faye's stubborn expression told her that any further questioning along that line would prove useless. Instead, she contented herself with pouring a small glass of wine for herself and settled into the armchair across from the couch.

'Okay, I won't push it...' She paused and took a sip of her wine, then added, 'for now. So how was Ghana, then?' She looked at Faye speculatively. 'You look...' she hesitated, 'really well. I mean you look a bit tired but, you know, glowing as well...' She ground to a halt and then giggled. 'You wouldn't believe I write scripts for TV would you, judging by that sentence?'

The sound of a key in the lock cut short Faye's reply and she scrambled off the sofa to launch herself at Marcus as he walked in.

'Hey, stranger!' He dropped his briefcase and hugged her. 'It's good to have you back,' he grinned. 'If I have to go clothes shopping with Caro one more time, I'll shoot myself!'

Ruffling his indignant partner's hair affectionately, he kissed her freckled nose and turned back to look at Faye.

'Don't move,' he ordered. 'Let me hang my coat up and take a good look at what Ghana's done to you.'

Hanging his coat neatly on the rack, he turned and peered at her over the top of his wire-rimmed glasses. Marcus was as tall and lean as Caroline was small and round. Although he was only thirty, his fair hair was already thinning and he stubbornly refused to change his old-fashioned glasses for more modern frames, or even contact lenses. His face had a rumpled, slept-in quality that belied the sharpness of a brain which looked destined to take him into the ranks of the hedge fund titans dominating the financial sector.

'You've definitely got a tan,' he pronounced as he eyed Faye critically. 'Apart from that, you don't look any the worse for wear,' he said. 'Although you might want to try sleeping a bit more – I distinctly see some little shadows under those gorgeous eyes,' he teased.

Faye grimaced and punched him lightly on the shoulder before returning to the sofa, her long legs outstretched.

'You'd stay awake all night too if you had to catch up on almost a month of filing,' she retorted. 'The wretched temp that was supposed to cover for me walked out after two weeks – not that I blame her, knowing what my boss is like. But, did she have to leave me *all* the filing?'

Caroline smiled in sympathy and poured some more wine into Faye's glass while waiting for Marcus to re-appear from the bathroom, where he had gone to wash his hands.

'Okay, dinner's ready.' She looked at the two of them in enquiry. 'Shall we start? I don't know what time Dermot's planning to get here – you know what he's like.'

'Well, I'm starving,' Faye declared, jumping off the sofa. 'Let's go ahead and he can join us when he arrives.' Seizing her wine glass, she led the way to the kitchen and sat down at the table. Marcus opened another bottle of wine and dutifully carried the basket of sliced baguettes to the table while Caroline dished up the baked salmon, pasta and mixed salad.

Faye eyed the serving dishes on the table gleefully, her mouth watering at the contents of the huge bowl.

'Ooh, I've missed eating pasta,' she exclaimed happily. 'This looks great. Can I start?'

Marcus shook his head indulgently as he watched her spooning a heap of the steaming pappardelle onto her plate. 'Well, some things never change. How on earth did you manage in Ghana?'

Faye swallowed before replying. 'Well, believe it or not,

I didn't actually notice after a while,' she said honestly. 'I really got into eating all the local food, even pigfoot! Caro, can you imagine?'

Caroline laughed, spooning a modest portion of the thick, flat ribbons of garlic pasta onto her plate. 'This stuff is incredibly fattening,' she said regretfully as she stabbed at her food. 'I'm supposed to be on a diet.'

Faye took a long sip of her wine and looked enquiringly at the other girl. 'Is this the same Caroline who said "Read my lips; no more diets. *E-ver*"?'

Caroline blushed. 'I know, I know! But I'm *not* walking down the aisle looking like a butterball.'

Faye continued chewing for a moment before the import of her friend's words hit her. With a shriek of astonishment, she stared in disbelief at Caroline's flushed face.

'You've set a date!' she cried. Caroline nodded, beaming happily, while Marcus raised his wine glass with a broad grin. 'Yes, that's what we wanted to tell you this evening. We're getting married on April fifteenth. I know the weather might still be a bit chilly, but we didn't want to put it off any longer.'

Faye jumped up from the table and rushed over to Caroline, enveloping her in a suffocating hug. Marcus stood up and opened his arms for a hug, stooping low for her to kiss his flushed cheeks. The sound of the doorbell cut through the general hilarity and Caroline sped downstairs to let Dermot in. The sound of his heavy boots clumping up the stairs preceded his arrival into the flat and within seconds he had swept Faye off her feet.

'Welcome back, my beautiful Nubian princess!' He swung her round and deposited her back on the ground, none too gently. 'Life has been horribly boring without you.'

Tossing his woolly hat onto the ancient rocking chair, he shrugged off his thick wool jacket and turned to the dining table, rubbing his hands purposefully.

'Okay, sister mine, what culinary delights have you fetched up for us tonight?' He peered into the serving dishes. 'I didn't need to ask, did I, since Faye's here,' he said with a laugh. 'Of *course* it's pasta.'

He sat down across the table from Faye and served himself, scooping liberal helpings of the salmon and garlicky pasta onto his plate while Marcus poured him a glass of wine.

'Never mind the food, Dermot,' Faye said impatiently. 'Have you heard their news or I am the only one who didn't know?'

Dermot looked at her in silent enquiry, his mouth full. She looked back at him with exaggerated patience while he continued chewing.

'Dermot!' she said in exasperation. 'Have you heard that they have set a date for their wedding?' She said the words slowly and distinctly as though she was speaking to a child.

'Yes, I have,' he said mildly, taking a sip of his wine. 'And very good news it is too. I've told them the band will play for them for free,' he added magnanimously, missing the look of dread his sister and her fiancé exchanged.

Caroline swiftly changed the subject. 'Faye, you'll be my bridesmaid, of course,' she said firmly.

'Only if you promise not to make me wear one of those awful frilly dresses,' was the reply.

Faye finished the remains of her salmon and pasta and took another sip of her wine, feeling distinctly light-headed. She smiled dreamily at her friends, listening to their familiar banter as Dermot ate his way through most of the food on the table. When even he had declared himself full, she stood up and helped Caroline carry the used plates across the kitchen to the dishwasher.

'So what finally brought on the wedding date?' she asked in a low voice as she scraped the remnants of the food off the dishes. Caroline giggled and glanced furtively across to where the two men were engaged in a loud discussion about the rugby match that had taken place the night before. Satisfied that they couldn't hear, she turned back to Faye.

'I was four days late last month and I was terrified that I was pregnant,' she whispered. 'Marcus went ballistic when I told him. You should have heard him.' She bit back the giggles that threatened to erupt. 'He just stood there staring at me, and the first thing that came out of his mouth was, 'No one in my family has ever been born out of wedlock and I'm not breaking that tradition now!'

Faye burst into giggles and Caroline, unable to hold hers back, joined in. Marcus and Dermot stopped talking and looked over in amazement at the two of them clutching their sides and literally weeping with laughter. The two men looked at each other, shook their heads in unison at the inexplicable behaviour of women, and carried on with their conversation.

Two hours later, Faye was yawning widely. 'Sorry, guys, I think I'm still suffering from jet lag.'

Caroline was sitting on the carpet, propped up against Marcus's knees. She sounded sceptical as she looked across to where Faye and Dermot had occupied the length of the sofa, their heads resting at opposite ends.'I thought you said Ghana is on the same time zone as us. How can you have jet lag?'

'I can, if I say I can,' Faye retorted, her head beginning to buzz from the multiple glasses of red wine she had consumed. Caroline looked meaningfully at Dermot, who rose with a sigh and dragged Faye to her feet.

'Come on, my princess,' he said resignedly. 'Since your chariot is out of commission, I'll drive you home.'

Faye looked at him, raising her eyebrows in disbelief. '*You've* got a car?'

'I'll have you know that thanks to all the gigs we've been getting this year, I'm now the proud owner of a nicely souped up Golf.' He grabbed his hat from the rocking chair and jammed it down over his unruly curls, then held out his arm to support her.

Caroline reached up for Faye's winter coat and handed it over to her.

'Call me tomorrow,' she instructed, walking with her to the front door and with Marcus close behind. 'We've got loads of catching up to do, not to mention shopping!'

Faye nodded and yawned again. Giving them a final hug, she stumbled down the stairs and followed Dermot outside to his car. Coming from the warmth of the house, the cold air cut like a knife, shaking off the drowsiness that threatened to engulf her. Shivering violently, she waited impatiently for Dermot to open the door, sliding into the car as soon as he released the lock.

'I cannot believe how cold it is,' she moaned, rubbing her hands together. 'Only a few days ago, I was in shorts and a T-shirt and I still felt hot!'

His teeth chattering, Dermot nodded and concentrated on demisting the windscreen before slowly pulling out into the road. The heater soon warmed the interior of the car and they were able to speak normally again.

'So, did you meet any hot guys in Ghana?' Dermot glanced over at her with a teasing grin. 'No holiday romance or anything?'

Faye bit her lip, unnerved by the unexpected question. 'I was only there for three weeks, for goodness' sake. Of course not!' she said shortly, and turned her head to look out of the window.

Dermot raised an eyebrow, taken aback by the abrupt reply. He said nothing further about it and changed the subject to talk about the bargain price he had negotiated for his new car. When they reached her house, Faye stumbled out, shivering once more as the cold hit her.

Dermot leaned out the window to say goodbye, his expression suddenly serious. 'I'm glad you're back, even if I'm not too sure it's in one piece,' he said quietly. 'Whoever the bastard is, I hope he realises what he's missing.'

Blowing her a kiss, he drove off, leaving her staring in astonishment at the disappearing tail lights of his car.

Waking up the next day with a head heavy from the effects of the red wine and a heart heavy from restless dreams of Rocky, Faye spent the morning finally unpacking the suitcase she had consigned to the bottom of her wardrobe on her return. Slowly unfolding the lightweight clothing, she mentally relived the events that had taken place with each outfit worn, before sorting out what needed washing, and packing the rest into the heavy trunk she used to store her summer clothes. By the time she had finished, the gold and bead bracelet – which had yet to leave her wrist – was the only physical reminder left of her trip.

Just before midday, she trudged down to the local garage to check on the state of her car, sighing in frustration as the mechanic cheerfully assured her that it would not be ready for collection before mid-week. She headed gloomily for the high road to catch the bus that would drop her close to Caroline's flat, and was almost at the bus stop when she noticed a young couple coming out of the large building that housed the local library. She stared thoughtfully at the imposing Victorian edifice for a few moments and then walked in quickly before she could change her mind.

She strode into the reference room and after asking for directions from the busy librarian, moved off in search of what she needed. She logged onto one of the computers and browsed through several websites before finding the information she was after. She quickly printed out a number of sheets, crammed them into her coat pocket, and logged off the machine.

After a hilarious afternoon of shopping with Caroline, Faye returned home exhausted and empty handed. Because most of her last pay packet had gone on taxis and shopping during her holiday, she had been forced to stick to window shopping and watching Caroline spend her own generous salary on what she referred to as 'my marriage wardrobe'.

Having turned down her friend's offer of dinner with the explanation that William and Lucinda had insisted on her joining them for dinner at home that night, Faye went off in search of her brother and found him lounging in an armchair in the spacious family room. He looked up from the legal magazine he was reading and smiled affectionately at her as she sauntered in and curled her long legs into the brown leather couch.

'Hi, kiddo,' he said, casually tossing the magazine onto the worn Persian rug. 'How many shops have you left stripped bare of merchandise in your wake?' he teased. With his long legs sprawled over the side of the armchair, his lean physique was clearly visible. Faye looked at him thoughtfully, thinking how remarkably similar in build he was to Rocky.

'What?' her brother asked, his eyes narrowing in amusement at Faye's prolonged scrutiny.

She laughed, shaking her head in apology. 'Sorry, I was just thinking about something.' Legs still crossed, she bounced up and down in excitement.

'Will, did I tell you about our cousin, Joshua?' Taking no notice of her brother's feigned not-another-story-from-Ghana expression, she continued excitedly. 'You won't believe this, but he's the spitting image of you!'

William sat up, clearly interested in this particular story. 'Really? What does he do? Don't tell me he's also a lawyer.'

Faye shook her head. 'No, he's a teacher and he's really sweet. He told me so much about the cultural traditions that were taking place when we went to the funeral in Ntriso.' Although she had spent hours talking to her father, Lottie and her brother about her trip, she was never sure whether she had included all the details.

Their reactions to her account of three weeks in Ghana had been varied. Lottie listened patiently to everything, asking questions and never minding if she repeated a story. In William's case, while he had been fascinated with her picture of the country in which he had been born, and moved by the details of their mother's early life, his reaction had been more detached and intellectual and less emotional than she had expected. Her father, on the other hand, had listened without interruption to her stories about Ntriso, her mother's family and the visit to the cemetery, often with tears in his eyes. Even her light-hearted stories about Frieda's engagement ceremony and the hilarious dinners she had shared with the Asantes and the Debrahs had been received with emotional self-recriminations about his failure in not giving her the chance to enjoy these experiences sooner.

She was brought back to the present by the sound of the chimes from the antique clock on the far wall. Exclaiming at the time, she shooed William off to get ready for dinner and rushed upstairs to change. After a quick shower, she pulled a long, grape-coloured dress over her head, letting its unstructured length fall loosely over her slender form. She brushed her hair and sighed wistfully, already missing the expert hairdressers in Accra who had put new life into her locks. Spraying herself liberally with her favourite perfume, she went back downstairs.

William had also changed and was wearing a pristine white shirt, open at the neck, and a pair of dark trousers. Lucinda arrived just as Faye was walking downstairs and looked radiant in a midnight-blue dress with a pair of tiny diamond studs in her ears.

Faye hugged her warmly and stood back to admire the other girl's sparkling beauty. 'You look gorgeous, as usual,' she said in admiration. Lucinda was so beautiful that there was simply no point being jealous of her. Tonight, she looked even more stunning than usual and was flushed with excitement, causing Faye to look at her curiously.

'Is there something going on that I should know?' Her gaze swung between Lucinda and William, her eyes narrow with suspicion.

'Good evening, everyone,' her father said, interrupting her attempted interrogation. He kissed Lucinda in greeting and led the way into the dining room. A stickler for punctuality, he insisted on dinner being served at exactly seven-thirty and had little sympathy for any excuses for lateness.

Lottie served the meal; a rich beef stew with lightly curried rice and a heaped bowl of steamed vegetables. While she was always welcome to join them for meals, she rarely did so, preferring to leave the family to spend time together during the doctor's infrequent spells at home. Tonight, however, William had insisted she join them and she sat down at the other end of the table from her employer, passing the serving dishes around the table before helping herself.

Faye chewed on her food and watched with mounting suspicion as her brother and Lucinda appeared content to just smile at each other, seemingly oblivious to the others at the table. Dr Bonsu was in a particularly good mood; laughing and joking throughout dinner and chatting at length with Lottie about their plans to start a rockery at one end of the garden. After yet another exchange of unusually adoring looks between William and Lucinda, Faye put down her fork with an audible clatter.

'Okay, that's enough!' she said in exasperation. 'What on earth is wrong with everyone tonight?' She wiped her mouth on her napkin and looked accusingly at her brother. 'You insisted that I should be here for dinner and all I can see is you and Lucinda making eyes at each other like you've been apart for six months. *What* is going on?'

William almost choked on his food and Lucinda giggled, her face turning pink with embarrassment. Dr Bonsu looked at his son and raised an eyebrow in amusement.

'I think you had better go ahead and say what's on your mind, William,' he said mildly. 'Otherwise, I don't think you're going to get to the end of your meal.'

William cleared his throat and looked sheepishly at his blushing girlfriend. Taking her hand in his, he turned to Faye.

'Okay, Dad already knows but we wanted to tell you and Lottie together,' he said. 'Lucinda and I are getting married next summer.'

Faye squealed in shock, while Lottie clapped her hands together in excitement and rushed around the table to hug the couple. Faye sat in a daze, trying to take in the news. Although she had always known her brother would eventually tie the knot and move out, she was ill-prepared for the rapid changes suddenly taking place in her previously well ordered life. Suddenly aware of everyone's eyes upon her, she smiled warmly at Lucinda and moved over to kiss and congratulate her, before hugging her brother fiercely.

'Have I been gone three weeks or three months?' she asked in bemusement, looking up into his smiling face. 'First it's Caro and Marcus, and now the two of you!'

Lucinda took a sip of her water and stared fixedly at Faye. 'You *do* know you have to be my bridesmaid, don't you?' she asked, her tone making it clear that it was a statement rather than a question.

The old adage *Always the bridesmaid, never the bride* popped into Faye's mind. 'Make me your maid of honour instead, and you're on,' she said hastily as she sat down. 'And *no* frilly dresses!'

'You never know,' William grinned. 'You just might catch the bouquet if you're lucky.' He pretended not to see the glare she directed at him and continued unabashed. 'Speaking of which, we called you one evening when you were in Ghana and they said you were out with someone called Rocky. What's the story with him, then?'

Faye tensed and stared blankly at her brother, unable to think of a response that would shut him up. At her continued silence, her father looked across at her in surprise before turning to William.

'Rocky is Mr Asante's son,' he said, and looked back at Faye curiously. 'He's a banker, I believe. Is that right, Faye?'

She nodded and took refuge in her glass, trying to breathe despite the sudden heavy weight that was pressing down on her chest. Lucinda sensed Faye's distress and quickly changed the subject back to the topic of their forthcoming wedding.

It was on the following Tuesday as she returned to the office from the nearby sandwich shop, that she thrust her hand into her coat pocket and came across the documents she had printed out in the library. Caught up in the excitement of both William and Caroline's impending nuptials, she had completely forgotten about her research. She walked into the empty staff sitting room and smoothed out the crumpled pages while she finished her sandwich.

She jumped at the sound of the door opening and sighed in relief when she saw Miss Campbell walking in, turning back to the sheets she had hastily turned over. The older woman was dressed in her customary twin-set and after making herself a cup of tea, came over to where Faye sat frowning in concentration as she went through the forms.

'What are you up to, young lady?' The older woman sat in the armchair opposite Faye. 'You looked terribly guilty when I walked in just now.' She raised an eyebrow in enquiry as she slowly sipped her hot tea.

Faye looked at her and hesitated for a moment before impulsively thrusting the sheaf of papers towards her. Miss Campbell put down her cup carefully, pushed her glasses back onto her pert little nose and slowly studied the documents. When she had read through them all, she took another sip of her tea and sat back in her chair. 'Now, why am I not surprised to see this?' Her eyes twinkled behind her rimless glasses. 'I've noticed something has changed in you since you returned to work and it's high time, if you ask me.'

Faye looked at her in surprise and reached out to take back the papers. 'Do you think I can do it?' Her eyes mirrored the uncertainty in her voice. The older woman looked back at her quizzically. 'The real question, my dear, is do *you* think you can do it?'

Faye thought for a long moment. 'Yes,' she said. 'Yes, I do.'

Miss Campbell nodded slowly. 'Well then, that's all that matters. Let me know how it goes, will you?' With that, she swallowed the rest of her tea, patted Faye's shoulder in gentle encouragement and left the room.

The next three weeks came and went, with life apparently carrying on as usual. Faye slipped back into the routine of life at Fiske, Fiske & Partners, spending most of her spare time with Caroline and going on occasional shopping expeditions with Lucinda.

Returning home after work on a Friday evening, she spotted the envelope addressed to her lying on the mantelpiece in the hall. With shaking fingers, she turned it over and read the address printed on the back of the envelope over and over again. Taking a deep breath, she tore the envelope open and scanned the contents of the single sheet inside before letting out a blood-curdling shout and jumping up and down unrestrainedly, her long legs flying.

'Faye! What on earth is the matter...?' Lottie stood in

the hallway, her hands covered in flour. The expression of alarm on her face rapidly turned into irritation as she realised that Faye was not, in fact, being murdered.

Dr Bonsu, who had been working on a research paper, hurried out of his study into the hall, clutching his reading glasses. 'Faye! Are you all right?'

She rushed over to hug him, still waving the letter in the air. 'I've never been better, Dad,' she said, almost squealing in her excitement. She handed over the letter and he stared at her for a moment before slipping on his glasses and reading it. He looked up in surprise to find her grinning at him.

'Faye...' he started, pausing in search of words that he suddenly couldn't find. Lottie wiped her hands on her apron and hurried forward to take the letter from him. Reading it swiftly, she looked at Faye in disbelief.

'Well, no wonder you made such a rumpus, you secretive thing!' she exclaimed. 'When did all this happen?'

Faye grinned in excitement. 'I went into the library a few weeks ago and looked it up. I had to go for an interview, but I didn't want to jinx my chances by telling anyone.' She seized the letter back from Lottie and kissed it soundly, twirling around with joy.

'Daddy, can you believe it? I'm finally going to college!'

21

Cultural Conclusions

It was unseasonably warm for March and as Faye walked briskly towards the faculty building where her lectures were held, she breathed in the fresh smell of spring, feeling lighter and happier than she had felt for ages. She nodded in greeting to a young woman dressed in jeans and a light jacket who walked past, recognising her as one of the students in her History of Art class.

It had been three months since she had started her degree course in interior design at the renowned College of Art, and she found it hard to believe that she was the same person as the gawky young girl who had been cocooned in Fiske, Fiske & Partners for so many years. Although she still kept in touch with Miss Campbell, her life was now packed with lectures, design projects and research, giving her little time to think about anything else. What spare time she had was spent shopping with Caroline and Lucinda and trying to help them plan their respective weddings. She had also made friends with some of the people on her course and occasionally crammed the odd design exhibition or group movie night into her crowded schedule.

Early for once, she walked into the large auditorium and took a seat in the middle of the front row. Looking dreamily around the half-empty hall, she marvelled yet again at the series of events that had brought her there. Her bold decision to phone the College and ask if she could be considered for late admission had taken every ounce of willpower that she possessed. When the call had come inviting her for an interview, she had been on the verge of phoning them back to say that she had changed her mind. It was Auntie Amelia's advice during a long phone chat that had helped her to push aside the awful memories of interviewing for secretarial jobs.

She smiled as she remembered the nerve-racking interview for the design course that had felt more like an interrogation. The three faculty members that made up the interview panel had fired questions at her, giving no indication as to whether or not they were impressed by her answers. Nevertheless, fuelled by a burning need to move forward with her life, she had spoken confidently and passionately about her desire to train for a career in interior design. Addressing their concerns about having missed the first few weeks of the course, she had assured them that she was prepared to put in all the hours needed to catch up on the lost time. At the end of the interview, still no wiser as to her fate, she had gone back to her office and to her life to wait anxiously for their response.

The days following the offer of the college place were

still a blur. She had rushed in early on Monday to see Mr Fiske Junior and to explain why she needed to leave, and leave immediately, and to beg him to release her from her notice period. Although shocked at the thought of losing Faye, his essentially kind heart had won the day and he'd agreed on the understanding that she would organise a replacement before she left.

On hearing her news, Miss Campbell had hugged her joyfully, promising to help whoever was sent to work with Junior. Having learnt their lesson from the last temp sent to cover for Faye, this time around the recruitment agency sent an experienced older woman who, much to Faye's relief, immediately and firmly took charge of her hapless boss.

Later that week, on her last day at Fiske, Fiske & Partners, Faye was touched when the other secretaries threw her a small farewell party. Drinking the warm white wine they had clubbed together to buy, she looked around with a smile at the women she had worked with for years and yet, with the exception of Miss Campbell, knew so little about. Junior popped into the staff sitting room and gave a short, emotional speech thanking her for all her help, particularly, he said, when he had been suffering from one of his many 'distressing physical ailments'. Three plastic cups of wine later, and after promising to keep in touch with everyone, she clutched her leaving present – a glossy hardback on famous designers – to her chest, and skipped out of Fiske, Fiske & Partners for the last time.

The hall was now almost full and as she looked around, Faye spotted the lecturer walking in and heading towards the front of the room. Switching off her mobile, she made a mental note to finish reading Amma's email after the class. As usual, Amma had written a long and detailed account of all the goings-on back in Ghana. Well, nearly all. For after confirming months earlier that Rocky had left Ghana, Amma never once mentioned her brother. Instead, she shared updates about her new job in a computer software company and Baaba and Stuart's continuing romance.

Edwin was working hard to finish a Masters degree and had found himself a part-time job. His love affair with America, although slightly bruised by some of his experiences since his arrival, had continued more or less unabated. The most surprising news in her latest email had been the blossoming relationship between Sonny and Clarissa. Faye was initially stunned by the news, but could see how they might be a good match. As Amma wrote, 'they've become inseparable and go everywhere together, because neither of them trusts the other one in the slightest!'

The tutor took his place at the podium and started the class. Faye forced thoughts of Ghana from her mind and turned her attention to the lecture, making notes throughout the ninety-minute class. When it was over, she gathered her papers together and was about to push them into the leather portfolio case her father had bought her as a congratulatory gift, when she heard someone coughing softly behind her.

She turned round to see a tall, athletically built black man smiling down at her. He wore a pair of fitted denims and a brown sports jacket and she recognised him immediately as one of the executive members of the

African-Caribbean Society. Although she had signed up to be a member shortly after starting at the College, her coursework had kept her so busy that she had only ever managed to attend two meetings.

'Hi,' he smiled. 'It's Faye, isn't it?' She nodded curiously and he held out his hand. 'I'm Brian – Brian Hearst.' He shook her hand with a firm grip. Faye returned his smile and he stood back for her to lead the way out of the auditorium.

'If you're not in a rush, would you like to go for a coffee?' He gestured towards the small building that housed the student cafeteria.

Faye hesitated for only a brief moment. 'I can't stay too long, but that would be nice.'

As they walked, they chatted about the lecture they had just sat through and once inside the cafeteria, Brian bought two large coffees from the counter before joining her at the table.

Faye stole a look at him from under her lashes and was forced to admit that his dark chocolate colouring, close-cut beard and even features were extremely attractive. He also had a wicked sense of humour and they were soon laughing and arguing good naturedly about some of his more radical opinions on art and design.

After about forty minutes, Faye glanced at her watch, exclaiming at the time.

'I'm sorry,' she said apologetically, 'but I've got to go now.' Gathering up her things, she stood up and smiled across at him as he rose to say goodbye. 'Thanks for the coffee, Brian. I'll see you in class on Monday.'

But before she could walk away, he placed a hand lightly on her arm and his dark brown eyes looked straight into hers. 'Hold on a minute, Faye. I'd love to see you again, and before Monday if that's possible. If you're free tomorrow evening, would you like to go out to dinner?'

For almost a full minute Faye stared at him blankly, completely taken aback by the invitation. Trying not to sound rude, she shook her head and forced a smile onto her lips. 'I'm so sorry, but that's not possible,' she said, almost babbling in her haste. 'I already have plans for tomorrow night. But thank you for asking me – maybe another time?'

Before he could respond, she turned on her heel and walked quickly out of the building. Her mind was racing as she headed to the station, and it was only once she was safely on the tube that she was able to take a deep breath and force herself to relax.

Calm down, Faye, he was only suggesting dinner, not an invitation to elope to Bermuda! She edged away as best as she could from the overweight man spilling out of the seat next to hers and tried to make sense of her overreaction to a harmless invitation. It was almost six months since her return from Ghana and, true to her fears, Rocky had never made contact. Even Amma, who had initially been optimistic that things would resolve themselves, no longer made any reference to him. Whatever their relationship had been, Faye thought sadly, it was time to accept that it was now clearly over.

Back at home and still feeling guilty about lying to Brian about her non-existent plans, she phoned Caroline to find out what she was doing the following evening. Marcus was away on a business trip and, for once, Caroline was open to the idea of leaving her couch and TV for a few hours.

'There's a new film that one of the guys in college was talking about the other day,' Faye remarked. 'The director is from Senegal and apparently it's won a couple of awards. Nick said it was really good – why don't we go and see it tomorrow evening?'

'Now you're starting to sound like Michael,' her friend replied, a teasing note in her voice.

Faye laughed. 'Very funny. *Not*. I'd like to go because I want to see the film, not because I think I have anything to prove. Besides, it's either that or going to watch Guns in Clover play.'

'Okay, fine,' Caroline agreed hastily. 'I love my brother dearly, but if I have to hear that band's greatest hits one more time—'

'By the way, I got asked out by someone on my course today,' Faye cut her short and tried to sound casual. There was silence at the other end and she repeated her statement, not sure if Caroline had heard her.

'And…?' Caroline sounded wary and this time Faye was the one who remained silent.

'Don't tell me you said no?' Caroline queried in disgust. Unable to keep anything from her best friend, Faye had eventually told her about Rocky and the disastrous way things had ended. Although initially she had understood Faye's reluctance to get romantically involved with anyone else, as the weeks and months passed and any hope of reconciling with Rocky faded, Caroline had becoming increasingly vocal about the need for Faye to move on.

Already regretting having mentioned Brian, Faye quickly changed the subject. After dinner, she spent the rest of the evening in her room working on a project that was due in three weeks, and eventually climbed into bed just before midnight.

The next evening, after giving in to Caroline's pleas to stay the night as she was on her own, she drove over to her friend's flat to deposit her overnight bag before they left for the cinema. The tube was packed with people on their way into town and they had to stand through several stations before they finally got a seat. Faye glared at a young couple sitting directly opposite them who had been kissing passionately since they boarded the train, totally oblivious to the other travellers and their surroundings.

'Why the hell don't they just get a room if that's what they're planning to do all evening,' she muttered in irritation.

Her friend shrugged and smiled. 'I think it's rather sweet, really. If *you* stopped behaving like Mother Teresa and joined the human race, you'd think so too,' she added pointedly.

Faye stared at Caroline indignantly. 'Just because I don't want to watch the underground version of the Kama Sutra does *not* mean I'm behaving like a nun.' Caroline shrugged, unperturbed. 'Well, if you won't go out on a simple date with someone, what else am I to think?'

Faye said nothing. Lost in thought for a moment, she looked across at the couple and glanced back at Caroline, a faint smile forming on her lips. 'I suppose I *am* being a bit cynical, aren't I?' she admitted grudgingly. 'But am I really ready to date someone? I just don't know!' She shook her head in frustration.

Caroline turned towards her. 'Look, Faye, you need to face the fact that Rocky is in the past. Look how well you've done by leaving your dead-end job and training for a real career doing what you love.' She sighed at Faye's downcast expression and her voice softened. 'Don't you think it's time to let go of a relationship that's obviously not going to happen?'

Faye bit her lip hard. 'I thought I had. But every time I think I'm over him, something happens and it feels as if it all just happened yesterday.'

Caroline sighed again and sat back in her seat. 'Well, then maybe you *should* go out with this new guy just so you have something else to think about.'

They train lurched to a stop at Leicester Square and they jumped out, pushing their way past a group of rowdy teenagers trying to make a grab for their seats. Once they were up at street level, they hastened along the main road, turning off into a small side street. A short queue had formed in front of the cinema and they joined the end of the line, studying the posters for the film while waiting to pay for their tickets.

When the movie started, Faye watched in fascination as the story unfolded. The rich colours and textures of the African landscape and the sounds and images in the city scenes transported her straight back to Ghana. The film told the story of two young men from the same Senegalese village who migrated to the capital city in search of work, but fared very differently in their ability to fit in and adapt to urban life. One of the men found a mentor and was encouraged to educate himself, and he rose to become a successful lawyer and later, a prominent judge. The other young man found it difficult to make the transition to the demands of the big city and soon fell by the wayside, eventually turning to a life of crime. The drama reached an emotional climax when the two men met again after twenty years. However, this time the meeting was in court, and the judge had been appointed to try his old village comrade who had been arrested for raping a young girl. Despite the use of subtitles, something Caroline usually detested, the acting and direction of the film was superb and they watched the movie in rapt silence until the credits rolled up on the screen.

The house lights came on and they stood up to leave.

'That was brilliant, Faye,' Caroline said. 'I really enjoyed it.' She struggled back into her coat and added mischievously, 'I think I should go to Ghana too, or maybe Senegal, after seeing that beautiful landscape. I can just imagine Marcus bare-chested and toiling in the fields.'

Faye was still laughing when she heard a high-pitched voice calling her name. She turned back sharply and stood still in shock, staring at the petite girl standing in the row behind them, her red gold curls tumbling over a black roll-neck jumper.

'Jasmine!' she exclaimed. Her eyes darted to the man standing beside her, but he was completely unfamiliar to her and Faye relaxed slightly, relieved not to have to exchange pleasantries with Michael.

'What a surprise, no? It's been ages since we last met,' Jasmine purred.

'Yes, it has,' Faye replied evenly. She buttoned her coat and continued along the row of seats, heading for the stairs that led up to the exit. Undaunted, Jasmine followed in the adjoining row, her companion trailing after her.

'So, how's everyone?' Faye stopped and asked politely when it became clear that Jasmine wasn't about to be shaken off easily. 'Have you seen Michael lately?' She felt no emotion when she mentioned his name.

Jasmine pouted in the manner Faye remembered so well from the night at the pigfoot restaurant. 'Oh, please!' she said, her voice heavy with scorn. 'I finished with him months ago – he is so terribly *insular*.'

Caroline had been waiting at the end of the row and waved impatiently at Faye. Jasmine's eyes noted the gesture and her expression immediately changed.

'Is that who you came with?' Although the question sounded harmless, the hostility in the look she directed at Caroline was unmistakable.

'Yes. Why do you ask?' Faye tried not to sound defensive, all the while wondering what was coming next.

Taking no notice of the warning cough from her companion, Jasmine pursed her lips and shrugged. 'Oh well, I just remember Michael talking about how hard he had tried to put you in touch with our culture. Of course, if your friends are *white*, then I suppose it does make it that much harder, doesn't it?' she said sweetly.

Faye gasped in outrage and gripped her handbag, forcing herself not to swing it at Jasmine's small head.

Then suddenly, inexplicably, she felt incredibly calm and she simply laughed.

Whatever reaction Jasmine had been expecting, judging from the angry flush that stained her cheeks, it didn't appear to include amusement. Faye laughed long and hard before fixing the other girl with a steely glare.

'Well, that has to be the most ignorant statement I've heard for a very long time,' she said, the humour seeping out of her voice. 'First off, Michael wouldn't know real culture if it got up and bit him, any more than *you* would, if that's the kind of rubbish you come out with.'

Jasmine's companion looked at his girlfriend in alarm as she stood rooted to the spot, staring at Faye in shocked disbelief. Caroline, tired of waiting, walked up to Faye and was just in time to catch the rest of her tirade. It was as if the years of pent-up frustration and irritation at the constant cultural put-downs she had endured had decided to unleash themselves, and Faye was now in full flow.

'Secondly, if you have enough sense of who you are and where you're from, it doesn't matter in the slightest what *colour* your friends are because, as any intelligent person will tell you, friendship doesn't come in colours. If it did, Michael shouldn't have been friends with either you or your precious brother, since both of you are even paler than my white friend here!'

Jasmine's jaw had dropped in shock and she gasped as Faye's words poured over her like a cold shower. Undaunted, Faye took a deep breath before continuing.

'And finally, for your information, in *my* culture, it is *not* acceptable to chase after other people's boyfriends.'

She paused briefly, then added sweetly, 'Oh sorry, I forgot, you're not from *Africa*, are you?'

Leaving a speechless Jasmine staring after her, she nudged a stunned Caroline into life and they walked quickly out of the cinema. They had barely left the building when they took one look at each other and collapsed into helpless giggles. Staggering along the dark street, they held each other up and laughed hysterically, tears streaming down their faces.

'Oh, oh, Faye,' Caroline cried. 'Did you see her *face* when you walked off? I thought she was going to faint!' She paused, holding her sides painfully and panting with laughter. Faye leant against a lamp post, shaking with mirth.

'Oh dear,' she said, finally calming down and wiping her eyes with the back of her hand. 'I think I went a little bit over the top there, Caro. But that girl is such a bitch, she had it coming.' She burst into fresh peals of laughter as she remembered the look of panic on the face of Jasmine's friend.

'Did you see the way that man kept looking at her?' she gasped. 'The poor guy looked ready to run for his life!'

They laughed all the way home, hardly noticing the discomfort of the hot tube packed with partygoers. Sharing a bottle of wine back at Caroline's flat, they chattered for hours as only old and true friends can, eventually falling into their respective beds in the early hours of Sunday.

A few days later, as she walked out of the faculty building at the end of the last lecture of the day, she heard her name and turned round to see Brian hastening towards her. She greeted him with a warm smile and walked along with him for a few minutes, readily agreeing to his offer of a cup of coffee to ward off the chilly March winds.

'Faye, I would really love to take you out.' Brian's warm brown eyes were serious as he looked at her. Faye stared back at him and, touched by the sincerity in his voice, she nodded slowly.

His face split into a huge grin and he stood up, picked up their empty coffee mugs and placed them on the trolley with the other used crockery. As they walked out of the busy cafeteria, he looked across at her curiously. 'By the way, where are you from?'

Without hesitation, Faye replied, 'From Ghana.' He nodded with interest and hoisted his heavy black rucksack over his shoulder.

'I'm from Barbados,' he said. 'Well, at least my parents are, but I like to think of it as my home too, even though the last time I went there I was only about ten years old. Have you visited Ghana?'

'Oh yes,' Faye smiled. 'I was there only a few months ago and I had a wonderful time.'

Brian walked with her to the tube station before saying goodbye, and they agreed to meet the following evening at a wine bar they both knew. Elated at her decision, Faye headed for home. Her father was away on yet another overseas trip and was not due back for at least another week. William and Lucinda had also decided to take a few days off together and had left that morning for a short holiday in the sun.

Lottie had decided to take advantage of an almost empty house and announced that she would be going up to Scotland to spend a long weekend with her disabled sister. Closing the front door behind her, Faye headed up to Lottie's room where she found her packing a small suitcase in preparation for her departure the next morning.

She gave Lottie an exuberant hug and sat cross-legged on the bed watching the older woman as she sorted out her clothes and carefully packed the gifts she had bought for her family in Glasgow.

'So what's put that expression on your face, then?' Lottie looked with amusement at Faye who was grinning irrepressibly.

'I was asked out today by someone on my course. We're going for a drink tomorrow night.' She tried to sound casual but the excitement that had been building up in her since agreeing to go out with Brian seeped into her voice.

Lottie paused in the middle of folding the white towelling dressing gown she was about to pack. Her curiosity piqued by this new development, she sat down next to Faye on the bed. 'So, what's he like then?'

'You mean, apart from the sexy, low-cut beard, great body and fantastic sense of humour?' Faye giggled. 'Pretty nice, I'd say.'

'Okay, but leaving all that aside, are you really sure you're ready to get involved with someone?'

She watched as Faye's face clouded over for a moment before a determined smile broke through. Troubled by the sadness she had seen in Faye's eyes after her return from Ghana, Lottie had eventually prised the details of what had happened with Rocky out of her. Now, she tried to quash the unsettling thought that Faye was trying just a little too hard.

Oblivious to Lottie's scrutiny, Faye described Brian in minute detail, including his easy acceptance of her dual cultural upbringing. 'He's *so* different from Michael,' Faye babbled on enthusiastically. 'I don't feel in the least bit pressured or judged when I'm with him. Actually, he's just like me, except his parents are from Barbados.'

Lottie considered Faye's statement for a moment before asking quietly, 'You don't still worry about your cultural identity, do you? I thought the trip to Ghana had changed all that.'

Faye shook her head with vehemence. 'Oh no, I'm way past worrying about that now. You know, Lottie, Michael made me feel as if I could only be culturally acceptable if I spoke a certain way or ate a particular type of food. It took me a while to sort things out for myself, but I know now that eating all the pasta in the world doesn't make you white, any more than eating all the pigfoot in the market can make you black.'

She paused for a moment, her forehead furrowed in thought. 'Besides which, from what I learned in Ghana, African culture is also going through change, and some of the people I came across were just as "Western" as me, if not more so. It really doesn't matter what I choose to eat or wear, or who I'm friends with; my culture is part of me, no matter what.'

Lottie's face mirrored her surprise at Faye's confident outburst. 'To be honest, Faye, I have to say that I'm stunned. I knew going to Ghana had changed something in you, but —' She shook her head and shrugged, suddenly at a loss for words.

Faye laughed, warmed by the look of new-found respect in Lottie's eyes. 'Well I couldn't expect you to keep rescuing me all my life now, could I? I mean, think about it, Dad even paid for my trip to Ghana! You were right, Lottie; it *was* well past time for me to grow up.'

She stood up to leave the room and let Lottie finish off her packing. 'You know, applying for college and getting the loan to pay for it is the first thing I can really say I've done for myself and by myself,' she said frankly. 'And I guess I've learned that if I want to be happy, I have to rescue myself.'

She felt a little less sure of herself the following evening when it was time to leave the house to meet Brian. Dressed in a black shift dress which she had teamed with a cherry-red cardigan, high-heeled ankle boots and a long double-stranded seed pearl necklace, she applied the barest minimum of make-up and drove down to Camden Town, finding a parking spot in a side street.

She walked the short distance to the wine bar, pushed open the door and peered through the small crowd of people in search of Brian. He was sitting at a table near the door and stood up as she walked over and gave him a hug. He looked even more attractive in the candlelit setting of the quiet bistro and she noted that the sexy beard had been freshly trimmed. He wore dark trousers and a thin grey turtleneck jumper that showed off his athletic physique.

She ordered a glass of white wine and they were soon chatting easily. She soon discovered that he had also seen the Senegalese film and they discussed the storyline, arguing noisily about their varying interpretations of the filmmaker's message. Brian was a keen traveller and had her in stitches with stories about some of the places he had visited.

The time flew by, and two hours and another glass of wine later, Faye looked at her watch regretfully and made her excuses, explaining that she needed to be up early the next morning to continue working on her project. Brian looked disappointed at the early end to the evening, but he shrugged good naturedly and called for the bill without protest. When the waiter came over, he pulled out his wallet and paid quickly, then led the way outside and walked with her back to her car.

'Can I give you a lift somewhere?' Faye asked when they reached her Fiesta. He shook his head with a smile. 'No, thanks. I'm all the way in South London. I'll just jump on the tube – it's much quicker than driving anyway.'

Faye nodded and reached up to kiss his cheek. Just as she did so, he turned his face swiftly, capturing her lips with his. For a long moment Faye remained motionless, feeling the sensation of his firm lips moving against her mouth and the strength of his arm drawing her against him. When at last he raised his head and looked at her questioningly, she looked back at him with regret, and shook her head slowly.

'I'm sorry, Brian,' she said softly, unable to pretend a passion she didn't feel. 'But thank you so much for asking me out tonight. I had a great evening. See you in class next week?'

He nodded, his wry smile showing that no harm had been done. He kissed her on the cheek, the soft touch of his beard lightly grazing her face, and stood back while she opened her car door and got in. She wound down the window and smiled up at him as she started the engine.

'Drive safely, Faye.' He stood back as she slowly reversed out of the parking space, and watched her drive away.

Faye woke up early the next morning and after a quick shower, padded downstairs to make coffee before getting back to work on her project. Although she still had a couple of weeks before it was due, she was determined to keep ahead of the gruelling schedule of coursework. After a few hours, she took a break and went downstairs for a quick snack, and then forced herself to go back to her room to continue with her task.

It was late in the afternoon when the insistent chimes of the front doorbell broke her concentration. For a few moments she didn't move, and then remembered that she was alone in the house and no one else was going to answer the door.

Tutting in irritation, she raced downstairs, not bothering to check through the peephole before opening the door. She stood speechless with shock as she looked up to see Rocky standing on the doorstep.

For what seemed like hours, neither of them spoke.

'Hello Faye,' Rocky said finally, his long-lashed, caramel-coloured eyes fixed on hers.

'Hello Rocky,' she echoed faintly, still unable to believe her eyes. She realised that she was blocking the doorway and moved back hastily to let him in.

He shrugged off the heavy jacket he'd been wearing and hung it on the coat rack near the door, then turned back to Faye who was still standing and staring stupidly at him.

'What are you doing here?' She blurted the words out, too surprised to care if she sounded unwelcoming.

Rocky looked at her steadily for a few moments and then pulled his wallet out from his back pocket. 'I came to bring you this,' he said, taking out a small piece of paper, which he unfolded and then handed over to her.

Faye looked with surprise at the picture Uncle Fred had taken of her on the day of Frieda Ansah's engagement ceremony. Dressed in her borrowed *boubou*, she was laughing, her face radiating happiness. Her head was thrown back, exposing her long slim neck, while her almond-shaped eyes gazed straight into the camera, their expression sultry and inviting.

'Where did you get this?' she asked in bemusement. 'Uncle Fred took this picture ages ago.'

Rocky sighed and ran his hands through his cropped wavy hair in the gesture that was at once so familiar and so painful.

'Faye, can I sit down, please?' he asked suddenly. She looked at him closely. He looked thinner than she remembered and tiny lines around his eyes betrayed his exhaustion.

She ushered him into the living room. 'Are you all right?' she asked anxiously. 'Can I get you something to drink?'

He waved away her concern, patted the seat next to him in invitation and turned to look at her as she reluctantly sat down.

'Faye,' he started – and stopped – almost immediately, shaking his head in frustration. 'Look, there's so much I want to tell you but first, and most importantly, I want to say I'm sorry.'

She stared at him, but before she could say a word, he

reached across and gently placed a forefinger against her lips.

'No, please, let me finish,' he said. 'I'm sorry for being such a stubborn fool and for not giving you the chance to tell me what really happened. I'm sorry for putting my own fears ahead of everything else and, most of all, I'm sorry for all the pain I've caused you by being such a total idiot.'

Faye surreptitiously pinched her arm to check she wasn't dreaming and welcomed the pain that confirmed that this was no illusion.

Rocky reached for the picture she was still holding and tapped it slowly with his finger. 'You know, Faye, for a long time I thought that if I worked hard enough and long enough, I'd be able to get you out of my head. For a while I even thought it was working, until the day I was downloading the pictures in my camera and saw this one.'

Casting her mind back, Faye remembered how Uncle Fred had borrowed Rocky's camera to take the pictures. Silently blessing the older man for his foresight, she tried to take in what Rocky was saying.

'The picture brought it all back and I realised that I was kidding myself if I thought that I was over you,' he said softly. 'Faye, I'm sorry. Really, truly, sorry. Can you forgive me?'

He looked deeply into her eyes and held his hand out to her. Trembling with emotion, her eyes filled with tears and she reached for his hand briefly before releasing it and flinging herself into his strong arms. He held on to her tightly and continued to murmur apologies under his breath.

Breathing in his familiar scent, she kept her head pressed against his strong chest until she felt his fingers gently lifting up her chin. Looking down into her eyes,

Rocky leaned forward and kissed her, tenderly at first, and then with barely suppressed passion. She wrapped her arms around his neck, her mouth hot against his searching lips, feeling a heady sensation flooding through her as she pressed herself up hard against him, clearly feeling the evidence of his passion.

With a groan, she dragged herself from the couch, pulling him up with her. He looked at her, his breathing ragged, and she nodded in unmistakable invitation before turning and leading him up the stairs to her room.

The long shadows of evening had crept across the bedroom as they lay quietly in Faye's large bed. Resting her head on his chest, Faye caressed his muscled shoulders, marvelling at the strength they had just displayed. Kissing his chest softly, she asked the question that she needed the answer to, now more than ever.

'Rocky, please tell me what happened with Celine,' she asked quietly. His hand had been stroking her hair and it suddenly stilled. He dropped a kiss on her head and sighed deeply before speaking.

'We met when I was in the States,' he said softly. 'She was on the MBA programme with me and we were in the same project group. She was very bright and incredibly attractive, and we soon started talking about more than our coursework.' His laugh was quiet and mirthless, and the sound rumbled in his chest against Faye's ear.

'After a few months, she'd more or less moved in with me and things started getting pretty serious, at least they did for me – I even mentioned her to my family. Anyway, a few hours after we finished our final exams, I came back to our apartment to drop off some books.' He paused briefly before continuing, his voice devoid of any emotion. 'She was in bed with one of our classmates – a rich American guy whose father owned a steel mill somewhere in Pittsburgh.'

Her arms tightened around him in sympathy and he sounded almost pensive as he continued. 'The funny thing was she didn't turn a hair. *He* was terrified and couldn't get out of the room fast enough. She just looked at me and shrugged. I can still hear her now, "Rocky, honey, you've got to understand. I'm smart and I'm a high achiever and I've got to be with another high achiever – that's the only way to get on in this world."'

Faye sat up abruptly, appalled at what she had just heard. 'But how could she say that, Rocky!' she exclaimed. 'You'd just finished an MBA, for God's sake. *Of course* you were going places!'

He shrugged, gently pulling her head back down against his chest. 'In her book, having someone with an MBA *and* access to millions of dollars was a much better bet than having some foreigner with an MBA and no job.' He laughed properly for the first time since his arrival.

'Anyway, I guess that's what made me so determined not to let another woman get to me. Until I met you, that is,' he added, kissing her hair.

'Er, hello! What about Clarissa, then?' Faye asked pointedly. He laughed again and pulled her closer still.

'Believe me, Clarissa was a non-starter,' he chuckled. 'She was good fun and easy to be with, but there was no way it was going any further and I didn't want to lead her on. In fact, she did me a favour by playing up to Stuart.

She knew Celine had left me paranoid about infidelity and Clarissa's attempts to flirt with Stuart gave me all the excuse I needed to end the relationship.'

He sat up slightly, peering at her in the semi-darkness. 'I'm just sorry that my paranoia also made me jump to the wrong conclusion about you and Sonny,' he said soberly. 'I should have known better.'

He moved to kiss her and she pulled away from him, pretending to sit up.

'I really think I should get up now. As your hostess, I don't want to abuse the situation,' she said with a teasing smile.

'Abuse me all you want,' he murmured, pulling her back to him and nibbling gently on the soft lobe of her ear. After several minutes, she sat up again.

'Rocky, you're definitely thinner than before,' she said in earnest. 'You looked really tired when you got here. You must be hungry – let me make you something to eat.'

'Okay, what do have in mind?'

She thought back to what she remembered of meals in Rocky's house. 'I could make *jollof* rice, if you like? Or I could cook some spinach stew with pigfoot – I've watched Martha make it and I'm sure I can get the ingredients together in no time.'

Rocky pulled her back into his arms and kissed her. Shaking his head, he smiled gently and said before kissing her again, 'I *hate* pigfoot. What about some pasta?'

Acknowledgements

While it is said that everyone has a book in them, it takes more than just the author to bring it out.

A huge thank you to the Jacaranda Books family for being the most positive and supportive publishers any writer could ask for. Jazzmine, thanks for loving the story from the start – you'll never know how happy your email made me! Rukhsana, thanks for believing in the characters so much, you wanted to punch them. Valerie, you have my deepest and most sincere gratitude for being such an insightful, brilliant, tough and encouraging Editor. You can bet that 'Show, don't tell!' will be engraved on my tombstone.

Thank you so much, Kate Forrester, for the brilliant cover design and your sensitive interpretation of the key points of the storyline.

My thanks to Melissa Mensah Abanulo for reading the manuscript and for loving it enough for me to risk letting it see the light of day.

My special thanks to Marcelle Akita for her inspired matchmaking – I will be eternally grateful.

I would also like to express my heartfelt gratitude and appreciation to everyone who took the time to review this book and offered their feedback.

To all my wingwomen and indefatigable cheerleaders, you know who you are and thank you for being there whenever. Chux, thanks for being the best friend anybody could have – we've come a long way since my first published book review in *The Voice*!

Finally, thanks to each and every one of you in my big, lovely, loving, scattered and supportive family. To my beautiful daughters, Seena and Khaya, you haven't quite yet mastered the art of not interrupting when I'm 'in the zone', but I love you anyway. Nana, thanks for giving me the motivation to go home, for a great day in Cape Coast and for the time to learn enough to tell Faye's story.

And finally, finally, my love and thanks to the beautiful country of Ghana, land of my birth and my spiritual home for ever. I hope I've done you justice and if I haven't, any inaccuracies are mine alone.

About the Author

Frances Mensah Williams was born in Ghana and grew up in the UK. After graduating from the University of Reading, she pursued a career in Human Resources Management, Training and Consultancy, which spanned the UK and Africa. She is now the Chief Executive of Interims for Development Ltd. and the Managing Editor of ReConnectAfrica.com, a careers and business website and online publication for African professionals in the Diaspora.

Frances is the author of the non-fiction titles *Everyday Heroes – Learning from the Careers of Successful Black Professionals* and *I Want to Work in Africa: How to Move Your Career to the World's Most Exciting Continent*. She is the recipient of several awards and in 2011 was nominated as one of the Top 20 Inspirational Females from the African Diaspora in Europe.

Frances has travelled extensively, having also lived in

the USA, Austria and France. She now resides in London with her family. *From Pasta to Pigfoot* is her first fiction novel.

To find out more about Frances Mensah Williams and for regular updates, visit her website and Facebook page:

www.francesmensahwilliams.com

www.Facebook.com/FrancesMensahWilliams